Michael Müller

God the teacher of mankind

Or Popular Catholic theology, apologetical, dogmatical, moral, liturgical, pastoral,

and ascetical, Volume 4

Michael Müller

God the teacher of mankind

Or Popular Catholic theology, apologetical, dogmatical, moral, liturgical, pastoral, and ascetical, Volume 4

ISBN/EAN: 9783741195105

Manufactured in Europe, USA, Canada, Australia, Japa

Cover: Foto ©Andreas Hilbeck / pixelio.de

Manufactured and distributed by brebook publishing software (www.brebook.com)

Michael Müller

God the teacher of mankind

GOD THE TEACHER

OF

MANKIND;

OR,

POPULAR CATHOLIC THEOLOGY,

APOLOGETICAL, DOGMATICAL, MORAL, LITURGICAL,
PASTORAL AND ASCETICAL.

EXPLANATION OF COMMANDMENTS CONTINUED.

BY

MICHAEL MÜLLER, C. SS. R.

VOL. IV.

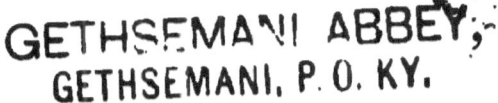
St. Louis, Mo.
Published by B. HERDER, 17 S. Broadway.
1889.

𝔍𝔪𝔭𝔯𝔦𝔪𝔞𝔱𝔲𝔯:

✠ *John Card. McCloskey*

ARCHBISHOP OF NEW YORK.

GETHSEMANI ABBEY,
GETHSEMANI, P. O. KY,

CONTENTS

CONTENTS.

CONTENTS.

v

THE COMMANDMENTS OF THE CHURCH.

THE SECOND COMMANDMENT.

" Thou shalt not take the name of the Lord thy God in vain."

Our true happiness in this world consists in being united with God by the divine virtue of charity. The principal obstacle to this union of God with man is idolatry and superstition. To remove this obstacle, God gave the first commandment: "I am the Lord thy God; thou shalt not have strange gods before me; thou shalt not make nor adore idols, etc.".

A person, however, might avoid the worship of idols, and still might not have due respect for God. Hence it is that God added the second commandment: "Thou shalt not take the name of the Lord thy God in vain."

Now, what is meant by the *name* of God?

When we have sufficient knowledge of a thing, we give it a certain name to distinguish it from everything else; that name expresses the idea and image we have of that thing. We, therefore, name things according to the knowledge we have of them. Now, we cannot see God, we can never fully comprehend his divine essence. We therefore can never give a name to God which fully expresses his divine nature; as, for instance, the word "man" represents humanity. We know God in different ways; we know him by the works of Creation, and by revelation. According to the different ways of knowing God, we give him different names. Knowing that he is the cause and origin of all things, we call him "the Creator," "the Lord and the King of Heaven and Earth," "the Lord of Hosts," "the Almighty," "the

Strong," " the Eternal Judge," and the like. Knowing that God saved us from everlasting perdition, we call him " the Redeemer," " the Saviour," " the God of Mercy," " the Source of all Goodness," "the Good Shepherd," " the Lamb of God," " Eternal Life," " the Food of Our Souls," " Holy Communion," " the Blessed Sacrament," " the Father of the Poor," " the Friend of Children," and the like. Knowing that God purifies our souls from sin, we call him "the Sanctifier of Souls," "the Comforter of the Weak," " the God of all Consolation," " the Light of the Understanding," " the Sweet Guest of the Soul," etc.

By the name of God we must also understand especially the name of " Jesus," for this name is far more venerable than that of God. The word " God " signifies Creator, but the word " Jesus " signifies God the Redeemer and Saviour."

Hence the name " Jesus " adds to the word "God" or " Creator " the new and greater title of " Saviour."

Now, when God says, " Thou shalt not take the name of the Lord thy God in vain," he does not mean any particular name of his which should not be taken in vain, but he means that none of the names which represent him as the cause and origin of all things, or designates one of his divine attributes, should be taken in vain.

But this command must not be understood as directed to the mere name of God, that is, to the letters or syllables of which that name is composed ; it is directed rather to the meaning of the word used to express the eternal Majesty of the Godhead. The respect of the Jews for the mere name of God—" Jehovah "—was so great that they did not consider their lips pure enough to pronounce the name " Jehovah," yet they did not hesitate to write it. This was rather a superstitious than true manner of observing this commandment ; for the power of God does not consist in the mere letters of which his name is composed, but rather in the meaning of those letters.

2. What are we commanded by the second commandment?

We are commanded: First, to speak with reverence of God, of his saints and priests, of religion, its practices and ceremonies, and of all holy things; and, second, to keep our lawful oaths and vows.

1. The God who created us—that God on whom we depend every moment of our existence—is a God of infinite majesty and glory.

Look around upon the heavens and the earth, how sublime an idea do they convey of their almighty Creator! What a stupendous mass is the ponderous globe upon which we stand; yet God poises it with one finger! How vast the abyss of its waters; yet he measures it, as Scripture says, in the palm of his hand! How awful is the roar of thunder! it is but the feeble echo of his voice. How terrific the glare of lightning; it is only a faint scintillation of his brightness. All that we see around us, the vast luminaries that roll above us, the earth which we inhabit, with its endless diversity of animals and productions, with man, the lord and master of the whole, once were not. The Almighty spoke one word and instantly we leaped into being, and we are. How must not the soul and all her faculties sink into insignificance before this idea of her Creator, God! How must not the soul long to honor the name of the one true, living God, who is the centre of all honor and glory! Yes, glory and honor essentially appertain to the name of God.

Amongst all creatures, man is essentially under obligations to glorify and honor Almighty God. Man is the masterpiece of the creation, a resplendent image of the three divine Persons. God has redeemed man preferably to the angels. In baptism, man is consecrated to the Father, to the Son, and to the Holy Ghost, by an inviolable character impressed on his soul. Man, therefore, is under the strictest obligation to honor the name of his Creator, of his Redeemer and Saviour, and the Sanctifier of his soul.

Now, the name of God may be honored in various ways:

1. The name of God is honored when we publicly and confidentially confess him to be our Lord, our God and our Saviour; when we defend his honor amongst blasphemers, and courageously check their insolence by a seasonable correction.

2. The name of God is honored when we devoutly listen to the word of God, which announces to us his sovereign will; when we make it the subject of our daily meditation, and practise what it prescribes.

3. We honor and venerate the name of God when we sing his praises, when we pray devoutly, or when we give him thanks for all his blessings and whatever happens to us by his appointment, whether prosperous or adverse, saying, with holy David, "Bless the Lord, O my soul, and never forget all he hath done for thee." (Ps. 102, 1). Such praise is most agreeable to the Lord, especially when, like holy Job, we bless his name in our troubles and afflictions.

4. The name of the Lord is not less honored when we call upon the Lord, in order that he may deliver us from our afflictions, or grant us strength to endure them for the glory of his name. This is in accordance with his own wishes, "Call upon me in the day of trouble," he says; "I will deliver thee, and thou shalt glorify me." (Ps. 49, 15).

5. We honor the name of God when we speak reverently of God, of the holy Mother of God, or of any of the

saints of God, of the mysteries and great truths of our holy religion, its practices and ceremonies, and of other holy things.

God feels insulted by every kind of irreverence that is shown to him or to his saints; he feels insulted by everyone who ridicules his holy religion and its holy practices and ceremonies. He has often inflicted very severe punishments on those who offered such insults to him. In the first week of November, 1870, a wicked Italian dressed himself up like the Pope on state days, and thus robed, entered a saloon and solemnly imparted the Benediction, singing the words and with his right hand made the sign of the cross over all the rabble in the saloon. He had just finished the sign of the cross in giving the Benediction, when his right arm, *dead and black*, fell down by his side—not only the hand but the arm. In the same instant his face began to burn with something like an awful cancer. It blackened, and his face was fast being consumed. He fell to the floor and cried, "I have sinned against God and his Vicar on earth; call the priest, quick, or I'll be damned. Forgive me, comrades, forgive my scandal; bring the priest." The priest came and gave him absolution. His face was black and burning, his arm dead and black. In a moment he was a corpse.—[Letter of a priest, written to the *Baltimore Mirror*, November 11th, 1870.]

Those who fear God always speak of him with great reverence; and those who truly love God always speak most affectionately of him and everything that, directly or indirectly, relates to him.

We read, in the life of St. Margaret of Cortona, that hundreds of sinners came to see her after her conversion from a very sinful life. She spoke to them so tenderly and affectionately of the goodness and mercy of our Lord that they entered into themselves, made a good general confession and became models of piety.

6. Finally we honor the name of God by keeping our lawful oaths and vows.

3. What is an oath?

An oath is to call God or anything sacred to witness that what we say is true, or that we will keep our promise.

An oath is an external act of religion by which we appeal to something divine. He who performs this act, or takes an oath, calls on God to witness the truth of what he affirms of things past or present, or of what he promises to do at a certain future time.

Since the fall of our first parents, men, in general, have a natural inclination to falsehood; hence, they distrust one another. "Men," says the prophet Jeremiah, "have taught their tongues to speak lies." (IX., 5). "Oaths," says St. John Crysostom, "were introduced amongst men, not at the beginning of the world, but long after, when vice had spread all over the world, when man went so far in debasing the dignity of his nature as to prostrate himself in degrading servitude to idols; then it became evident that man could not be induced to believe the assertion of his fellowman unless he called on God as a witness of the truth which he asserted" (Hom. 26, ad. pop. Antioch). An oath, then, is considered by all as the greatest pledge that a man can give of the truth of his words. He who calls on God as a witness to the truth of his words, means to say: *"May God bless or punish me according as my words are true or false."*

The form of an oath is not the same everywhere, for that depends on the laws and usages of each country. But whatever the form of an oath may be, it is an oath to call God to witness. To say "God is my witness," is just as much as to swear by his holy name. To swear by the holy Gospel is to swear by God himself, whose revealed word it is.

It is also an oath to swear by such objects in which the divine power, majesty or goodness shines forth. Hence it is an oath to swear by the saints, who are the temples of God, who believed the truth of his Gospel, were faithful to its dictates, and spread its doctrines amongst the remotest nations of the earth; it is an oath to swear by the cross, or by the relics of the saints. It matters very little what form of words or what ceremonies are used to express that one calls on God as a witness of the truth of his words, provided such form or ceremony is meant and understood as being an appeal to God to witness the truth.

Is it an oath to say "God lives," "God sees it?" If these and similar expressions are used by way of assertion, without calling God as a witness, then any such expression is not an oath. But if anyone uses such an expression to call God as a witness of the truth of his words, it is an oath.

Neither is it an oath to say "By my conscience," or "By my faith," unless divine faith is expressed or understood.

It is not an oath simply to say, "I swear such is the case," provided the person who makes use of these words, is not asked to swear by God or anything sacred.

Is it lawful to take an oath?

There were, at different times, certain heretics, as the Pelagians, Wicliffites, Anabaptists and Quakers, who asserted that it was never lawful to take an oath. They based their opinion on the words of our Saviour, "You have heard that it was said of them of old, thou shalt not forswear thyself, but shalt perform thy oaths to the Lord. But I say to you not to swear at all; neither by heaven, for it is the throne of God; nor by the earth, for it is his foot-stool; nor by

Jerusalem, for it is the city of the great King. Neither shalt
thou swear by thy head, for thou canst not make one hair
white or black. But let your speech be yea, yea, no, no, for
whatsoever is more than these cometh from evil." (Math. v.,
33—37). Now, in these words our dear Saviour does not condemn oaths, generally, and under all circumstances. What
he reproves is the perverse opinion of the Jews that truth
alone was a sufficient reason to take an oath. Hence, they
did not hesitate to make frequent use of oaths, and exact
them from others on the most trivial occasions. Such frequent recurrence to oaths without weighty reasons is as highly
prejudicial as the too frequent use of medicine. This practice, therefore, is condemned by our Saviour. He teaches
that no one should swear by God, or heaven, or earth for a
trivial reason, but only when necessity requires so solemn a
pledge. When he says, "Let your speech be yea, yea, no,
no," he evidently forbids the habit of swearing in familiar conversation and in trivial matters. He, therefore, admonishes
us against an habitual propensity of swearing, as countless
evils grow out of the unrestrained habit of swearing. "Let
not thy mouth," says Holy Scripture, "be accustomed to
swearing, for in it there are many falls." (Eccl. xiii., 9).
And again, "A man that sweareth much shall be filled with
iniquity and a scourge shall not depart from his house."
(Eccl. xxiii, 12). Now, by condemning the unrestrained
habit of taking an oath on every trivial occasion, our Lord,
by no means, condemns the taking of an oath when there is
a necessity for it.

Such an oath is not only permitted, but even commanded
by the law of God. "Thou shalt fear the Lord, thy God,"
says Moses, "and shalt serve him only, and thou shalt swear
by his name." (Dent. vi., 13). "All they," says holy
David, "shall be praised that swear by him (the Lord)."

(Ps. 62, 12). We are also told in Holy Scripture that the Apostles themselves made use of oaths. "The things which I write to you," says St. Paul, "behold, before God I lie not." (Gal. i., 20). And again; "The God and Father of our Lord Jesus Christ—knoweth that I lie not." (2 Cor. xi., 31). Even the angels have sometimes sworn. "The angel," says St. John, "swore by him who lives forever." (Apoc. x., 6.)

In fine, God himself, has often sworn, and as we read in many passages of the Old Testament, has confirmed his promises with an oath. (Heb. vi., 17; Ps. 109, 4). Indeed, he who attentively considers the origin and object of an oath will easily understand why it is not only lawful, but even praiseworthy to take an oath. An oath has its origin in faith. We believe that God is the author of all truth, that he can neither deceive nor be deceived, that all things are naked and open to his eyes, and that he superintends all human affairs. This faith induces us to appeal to God as a witness of the truth whom every one is bound to believe. To profess this faith by an oath is a very praiseworthy act of religion.

The object of an oath is not less praiseworthy, for its object is to establish the justice and innocence of a man, and to put an end to disputes and contests.

4. When is an oath lawful?

When it is necessary to take it for a just cause.

An oath to be lawful must have three conditions. "Thou shalt swear," says the prophet Jeremiah, in *truth*, and in *judgment*, and in *justice*. (IV., 2).

1. "*Thou shalt swear in truth.*" Truth, then, holds the first place in an oath, that is to say: he who swears must be certain of the truth of his assertion. He who swears and at

2

the same time doubts whether that which he swears to is true, commits a sin.

2. " *Thou shalt swear in judgment*," that is, if we swear we must have a reasonable cause for taking the oath. Such a cause is when God's honor, or our own good, or the good of our neighbor, or our lawful superior ecclesiastical or civil, demands that we should take an oath. We must swear only after mature deliberation and calm reflection. Hence, in taking an oath, we must not be influenced by love or hatred, or any other passion, but by the nature and necessity of the case. Without this calm and dispassionate consideration, an oath is rash and hasty; and of this character are the irrelegious affirmations of those who, on the most unimportant occasions, swear from a mere habit of swearing. This criminal abuse is but too prevalent amongst buyers and sellers. In order to purchase at the cheapest rate, buyers make no scruple to strengthen with an oath their dispraise of the goods in question, whilst sellers in order to sell at a high price, do not hesitate to strengthen with an oath the praise of their goods. Judgment and prudence, therefore, are necessary in an oath. Hence, Pope Gelasius decreed that an oath should not be administered to children before their fourteenth year, because it is generally believed that children, before that age, are not competent to perceive clearly the proper distinctions of things.

3. " Thou shalt swear in justice." The third and last condition of an oath is justice, that is, that which one promises to do on oath must be just and lawful. Hence he who swears to do what is unjust or unlawful, commits sin, and if he keeps such an oath, he commits another sin. Herod bound himself by oath to grant the request of Herodias as a reward for the pleasure she afforded him by dancing. This oath was both rash and unjust, for he knew not what unrea-

sonable or unjust thing she might ask. As she demanded the head of John the Baptist, Herod sinned again, and far more grievously, by keeping the oath—by commanding the head of John the Baptist to be given to her. (Mark vi., 21-28). Such was also the oath taken by those Jews who swore not to eat until they had shed the blood of St. Paul. (Acts xxiii., 12).

There are four kinds of oaths, namely: *affirmative, promissory, imprecatory, and cominatory* oaths. An oath is affirm. atory, when, under its solemn sanction, we affirm anything past, present, or to come; as, for instance, St. Paul does in his epistle to the Galatians: "Behold, before God, I lie not." (I., 20).

An oath is promissory when we promise for certain to do something, as, for instance, holy David did, when he swore to Bethsabee, his wife, that Solomon should be heir to his kingdom, and successor to his throne. (3 Kings, i., 17). He, therefore, who promises on oath to do something without having the intention to fulfil his promise, commits a sin. But if, in a matter of little moment, a person swears with the intention of keeping his promise, but afterwards does not fulfil it, he is not guilty of a mortal sin, because he calls on God as a witness of his present intention, and not of the future execution of his promise.

It is necessary to remark:

1. An oath can never bind a person to do what is unlawful.

2. It is never lawful to swear without having the intention to take an oath.

3. When the punishment threatened with an oath is unjust, the oath is not binding.

4. He who swears falsely before a judge in a court of justice is guilty of a double sin; and should his false

testimony cause a certain loss to his neighbor he is bound to make restitution for the damage done. A witness is always bound to make true answers whenever he is lawfully interrogated by a judge. But some one may say: "Father, if I tell the truth, my neighbor will suffer a great loss. So, out of charity for him, I will say that I know nothing about him." This is no charity. By such perverse charity you condemn yourself to hell. If witnesses conceal the truth, malefactors are acquitted, and thefts, murders and other crimes are multiplied. If guilty persons were always punished, crimes would not increase so rapidly.

5. He who is subordinate to another is not his own master. He therefore cannot bind himself by an oath to do what he pleases. Hence, if he has taken an oath in a matter in which he is dependent on the will of his legitimate superior, his oath can, even without just cause, be declared null and void by his superior (father, or guardian, prelate, etc.)

6. For a just cause, the Pope, or bishop can dispense from an oath, or impose another good work instead.

7. One may also be released from the obligation of an oath by him in whose favor it was taken.

5. What is a vow?

A vow is a deliberate promise made to God, to do or omit something that is possible and more perfect than its opposite.

1. A vow is a *promise* made with the intention that it should be binding under pain of sin to keep the promise. Hence, such a promise greatly differs from a mere resolution, which is but a purpose to do or to omit something without the intention that it should be binding under pain of sin to do or to omit it. It is, for instance,

a mere resolution to say, if I am quite well again, I will serve God better, I will pray more, and receive the sacraments more frequently. Such a resolution is not binding under pain of sin. But it is a vow to say, if God restores my health, I will have three Masses offered up in thanksgiving, or give fifty dollars to the poor.

If a person doubts whether he had an intention of binding himself under pain of sin in promising or omitting something, he is supposed he had the intention because every act is supposed to have been done as it ought.

When it is doubtful whether a person made a vow or only a simple resolution, his promise must be considered as a true and valid vow, if he is under the impression that, were he to violate it, he would commit a grievous sin.

2. A vow is a *deliberate* promise; because a vow supposes the perfect use of reason and a free agent. Human reason is the principal faculty which deliberates upon, chooses and commands, the performance of an action by the co-operation of the will; and as a vow implies a moral obligation to do, or omit a certain thing, it must be a voluntary act. Hence a vow essentially depends on the perfect use of reason and the free agency of the will. Vows, therefore, which are made before we have the full use of reason, are null and void, and the same is true of vows which are forced upon a person by menaces or violence. The person binding himself by vow must be free to do so. Before the age of sixteen no one is allowed to make solemn religious vows. Boys under the age of fourteen, and girls under the age of twelve, cannot engage themselves irrevocably by a simple vow, without the consent of their parents, and in some cases, without the consent of their tutors.

A wife cannot, without the consent of her husband, vow to do things that may, or do, occasion disorder in her

household affairs, such as to rise by night to pray, to make
pilgrimages, etc. She can, however, vow to do things con-
sistent with her duties as a wife, such as, the reception of the
sacraments, abstinence from balls, theatres, shows, etc.
The same may be said of servants.

3. A vow is a promise made *to God*, or to any of his
saints in honor of God, because a vow is an act of religion
by which we honor God, dedicating to his service our will
and liberty in the thing that we vow.

4. A vow is a promise *to do or omit something that is
possible and more perfect than its opposite*. The promise
must be of something that can be done. Hence, if that
which is promised is impossible, the promise is not binding.
A person, for instance, makes a vow, to avoid all, even the
least venial sin. This vow is not binding, because no one
can, without a particular grace, avoid every venial fault;
but if he vows to avoid all mortal sins, or every *wilful*
venial sin, his vow is valid, because he can keep it with the
ordinary assistance of God's grace. If a person makes a
vow to do something, and the principal part of it cannot be
done, the vow is not binding; but if the principal part of
it can be done he is bound to accomplish it.

What is vowed must also be *more perfect than its opposite*.
To vow, for instance, to fast is better than not to fast; to
vow to give alms is better than not to do so; to vow to
remain single is better than to marry. Hence, should a person make a vow not to hear Mass on a week day, or to go
but once a year to confession and communion, or to marry,
or never to make a vow, such a vow would be invalid because
its opposite is better; for to promise God to do something
trifling, or indifferent, or an inferior good is to dishonor God
rather than to please him, unless circumstances or the motive
of making such a vow render its fulfilment more perfect than

the omission of it, as when a person vows not to assist a poor man who is not in great need, in order to be able to give more assistance to·those who are in extreme necessity and in danger of starvation, or to marry in order to escape the danger of incontinenty and everlasting damnation.

Now, there are different kinds of vows. There are *real, personal, mixed, absolute, conditional, temporary, perpetual, solemn,* and *simple* vows. A *real* vow is one the matter of which is something external; for example, a person promises God to give one hundred dollars of his inheritance to the poor, or to make a present of a chalice to a church. In this case the money or the chalice is the matter of the vow, and if the person who made the vow does not give the money or chalice, his heirs are obliged to fulfil the vow.

A *personal* vow is one that regards the person who makes it; for example, I promise God to fast once a week for a whole year, or to make a pilgrimage. In this case, the obligation is personal.

A *mixed* vow is both personal and real; for instance, I promise God to visit the sick and aid them with my money.

An *absolute* vow is such a one as does not depend on any condition; for instance, a person promises God never to enter, on any account, a drinking saloon, because he often became drunk there.

A *conditional* vow is one the obligation of which depends on a certain condition; for instance, a sick person promises God to give five hundred dollars to an orphan asylum if he recovers from his sickness. This is a conditional vow which is binding only if the sick person recovers from his illness.

A *temporary* vow is one by which a person promises God to do, or to abstain from, something for a time; for instance, a person promises God to hear Mass every day for six months.

A *perpetual* vow is one by which a person binds himself to do, or to abstain from, something forever, as when a person promises to observe chastity, or virginity until death.

Solemn vows are those which are made in some religious Orders, in which the Church has sanctioned the making of this kind of vows. They are then accepted and considered by the Church as solemn, and made by the novice, after at least one year of novitiate, with the intention that they are so accepted and considered. Similar is the vow of chastity made by those who receive holy orders, and the vows of chastity, poverty and obedience made by the Carthusians, Cistercians and some other religious Orders.

Simple vows are those which the Church does not recognize as solemn, or accept as such.

Now, he who has made a vow, is bound in conscience to keep it. If we are obliged to keep the engagements and promise which we made to our fellow-men, how much more obliged are we to fulfil our engagements and promises made to God? "When thou hast vowed anything to God, delay not to pay it." (Eccl. v., 3.)

And St. Paul assures us that those widows who have been consecrated to God by a vow of chastity, and afterwards marry, have "damnation because they have made void their first faith." (1 Tim. v., 12). As a vow is strictly binding on conscience, young people in particular should be very cautious in making vows, especially such as are perpetual. If they wish to make an offering of something to God, let them make only a simple resolution which imposes no obligation. If they faithfully keep their resolution for a considerable time, they may, by the advice of a prudent priest, change their simple resolution into a temporary or perpetual vow.

How long can a person delay the fulfilment of a vow

without committing a mortal sin? According to the opinion of many theologians, a person is guilty of a mortal sin if he defers the fulfilment of his vow longer than three years. This, however, is to be understood of those vows only, the matter of which is not perpetual — such as the vow to visit a holy place, to have Masses said, and the like; but to put off, for more than half a year the fulfilment of a vow the matter of which is perpetual, is regarded a grievous sin.

If a person does something which he bound himself by vow to perform, but does not at the time advert to the vow, he is not bound to do it over again in order to fulfil the obligation of his vow, because every one has a general intention to do first what he is bound in conscience to do, and then only to do what is a mere act of devotion.

If a person is in doubt as to whether he made a vow he is not strictly obliged to fulfil it, but it is safer for him to fulfil it. But if a person is certain of having made a vow, but is uncertain of having fulfilled it, he is obliged to do what he has promised, because, the obligation of the vow being certain, he remains under this obligation until he has complied with it.

If a person knows that he cannot comply with the obligation of a vow, he should apply to competent authority that may either release him from it altogether, or impose upon him some other good work instead. A vow, says St. Thomas, is a promise to perform some particular good work. Now, he who makes such a promise, may be placed in such circumstances that he cannot accomplish the good, without committing a sin, or without omitting some other good work, equally important, and more pressing. In such a case it is necessary that he be released altogether from the obligation of his vow, or that he perform some other prescribed good work instead of that which he vowed to do. In such a case, as we have just said, a person must have recourse to competent authority.

Now, who has power to release a person altogether from the obligation of a vow, or change the matter of a vow into some other good work?

A father can declare, without any cause, a vow null and void which was taken, without his consent, by one of his children under age. A husband can, without any cause, annul a vow, taken by his wife, without his consent, in a matter in which she is depending on him. Any lawful superior can annul a vow taken, without his consent, by one of his subjects in a matter in which his consent is required for the validity of the vow.

In virtue of his supreme authority, the Pope can, for a just cause, release a person, in any part of the world, from the obligation of a vow, or impose another good work instead. If a person, from love of virtue, has vowed to observe perpetual chastity, or to enter a religious Order, or to make a pilgrimage to the sepulchre of our Lord in Jerusalem, or to visit the Churches of Sts. Peter and Paul in Rome, or the Church of St. James of Compostella in Spain, he cannot be released from the obligation of any of these five vows, except by the Pope.

Every Bishop can, in his own diocese, grant a dispensation in simple vows, or commute them, except those just mentioned, because they are especially reserved to the Pope.

But if any of these vows is only a penal or conditional vow, the dispensation from it is not reserved to the Pope; if a person, for instance, makes a vow to become a religious if he gambles again, or on condition that he is delivered from a certain illness, the vow is not reserved. The Bishop can, for a just cause, grant a dispensation or impose another good work instead, because the vow was not made through love of virtue; nor is any of those five vows reserved, if it was made through great fear, and on account of some evil justly threatened. A priest can release a person from the obligation of a vow or impose another good work instead, if he is especially authorized by a Superior who has power to do so.

6. Are vows pleasing to God?

Yes, but not always: hence we should ask the advice of our confessor or some prudent priest, before making a vow.

Nothing is more earnestly recommended in Holy Scripture than the performance of good works. "Let your light shine before men," says our dear Saviour, "that they may see your good works," (Matt. v., 16.); and again he says: "Every tree that does not yield good fruit shall be cut down, and cast into the fire." (Matt. iii., 10). The performance of good works, is most pleasing to God. Now, St. Thomas assigns three reasons why good works which are performed in compliance with vows are more agreeable to God than others.

The first is, that religion being the most excellent of all moral virtues, and a vow being an act of religion, it clearly follows that a vow increases the merit of every good work done in compliance with a vow. There is, for instance, a person, who vows to fast on a certain day. Now, to fast is a very good work in itself, because it is an act of temperance; but if this act is vowed, it is at the same time an act of religion. To this act of temperance, therefore, is attached a double merit — the merit of this good work and the merit of an act of religion. He, therefore, who performs a good work which he vowed to perform gains more merit than he who performs the same work without having vowed to perform it.

The second reason why good works which are done in

compliance with a vow, are more pleasing to God than others is because, in their performance, we offer more to God than in the performance of others. He who does a good work which he has vowed gives to God not only the good work itself, but he offers him also the sacrifice of his liberty of doing otherwise, and this oblation is the best that we can make to God.

The third reason why good works performed in compliance with a vow are more agreeable to God than others is because they are more perfect. The perfection of all exterior actions is in proportion to the perfection of the will, that is to say, the better the will is, the better also are its works. Now the perfection of the will is in proportion to its firmness and constancy in doing good. The more determined the will is in carrying out what is right, the more perfect it is, because it is farther removed from the defect which the Holy Ghost reprehends in timid persons when he says through the Wise Man : "*The slothful man wills and wills not.*" (Prov. xiii., 4.)

All theologians say that the more hardened the will is in crime, the more grievous are the sins which it commits. In like manner, the more firm and determined the will is to do good, the holier and more perfect are all its actions. Now, there is no better means to increase and keep up this firmness and determination of will than vows, for vows check the fickleness of the mind and fix the will and heart to serve the Lord faithfully and perseveringly, and consequently, make all its good actions more pleasing in the sight of God.

Now, if good works become more pleasing to God by vows, it is evident that vows must be very agreeable to him. St. Teresa bound herself by vow to perform all her actions in a manner as perfect as possible. St. Alphonsus made a vow to spend every moment of his life in a profitable manner. St. Francis of Assisi vowed never to refuse an alms which was asked of him in the name of Jesus Christ. However, as the obligation of vows is very strict, it is not advisable to make a vow except after mature deliberation. It often happens that certain persons make vows without much previous reflection. The consequence is that they either soon break them, or fulfil them only after a long time. "It is much better," says Holy Scripture, "not to vow, than, after a vow, not to perform the things promised." (Eccl. v., 4.)

7. What is forbidden by the second commandment?

The second commandment forbids all profanation of the holy name of God.

The second commandment, as we have seen, ordains that we should revere the holy name of the Lord, and always speak of God and holy things with profound respect. Let us now see what is forbidden by this commandment. The second commandment forbids all profanation of the holy name of God.

Now, the name of God is profaned:

1. By pronouncing it *irreverently*, that is, by using it in jest, or in anger, or in any other careless manner; or by speaking irreverently of Holy Scripture, the saints, the sacraments, and other holy things; for to speak irreverently of holy things is to speak, in an indirect manner, irreverently of God himself, because he is the author of all holy things. There are many who carelessly and irreverently use the holy name of Jesus in every conversation. This is a detestable habit, which is condemned in Holy Scripture. "Let not the name of God be usual in thy mouth; and meddle not with the names of the saints;" (Eccl. xxiii., 10), for the Lord will not hold him guiltless, that shall take the name of the Lord his God in vain." (Exod. xx., 7).

2. The name of God is profaned by behaving irreverently

in church.   One of the chief reasons why many behave
irreverently in the house of God, is because, on their way to
church, they think and speak of immodest things, and then
continue to do so even in the house of God.   Many are not
ashamed to speak aloud, to give full liberty to their eyes,
nay, many go to church there to make love, in spite of the
Real Presence of Jesus Christ in the Blessed Sacrament.
What execrable irreverence this for the Lord of heaven and
earth!   How can we complain, if God sometimes sends
heavy punishments upon a whole congregation or family, if
there are some who dare commit sins even in the presence of
the most Holy Sacrament and the angels of heaven.   Many
authors assert that in punishment for irreverence committed
in the church, the Kingdom of Cyprus was lost and fell into
the hands of the Turks.   Verme relates, in his " Instructions,"
that in a certain church in which irreverences were committed, during the elevation of the Host, a terrible voice was
heard, saying, "Christians, I am going to depart."   Immediately after, the Host was raised in the air, and the voice
repeated, "Christians, I am going to depart."   Finally,
when the Host had reached the roof of the church, the voice
again repeated: "Christians, I depart."   The Host was seen
no more, and the church instantly fell on the unhappy congregation.   Ah, how can God bear with us, if he sees that
we offend him even in the church in which he dispenses his
graces.   It is not thus that pious and saintly christians have
acted.

We read of St. Nonna, the mother of St. Gregory Nazi-
anzen, that her reverence for the house of God was so great,
that she never, even in leaving the church, turned her back
to the altar or spat on the floor.   The hermits of Egypt
and Thebais observed the greatest silence in the church;
they avoided most carefully the least distracting noise, such

as unnecessary coughing, audible sighs or anything that might in the least disturb the devotion of others. No other voice was heard than that of the priest reciting the prayers of the Mass. When St. John the Almoner saw anyone talk in the house of God, he made him leave it, saying: "If you have come hither to pray, do not employ your mind and tongue in anything else; but, if you have come hither to talk about vain subjects, hear what our dear Saviour says in the Gospel: 'My house is a house of prayer. Beware of turning it into a den of thieves.'"

8. The name of God is profaned by ridiculing religion. In my work "The Greatest and the First Commandment," when speaking of sacrilege, I have shown how Almighty God is accustomed to punish most severely those who profane his name by ridiculing religion, or anything sacred. Not long ago it happened, that a Protestant lady went into a Catholic church at the time when the holy Rosary was recited. As she heard the Hail Mary constantly repeated, she began to ridicule the devotion by repeating the words: Hail Mary, hail Mary, holy Mary, holy Mary. What happened? All on a sudden she became insane. She was taken to the insane asylum, where she constantly repeated the words: Hail Mary, holy Mary.— It was evident to every one that her insanity was a punishment of God for her sin of ridiculing religion.

La Sémaine religieuse, of Arras, tells of scandals at Boulogne-sur-Mer, and of the punishment that followed them:—

"Two scandalous things happened at Boulogne some months ago — the first on the Thursday of Holy Week, the second on Good Friday. On Thursday thirteen young men (for the most part English) met in a tavern and held a banquet, aping the picture of the Last Supper by Leonardo da Vinci. On Friday about forty Freethinkers met, with the same intention, and had a meat-dinner. Several of the sacrilegious young men who had imitated the Last Supper were stricken with small pox in the succeeding week, and died so impiously and in such agony, that it was not hard to see that the finger of God was there. The first man attacked was the Englishman who had played the part of Jesus Christ. He was carried to the hospital, where he died — his body absolutely corrupted, his flesh actually hanging in shreds. The English physician attending him did not hesitate to say that the death of this young man was unnatural — that it was a blow of divine justice. This doctor was a Protestant, and a Protestant verging on Rationalism. It is stated that ten out of the thirteen died of the disease.

"Another scandal occurred on Holy Saturday. A young owner of a fishing-vessel, Demay, a Radical member of the Municipal Council of Boulogne, recently initiated into the Masonic Order, had been invited to the feast on Holy Saturday. As he was obliged to start on a yearly fishing-expedition on that day, he was unable to be present at the Masonic banquet, but he declared he would take his meat out to sea with him and eat it thinking of his Masonic brethren and friends. He was careful, before setting sail, to take down all the images of Our Lord and His Mother on board his vessel and to replace them by Masonic emblems. In place of the usual prayer in departing, he had the 'Marseillaise,' sung. The twenty men forming the crew saw these profanations with sadness; and one of them said to his wife:— 'How unfortunate it is that I have engaged to sail with Demay! The good God will punish us.' Of all the boats that set out from Boulogne, that belonging to Demay was the only one lost. The mariners on board left sixty-three orphans. The faithful of Boulogne saw in this an instance of divine justice. Another master of a fishing-vessel, who had likewise been received among Freemasons, was abandoned by his crew; and, so terribly have these facts impressed the people that, when anybody dies suddenly, they exclaim, ' He must have been one of the thirteen, or been present at the banqnet on Holy Saturday.' The arm of God fell with terrible weight on these two cases. The patience of God is great, but his punishments severe!"—[*Freeman's Journal* of New York, Nov. 12th, 1881.

The Paris correspondent of the *Catholic Times* contributes three more instances of evidences of Divine Providence:

"At Mont d'Or, in Auvergne, a woman and her daughter kept a book and newspaper shop. As is usual in French watering-places, the building was of wood. Amongst other papers sold was a blasphemous and immoral pamphlet full of calumny and outrage against Pius IX. Not many days ago the shop was struck by lightning; the daughter was killed on the spot, and the mother is only just out of danger. Strangely enough, the shop, which was joined to some others, was burned to the ground, but the others were untouched. The people of the place have been much impressed by what appears to be an evidence of the anger of God.

"At Neuville Sous Carbie, in the diocese of Amiens, two Municipal Councillors impudently interfered when the Catholics were about to raise a cross in their cemetery. One of them expressed a hope that the figure of our Lord would fall and break its neck. A few days afterwards the blasphemer fell under a cart-wheel which literally passed over his neck and broke it."—[From the *New York Tablet*, Dec. 24th, 1881.

4. The name of God is profaned by blaspheming, that is, by speaking ill of God, or the saints, or holy things. Thus it is blasphemy to say of God, that he is a tyrant, or

3

that he rejoices in the misfortune of men, or that he is partial, or that he favors some men too much, whilst he treats others too harshly, or to say, that, if God does not punish that wicked man, I do not believe that he is just; or to say, it seems that the servants of the devil are better off than the servants of the Lord.

To be guilty of the sin of blasphemy, it is not necessary that one should speak directly against God. He who speaks of God's saints, or of sacred things in a contemptuous and injurious manner, is guilty of the sin of blasphemy, because God looks upon an insult offered to his mother or any other saint or sacred thing as offered to himself. Hence a person may become guilty of the sin of blasphemy in the following different ways :—

1. By denying any of God's perfections; as, for instance, by saying that God is not all-wise, nor all-powerful; that he is not good, nor just, nor kind, nor merciful; that he takes no interest in us here below; that he cares not for what we do; that there is no Providence, and the like.

Certain persons who labor under the affliction of wrong, and are in destitution and misery, sometimes fall into this kind of blasphemy.

2. The sin of blasphemy is committed by those who ascribe to God some fault or imperfection, by saying, for example, that he is an unjust God — that he is a despotic God — that he takes pleasure in the miseries of his creatures — that he cannot aid us in our troubles. Of this kind of blasphemy the children of Israel were guilty when, tired with the manna sent them from heaven they wanted flesh; for they spoke ill of God; they said, " can God furnish a table in the wilderness?"

3. The sin of blasphemy is committed by ascribing to creatures any of the attributes of God; for example, by

saying that the devil is omnipotent—that he knows everything to come, or that he knows as much as God himself; or by saying that such a person is a God, a second Messiah, as beautiful and as amiable as God. Of this sort of blasphemy the Jews were guilty when they attributed the miracles of our Lord to the devil.

4. The sin of blasphemy is committed by cursing God or wishing him ill; as, for example, by saying, death to God! would that there was no God, no Redeemer! This is the blasphemy of the damned souls; for St. John tells us, that "they bit their tongues for pain; and they blasphemed the God of heaven, because of their pain and wounds." (Apoc. xvi., 10). To speak contemptuously of God, or of his Son, Jesus Christ — to speak in a tone of mockery and contempt of the holy name of Jesus, or of the wounds, blood, passion, or death of Christ, is also to be guilty of the sin of blasphemy. Of this kind of blasphemy those were guilty who derided Christ hanging on the cross: "They that passed by blasphemed him, wagging their heads, and saying, vah, thou that destroyest the temple of God, and in three days buildest it up again, save thyself; if thou be the Son of God, come down from the cross." (Matt. xxvii., 39). Such was the blasphemy of Julian the Apostate, when, on the point of death, he cast some of his blood against heaven, crying out in his rage: "Well! Galilean, you have conquered." This was the expression he uttered against God when his perjured soul was about falling into the arms of the devil.

5. The sin of blasphemy is committed by saying something of the Blessed Virgin, or of any other saint, that is an outrage on their sanctity and memory; as, for example, by saying, that they were cruel and wicked during their lives, and that they are undeserving of the honors which are paid to them; that they caused, whilst they lived, a great deal of

disquiet, and brought about much misery and wretchedness. The worst species of blasphemy against the saints is that which infidels pronounce against the Blessed Virgin, the Queen of all saints, by denying that she was always a virgin, and saying that she was no other than an ordinary woman.

6. The sin of blasphemy is committed by those who speak injuriously of sacred things and religion, for example, by saying, that the sacraments of the New Law are of no use or benefit to man — that the holy Scriptures are not the work of God — that they contain falsehoods — that religion is the work of man, and the invention of interested priests — that it is of no use or benefit to man — that all those who practise religion are just as bad as those who have no religion — that the Catholic Church is no better than the Protestant Church — that one form of religion is as good as another. It is, also, blasphemy against religion to mock and deride the ceremonies of the Church, to speak contemptuously of its holy practices, calling her sacraments and ordinances the mummeries of superstition. All such blasphemies dishonor God himself, and are so many outrages against his infinite majesty and holiness. Of such kind of blasphemies Antichrist will be guilty, for of him it is said by St. John : " He opened his mouth in blasphemies against God, to blaspheme his name, and his *tabernacle*, and them that dwell in heaven." (Apoc. xiii., 6.)

7. The sin of blasphemy is committed by cursing those creatures of God, in which the power and goodness of God shine forth in an especial manner, as they do in heaven and in the human soul. Hence it is a blasphemy to curse the world, unless the curse is meant only for the wicked world, of which St. John says : " The whole world is seated in wickedness." (1 John, v., 19). It is also a blasphemy to say : " God damn my or your soul,"—or to say : " Cursed be

the wind, or rain or day of God." But to curse simply creatures, such as the wind, the rain, the year, the dead and the like without referring any of these creatures to God, is no blasphemy, but only a vénial sin, says St. Alphonsus.

8. Of the sin of blasphemy are guilty not only those who formally utter it, but also those who provoke or applaud it. There was once a very good and virtuous father. He had several children. For each of them he provided a large inheritance. In a word, he left nothing undone to make them comfortable and happy. Now, this good father had a great enemy who said all kinds of bad things against him in public speeches, which were printed in many newspapers. His children took great delight in all that was said and printed against their father; they went even so far as to congratulate this enemy of their father on the courage he had shown to speak against him, and what was worse, they paid him for his speeches, and bought thousands of copies of them to circulate them everywhere, in order that everybody might hate and detest their father as much as possible. What do you think of those wicked children? Are you not highly indignant and incensed against such conduct? This good father represents God the Father, who is the greatest benefactor of mankind; but alas! how is he treated by thousands of his children. Some of them blaspheme him in so shocking a manner that one is made to believe that they are possessed by the devil.

But there are others who applaud these devilish blasphemies; others publish them in newspapers, pamphlets or books; others read them with pleasure; others, without reading them favor their publication by subscribing to them, or by paying for admission to blasphemous lectures; others, whose duty it is to prevent and oppose the sin of blasphemy, tolerate it. All these are guilty of the sin of blasphemy.

Now, blasphemy has always been regarded as one of the greatest sins in the sight of God, because it directly attacks his infinite majesty and perfections, and insults and outrages his sacred name. To insult a king of this world, to load him with indignities, and to scoff and ridicule him, is considered a very great offence; but how much greater is the offence of one who dares to give expression to insults and indignities against the King of kings and the Sovereign Master of heaven and earth. Hence, we find blasphemy severely condemned in Scripture.

St. Paul says: "Put away . . . . . blasphemy — filthy speech out of your mouth." (Col. iii., 8). This great Apostle delivered Hymenæus and Alexander over to satan that they might learn not to blaspheme. (1 Tim. i., 20).

St. Jerome says that, compared with blasphemy, every sin is small: "In fact, every sin, compared to blasphemy, is trifling." And St. Chrysostom says that, when a person blasphemes, his mouth should be instantly broken to pieces: "Give him a stripe — break his mouth."

"Blasphemers," says St. Alphonsus, "are worse than the damned." Those who are in hell always retain a perverse will in opposition to God's justice which condemned them to eternal torments. They are always filled with hatred and malice. If they feel any regret for past iniquities, it is only because iniquities were the cause of their eternal damnation. They died in sentiments of impiety, impenitence and in great hatred to God and his holy Church, which is real blasphemy. Hence they are in a state of satanic rage and despair. Even after the general Resurrection, they will never cease uttering groans of imprecation and blasphemy against God and all the angels and saints of heaven. The blasphemies of the damned, therefore, consist in the detestation of God's justice; but the blasphemies of the wicked on

earth principally consist in the detestation of God's goodness. The damned blaspheme the author of their torments;
but the wicked of this world blaspheme their benefactor;
they blaspheme him who keeps them alive. Instead of thanking God for preserving their life in order to give them time
to repent and be saved, they blaspheme his divine Majesty.
The sin of blasphemy, therefore, is so great, says St. Alphonsus, "that I wonder, why the earth does not open and
swallow the blasphemer." St. Louis, King of France, enacted a law which condemned all blasphemers to have their
tongues pierced with a red-hot iron.

Ah! how frightful are not the chastisements which God is
accustomed to inflict upon blasphemers! In the Old Law it
was God's ordinance that blasphemers should be stoned to
death. In the book of Leviticus we read that a young
Israelite, who had blasphemed, was brought to Moses, and
that Moses, having consulted the Lord, the blasphemer was
ordered to be stoned: "And the Lord spoke to Moses,
saying, Bring forth the blasphemer without the camp, and
let them that heard him put their hands upon his head, and
let all the people stone him. *And thou shalt speak to the
children of Israel, ' He that blasphemeth the name of the Lord
dying let him die; all the multitude shall stone him, whether
he be a native or a stranger.' "*

"And Moses spoke to the children of Israel, and they
brought forth him that had blasphemed without the camp,
and they stoned him. And the children of Israel did as the
Lord had commanded Moses." (Levit. xxiv., 10-23.)

The holy king Ezechias, who ruled over the kingdom of
Juda shortly before the time of the Babylonian captivity,
was on one occasion besieged in Jerusalem by the Assyrian
general, Rabsaces, who had been sent by King Sennacherib
to demand the surrender of the city. Rabsaces, in the name

of his master, uttered horrible blasphemies against the God of heaven, who, he assured the Jews, would be no more able to protect his people than the idols whom they worshipped had been able to protect the neighboring nations. Being compelled to abandon the siege, in order to lead his army against the King of Ethiopia, he wrote a letter to Ezechias, in which he repeated his former blasphemies, and threatened, upon his return from his expedition, to destroy the holy city, if it did not appease his master's anger by a timely submission. The pious Ezechias was struck with horror at the words of the letter, and, carrying it into the temple of God, he there spread it open, and, with many tears and fervent prayers, begged of the Lord to avenge the insult offered to him on the head of the blasphemer. He then repaired, for consolation and advice, to the holy prophet Isaias, and was assured by him, on the part of God, that the blasphemies uttered against the Lord should not remain unpunished.

"And it came to pass that night," says the sacred writer, "that an Angel of the Lord came and slew, in the camp of the Assyrians, one hundred and eighty-five thousand. And when he rose early in the morning, he saw all the bodies of the dead. And Sennacherib departing, went away, and he returned and abode in Nineve. And as he was worshipping in the temple of Nesroch his god, his sons slew him with the sword, and Asarhadden his son reigned in his stead." (IV. Kings, xix., 37.)

We read in the second book of Machabees, that the impious Antiochus died a wretched death, his flesh rotting away, and worms growing out of all the parts of his body. "Thus, the murderer and *blasphemer*, being grievously struck, died in a miserable state in a strange country." (2 Mach. ix., 28).

When Benedad, King of the Syrians, was defeated in battle

by the Israelites, his servants said to him: " The God of the Israelites is only a God of the hills, and not of the plains. It is on this account that we have been defeated. It is, therefore, better for us to fight against the Israelites in the plains, and we shall overcome them." Thereupon a man of God came to the King of Israel and said to him: " Thus saith the Lord. Because the Syrians have said the Lord is God of the hills, but is not God of the valleys, I will deliver all this great multitude into thy hand, and you shall know that I am the Lord." (8 Kings, xx.) What happened? God destroyed 127,000 Syrians for having blasphemed the Lord.

Demetrius, king of Syria, being at war with the Jews, in the time of the brave Judas Maccabeus, sent against them his general, Nicanor, their most implacable enemy. The latter did not spare them in any way, and prepared to attack them on the very Sabbath day. Some Israelites, whom the calamities of the time kept in his army, represented to him that it was wrong for him to violate the Lord's Day. " And who is this powerful God who commands the day to be respected?" " My Lord, he is the living God, the Master of heaven." " Well! if the Master of heaven forbids you to fight, I, who am master here on earth, command you to take up arms and march." What happened to this blasphemer? When he gave battle, he was completely routed, perishing himself in the combat together with 85,000 men of his army. (2 Maccab., xv.)

It is true, the punishment of death for the sin of blasphemy does not exist in the New Law; yet Almighty God has often inflicted very severe punishments on blasphemers.

Cardinal Baronius tells us, that an inhabitant of Constantinople, after having uttered a blasphemy, went to take a bath. He suddenly rushed out of the bath, saying that he felt the stroke of death; and while he continued to cry out that death was on him, he tore the flesh off his ribs and arms with his nails and teeth. To mitigate his pain, he was wrapped in a white sheet, but his torture was only increased. The sheet was taken away, and the skin came with it; and the miserable man, screaming and swooning away through pain, died in the hands of devils, who carried him off to be punished with the eternal torments of the damned.

In the month of February, 1847, an instance of this kind occurred in France, in the department of Lower Seine. Some persons were sitting at table in a tavern kept by a man named Sylvain Levaillant. Amongst the workingmen present there was one who kept swearing continually, more from custom, as it seemed, than from any bad intention. The tavern-keeper remonstrated with him several times in a friendly way, and his advice was taken in good part by the tradesman, who was not without some feelings of religion. But another, a weaver, named Huberel, desirous of showing off, as it were, before the others, spoke in his turn, and commenced by denying that there was a God; from that he proceeded to belch forth all sorts of blasphemies against God and his religion. Levaillant endeavored to soothe away this frenzy by words of mild persuasion, but the weaver answered in a scoffing tone: "Your God! I will sup with him to-night!" Alas! he had scarcely uttered this blasphemy when he fell on his face as if struck by lightning. They hastened to raise him up. The unhappy wretch was dead. Every one felt sure that this awfully sudden death was a punishment from heaven. (Noel, *Cat. de Rodez*, iv., 336.)

On Sunday, the 14th of February, 1841, a party were seated around a table, in a public-house in a *commune* of Yonne, one of the departments of France, at the hour of the celebration of High Mass. At the moment when the tolling of the church bell announced the elevation of the Sacred Host, one of those seated at the table — and who was well-known for the irregularity of his life, the corruption of his morals, and the sarcasms and the blasphemies that he was daily vomiting forth against God and religion — arose suddenly from the table, and gave vent to the most blasphemous expressions: "I must show you," said he, "what the priest is now doing." And then he commenced a blasphemous mockery of the most august ceremony of Christianity. In derision of the ceremony of consecration, and the act of adoration, he inclined over the table, and then bent the knee, pronouncing, at the same time, with a blasphemous tongue, the form of consecration. Again he made a second genuflection, and, to the amazement of all around, he did not arise, but remained motionless in that position, as if he were fastened to the floor! At first it was thought that he purposely remained kneeling, but it was soon seen that he was unable to arise unaided, and that he required the support of two persons to arise from his kneeling posture. Everyone became alarmed at what had happened to the blasphemer, and a perfect stillness reigned around. When those present recovered from their terror and surprise, and breathed a little more freely, they began to examine the cause of this extraordinary effect, and it was found that the blasphemer's knee was fractured, and the knee-pan shivered into two parts. The surgeon who examined the fracture said that, in his long experience, he had never seen one like it. All who heard of the accident, and those who were present when it occurred, agreed in thinking that the stroke came from God in punishment of the blasphemies uttered against him. Of the circumstances thus related we have the strongest proof and the most authentic evidence. The parish in which this signal punishment of blasphemy was inflicted is

called Venisy; the blasphemer is named S——, but is called
by the people the "*Terrible*," on account of his audacity and
impiety.

About the beginning of the present century there lived in
Lancashire, among the Aughton congregation, a good religious Catholic woman named Mrs. Ann Spencer, who occupied
a farm-house on the Prescot road. In the same neighborhood there dwelt with his father a young farmer named
Charles King, who died a few years since at an advanced
age, in the adjoining parish of Lydiate. The following history was related by Mr. King to the priest who attended him
on his death-bed, and is given in his own words:

"About sixty years ago it happened that my neighbor,
Mrs. Spencer, had a boat-load of manure to be carted from
the canal. It was customary then, as indeed it is now, for
the neighbors to help with their teams, in order that the work
might be got through speedily. I accordingly brought my
father's team to assist, but, having to go to Liverpool in the
afternoon, I did not stay for the dinner given on such occasions. The next morning I went again, and found Ann
Spencer very indignant at some impiety which her company
had been guilty of the previous day. It seems that, after
dinner, when most of the party had left, there remained five
young men, Protestants, in the room. Now there happened
to be a crucifix over the chimney-piece, which they took
down and began to ridicule. They said it was the Papists'
God, etc. 'Let us go,' said one, 'and bury it, and see if it
will rise again in three days.' They carried their blasphemy
into effect, and actually dug a hole in the ground, into which
they thrust it. Mrs. Spencer, who was engaged in another
part of the house, did not hear of the profanity till afterwards. In relating it to me she was very much moved, and
said, 'Mark my words, not one of those who took part in

this blasphemy will die in his bed.' I did mark her words, and have lived long enough to witness their exact fulfilment. These men are all dead, and not one of them died in his bed. Two were brothers (he mentioned their names); one was killed by falling out of his cart, the other cut his throat in a barn. A servant-man of theirs was also present, and he was killed by his team. Another drowned himself in a pit, and the fifth died in his chair."—[*Rev. H. Gibson's Catechism.*

St. Alphonsus relates in his Catechism that, in the Kingdom of Naples, a man who had blasphemed the Crucifix of a certain place, suddenly fell dead as he was passing by the Crucifix, and that, in Vallo Novi, a certain coachman, upon blaspheming a saint, was immediately upset into the water. The pole of his carriage pressed upon his neck and he was drowned. "I have spoken," says St. Alphonsus, "with an eye-witness of this punishment."

Some years ago, there lived, in a town of England, a certain tradesman who was well-known among the spiritualists as a successful medium, and who addressed the meeting on the subject of his past experiences. Among other things, he declared to them that at a certain *seance* he had shaken hands with the Apostle Peter, and that he had on that occasion felt the Apostle's hand firmly clasped within his own. From this he went on to argue that it was very easy to understand how the Apostle Thomas put his hand into our Lord's side, or rather into that which was a representation or personification of our Redeemer. No sooner had he uttered this awful blasphemy than he fell back upon his chair a corpse. This terrible judgment produced a vivid impression on all who were present, and the meeting broke up in the wildest excitement.

At the inquest, held a few days after, over the body of the

deceased spiritualist, the usual verdict. was declared, the words of which, in such a case, cannot fail to strike the mind as having a special and terrible significance, " Died by the visitation of God."—[*Liverpool Mercury and other Journals*.

A young gentleman of Abbeville, named John Francis Lefevre de Labarre, had had the misfortune to read some works of Voltaire, and had imbibed from them, the very worst sentiments. Not content with ruining himself he succeeded in seducing some other gentlemen of his own age. These wretches, mutually encouraging one another in crime, came at last to throw aside all decency and decorum : they uttered publicly the most horrible blasphemies against God, his holy religion, and all that is sacred in the world. Public morality was outraged, and the parliament of Paris caused these wretches to be arrested, tried, and condemned. Labarre especially, being the author of this frightful scandal, was treated with all the severity of the laws of France. By a warrant, dated the 4th of June, 1766, he was condemned to give satisfaction in the public street, to have his head cut off, and his body burned to ashes, together with the bad books from which he had drawn doctrines so pernicious. This sentence was executed to the letter ; whilst the blasphemer stood to give public satisfaction to the outraged multitude, there was affixed to him a placard bearing the inscription in large characters: "*Impious and sacrilegious Blasphemer*."—[*Feller, Biographie Universelle*, ii., 85.

In the St. Louis *Republican*, of November 14th, 1881, we read the following :

A strange story comes from Union county, Arkansas, but it is as true as it is strange, to-wit : That three young men were sitting on their horses in the road, discussing the probabilities of rain from a cloud which just then was rising in the west. The youngest of the group, named John Freeman, referred to the drought, and remarked that a God who would allow his people to suffer thus couldn't amount to much. As he was speaking this the boys were encircled with lightning and the speaker stunned severely, though his companions were unscathed. Recovering, he renewed the subject, bitterly reviling the Supreme Power. Instantly a bolt of lightning flashed from the cloud overhead, and the young man fell dead in his tracks. Nearly every bone in his body was mashed to a jelly, while his boots were torn from his feet and the clothing from his lower extremities. The body presented a horrible appearance, being a blackened and mangled mass of humanity. His companions were stunned and thrown on the ground, but not seriously injured. The funeral of the unfortunate young man occurred the next day, and attracted a large crowd, the larger portion of whom were drawn thither by the rumor of the strange events preceding the death of the deceased. When the body was deposited in the grave and the loose earth had been thrown in until the aperture was filled, and while the friends of the dead man yet lingered in the cemetery, a bolt of lightning descended from a cloud directly above the burial place and struck the grave, throwing the dirt as if a plow had passed lengthwise through it. No one was injured, but those present scattered, almost paralyzed with terror. The incident is exciting a great deal of attention, ministers and religious people generally holding that the young man was the victim of the wrath of an offended God.

If a blasphemer is not punished in this life, he will be so much the more severely punished in the next. Our Lord showed to St. Frances of Rome the special and horrible torments of the tongue which blasphemers suffer in hell.

If it is not in your power to punish the blasphemer, if you cannot silence his impious tongue, or raise your voice against

him, then at least repair in some measure,. the insults offered
to God by saying in your heart: "Praised be .God,"—or
"Glory be to the Father and to the Son, and to the Holy
Ghost," or perform some other good work.

4. The name of God is profaned by *breaking a lawful oath*
and *by sinful swearing*.

We have seen that, when we swear we call on God to witness that we intend to do what we promise. Now, not to keep
such a promise, when it is in our power to keep it, is to do
as much as we can, to make God palliate our knavery, to
patronize our lies and to support an untruth. What can be
more injurious to him than to endeavor to make him bear testimony to what is not true?

We dishonor the name of God by sinful swearing when
we swear against *truth*, or against *justice*, or against *judgment*. Now, a person swears against truth when he asserts
under oath *what he knows to be untrue*, or when he promises
with an oath *what he does not intend to perform*, or when he
asserts under oath *what he does not know for certain* to be
true. Now, to break a lawful oath when it is lawful and
possible to keep it, or to take knowingly a false oath is the
dreadful crime of *perjury*. He who commits perjury calls on
God to witness what is not true. And is there anything
more detestable than that of using God's name and authority
to confirm a lie? He who calls on God in this manner must
suppose either that the Lord does not know the truth, or that
he can be bribed to serve as a false witness, and give testi-.
mony to a lie, or that he does not mind whether his holy
name is abused to test lies or not. Now, is not this to brave,
as it were, the Wisdom and Power of God? Is it not to
insult and mock his holy Name? "Thou shalt not swear
falsely by my name," says the Lord, " nor profane the name
of thy God: I am the Lord." (Levit., xix., 12.)

But perjury is a very grievous sin not only because it is most injurious to the Truth and Holiness of God, but also, because it is very injurious to society and to ourselves. By perjury our neighbor is greatly deceived by that very means which is considered as giving the greatest security of truth. How can society exist, how can business be transacted without having certainty of the truth by oaths or solemn affirmations!

Perjury is also very hurtful to our own soul. He who commits this sin gives consent to his own condemnation, and even prays for it. He who swears falsely even in a trifling matter commits a mortal sin, because to call on God to witness any kind of a lie is to offer a great insult to him. "Behold, you put your trust in lying words;" says God through his prophet; "such words shall not profit you; to steal, to murder, to commit adultery, *to swear falsely* . . . . And now, because you have done all these works, saith the Lord . . . . I will cast you away before my face." (Jerem. vii., 8-13-15.)

However, should a person swear to something which he sincerely believes to be true, but which afterwards turns out to have been untrue, he is not guilty of a false oath because he swore according to the conviction which he had at the time. But if a person swears to something which he th'nks is untrue, but which afterwards turns out to have been true, he is guilty of perjury in the sight of God, because he swore against his conscience. It should also be remembered that a false oath, deliberately taken, is always a mortal sin, even though it may be about a trifling matter, because it is a great irreverence to God to call on him to witness the truth of anything that we believe to be untrue. One day two sisters came to the emperor Charlemagne, and told him that their brother, who was a duke, retained in his possession a

4

considerable portion of their inheritance. The emperor ordered the duke to give up to his sisters all that belonged to them. The duke told the emperor that he did not owe a cent to his sisters, and confirmed his words by an oath. But as he swore falsely, he was punished immediately for his crime. He fell instantly to the ground, and two hours after he was a corpse. (Paed. Christ. P. C., v., § 1.)

There were three men who plotted the ruin of St. Narcissus, bishop of Jerusalem, and accused him publicly of a heinous crime. In order to give yet greater weight to their accusation, the first of them prayed that he might be burned alive, if he did not tell the truth; the second cried: "And that I may be seized with the most frightful malady, if I have spoken falsely;" finally, the third said: "That I may lose my sight, if my testimony is not true!" St. Narcissus, seeing that his influence was daily decreasing, under these degrading accusations, quitted Jerusalem and retired into solitude. But what happened? The three impostors did not escape the punishment they had voluntarily called down on themselves. The first was burned to death in a fire which broke out in his own house; the second saw himself covered with ulcers from head to foot, and his whole body became one mass of putrefaction. The third was so shocked by the terrible chastisement of his two companions that he repented, confessed his crime and completely exculpated by the holy bishop. Nevertheless, the abundant tears he shed as the natural consequence of his repentance, made him afterwards lose his sight.—[*Godescard, Vies des Saints,* 7th August.

A person swears against *justice* when he promises under oath to do what is evil, or against the law of God. As everything that is against the law of God is an offence against God, it is clear, that, to swear or call on him to witness such an offence must be very injurious to him; for, if a simple promise to do what is evil is injurious to God, how much more injurious to God is not that promise when made with an oath. Of this sort of oath those Jews were guilty who swore that they would neither eat nor drink till they had killed Paul. (Acts xxiii., 12). A person swears also *against justice* when he promises under oath that he will do what he knows to be injurious to himself or to his neighbor, as, for instance, when he swears that he will kill himself, or burn his house, or shoot his horse, or destroy his property, or do to himself or to any other person some harm.

Now, it is, indeed, surprising how frequent these oaths are among people when they get into a sudden passion against anything. Such oaths are often taken by fathers and mothers against themselves and their children when vexed by them, by masters against their servants, and by servants against cattle. They swear by God that they will beat them ; by Christ that they will kill them, or by the cross of Christ that they will turn them out of the house, and never more give them anything to eat. A person also swears against justice when he swears not to do what is good, as, for instance, when he promises under oath that he will not be reconciled to his enemy, or that he will not fast, or pray till a certain time ; or that he will not give alms, or assist his friends in necessity, or that he will not speak to this or that person, or that he will never show him an act of kindness.

A person swears *against judgment*, when he takes an oath without necessity, without deliberation and proper attention ; asserting under oath the most trifling things. Such an oath is called rash. Many a person when taking a rash oath, is accustomed to add a curse to it, by saying : " May I never see God — may I fall down dead — may I never stir out of this place, if what I say is untrue — may I never have luck — may God strike me dead if I do not keep my promise, and_ the like." However, rash and unnecessary oaths which are free from contempt for God's name, or the danger of scandal or perjury, are only venial sins, because there is no great irreverence to God in them.

In England there is a law forbidding all kinds of swearing under a certain penalty. A man who was much addicted to that vice, being at table with some others, went on cursing and swearing as usual, without the least attempt to restrain himself. Every time he spoke he added an oath, or something equivalent thereto. On the following day he was summoned to the court without knowing for what. He had scarcely made his appearance in the hall, when he saw an individual take a little bag from his pocket and gravely count out some beans on a table. When he had finished, he said to the magistrate, "I hereby prove that this man whom you see before you, swore 487 times yesterday evening in such an inn." Being asked how he knew so exactly, he answered: "I chanced to have the left pocket of my coat full of beans yesterday, and when I perceived that this man cursed so often, I took it into my head to drop one into the other pocket every time he uttered an oath. In this way it was that I reckoned 487, and that number is under the truth, because my beans ran out, so that I was unable to continue my count." The accused could not, of course, deny the fact; he paid a large fine, reddened to the eyes with shame, and retired fully resolved to correct so shameful a habit.—[*Schmid et Belet, Cat. Hist.*, ii., 146

5. The name of God is profaned *by cursing*. To curse means to call down some evil upon ourselves, or our neighbor, or any of God's creatures. It is a curse to say: "May you be struck dead," or "Bad luck to you," or "May the devil take you," or "May God damn you," and the like. A curse, therefore, contains not only a mere wish of evil to

others, but also a prayer either expressed or implied that the evil may happen. Such an evil wish is not only contrary to the precept of charity, but also to the second commandment. No doubt, to call on God that he may execute our evil wishes is very injurious to his Holy Name.

Almighty God says to us in Holy Scripture: "Revenge is mine and I will repay;" (Rom. xii., 19.) that is, leave all revenge to me. I shall punish those who injure you with strict justice unless they sincerely repent. But the curser says: "No, O Lord, revenge is mine; it is for me to will it and for thee to execute it. Thou must not give this man time to repent; must punish him at once, because I wish it. Thou who gavest sight to the blind and didst raise the dead to life, must strike this man dead and that other one blind because I say so; thou who didst shed thy blood to save the poor sinner from hell, must condemn this enemy of mine—this wretched being to eternal damnation, thou must not give him any longer any hope of salvation.

Such language is horrible! Do you think perhaps that it is impossible for any man thus to pray to God? Alas! such bad prayers are made very often. Not long ago the poor wife of a drunkard, in a city of Georgia, was often ill-treated by her drunken husband. One day she went to the bar-keeper's wife to expostulate with her for selling liquor to her unfortunate husband. She was turned away without any satisfaction. In a fit of passion she knelt on the bare ground and called down the curse of God on the bar-keeper's wife and house. Three days after the bar-keeper's wife was struck by lightning in her house and killed. A few days after the house was burned to the ground. The unfortunate woman who cursed said that she sees every night the ghost of the dead woman all on fire, and threatening her with revenge.

There are many persons who have contracted the most

shameful habit of cursing. Is it not most shameful to curse
God's creatures, to speak the language of the devil, to be
addicted to a sin from which no gain, no pleasure, no satisfaction can arise, to praise and profane with the same tongue
the holy name of God, to call down great evils upon ourselves
and others? What great vulgarity to speak scarcely one
sentence without some profane words, and scandalize all
those who hear them! Ah! how delighted the devil is with
all those who speak the language of his country and teach
also others, especially the little ones, to speak it well!

A certain habitual curser was condemned in a court of
justice to be hanged for a crime which he had committed.
He was already on the scaffold, ready for the rope to be put
round his neck. By some accident he was thrown off the
scaffold and fell down. Now, see how strong his habit of
cursing and swearing was. At the very moment when he
began to fall, he cursed and swore. The next moment he
was on the ground, his neck was broken, and he was dead!

St. Gregory tells us that a child accustomed to curse and
swear, in his impatience, uttering the name of God, was
seized with a mortal distemper, and assaulted by evil spirits,
which caused him to depart this life in his father's arms.
The father being too indulgent to him, neglected to correct
and reprehend him for his vice, and so, as the same saint
observes, had bred up in this child a great sinner for hell.
(L., 4; Dialog. c. 18)

Nothing is more common than to hear carters, coachmen,
and people of that kind cursing and swearing. Now, when
their attention is drawn to their bad habit, they often excuse
themselves by saying that their horses are so used to hear
curses that they will not go on without hearing such language.
One day, the pastor of a small country parish was walking
along the road reading his breviary. All at once he heard

one of his parishioners urging on his horses with voice and whip, and swearing like a trooper. The priest goes up to him and says: "Well! my good Francis, it appears your load is hard to pull."—"You may say that, Father, especially for beasts so wretched as these."—"Nevertheless, friend Francis, I cannot think that any reason why you should curse and swear as you do." "Oh! it is easy seen, Father, that you know little of driving, or you'd know as well as I do that the horses won't go at all without that."—"My good friend, you are entirely mistaken, and I will prove it to your satisfaction; give me your whip." So saying, the good priest put his breviary in his pocket, takes hold of the whip, and gives the horses two or three good blows, crying as loud as he could: "Get along there, old horse!" The horses instantly started forward at so rapid a pace that Francis was obliged to run in order to keep up with them. The priest returned him his whip laughing: "Well! my good friend," said he, "you see horses can be made to step out without hearing cursing." —[G. S. G.

Sometimes we hear the curser excuse himself by saying that he curses by habit, and that he does not really wish any evil from his heart, nor really mean what his curses imply. Such an excuse is not accepted by God. A person who sins through habit is more guilty than one who sins through sudden passion. The habit of sinning shows the extreme weakness of the will to resist evil. Now, the more ready the will is to commit sin, the worse it is in the sight of God. A person, therefore, who has formed the evil habit of cursing cannot be excused from mortal sin; and if he does not sincerely strive to correct this bad habit, he is accountable for all the curses and profane words which he utters through habit.

It happens not unfrequently that the habitual curser, besides invoking the curse of God on his work, his cattle, his

neighbors, his children, his wife, actually in as many words
calls it down upon his own head; in other words, he prays
God, who is infinitely just and infinitely powerful, to send
him bad luck, to strike him dead, or to damn him for all
eternity. This kind of cursing is what the Jews were guilty
of in the desert, when they murmured and cried out, "Would
to God that we may die in this vast wilderness!" (Numb. xiv.
3.) And they were guilty of the same when they sought our
Lord's death, calling out to Pilate, who strove to release him,
"His blood be upon us and upon our children!" (Matt. xxvi.
25.) Almighty God heard their wicked prayers and granted
them. Of the mighty multitude who came out of Egypt, all
who had attained the age of manhood, except Josue and Caleb,
perished in the wilderness; and we know how the innocent
Blood of the Lamb of God, shed by the hands of the Jews,
has drawn down the divine vengeance on this guilty nation.
Driven from their country, and scattered over the face of the
earth, they are a living monument of the justice of God on
those who insolently brave the justice of God. And so it
will be, no doubt, with those wicked sinners who have the
habit of invoking the divine vengeance on their own heads.
Often, as we read in history, has God heard their prayer,
and granted them the evil they asked for, even while the
words of their curse were yet upon their lips; and if sometimes in his mercy he delays his vengeance, there is no doubt
that, if they do not sincerely repent, the punishment will fall
upon them with still greater severity either in this or in the
next life.

When St. Edward the Confessor sat on the throne of
England, his younger brother Alfred, whom he tenderly
loved, was one day cruelly and treacherously murdered.
The perpetrators of this foul deed remained undiscovered,
but several historians attribute the guilt of it to the powerful

Earl Godwin, who was the father of the queen. Some years after, when the king was seated at table with his nobles, the conversation happened to fall on the death of Alfred. St. Edward declared that he would always regard with horror those who had been guilty of so black a crime. As he uttered these words he cast his eyes towards Earl Godwin. The latter, fearing that he was suspected, took up some bread, saying: "If I had any hand in that foul deed, may this be the last morsel I ever swallow." No sooner had he uttered these words than he fell dead at the table with the morsel in his mouth.—[*English History.*]

The habit of cursing is, no doubt, most detestable in every one who has contracted it; but it is far more so in fathers and mothers on account of the great scandal which they give to their children by teaching them a devilish language. What can be more unnatural for parents than to curse those whom they are strictly bound to love. Such curses have often been heard by God to the great shame and confusion of both parents and children.

Surius relates in the life of Zenobius that a certain mother had a son who was very sick with a malignant fever. One night she was obliged to rise forty times to give a drink of water to her suffering child. She was at last overcome by impatience, and instead of sympathizing with her son in his great pains, she flew into a passion and said, on presenting to him the cup of water: "Take and drink with it the devil." No sooner had she uttered this imprecation than her sick child was possessed by the devil.

There lived in Cæsarea, in Cappadocia, a widow with ten children, seven boys and three girls. They were of an honorable family. One day the oldest son insulted his mother and even struck her, while the others looked on without defending her. The mother in a rage cursed her children;

she even went to the church and there on her knees before
the baptismal font, with her hair dishevelled and her breasts
bare, she cursed her children and prayed that they might be
made an example to the whole world, that they should be
forced to wander everywhere without ever finding any rest.
This horrible prayer was instantly heard. First the eldest
son and then the other children one after the other were
seized with a strange trembling in every limb. They could
not rest anywhere and thus traveled through the greater part of
the Roman Empire. The mother seeing the terrible consequences of her curse and stung with shame and remorse, as
well as the reproaches of her neighbors, hanged herself in
despair.

Two of the children, Paul and his sister Palladia, came to
Hippo in Africa, where St. Augustine was then bishop.
Every day for two weeks they went to a chapel, where the
relics of St. Stephen were preserved, and prayed for their
cure.

The second week, it was Easter Sunday, as the young
man was praying in the presence of the congregation, he
fell into a swoon; after some time he came to himself and
arose perfectly cured. The joy of the people was unbound-
ed; they sang hymns of praise and gladness.

Next day the brother and sister appeared in church in
presence of all the people, while St. Augustine related their
sad story. The young man remained perfectly cured, while
his sister still trembled in every limb. After the sermon
she too went to the chapel of St. Stephen and conjured the
Saint with the greatest fervor to restore her to health.
Presently she fell into a swoon like her brother, and after
some time rose perfectly cured.

Afterward the eldest son was cured at Ravenna through
the intercession of St. Lawrence.—[*City of God, A.D.* 425.]

St. Augustine, in his sermon on this subject, makes the following remarks: " It is to be hoped," says he, " that the other brothers and sisters (who were all, upon their mother's curse, struck by the hand of God for abusing her) may regain their health and cure, as this young man has done, for whose recovery we now rejoice. Nevertheless, let children learn henceforward to be obedient and respectful to their parents, and let parents tremble to be thus angry. The mother prayed against her children, and she was heard, because God is truly just. But what became of her, miserable wretch? Ah! the sooner she was heard, the more severely she was punished."—[*De Civitate Dei.*]

Now, curses may be mortal or venial sins. A curse, implying a great evil which a person wishes from his heart to his neighbor or to himself, is a mortal sin; but a curse, implying but a slight evil, is only a venial sin. But if a curser sincerely repents of his evil habit of using profane language, and earnestly tries to overcome it, he may be excused from the sin of a bad word that slips out of his mouth against his will.

A certain soldier was in the habit of cursing and swearing. One morning a fellow-soldier said to him: " I will give you a dollar to-night if you do not curse and swear in the course of the day." The offer was accepted; it prevailed upon the curser to stop his evil habit for that day. On receiving the promised reward he was told: " For the love of one dollar you have not cursed to-day. Will you not, for the love of God, overcome your evil habit of cursing for the future?" This charitable correction had the desired effect. Indeed, if a person can check the evil habit of cursing for the sake of some temporal gain, it would be a great shame to make no efforts to overcome it for love of God and heavenly gain! Where there is a will there is a way. Let the curser firmly resolve to give up cursing; let him impose a little penance upon himself for each curse he utters; let him say, for instance, a "Hail, Mary!" or give a cent to a poor person, and he will soon be cured of the evil habit of cursing.

THE THIRD COMMANDMENT.

" Remember that thou keep holy the Sabbath-day."

The occupation of the blessed in heaven is to honor and praise God forever and ever. I heard all saying: "To him that sitteth on the throne, and to the Lamb, benediction and honor, and glory, and power, forever and ever." (Apoc. v., 13.)

Their Allelujas, their hymns of gladness, are ascending before the throne of God forever and ever. All that is in heaven, on earth, and under the earth, says St. John, sing in concert the praises of God. (Apoc. v., 13.) Indeed, adoration, honor and glory essentially belong to the Lord. The souls in purgatory show their profound esteem and homage to God by their intense desire of enjoying and glorifying him in heaven.

Even hell itself glorifies the Lord, for the reprobate are constrained, in deploring their eternal loss of all the benefits of nature, grace and glory, to offer a reparation of honor to the power of the Father, the author of nature; to the wisdom of the Son, whose grace they have despised, and to the goodness of the Holy Ghost, whose saving inspirations they have criminally rejected.

But, of all creatures, man is especially obliged to honor, praise and glorify God—his Creator, Redeemer, and Glorifier.

As the voice of reason universally proclaims the existence of God on whom all creatures depend for their support and preservation, so also does it dictate that man should acknowledge the supreme power and dominion of God by interior sentiments of his heart, as well as by exterior acts of religious worship.

The voice of reason, however, or the natural or moral law, as it is called, gives only general principles of right and wrong. It is, for instance, a law of nature, that malefactors should be punished; but this law does not determine the mode and kind of punishment. In like manner, it is a law of nature that we should honor and worship God; but this law does not determine the mode and the time of worship. Hence it is necessary that the real obligations of the natural law should be determined by divine or human law.

If it were left to men to choose their particular portion of time for the special worship of God, they would be too apt to neglect it, by giving to earthly cares *that time* which ought to be given especially to the immediate worship of God. In order, therefore, to prevent such neglect, God has specified and fixed, by the third commandment, the time which he requires to be thus given to him.

The commandment, given at length, is: " Remember that thou keep holy the Sabbath-day: six days shalt thou labor and do all thy works; but on the seventh day is the Sabbath of the Lord thy God: thou shalt do no work on it, thou, nor thy son, nor thy daughter, nor thy man-servant, nor thy maid-servant, nor thy beast, nor the stranger that is within thy gates: for in six days the Lord made heaven and earth,

. . . and rested on the seventh day; wherefore the Lord blessed the seventh day, and sanctified it." (Ex. xx. 8.)

Now, this commandment of devoting a specified time to the external service of God is here especially given to the Jews. Inasmuch as it prescribes the duty of worshipping God externally, it is part of the natural or moral law, like any other of the ten commandments, and cannot be changed, binding as it does all men, without respect to time or nation. But inasmuch as it prescribes the day and manner for the external worship of God, it is a ceremonial precept.

In the Old Law, God ordained that the last day of the week should be kept holy, and it was called Sabbath, or Saturday, as we call it. The word "Sabbath" signifies rest from labor, for God, after having created the world, in six days, rested on the seventh or Sabbath.

The creation commenced on the first day of the week, which is called Sunday, or the Lord's Day; it was concluded on Friday; and God rested on Saturday, that is, ceased from creating. Saturday or the Sabbath is, then, the repose of God; and it is on this account, that, in the Old Law, he commanded all men to keep that day holy, in memory of the great work of the creation, and of the rest or repose which he took from his work after all was finished. Now, on this account, the seventh day had been kept holy by the servants of God from the beginning, and though it was interrupted during their captivity in Egypt, yet we find it renewed again immediately when they came into the wilderness, even before the commandments were given on Mount Sinai.

In the rehearsal of the Law another reason is assigned for observing the Sabbath-day: "Remember that thou also didst serve in Egypt, and the Lord thy God brought thee out from thence with a strong hand and a stretched-out arm. Therefore hath he commanded thee that thou shouldst observe the

Sabbath-day." (Deut. v., 15.) The Jews, then, by resting from labor on the seventh day, commemorated their deliverance from Egyptian bondage, and testified to the surrounding nations that Jehovah, the God whom they worshipped, was the Creator of all things.

As the Sabbath-day reminded the Jews of the stupendous work of creation, and of their miraculous deliverance from the Egyptian bondage, the Lord called it a sign between him and them. "I gave them a sign," says he, "my Sabbaths to be a sign between me and them, and that they might know that I am the Lord that sanctify them." (Deut. v., 15.) And again he says: "See that you keep my Sabbath. It is an everlasting covenant between me and the children of Israel, and a *perpetual sign.*" (Exod. xxxi., 13-17.) As the Sabbath-day was especially dedicated and consecrated to the Lord, it was also to serve as a sign to remind the Jews of their duty of dedicating and consecrating themselves to the Lord.

The Sabbath-day was also a sign to remind the Jews of the celestial Sabbath. According to the narrative of Moses, each of the six days lasted "from the evening to the morning." Now, it is not mentioned that the seventh day ended at the morning of another. And this seventh day still lasts, according to the belief of the Fathers of the Church. It has lasted for nearly six thousand years, and will only end from the evening of time to the morning of eternity; or rather it will never end, but become one with the eternal day—the celestial Sabbath-day, which is celebrated in heaven where God crowns, with eternal glory, all those who, on earth, have done his holy will.

However, since the promulgation of the Gospel, the ceremonial precepts of the Mosaic Law are no longer binding. They were abolished by the New Law of Christ—the law of grace. The Church of Christ, therefore, having received legislative power from Christ (Matt. xvii.) could substitute another day for the Jewish Sabbath; and this was done even in the time of the Apostles, who were inspired by the Holy Ghost to transfer the obligation from the seventh to the first day of the week—to choose Sunday in place of Saturday. This change was made by the Apostles in honor of Jesus Christ, and, therefore, the first day of the week is called "*The Lord's Day.*" (Apoc. I, 10.) It was on the first day of the week (Sunday) that Christ rose from the dead,—that he commissioned his Apostles to teach all nations,—that he empowered them to forgive sins,—that he sent down upon them the Holy Ghost; it was on this day that the Apostles began to preach the doctrine of Christ and to establish the Christian religion; it is also on this day that the creation itself is most fitly commemorated, because this great work of God was begun on the first day of the week. Under the Christian Dispensation, therefore, we commemorate far more and far greater mysteries and blessings on the first day of the week, than were commemorated by the Jews on the seventh day.

Another reason for this change from Saturday to Sunday was this: the seventh day was appointed for the Israelites, to be a sign that they were the people of God, as we have already seen; but, as on the coming and death of Christ they were no more his people, the observance of Saturday was no more necessary. Again, as the observance of the seventh day was a figure of the rest of Jesus Christ in the grave, this figure was fulfilled by his death and burial; and, therefore, like all the other ceremonials of the Old Law, which were figures of Christ, it was done away with on being fulfilled by him.

. The Sabbath, then, no longer exists for us Christians; it

has passed away with other Jewish feasts. This the Apostle plainly declares: "Let no man judge you in respect of a festival day, or of the new moon, or of the Sabbath, which are a shadow of things to come." (Col. ii., 16, 17.) On the other hand, we know for certain that it was the practice of the Apostles and first Christians to observe religiously the first day of the week. "Eight days after the resurrection the disciples were within, and Thomas with them, and Jesus came and stood in the midst." (John xxi., 26.) Later, in Acts xx., 7, we read that upon the first day the disciples assembled to break bread. Again, we find St. Paul commanding the Corinthians: "On the first day of the week let every one of you put apart with himself, laying up what it shall well please him." (1 Cor., xvi., 2.) And the first day is recognized as the Lord's day. "I was in spirit, on the Lord's day," says St. John. (Apoc. i, 10.) The Church, therefore, following this custom, has given a special precept to observe the third commandment by keeping holy the first day of the week.

How are we to keep the Sunday holy?

By resting from servile works, and hearing Mass.

1. *To rest from servile works.*

Works or worldly actions may be divided into three classes, namely—1. *Servile works;* 2, *Liberal works;* 3, *Common works.*

Servile works, which are prohibited on Sundays, are all such bodily works as are commonly performed by servants, tradesmen, and laborers, for gaining their bread, and which, as they regard the concerns of the body and of this world, naturally engross our minds, and call off our attention from those duties which the santification of the Sunday requires from us. Carrying loads and burdens, either by oneself or

5

with cattle, and, as a consequence, markets, fairs, buying and selling, may be classed under the works called *servile. Liberal works* are those which engage the mind more than the body, and which, consequently, are usually performed by *free* and *independent* persons. Under this class may be placed *drawing*, writing, and the like. *Common works* are those which engage the mind as well as the body, and which may be performed by all classes of persons, as they require neither profession nor trade. In this class are comprised walking, playing, hunting, fishing, and the like.

"Servile works," and only *servile* works, are strictly prohibited on the Lord's day. "Thou shalt not do any work therein," says the Lord; "thou, nor thy son, nor thy daughter, nor thy man-servant, nor thy maid-servant, nor the stranger that is within thy gates; that thy man-servant and thy maid-servant may rest, even as thyself." (Deut. v., 14.) All unnecessary *servile* works, then, are strictly forbidden, such as ploughing, sowing, reaping, mowing, digging, weaving, planting, building, and the like.

By the third commandment are also forbidden all courts of justice, trials, examination of witnesses, pronouncing or executing sentences, and all public transactions of business, such as selling and buying goods in shops; all such occupations are forbidden on Sundays, because they take up much time, engross the mind considerably, and prevent the due observance of the Lord's day, or tend to profane it. To do servile work on a Sunday or holy-day of obligation, without sufficient reason, for two hours, is considered a mortal sin; but to do such work, without sufficient reason, for a shorter time, is but a venial sin.

There are three reasons, for which it is allowed to do servile work on the Lord's day. The first is *real necessity;* as for example, to prepare food for man and beast, which could not be provided before, and which, if a person did not work on Sunday, could not be procured for the day; or when a person works in order to avoid a grievous loss. Thus, our Saviour excused his disciples for plucking the ears of corn and eating them on the Sabbath-day, and declared them innocent in doing so. Hence, it is lawful to do whatever is necessary for the day, such as to cook food, to arrange and put the house in order. It is lawful, too, to reap corn, to gather fruits, when these things are in danger of being destroyed by wind or water.

Should children be beaten or ill-treated by their parents if they were not to work on Sundays or holy-days of obligation, they are excused from sin if they work. In like manner, servants and laborers, who would lose their situations if they were not to work on Sundays and holy-days of obligation, are excused from sin if they work on those days; but they should try to obtain, as soon as possible, other situations in which it is possible for them to keep the third commandment.

A mother of a poor family, who has to work hard every day of the week in order to earn bread for her children, commits no sin by mending, on Sundays, the clothes of her children. In like manner, a poor girl who lives out, and to whom no time is left for herself, commits no sin by doing, on Sundays, such sewing for herself as is necessary. Such a person, however, should do her work as privately as possible to avoid scandalizing those who do not know the reason why she is permitted to work.

The second reason for which it is allowed to work on the Lord's day, is *charity*, in assisting the poor and distressed, provided this be done without any return, either in money or work, as a reward or payment for it; for if one should assist a poor person on Sunday or a holy-day, on condition that the poor man should give him a day in return, it is the same in the sight of God as if he had worked on the Sunday or holy-day himself. We find our Saviour doing works of charity on the Sabbath, and defending his conduct by unanswerable arguments, against the Pharisees, who censured him for what he did. "What man shall there be among you," said our Lord, "that hath one sheep, and if the same fall into a pit on the Sabbath-day, will he not take hold of it and lift it up? How much better is a man than a sheep? Therefore it is lawful to do a good deed on the Sabbath day." (Matt. xii., 11.) The reason is, because works of charity sanctify rather than profane the Lord's day.

The third reason for which it is allowed to do servile work on the Lord's day, is *piety;* when, for instance, such work is done for the service of God and the interests of religion, without any view to temporal gain or reward. Thus our Saviour says: "Have ye not read in the law, how that on the Sabbath-day the priests in the temple break the Sabbath, and are without blame?" (Matt. xxi.)

Now, though real necessity justifies persons in working on Sundays and holy-days, those cannot be excused who undertake more work than they can perform within the six days of the week, and on that account habitually remain up after twelve o'clock on Saturday night, and trespass for a considerable time on the Sunday. Neither can agriculturists be excused from sin who require their men to work on Sundays and holy-days, falsely persuading themselves that there is necessity for so doing, when in reality the work could, without any great inconvenience, be deferred until the following day.

Liberal works are allowed on Sunday, so that after having heard Mass, and attended other exercises of piety, we can, without sin, read, write, design, compose, or play music, and the like. All such works, as well as *common* or *intermediate* works, are permitted on Sundays and holy-days, even though performed for gain. This is the doctrine of theologians who follow the opinion of St. Thomas. "For corporal works," says the saint, "which belong not to the spiritual worship of God, are termed servile, inasmuch as they appertain to those who are in servitude; but inasmuch as they are common to servants and freemen, they are not termed servile."

Hence, according to the more common and probable opinion, it is not forbidden on Sundays and holy-days to travel, or to go fowling, or to fish; that is to say, that the Church, though not absolutely approving of these things, does not in positive terms condemn them, when they are done for recreation, and when a greater part of the day is not taken up with such amusements, because such works are at least common to persons in a servile and liberal condition of life. But fishing and fowling, when attended with great preparation and labor, appear to be *servile* works, because too much dissipation—incompatible with "the due observance of the Lord's day"—results from them. This, too, may be inferred from the Canon Law, in which the Pope has given a *dispensation* to fish for *sardines*.

The sanctification of the Sabbath-day is repeatedly enforced in Holy Scripture. "Remember that thou keep holy the Sabbath-day." (Exod., xx., 8.) "Six days shall you work; on the seventh day is the Sabbath, *the rest holy to the Lord*" (Exod., xxxi., 15) The punishment for the violation of the Sabbath was death. "He that shall profane the Sabbath, shall be put to death. He that shall do any work in it, his soul shall perish out of the midst of his people." (Exod., xxxi., 13-14.)

"When the children of Israel were in the wilderness, they

found a man gathering sticks on the Sabbath-day. They brought him to Moses and Aaron and the whole multitude. He was put in prison until the Lord said to Moses: 'Let that man die; let the multitude stone him without the camp.' And when they had brought him out, they stoned him; and he died as the Lord had commanded." (Numb., xv., 82-36.)

Nothing, indeed, is more odious than the ingratitude of those who, having received from God the six working days of the week, refuse to consecrate the seventh to him. This we clearly see from the following little story: A peasant was ridiculing his neighbor because he would not, like himself, work occasionally in the fields on Sunday, but endeavored, on the contrary, to sanctify the Lord's day by attending the several offices of the Church. "Suppose," said the neighbor, with a view to enlighten and convince him, "I have seven gold pieces in my pocket, and that, meeting a man on the road, I give him six of them, what would you say to that?" "I would say that you were very generous, and that the man who was lucky enough to find you so would owe you a debt of gratitude." "Very well; but suppose, instead of that, he knocked me down and robbed me of the one gold piece I had kept for myself, what would you say then?" "The wretch! hanging would be too good for him!" "Yet, my friend, it is your own story; you are that man: God has given you six days to work for your living, he has only reserved the seventh for himself, and he commands us to keep it holy; but you, instead of being grateful for his gifts, and respecting his will, rob him of the seventh day. Don't you think it is just the same case?" The peasant acknowledged his fault, and avoided it for the future.—[*Daily Rewards*, No. cxix., p. 5.]

It is true, the punishment of death for the violation of the Sabbath does not exist in the New Law; yet Almighty God

has often inflicted very great punishments on those who outrage him by working on Sundays and holy-days of obligation.

A miller of the parish of St. John de Corconé, in Vendee,
was so possessed of the demon of avarice, that there was
scarcely a Sunday on which he did not work. During the
High Mass and other offices, he was seen working at his mill.
On one particular festival he went as usual, and began to
work away. In the evening he returned not. His wife was
every moment expecting him, but in vain, for he appeared
not. When it was becoming rather late, she went out to look
for him, and—frightful spectacle !—she beheld him dead and
extended on the ground, with his entire body pierced with
something like stakes. In setting out from his house in the
morning, he complained of there being no wind, and said
that he was going to arrange the wind-mill, so that an advantage might be taken of the first breeze that would spring up.
He waited some hours in expectation of the wind ; he saw
the country people going to church, and through shame—for
he knew he was doing wrong—hid himself. When they had
passed on, he stood up and began to watch the clouds. On
a sudden the wind sprung up, the wings of the wind-mill
turned immediately around, and the points coming in contact
with his body, he was cast violently some distance from the
place in which he was standing, and died in pain and agony !
His death produced a great sensation in every part of the
country around ; for it was considered, and justly, a stroke
from the hand of God, to mark his horror of the profanation
of Sunday.—[*Noel.*, *Cat. de Rodez.*, v., 21.]

"There are many," say the bishops of the sixth Council
held at Paris, in 829, "who have been struck by lightning
for working on the Lord's day. We ourselves have been
eye-witnesses of several of such punishments, and others have
related to us most terrifying instances of divine chastisement

inflicted on those who outraged the Lord by the servile work which they performed on Sundays or holy-days of obligation. Some were punished by a sudden contraction of the nerves; others were burnt alive, etc."

St. Gregory, a celebrated bishop of Tours in the sixth century, relates that a laborer of Auvergne, having yoked two oxen to his plow, feared not, to the great scandal of his neighbors, to go and work in his field on a Sabbath-day. Whilst employed at this forbidden work his ploughshare broke. Instead of desisting from his criminal undertaking, he took his axe to mend it; it was then that God punished him in a most remarkable manner. He permitted that the laborer's hand should close convulsively on the handle of the axe. Notwithstanding all that could be done to take the axe from his hand, it remained the same, so that for two whole years the unhappy man bore that visible mark of the wrath of God. But at length, at the end of that time, he conceived the happy idea of going to pray in the church of the famous martyr, St. Julian, at Brioude, now in the Department of the Upper Loire. He passed in prayer the night between Saturday and Sunday, according to the custom of that time, and, on the following day, in presence of all the people, his hand was cured; it opened miraculously of itself and let fall the piece of the axe handle which for two years had remained in its grasp. This striking example of divine chastisement encouraged all those who knew of it to continue sanctifying the Lord's Day in the best way they could.—[*St. Gregory of Tours, Glory of the Martyrs,* Book ii., Chapt. 11.]

St. Alphonsus relates that a farmer of Fano, Italy, ploughed on a holy-day of obligation—the feast of St. Ursus, the patron of the diocese. Being asked why he showed so little respect for the festival of the patron, he answered:

"Let him be a saint; I do not care; I am in want of bread."
No sooner had he uttered these words, than the earth opened
and swallowed him together with the plough and his oxen.
In the place, called Villa of Rosano, where this happened.
are seen to this day the marks of the chasm in which that
farmer was swallowed up.

By these terrible judgments of the Lord we clearly see how
grievously he is offended by the profanation of the Sunday.
No man ever became any richer by Sunday-work; bad will
come from it sooner or later. Let us rest assured that it is
God alone, and not sin, that can help us in our wants. He
provides plentifully for all those who keep his commandments, but not for those who despise and transgress them.
Woe to you, if you have any success in work done on Sundays. Such a success, say the Fathers of the Church, is a
sign that God will punish you most severely for your sin in
the world to come.

The design of Almighty God in forbidding us to work on
the Lord's day is that we may spend the entire day in the
performance of such religious acts and good works as relate
to the divine worship and the sanctification of our soul.
Hence it is a great mistake to imagine that, if we abstain
from servile work, and have heard Mass, the rest of the day
may be spent in idleness, lounging about, or in vain amusements.

It is true, as Sunday is a day of rest, we can on that day,
after having attended to our chief religious duties, take some
innocent recreation — we can take a walk, pay a visit to a
good friend, etc.; but it must be remembered that amusements and recreations are not the proper means of sanctifying
the time which is spent at them, and therefore they are only
allowed when one's state of body or mind requires them.

We must, therefore, in keeping the Sunday holy, attend

more to the spirit than to the letter of the law. We keep
the letter of the law by abstaining from servile work and
hearing Mass; but we keep the spirit of the law by spending
the day in exercises of devotion, and works of piety; that is,
in receiving the sacraments, hearing sermons and religious
instructions, in attending the public services and devotions
of the Church, in reading the lives of the saints, or some
other edifying and instructive book, in visiting the sick, or
in instructing those who are ignorant of their religious duties.
Those who thus keep the Lord's day holy, are more willing
and faithful to keep the other commandments. It is
especially for this reason that God so emphatically inculcated
the keeping of the Sabbath-day.

In the commencement of the present century, there lived
at Lyons a shoemaker named Berthier, who was seen working in his stall every Sunday morning. A merchant lived in
the house opposite the stall of Berthier, and being a religious
man, and most observant of the sanctification of the Lord's
day, was grieved at seeing it profaned by his neighbor. One
day he spoke to him on the subject, and represented to him
how much he offended God by working on Sunday; but the
shoemaker made answer that it was necessity that compelled
him to work. "You sir," said he, "are a very rich man,
and you can afford to remain idle on Sunday; but I am poor,
and have a large family to support, and it would be a great
loss to me if I did not work on that day; besides, I am never
able to finish on Saturday night the work ordered during the
week, and my customers must be supplied on Sunday."
The merchant, shaking his head at these excuses, kindly said
to him: "It is very far from my intention that your family
should suffer any loss; and I now promise you, that if you
do not work on Sunday, and regularly attend church for the
next six months, I will compensate you for any loss that you

may thereby sustain. Do you accept my offer?" "Willing-ly," said the shoemaker; "for it is much easier for me to sit in the church than to work, particularly when you are so kind as to compensate me for any loss that I may suffer." They both then shook hands, and the engagement was closed. When the six months had passed by, the merchant sought out the shoemaker, and said to him: "Very good, neighbor; you have faithfully kept your word, and I, too, will keep mine. Now tell me the loss you have suffered for the last six months by not working on Sunday, and I will make up for it to the last farthing." "Indeed," replied the other, "I must candidly say, my dear sir, that I have suffered not the loss of a cent, and all the claim I have on you is that of your accepting my best thanks for the advice you gave me. During those last six months everything has gone on well with me. At first I experienced some little inconvenience in not having my work finished on Saturday night, but the con-sideration that you would recompense me for any loss, and also the promise I made you, made me faithful in the due observance of the Sunday. I have been regular in my attend-ance at church, and the instructions given there every Sunday have made good impressions on my mind. I have learned many things with regard to my salvation, of which before I was completely ignorant. Having, during the past months gone to confession, and been nourished with the body and blood of our Lord, I now experience a content and happiness to which before I was a stranger. Hitherto I was of a violent temper, but now I am mild and gentle; and yet my frame is stronger and my arm more vigorous than before." "But, my good friend," said the merchant, "how are mat-ters going on between you and your family, for formerly you must allow that there was scarcely anything heard in your house but quarrels and bickerings?" "True, indeed," replied the shoemaker, with a blush upon his cheek; "but the case is altered now. Before, I always believed that my wife was always wrong, and that I was always right, and my anger and obstinacy was such as to cause scenes, the very thought of which now makes me blush; but now peace and concord reign always in the house." Very much moved at this recital, the merchant drew forth his purse, and offered him two ducats, saying: "Take this as a remembrance of my affection. As when you made the promise I could not anticipate the happy results, I, since then, laid by every month a sum to compensate you for the loss you might have sustained. Here is, then, what has been laid by for the six months, and receive it as a token of the delight I feel at your following my counsel. You have now seen from your experience that God will aid those who endeavor to do to the best of their ability what he requires of them."—[*Power's Catech.*

Oh, what great happiness and peace would reign in all Christian families if they kept holy Sundays and holy days of obligation, according to the spirit of the law! But alas! there are so many who keep but the letter of the law. They abstain from servile work, and go to hear Mass, but spend the greater part of the Lord's day in idleness and frivolous, sinful amusements. A great and learned man used to say that "Sundays and holy-days of obligation are the devil's best working-days." And he was right; for on Sundays more sins are committed than on any other day of the week, by gambling and dancing, by eating and drinking to excess, by night-revelling, and flirting, by immodest discourses, and blaspheming, by reading irreligious and most shameful articles in newspapers published on the Lord's day for the purpose of destroying all sentiments of religion in a large portion of the people. "They grievously violated my Sabbath," says the Lord, "I therefore said to them, that I would pour out my indignation upon them, and would consume them." (Ezech., xx., 13.) When the saintly bishop Stephen, of the city of Dia, saw himself unable to prevent a great number of his people from spending Sundays and holy, days of obligation in gaming, dancing, and drinking to excess, he besought Almighty God to make, on a certain day, a multitude of devils appear in their hideous forms. God heard his prayer. When the people saw the hellish monsters threatening to carry them along into hell, they all cried aloud for mercy, promising to amend their lives. They were by the prayers of their holy bishop delivered from the evil spirits. (Surins, Tom., v., cap. ix., 7th Sept). Let us rest assured that if Almighty God does not permit the devil to seize, in this world, upon all those who thus profane the Lord's-day, he will give him full power to do so in the next, where he will make them suffer in the eternal flames of hell for having so atrociously violated the Sabbath-day.

2. To hear Mass.

It cannot be doubted that many Catholics neglect hearing Mass on Sundays and holy-days of obligation, because they are very ignorant of their most essential duty towards God, which consists in paying to God the honor of divine adoration by offering sacrifice to him. I will, therefore, give here a plain, concise explanation of sacrifice, and especially of the holy sacrifice of the Mass.

A great lord of this world requires all his servants to honor him by obeying all his just commands. In like manner, God, the Lord of all lords, has, at all times, required men to pay him the honor of divine adoration as due to him alone, by doing all that he commands, by acknowledging him as the Supreme Lord of heaven and earth, and the Sovereign Master of life and death, upon whom all things depend. Our first parents, Adam and Eve, grievously sinned against this most essential duty of man towards God when they disobeyed him in Paradise.

By this disobedience they became the enemies of God, and as such could no longer please him. But God was merciful to them. He gave them the grace to be truly sorry for their disobedience. They asked his pardon, and were ready even to lay down their lives to repair the insult they had offered to God. But God gave them to understand that all the penances and good works which they could perform, together with the sacrifice of their lives, would not be enough to cancel their great debt. He consoled them, however, by promising them a Redeemer who would live and die in perfect obedience to his holy will, in order to blot out their sin and who, by his obedience, would honor him far more than he had been, or could be dishonored by them or by their posterity.

After this consoling promise, Adam and Eve firmly resolved always to honor and worship God as their Supreme Lord by living up to his holy will for the remainder of their life, and hoped, by so doing, to obtain forgiveness and life everlasting through the merits of the coming Redeemer.

But by their sin, our first parents had become much inclined to evil; they were very apt to break their good resolutions even so far as to neglect to give God the honor of adoration.

To strengthen them in their good resolution, he gave them a positive command to offer sacrifice to him, that is, such outward acts of divine worship as would fittingly express the sentiments of their hearts towards him. Hence he instructed them, to offer him, instead of their lives, other sensible objects, such as animals, fruits, oil, and the like;

to destroy or otherwise change the same: animals, for instance, should be slain, oil and similar offerings should be poured out, combustible things should be burned, in order to declare and acknowledge, by the destruction or change of the things offered, that he was the Supreme Lord of the Universe who could destroy all things, as he called them into existence out of nothing.

God also gave our first parents to understand that these sacrifices were to remind them of the Redeemer to come, and of the sacrifice which he would offer to take away their sin; that these sacrifices of theirs, as figures of the Redeemer to come, would be pleasing to him if made in said manner and intention.

Moreover, sacrifices were also made to God for the purpose of thanking God for graces received, or of obtaining particular favors, or of appeasing God after having offended him. This original revelation or command of God concerning sacrifice became very much corrupted in the course of time. Men, supposing that, what they loved and prized the most would be the most pleasing to God, went at last so far as to sacrifice their fellow-men, nay, even their own children, and thus, instead of honoring God by sacrifice, they only dishonored him in the highest degree.

Now, in order that sacrifices might always be made in the manner and with the intention which God had taught our first parents, he chose the Jewish nation as his people, and gave them particular laws about the sacrifices they were to offer.

By these laws, God determined:
1. The things to be offered in sacrifice.
2. The intention with which sacrifices should be offered.
3. The priests who were to offer sacrifice.
4. The manner in which sacrifices should be offered.

Now, the things offered in sacrifice by the Jews were certain animals, bread, salt, fruits, wine, oil, etc.

The priests chosen by God to offer sacrifice were Aaron, his sons and their descendants.

The manner in which things were offered in sacrifice was the same that God ordained in the beginning of the world, namely, that men should either destroy by fire the things offered, or otherwise change and render them useless.

The intention with which the people should offer sacrifices was also the same as in the beginning, namely, to declare, by the destruction or change of the things offered, that they wished to give to God the supreme honor of adoration, and to express and acknowledge, that, on account of their sins, they had deserved everlasting destruction.

These sacrifices were called *burnt-offerings* or *holocausts*. They were also made with the intention of *thanking God* for blessings received, or of appeasing him after having offended him, or of obtaining particular favors from him.

A sacrifice offered with the intention of thanking God for his blessing was called *thank-offering*.

A sacrifice offered with the intention of appeasing God after having offended him was called *sin-offering*. Sin-offerings were ordained to remind the people of their guilt in the sight of God, and of the hope which they should place in the Redeemer to come, by the merits of whom alone they would be pardoned, and received again into the friendship of God.

A sacrifice offered to obtain from God certain graces and blessings was called a *sacrifice of impetration*. Sacrifices of impetration were ordained to remind the people of the necessity of praying to God, in order to obtain the graces necessary to live and die in the friendship of God.

Now, as God, in the beginning of the world, instituted

sacrifice, in order that men should, thereby, give him the supreme honor of adoration, thank him for his blessing, appease him after having offended him, and obtain from him the graces necessary for their spiritual and temporal welfare, it was his will that men, to the end of the world, should offer sacrifice to him for the same sacred ends.

But, how can this be, you may ask, since the sacrifices of the Old Law are no longer offered to God? It is true, the sacrifices of the Old Law are no longer offered. Jesus Christ, our Blessed Saviour abolished them, because they were imperfect. God ordained them only as emblems, figures and representations of the perfect sacrifice, that undefiled oblation which was to succeed them. Those sacrifices were good in themselves because appointed by God, " but it is impossible," says St. Paul, " that sin should be taken away with the blood of oxen and goats." (Heb., x., 4.)

Those sacrifices, therefore, were to last only for a time, and then to give way to the perfect sacrifice which was to take their place. God himself announced this truth by the prophet Malachy, in these words: " I have no pleasure in you (Jews), and I will not receive a gift from your hand. For, from the rising to the setting of the sun, my name is great among the heathen, and in every place there is a sacrifice, and there is offered to my name a clean oblation."—(I., 10.)

Now, when God says to the Jews: " I will receive no gift from your hand," he plainly tells them that their sacifices will be rejected; and when he says: " In every place there is a sacrifice offered to my name," he expressly declares that another sacrifice will be substituted for the Jewish sacrifices; and when God calls the new sacrifice " a clean oblation," a pure sacrifice which will be offered to him " from the rising

6

to the setting of the sun," he clearly tells that this perfect sacrifice will take the place of the Jewish sacrifices.

Now, when Jesus Christ abolished the Jewish sacrafices because they were no longer pleasing to his heavenly Father, he did not, at the same time, abolish altogether the law to offer sacrifice. Our divine Saviour came on earth not to destroy the law of offering sacrifice, but to fulfil it, to make it perfect.

Whatever, was essential to the right worship of God in the Old Law—in the Jewish religion—remained essential also in the New Law, the Christian religion. Now, as sacrifice was the very essence of the Jewish religion, it continued also to be the essence of the Christian religion ; in other words, as God wished that the Jews should give him the supreme honor of adoration by offering sacrifices to him, as he wished that they should appease him by sacrifices, thank him, and receive spiritual and temporal favors by offering sacrifices, so, also, God wishes all Christians to render him the honor of adoration, atone for their sins, thank him for blessings received, and obtain all necessary graces by offering sacrifice to him.

Now, how did our Saviour fulfil the law of offering sacrifice and make it perfect? He substituted a perfect victim—himself—for the victims offered up in the Old Law—for sheep, oxen, lambs, and the like.

The Son of God is equal to his Father in all things. He, therefore, deserves the same honor and worship as his heavenly Father, and cannot give him the honor of adoration, or thank him for us ; he cannot appease him for our sins, or obtain favors from him for us. So he became man, and as man he honored and worshipped his Father for us, thanked him, appeased him, and prayed to him for us.

No doubt, the honor of adoration which Jesus Christ gave to his heavenly Father for us, the offering which he made of himself for our sins, the prayers and thanksgivings which he offered for us, were more pleasing to his heavenly Father than all the sacrifices which were offered in the Old Law to honor God, thank him, appease him, and obtain favors from him; for, whatever Jesus Christ did as man, is attributed to his Divine Person which is infinite. Hence, all that he has done for us is of an infinite nature. The honor of adoration, paid by him for us to his heavenly Father, is infinite; his atonement for our sins is infinite; his thanksgivings are infinite, and his prayers are infinite in merit and in value.

Now, Jesus Christ honored and worshipped his heavenly Father for us, thanked him, appeased him for our sins, and prayed for us quite particularly when he was about to die on the cross. He, then, offered to his heavenly Father, in our behalf, his life and death, together with all he had done for us on earth during thirty-three years, exclaiming in a loud voice: "*It is consummated.*" By these words, our Blessed Saviour meant to say that he had done all that was necessary: 1, To honor his heavenly Father for us, and repair the insults offered to him by our sins; 2, To appease him for our sins; 3, To thank him for all the blessings bestowed upon us; 4, To obtain for us all possible spiritual and temporal benefits.

This offering which our Blessed Saviour made of himself on the cross is called *the visible, bloody sacrifice, or offering of Jesus Christ on the cross,* because he shed his blood for us in a visible manner.

As the true character or essence of sacrifice consists in the destruction or change of the thing offered, it is clear, that the bloody sacrifice of Christ on the cross, was perfected, or entirely accomplished the moment in which the separation of his blood from the body caused his death.

Now, Jesus Christ wished to offer himself for us every

day even to the end of the world for those intentions for
which he offered himself on the cross in a visible and bloody
manner; for he knew that he was "*that clean oblation,* foretold by the prophet Malachy to be offered to the heavenly
Father 'in every place,' *from the rising to the setting of the
sun.*"

But how could this be done, since our Blessed Saviour
knew that, after his resurrection he could die no more, and
that, forty days after, he was to be in heaven, and not on
earth to offer himself in sacrifice for us to his heavenly
Father? His love for the honor of his Father, and his
charity for us found an easy means to sacrifice himself *every
day* and *everywhere* to the end of the world, not, indeed, in
a visible and bloody manner as on the cross, but in an *invisible* and *unbloody* manner.

Now, Jesus Christ sacrificed himself in an invisible and
unbloody manner at the Last Supper when he took and
offered bread and wine, changed the same into his body and
blood, and under the appearances of bread and wine, offered
himself for us to his heavenly Father, for the four intentions
mentioned above, and then, as St. Thomas Aquinas says,
"received his own body and blood, and gave the same also
to his Apostles." (De Humanit. Christi, Art. xvii.) This
sacred action of our Lord is called the *unbloody* or *Eucharistic sacrifice* of Jesus Christ, or the Holy Mass.

Christ, then, offered his body and blood for us not only
whilst he was upon the cross, but also when he celebrated the
Last Supper. This appears clearly from these words of our
Lord: "This is my body which is given for you."
(Luke, xxii., 19.) Here our Saviour does not say:—This
is my body which *will* be given for you, but he says, *which
is given* for you *now*, at the moment in which I am speaking.
This great truth appears still more clearly from the words

which Jesus Christ pronounced when holding the chalice, saying: "This is the chalice, which *is shed* for you."

Now, the chalice was not shed for us on the cross; therefore it was shed at the Last Supper.

Now, there is no essential difference between the bloody sacrifice of Jesus Christ on the cross, and his unbloody sacrifice at the Last Supper. The only difference is in the manner in which Jesus Christ offered himself on those two occasions. At the Last Supper the manner in which he offered himself was *unbloody* and *invisible*, whilst on the cross it was bloody and visible. In each instance, the priest was the same, and the victim offered was also the same—Jesus Christ himself.

We have said above, that the true character or essence of sacrifice consists in the destruction or change of the thing offered in sacrifice, as without this destruction or change it seemed that man did not fittingly express his inward acknowledgment that God was the Supreme Lord of the Universe, the Sovereign Master of life and death, and as such worthy of being honored by the sacrifice of man's life, were he to require it. Hence we said, that the sacrifice of Jesus Christ on the cross was perfect or entirely accomplished only at the moment of his death. Now, since his resurrection, Jesus Christ can die no more. How, then, can he be a perfect sacrifice under the appearances of bread and wine, since a sacrifice cannot be perfect without the loss of life?

Jesus Christ, it is true, can no more die or lose the glorious life which he possesses in heaven. But under the appearances of bread and wine, he possesses a kind of life—called his sacramental, or mystic life—which he can lose, and does lose as soon as the appearances of bread and wine cease to exist. The essence of this unbloody or Eucharistic sacrifice, therefore, consisted in rendering present, by the words of consecration, the holy Victim—Christ's sacred body under the two species and in the oblation which he made of it. Now, the same words, by which Christ rendered his sacred body present under the two species, served also to make the oblation thereof. This unbloody sacrifice of Jesus Christ was entirely accomplished only at the moment in which he lost his sacramental or mystic life, that is, soon after he and his apostles had received his body and blood.

This unbloody sacrifice of Jesus Christ consisted of three parts: 1, The offering of bread and wine; 2, The change of bread and wine into the body and blood of Jesus Christ; and 3, The eating of the flesh and drinking of the blood of our Saviour. Christ, therefore, at the Last Supper, celebrated the first Mass on earth. The Holy Mass, then, is the unbloody sacrifice of the body and blood of Jesus Christ under the appearances of bread and wine.

But how could Jesus Christ offer himself in Mass "in every place from the rising to the setting of the sun" after his ascension into heaven? He did it by instituting a new and perfect Order of priesthood to offer up the *unbloody sacrifice* in every place of the world.

In the Old Law there were two distinct classes of the priesthood: one—the priesthood of Aaron, who offered the blood of animals; the other, the priesthood of Melchisedech, who offered bread and wine. Now, our Blessed Saviour united in his own divine Person both of these classes of the priesthood, as was foretold by the royal prophet David, who called Jesus Christ a "*Priest forever according to the Order of Melchisedech.*" (Ps. 109.) Our Blessed Saviour is justly called a priest "according to the Order of Melchisedech," because, at the Last Supper, he used bread and wine, according to the rite of Melchisedech.

Jesus Christ is also a priest according to the rite of Aaron, because, on the day after the Last Supper, he offered up himself in a bloody manner as the victim of our sins, according to the rite of Aaron.

As Christ united in himself both kinds of the priesthood of the Old Law, so he also united the two kinds of sacrifice of the Old Law—the bloody or the sacrifice of animals, and the unbloody or the sacrifice of bread and wine, of the fruits of the earth, in the one adorable sacrifice of his body and blood which he offered up under the appearances of bread and wine.

But how is the bloody sacrifice of Christ, or his death on the cross caused by the separation of the blood from the body, particularly represented in his unbloody sacrifice—in holy Mass? The death of Christ which was caused by the separation of the blood from the body, is strikingly represented by the two distinct consecrations. By the virtue of the words which the priest pronounces, the *body* of Christ becomes present under the appearance of bread, and *his blood* under the appearance of wine; and both these appearances being visibly *separated* from each other—the separation of the blood in the chalice from the body under the appearance of bread, represents the bloody death on the cross in an unbloody mystical manner. Jesus Christ is also justly called by David "*a priest forever,*" because he continues to the end of the world to offer up the unbloody sacrifice of his body and blood by the hands of the new and perfect order of priests which he instituted at the Last Supper; for, after he had sacrificed his body and blood in an invisible and unbloody manner, he, at that very time, empowered and commanded the Apostles to do the same, and thus instituted the new and perfect Order of priests.

Jesus Christ gave this power and command to his Apostles in these words: "Do this in commemoration of me;" that is, as I took bread and brake, and gave to you, saying, this is my body, and really and substantially made it my body, which is given for you—and as I took the chalice, gave thanks, and said: This is my blood, and really and substantially made it my blood, which shall be shed for many, and as I thus offered to my heavenly Father in a mystic and unbloody manner, my real body and blood—that same victim which is to be immolated on the cross in a visible and bloody manner, so do you also take bread, and blessing it, make it my body; and taking wine, bless it, and make it my blood; and thus continually present to my Father, in an unbloody manner, not a different, but the self-same sacrifice which shall be offered up in a bloody manner once upon the cross. Do this for a commemoration of me; for, as often as you shall eat this bread, and drink this chalice you shall show the death of the Lord until he come.

The Apostles obeyed this command of Christ to offer up the unbloody sacrifice, as we can clearly see from the Acts of the Apostles (Chap. xiii., 2.) where St. Luke informs us that, as the Apostles were ministering—that is to say, as *they were sacrificing to the Lord*, the Holy Ghost said to them: "Separate me Saul and Barnabas."

The same sacrifice which the Evangelist distinguishes by the term "ministration," we Catholics, at the present day, call the "Mass." St. Matthew, the Apostle, as history informs us, was pierced with a lance whilst celebrating the holy sacrifice of the Mass.

This holy sacrifice has been offered from the time of the Apostles up to the present day, and will so continue to be offered to the end of the world.

We see, therefore, the prophecy of Malachy, that "from the rising of the sun to the going down, there is offered to my name a clean oblation," (Chapt. I.) is fulfilled only in the

Catholic Church, whose priests daily offer the holy sacrifice of the Mass, the clean oblation for the living and the dead. "This holy sacrifice," says St. Augustine, "was substituted for all the sacrifices of the Old Law." (De Civit. Dei, Lib. 17.) "The Apostles received this sacrifice from Jesus Christ," says St. Irenaeus, "and the Church having received it from the Apostles, celebrates it at the present day throughout the world, according to the prophecy of Malachy." (Lib. iv., c. 32.)

Jesus Christ, however, instituted only the principal parts of the Mass, that is: the offertory, consecration and communion. The accessory parts or the ceremonies of the Mass, come from the Church.

At the offertory the priest offers bread and wine.

At the Consecration, the priest pronounces, in the name of Jesus, the sacred *words of consecration*, by which the bread and wine are changed into the body and blood of Jesus Christ; and at the Communion, the priest receives the body and blood of Christ.

Here it may be asked: "If the sacrifice of the Mass and the sacrifice of the cross are but one and the same sacrifice, as was said above, why then is the same sacrifice daily renewed? Was not the sacrifice of the cross sufficient for the redemption of the whole world?" The sacrifice of the Cross is, indeed, of infinite value, and more than sufficient for the redemption of all mankind; but, to be of profit to us, we must make use of the means necessary to apply it to our souls, and these means are the sacrifice of the Mass, the sacraments, prayer, and good works.

We must, therefore, consider the holy sacrifice of the Mass, as an efficient means by which the merit of the sacrifice of the Cross is, in especial manner, applied to our souls. Now, Christ at Mass applies to us the merits of his bloody sacrifice by offering for us to his heavenly Father all that he offered on the cross for us (that is, the labors, the prayers and the sufferings of his life, and at last his life itself, in order thereby (1) to honor his heavenly father for us; (2) to thank him for all his blessings; (3) to atone for our sins, and (4) to obtain for us abundant graces. Mass, therefore, is (1) a sacrifice of adoration and praise of the divine Majesty; (2) a sacrifice of thanksgiving for divine blessings; (3) a sacrifice of propitiation, obtaining for sinners the grace of repentance and the remission of temporal punishment for the living and the dead; and (4), a sacrifice of impetration, obtaining for us abundant spiritual and temporal blessings.

As the acts of adoration and praise, of thanksgiving, of atonement and of impetration of Jesus Christ at Mass are of an infinite value because they proceed from his infinite divine person, it clearly follows, that, when offering up Mass to our heavenly Father, we offer him acts of infinite adoration and praise, of thanksgiving, of propitiation and of impetration. The best means, therefore, to worship God and praise him, to thank him for his blessings, to appease him for our sins, and to receive great graces from him is to offer up the holy sacrifice of the Mass. No doubt, if God, for four thousand years, required men to give him, by special though imperfect sacrifices, the honor of adoration, and to thank and appease him, and obtain from him the necessary graces to live and die in his holy fear and love, how much more does he not require Christians to offer to him that clean and perfect oblation of the body and blood of his son Jesus Christ, in honor of his divine Majesty, in thanksgiving, in atonement for their sins, and to obtain all necessary graces for their spiritual and temporal welfare!

For this, then, the Mass is given, and for this we are

required to be present at it, that we may, in a perfect and fitting manner, recognize God's sovereignty and our dependence on him. When we hear Mass the meaning of our action, if put into words, would be something of this kind: "I acknowledge Thee, O my God, for my Sovereign Lord and the Supreme Disposer of my life and death: and because I am not able worthily to express thy greatness, I beg of thee to accept as if it were my own, all the submission with which Thy Son honored on the Cross and now honors thee in this Holy Sacrifice. I intend, moreover, by this divine Victim to propitiate Thee for my sins, to lay my wants open to thee, through the pleading tongue of Jesus; and to thank thee as becomes me and as is worthy of Thee, for all the blessings Thou hast bestowed upon me and upon the whole world."

The spectacle is beautiful, indeed awful, in its sublimity. "Have I not said, you are gods!" comes up before one's mind when we think of it. All nature seems to turn to us at that moment: each of us is its representative. Intelligent and unintelligent, in heaven above, on earth, and under the earth, they all turn towards the priest, who gives expression to their feelings and their dependence, who represents their desires at the throne of eternity. The saints and angels look down with Holy Mary at their head, because we bring them increased glory and honor; the souls in purgatory look up to where we kneel, because we are about to make the Blood of the Lamb plead for the eternal union to which their holy souls are tending; the wants and woes and sorrows, the crimes and penitence of the universe turn to us, because everything, outside hell, is interested in the adorable Sacrifice, which it is given us to offer up. At Mass we are enabled to place in the Sacred Heart of the divine Lamb all our thoughts, words, and actions, that they may be purified

and sanctified.   In this Sacred Heart of the divine Victim at
Mass we find a supplement for our deficiencies, and a substitute for our incapabilities.   In the Mass we can offer to the
eternal Father, to atone for the coldness and distraction of
our prayers, the petitions which this compassionate heart of
Jesus poured forth in the silence of night on the lonely mountains of Judea, its supplications in the garden of agony, its
piteous appeals for mercy for men on the Cross.   At Mass
we can offer the burning zeal and love of the Heart of Jesus
to supply for our insensibility to the divine attractions, our
indifference to heavenly things, our fatal self-love, which
blinds the understanding and enslaves the affections; at
Mass we can clothe ourselves in the virtues of Jesus Christ,
and hide our miseries under the mantle of his perfections.

If we often go to Mass, this holy Sacrifice will correct our
faults without bitterness ; it will heal our wounds without pain ;
it will purify our heart without violence ; it will sanctify our
soul without alarm, and almost without a struggle ; it will de-
tach us from ourselves without the convulsion of death ; it will
withdraw us from creatures and unite us to God without
agony.   It is the remedy which Jesus Christ has left us in
all its sweetness.   The poor and the rich, the mechanic and
the merchant, the married and the unmarried, the sick and
the strong, all can easily participate in this adorable Sacrifice without leaving the world, without injuring their health,
or abandoning their family, or employments.   The holy Sacrifice of the Mass, then, is the most beautiful, the most sublime, the most powerful, the most acceptable, and withal the
easiest worship that we can ever offer to God.

THINGS REQUIRED TO COMPLY WITH THE DUTY OF HEARING MASS.

Two things are required to comply with the obligation of
hearing Mass on Sundays or holy-days of obligation.   First,

It is necessary to have the intention of hearing Mass. Hence a person who is forced into the church against his will, or who enters only to look around, and see the place, or to wait there for a friend or for any other purpose except hearing Mass, such a person does not fulfil the obligation of hearing Mass.

Secondly, to fulfil the obligation of hearing Mass, it is also necessary to hear it with devotion, that is, we must be attentive to the sacrifice whilst it is going on. A person, therefore, who, during Mass is asleep, or drunk, or employed in writing, talking, or performing other external actions, does not fulfil the precept of hearing Mass.

It is well to know that in order to satisfy the obligation of hearing Mass, it is not necessary that we should see the priest at the altar. Hence a person may hear Mass behind the altar, or behind a wall or pillar in the church, or immediately outside the church, provided, however, he is united with the people in the church, and knows, by their movements, prayers, or singing, at what part of the Mass the priest is.

Now, Mass may be heard with attention and devotion in different ways. Those who can read, will generally follow the priest by using the Missal, or a book containing suitable prayers. Another good way to hear Mass is to meditate on the Passion of Jesus Christ, for Mass is the renewal of the sacrifice which our dear Saviour offered on the cross; or to meditate on some great truth of salvation—on death, judgmedt, or hell.

Those who can neither read nor meditate, may hear Mass with attention by saying the Rosary, or other prayers; they may say: 1, fifteen Hail Marys and add after the word Jesus: "Whom I offer to God in honor of his divine Majesty;" 2d, again, fifteen Hail Marys and add, after the word Jesus: "Whom I offer to God in thanksgiving for all his benefits; 3, again, fifteen Hail Marys, and adding after the word Jesus: "Whom I offer to God in satisfaction for my sins, and the sins of the living and the death;" 4, again, fifteen Hail Marys, and adding after the word Jesus: "Whom I offer to God to obtain the spiritual and temporal blessings necessary for my salvation." Finish each Hail Mary in the usual manner: "Holy Mary, Mother of God, etc." At the elevation of the Sacred Host, you may say: "O my God! for the love of this, Thy Son, forgive my sins, and let me live and die in thy grace;" and at the elevation of the blood of Jesus Christ in the chalice, you may say: "O my God! through the blood of Jesus Christ make me love Thee more and more, and grant me a happy death." When the priest receives communion, you may say: "O my Jesus! I love Thee, and wish to receive Thee. I embrace Thee; let me never more be separated from Thee."

As the Church does not command us to say certain prayers on Sundays or holy-days of obligation, but commands us to hear Mass, that is, to join in the act of sacrifice, it is clear that the omission of this duty can never be supplied by any other devotions whether public or private. Why this strict obligation of hearing Mass? Can we not worship God just as well at home? No! For, although God, is present everywhere—yea, even in hell—nevertheless he is present on our altars *in a most special manner*. He is present there as God and man, as our Redeemer, our Intercessor, our High Priest, who offers his own innocent Heart's Blood as the atonement for our sins.

This is the reason why Holy Church commands her children under pain of mortal sin to hear Mass, at least every Sunday and holy-day of obligation; why she forbids us to come too late to Mass; why we always find good Catholics so eager to be present at the divine Sacrifice. This explains also the great difference between Catholics and Protestants while on their way to their churches. One may see Protestants taking their time, loitering on the way as if they were going to a lecture-room, which, in fact, is really the case; while, on the contrary, good Catholics are hastening on to church with a certain eagerness, as having some very important duty to perform.

What a consolation to know that as the sun in its course brings the light of day to each successive spot on earth, it ever finds a priest girding himself for the altar, preparing to celebrate holy Mass. Thus, from the rising to the setting of the sun, the pure oblation is offered up to God. Each day, as the busy din of the world begins, as the groan of the downtrodden and the wail of the heart broken, the tear of the helpless victim and the insolent boast of pride, rise up before the throne of God, there also ascends before that throne from our altars the sweet voice of Jesus supplicating for pardon and for peace.

Moreover, as the Church prescribes to hear a whole Mass, it is not enough to be present during a part of the Mass. Hence it is a mortal sin to miss wilfully, without sufficient reason, a *considerable*, or an *essential* part of the Mass. To be absent from the beginning of the Mass to the end of the offertory, through one's own fault, is to miss a *considerable part* in point of length. Hence theologians say that such a wilful omission is a mortal sin; and as Consecration and Communion are the essential parts of Mass, it is a mortal sin wilfully to miss through one's own fault, either of these parts.

To be absent, through one's own fault, from the beginning of the Mass to the end of the Gospel, or to leave without sufficient cause after the communion of the priest, is a venial

sin. If a person enters the church after the consecration of
the Mass is over and continues to hear the remaining part
of the Mass, and afterwards hears another Mass until the
consecration is over, and then leaves the church, he does not
comply with the obligation of hearing an *entire* Mass, because
he was not present at the essential parts (consecration and
communion) o f *oe entire sacrifice;* but should he leave only
after the communion of the second Mass, he has complied
with his obligation of hearing Mass.

It is no sin whatever to miss Mass on Sundays or holy-
days of obligation, if we are physically or morally prevented
from hearing it. A person, therefore, who is confined to bed
by sickness, or is in prison, or is blind and has no one to lead
him to church, is excused from hearing Mass.   In like manner a person who cannot go to church without exposing himself or others to the danger of some great spiritual or temporal loss, is also excused from hearing Mass; for instance,
persons who are on duty in cities, or in armies, or intrusted
with the care of herds of cattle, or of houses, or of infants,
or of the sick, all such persons are exempt from the obligation of hearing Mass when they have no one to take their
place; also sick people who are convalescent and unable to
go to church without great pain or danger of relapse, or
servants who cannot leave the house without great inconvenience to their master, or to themselves, are excused from
the obligation of hearing Mass; in a word, no person is,
strictly speaking, bound to undergo a great inconvenience
in order to hear Mass.   Hence a considerable distance from
church (three or four miles), is a sufficient reason to exempt
one from the obligation of hearing Mass; even a less distance is a sufficient excuse, if it is raining or snowing, or
when the roads are in a bad condition.

There are many, who live quite close to the church, and

they are, generally speaking, the very persons to be regularly late at Mass. They seem to be afraid of being a minute
too soon in church. Others are in the habit of standing outside the church until the organ commences to play, and then
noisily rush in so as to disturb the priest at the altar, and
the devout worshippers in their prayers. As all these come
to Mass without preparation, they assist at it, of course,
with little or no devotion. Many of them remain behind in
the church. They have eyes, and see not; ears, and hear
not what is going on at the altar. They have hearts, and
feel not, lips and pray not. They have neither prayer-book
nor rosaries in their hands. They are there like marble
statues. Like these, they neither hear nor draw the least
profit from Mass. They do not comply with the command
of the Church, prescribing *to hear Mass with devotion.* How.
sad it is to see Catholics manifest less devotion and recollection at the tremendous Sacrifice of the Mass than heathens
manifest at their idolatrous worship!

There are others whose preparation for Mass is still
worse. It frequently happens that the nearest neighbors of
a Catholic church are generally the proprietors of drinking
saloons. It was not the Holy Ghost, but the devil, the
enemy of God and of prayer, that inspired these men to
establish the offices of Satan as close to the church as possible, so as to make it convenient for lukewarm Catholics to
enter first these little chapels of the devil, and pay their homage to the god of their belly before entering the house of the
Lord. What is still worse than all this is, that the near
neighborhood of these houses causes lukewarm Catholics
sometimes to leave the church during the time of the sermon,
in order to spend it in these chapels of the devil. They are
afraid of listening for half an hour to the word of God, which
might make them become better Christians; they prefer to
7

listen to the word of the devil, to the obscene language which
prevails in these establishments. Some of these lukewarm
Catholics remain there during the whole time of High Mass,
and leave but too often in a state of intoxication; while others leave when they think that the sermon is over. It is
hardly necessary to say that to this class of Catholics the
words of the Gospel apply: "This people honoreth me with
their lips, but their heart is far from me." (Mark vii., 6.)
They leave the church as litttte touched and benefited by the
sacred mysteries as the stones in the wall. But woe to the
men who thus draw Catholics from the worship of God! Can
there be a greater blindness, a greater cruelty to one's-self
and to our fellow-men than that of making a living by offending Almighty God, and ruining many souls redeemed at the
infinite price of the most precious blood of Jesus Christ?

We read in the Holy Scripture that the two sons of Heli,
Ophni and Phinees, "withdrew men from the sacrifice of the
Lord. This sin was exceeding great before the Lord." And
as Heli neglected to punish his sons for this great crime, the
Lord punished them and their father by a sudden death.
Now, to withdraw Catholics from the holy sacrifice of the
Mass is a greater sin than the sons of Heli committed by
withdrawing many Jews from the sacrifice of the Lord; for
by the sacrifice of the Mass God is infinitely more honored
than by the Jewish sacrifices. Those, therefore, who prevent Catholics from attending Mass will be far more severely
punished than the sons of Heli.

EXCUSES OF LUKEWARM CHRISTIANS FOR NOT GOING TO MASS.

The holy sacrifice of the Mass is an inexhaustible treasure
of graces. Yet how little is this most august sacrifice valued
by the greater part of men? If it were said, "At such a
lace and at such an hour a dead person will be raised to

life," men would run to witness the miracle. But is not the consecration which changes bread and wine into the Body and Blood of Christ, a far greater miracle than the raising of a dead person to life? If Christians only knew the value of the holy sacrifice of the Mass, or rather, if they had more faith, assuredly they would not stay away from it for the most trivial pretexts.

There are some who say: "There is no need of going to Mass; we can pray just as well at home."

Now, do we really pray to God at home? But, whether we do or not, the question is *not* can we pray well at home, but whether God requires us to hear Mass on Sundays and holy-days of obligation. God *does require* this. God speaks to all Christians through his Church, and the Church of God commands us to hear Mass on Sundays and holy-days under pain of mortal sin, that is, she commands you under pain or eternal damnation to be present, with attention and devotion, at the principal parts of the Mass.

It is true that we are distinct individuals, with distinct individual duties, but it is also true that we are a religious body. This society, this Church of which we are members, has certain duties to fulfil towards God, one of which is public worship; and the public worship of this Christian society is precisely the holy Sacrifice of the Mass. To stay away from this act of public worship is to neglect a most sacred duty; it is, in a certain sense, to renounce all our share in the merits of Jesus Christ. For our sake the heavenly Father sends his well-beloved Son upon the altar; for our salvation, the Holy Ghost changes bread and wine into the Body and Blood of Jesus Christ; for our sake the Son of God comes down from heaven, and conceals himself under the species of bread and wine, humbling himself so much as to be whole and entire in the smallest particle of the Host.

For our sake he renews the Mystery of his Incarnation, is born anew in a mystical manner, offers up to his heavenly Father all the prayers and devotions which he performed during his life on earth, renews his Passion and Death to make us partakers of its merits, cancelling our sins and neg-ligences, and remitting many temporal punishments due to the same. And we reject these graces and blessings, despise this offering every time that we carelessly stay away from the holy Mass.

Now, can we think that God will allow this carelessness of ours to go unpunished? Listen to the following example: St. Anthony, Archbishop of Florence, relates that two young men went hunting on Sunday. The sky was cloudless, not a leaf was stirring. Presently they heard the low rumbling of distant thunder. A dark smoke like a vapor began to spread over the face of the heavens. Flashes of lightning succeeded one another rapidly, and the voice of the thunder was heard in one continuous roar. In a few moments the sky grew black as sackcloth. Soon the vivid flashes of lightning lit up the heavens with a lurid preternatural glare. At times the whole universe appeared to be on fire; the peals of thunder followed one another with astounding rapidity. Many trees were struck by the lightning within view of the hunters, and presently one of the largest trees was shivered to splinters directly in their path. Suddenly they heard above them in the air a wild unearthly yell. "Strike! strike!" cried the voice, and instantly a flash of lightning killed one of them—the one that had not heard Mass. The other young man was panic-stricken at this, especially as he heard at the same time, a voice saying: "Strike him too." A little after he felt encouraged by another voice, which said, "I cannot strike him because he heard Mass this morning." (Ant. ii., p. Theolog. ix., c. 10.)

We know that we can do nothing better for our parents, friends, for the poor and distressed, for our benefactors, for the dying, for the conversion of sinners, for the just, for the souls in purgatory, than to hear and offer for them the holy Sacrifice of the Mass; and that we cannot give greater glory and joy to the blessed Trinity, to the Blessed Virgin, and to all the saints, than by hearing Mass with devotion. But whenever we stay away from Mass through neglect, especially on Sundays and holy-days of obligation, we thereby give to understand that we do not care to give glory to God and his saints, as little as we care to obtain the graces of God for ourselves and others by so powerful a means as that of the Mass. And do we imagine that this contempt of ours for God's glory and his blessings will go unpunished? We cannot complain that the Almighty should treat us with similar neglect, if he bestows his choicest gifts upon others and passes us by unnoticed. We made the choice and we must abide the issue.

Three merchants of Gubbio went to a fair held in the town of Cisterno, and having disposed of their goods, two of them began to speak of returning home, and arranged to start the next day at dawn, so as to arrive by evening in their own neighborhood. But the third would not consent to start at that time, protesting that the next day being Sunday he would never think of beginning a journey without first having heard holy Mass. His companions refused to wait for him, and set out by themselves. But when they arrived at the river Corfuone, which had risen to a great height in consequence of the rain that fell during the night, the bridge gave way and they were drowned. The third, who had waited to hear Mass, found his two companions dead on the bank of the river, and gratefully acknowledged the grace which he had received on account of having heard Mass.—[*Lohner.*

We may rest assured that whenever we miss Mass through carelessness, we expose ourselves to the greatest dangers of soul and body; for it is then that the devil obtains from God great power over both; which power is refused him in regard to those who comply with their duty of hearing Mass with devotion on all days of obligation. It is an unquestionable truth that devout attendance at Mass has protected many souls from vices into which they would otherwise have fallen; it has saved many a one from sudden death and calamities which God has permitted to fall on others; it has conferred a blessing on many a family—given peace and unanimity, where discord would otherwise have reigned; and in the conduct of children made parents happy, whose hearts would otherwise have been broken by their disobedient and disorderly behavior.

It is related of Drahomira, the mother of St. Wenceslaus, a very impious duchess of Bohemia, how she one day went in a carriage to Saes in order to take a solemn oath on her father's grave, to extirpate all the Christians in her dominions. Passing a chapel in which Mass was being said, the driver, on hearing the bell ring for the elevation of the Host, stopped the carriage and knelt down on the ground to adore our Lord Jesus Christ on the altar. At this the impious duchess flew into a violent passion, cursing the driver and the Blessed Sacrament. In punishment for her horrible blasphemies, the earth opened and swallowed her and her whole escort.* They cried for help, but in vain. In a moment they were gone forever. The driver was glad indeed for having stopped the carriage to adore our Lord in the Blessed Sacrament; his faith and devotion saved him from destruction.—[*Hagec in chronic. bohemic. ad. ann. 9. 30.*

There are, as we have said, grievous reasons which dispense with the obligation of hearing Mass. But there are many persons for whom a little rain, a damp mist, the slight inconvenience of heat, a little moisture under foot, rise up as a sufficient excuse. They will be judged by St. Elizabeth, who, as Rutebeuf tells us, repaired early in the morning to Mass so poorly and humbly, through the mire of the road, without horse or carriage, holding her lighted taper in her hand.

The lukewarm Christians will be judged by that Christian young woman, who, when on her way to Mass, was perceived by the guard of the Emperor Diocletian; he was struck with her modesty, and going rudely up to her he said: "Stop! whither are you going?" The young woman was frightened; she feared that he would insult her. She made on her forehead the sign of the Cross, in order to obtain the divine protection. The soldier, deeming himself affronted by her silence, seized her violently and said: "Speak! who are you? whither are you going?" She courageously replied: "I am a servant of Jesus Christ, and am going to the assembly of the Lord." "You shall not go," said the soldier; "you must sacrifice to the gods; to-day we worship the sun; you must worship with us." He then attempted to pull off the veil which covered her face. This she endeavored to prevent, and said: "Wretch, Jesus Christ will punish you!" At these words the soldier became furious, and plunged his sword into the heart of the Christian virgin. She fell, bathed in her blood, but her holy soul flew up to heaven, there to receive an unfading crown of glory.—[*Fleury.*

There are also many who find an excuse in the fact that their friends and acquaintances, as well as occupations, make large demands upon their time. But these will be judged by Sir Thomas More, who never omitted hearing Mass, notwithstanding his numerous friends and occupations. One day, while he was hearing Mass, the king's messenger

came and told him that his majesty required his immediate
presence, in order to transact with him business of the greatest importance.   The Chancellor said to him : "Yet a little
patience.   I have to present my homages of respect to a sovereign of greater power and authority ; and I think it necessary to remain at the audience of heaven until it shall be
over."   He considered it a high honor to serve Mass.   "I
deem it," he used to say, "a high honor to have it in my
power to render this slight service to the greatest of
sovereigns."

   There are others who say : "Father, I oversleep myself."
Shame on such!   Let them break off useless conversations
and go to bed in due time ; not turning night into day and
day into night, and they will awake easily enough, as they do
when there is question of some temporal gain.   But when
the question is one of obtaining the blessings of the Mass,
graces and blessings which have cost our dear Saviour His
most precious Blood, they are too lazy to get up in time.
Certainly they will will be judged by that good and faithful
Christian who, as Gillois relates, lived in Roibon, a town of
the diocese of Grenoble.   He was a peasant whose great devotion at Mass edified every one who saw him.   Although
living three miles from the church, he never failed to be one
of the first worshippers in the morning.   In the latter years
of his life he was subject to severe pains in his limbs, which
prevented his walking so far in the winter season, but as
soon as the spring came, he used to rise about one o'clock
in the morning, and supporting himself by means of crutches,
he would reach the church after a painful and laborious walk
of four hours.

   But some may say, "It is more necessary for us to labor
than to hear Mass ; because, without work, we cannot even
earn a subsistence for ourselves and family."   On the con-

trary, it is even more necessary to hear Mass than to labor, because it is a most powerful means of keeping oneself in the state of grace, and obtaining the blessings of God. This does not mean that men are to neglect their work, but they can easily break off for half an hour, and devote that short time to God. Those who do so will soon find that their business will not suffer, as God's blessing will be upon it. Men who neglect to hear Mass, either from temporal interest or from sloth, inflict upon themselves a loss for which there is no compensation; they lose a hundred-fold more than the work of a whole day could bring in.

In the life of St. John the Almoner is an instructive narrative of two artisans who pursued the same trade; one was burdened with a family: wife, children, grandchildren; the other was alone with his wife. The first brought up his family in great comfort, and all his transactions turned out wonderfully. Thus he went on till he found himself putting by every year a good round sum, to serve in time for marriage portions for his daughters. The other, who was without children, at one time got very little employment, was half famished, and in short, a ruined man. One day he said confidentially to his neighbor: "How is it with you? On your home rains down every blessing of God, while I, poor wretch, cannot hold up my head, and all sorts of calamities fall on my house." "I will tell you," said his neighbor; "to-morrow morning I will be with you and point out the place from which I draw so much." Next morning he took him to church to hear Mass, and then led him back to his workshop; and so for two or three days, till at last the poor man said: "If nothing else is wanted than to go to church to hear Mass, I know the way well enough, without putting you to inconvenience." "Just so," said the other; "hear holy Mass, my friend, with devotion every day, and you will see a change in the face of your fortune." And, in fact, so it was. Beginning to hear holy Mass every morning, he was soon well provided with work, shortly after paid his debts, and put his house once more in a prosperous condition.

Some again say: "Father, I am in a place where I have too much work to do; after I have finished it is too late for Mass; and were I to leave my work unfinished and go to Mass, the family I live with would be much displeased with me, and might discharge me."

Now, there is good reason for believing that this difficulty is not so great as is imagined by those who raise it. If the family they live with are Catholics, they know that it is their duty to see that all Catholics get to Mass in due time; if they are Protestants or Jews, they will be glad to see those in their employ anxious to comply with their religious duties, knowing that if their employees are faithful to God, they will also be faithful to them; and this is the reason why they like to have Catholic workmen and servants. Should, however, the demand to go to Mass be refused, other places are open, and sensible employers will scarcely object at the risk of parting with a conscientious Catholic workman or servant. In order to avoid all difficulties, it is best to tell the family into whose service one is about to enter, that he or she only enters on condition that full liberty be given to comply with religious duties on Sundays and holy-days of obligation. Should they not agree to this, one should not go to them so long as there are prospects of finding another situation. However, it may be taken for granted that generally speaking, a good Catholic laborer or servant who is very anxious to hear Mass on Sundays and all holy-days of obligation, easily finds a good situation, for this is a blessing which Jesus Christ grants to those who never miss Mass through neglect. It may be also taken for granted that those who really value and rightly appreciate the blessings of Mass, will know how to arrange their work so as not to allow it to interfere with their regular attendance at Mass. Show a little more anxiety to serve the Lord, to keep the soul in the state of grace, and to advance in holiness of life, and all imaginary difficulties in this matter of staying away from church will soon disappear. Be just as careful and desirous to obtain the blessing of God as to avoid a little temporal loss, and you will soon be a better Catholic.

St. Isidore was hired by a wealthy farmer to cultivate his farm. He would, however, never begin his work in the morning before he had heard Mass. He was accused to his master by some of his fellow-laborers, of staying too long in church, and on that account of being always late at work. His master, in order to examine for himself the truth of the accusation, went out early in the morning to see whether or not Isidore came in due time to the farm; but how great was his astonishment when he beheld two angels, dressed in white, ploughing with two yoke of oxen, and St. Isidore between them. From that time forward Isidore was held in great veneration by his master as well as by all those who heard of the wonderful occurrence.

Why is it that Mass is said, especially on Sundays and holy-days of obligation, at different hours, from break of day till noon? Precisely for the convenience of the early traveller, laborer, the domestic, the student, the charitable matron, the pious father of a family, the children; to remove as far as possible every pretext for missing Mass. Indeed, there have been many Catholics who have heard Mass under greater difficulties and inconveniences than those who are so ready with excuses. They will judge and condemn on the day of the last judgment all who neglect this most important duty of their religion.

After the miserable Henry VIII., King of England, had consummated the schism and heresy of the Anglican Church, there were enacted several penal laws against those who had the courage to practise the Catholic religion; even a heavy fine was imposed on those who attended Mass. It happened one day that a fervent Catholic, who enjoyed a large fortune, was condemned to pay five hundred gold pieces, because he had dared to fulfil publicly that duty of religion. The gentleman was very happy in that he was judged worthy to endure this persecution. He sought out the finest pieces of Portuguese gold that were to be had, because they bore the impress of the Cross, and went himself to present the entire sum in the court of law. As he counted out the new coins before the Protestant official, the latter asked him, in a jeering tone, what was the reason of his selecting such beautiful pieces to pay the fine. To this ironical question the Catholic gentleman merely replied: "I would think it wrong to pay with common and ordinary money the favor I received in being enabled to adore my Lord and Saviour in the holy Sacrament of the Altar. Know, sir, that between the Cross you see stamped on this coin and the holy Sacrifice of the Altar, there exist numerous points of analogy; both are, in fact, monuments of our Saviour's infinite love, and no Catholic may ignore them." And so saying he went on quietly counting out the five hundred gold pieces; this was the price of assisting at the holy Sacrifice.—[*Schmidt's Histor. Catech.*]

But, granting that our facilities for hearing Mass may not always be so great as our wish, yet if we understand and value the gift of God to us in the Mass, we shall not only think it well worth some additional trouble in the purchase, but feel that the sacrifice of a life would be too well repaid by the high honor and unsurpassed happiness of attending even once at the most adorable Sacrifice. There is no Christian incapable of feeling the pleasure that is produced by the knowledge of what is contained in the holy Sacrifice of the Mass. All that is necessary for that is to esteem the blessings of grace, to desire your salvation, to sigh after heaven, and to remember that the august Sacrifice is the source of all temporal and spiritual riches, and the most efficacious means of satisfying all holy desires.

Unless so circumstanced that to hear Mass even daily is a moral impossibility, or a decided infringement on the duties of your state in life, maintain inviolably the good habit of hearing Mass every day. Go gladly to the altar of God, there to draw down the multiplied graces of which it is the copious source, thence to extract the spiritual treasures of which it is the inexhaustible mine; thence to procure a balm for all miseries and a remedy for all wants. Think seriously of all that we have in the wonderful and adorable Sacrifice, thus to enliven faith, to reanimate confidence, to inflame devotion, and powerfully to confirm the determination to be ever the fervent, devoted, loving adorer of Jesus, the divine Victim of the Altar. If circumstances render it really impossible to hear Mass daily, endeavor at least, as far as in you lies, to idemnify yourself for the very great privation. Desire with all the ardor of your soul to enjoy so great a happiness.

It is well for those who can do so in the course of the morning to retire to their room nearly at the time which they know to be the hour when the holy Sacrifice of the Mass is offered in the church, and, after having implored the grace of God, to perform with recollection and fervor the duty of religion, to kneel before the crucifix, and with all the sentiments of devotion possible to unite heart and soul to the Heart of Jesus in the holy Mass, and then read or say the same prayers that they would have said had they been actu-

ally present in the church, never forgetting to make the spiritual Communion, which may be made in any place, and at
any hour of the day or night.   The good Catholic, then, will
always feel himself impelled to hear Mass, unless a very
urgent reason prevents him from so doing.

In the South of Ireland, County Cork, there are two islands
with only one church.   When the sea is too stormy the inhabitants of one island assemble upon the beach at the appointed hour and turn to the church.   There they kneel in
the sand, arise at the Gospel, bless themselves at the Consecration, and thus unite themselves in spirit with the holy
Sacrifice from which they are separated by the wind and
waves.

St. Louis, King of France, used to hear two Masses every
day; sometimes even three or four.   Some of his courtiers
murmured at this, but the king gave them a sharp repri-
mand, saying: "If I were to ask you to play, or to go
hunting with me, three or four times a day, you would find
no time too long, and now you feel weary of staying in the
church during one or two Masses for the honor of our Lord
and Saviour."—[*Reinaldus in Annal.* 1270, *No.* 19.]

Henry III. of England used to hear each day three High
Masses, besides several Low Masses.   One day St. Louis
conversed with him on this devotion and observed that it
was not always necessary to hear so many Masses, but that
as many sermons as possible should be heard.   King Henry
replied, "I prefer seeing my friend often to hearing any one
speak of him, however excellent may be his discourse."

When St. Anselm, Archbishop of Canterbury, was no
longer able on account of his old age to say Mass, he had
himself carried to the church every day to hear it.—[*His
Life, by Eadmer.*]

Blessed Armella was a poor, but holy servant girl.   We

read in her life that whenever she was prevented from going to church, she used to kneel in the place where she had to work, with her face turned towards Jesus in the Blessed Sacrament, and thus performed her devotion. She used to do this particularly at the time when she knew the Holy Mass was celebrated, or that the Blessed Sacrament was exposed on the altar.

Would that we had some of this spirit of the saints still left among us! Has devotion forsaken the greater part of Christians altogether, that they leave Jesus at present such a stranger upon our altars? Are their necessities less numerous or less urgent than were those of old? No, but it is true that their weaknesses are greater and they are less sensible of them. They take less pains to acquire strength. If there was a day on which they would not be exposed to sin; a time in which they would not be surrounded by enemies; if they had no virtues to acquire, no homage to pay, they might be excused from hearing Mass. But if, on the other hand, they are pressed by all these motives, let them not be so thankless to the Almighty, so thoughtless of themselves, as to neglect the only means they have of performing all these duties. Let us endeavor to imitate the saints in their zeal in hearing Mass. Early in the morning, when angels are descending from heaven to take their stand around the altar of the Most High, let us too set out to assist at Mass, and emulate their devotion during the performance of this stupendous mystery.

Let us not think the time is lost which is spent in hearing Mass; it will prove most profitable to us in this life and in the next. See how many sins are expiated by it! how many punishments averted! how many graces drawn upon ourselves and others! how many merits stored up for heaven! Let us be diligent in hearing Mass, and we shall surely find

in it all that we need, our happiness here below and our happiness hereafter.   Amid all the vicissitudes of life, at the
altar we shall find true peace and support.   At one time it
will be Mount Cavalry for us, where we may weep tears of
sympathy for our Saviour, and of grief for our sins and for
those of others; at another time it will be Mount Thabor,
where heavenly joy will be poured into our sorrowing heart,
and tears will be wiped away from our eyes.   Again, that
same altar will be a crib of Bethlehem, where we may gather
strength to bear contempt, poverty, pain, and desolation.
Yes, at the altar we shall find that Mount of Beatitude,
where we may learn the vanity of all earthly things, and the
way to true and lasting pleasure.   In fine, it will be to us
Golgatha, where we may learn to die to ourselves and to
live to him who died for us!   All this and more we find in
the Mass, if we cherish a tender devotion to it: let us perse-
vere in this devotion, and we will soon taste the sweets of
those inspired ejaculations: "How lovely are Thy Tabernacles, O Lord of Hosts!   Thou hast prepared a table before me against those that trouble me.   Better is one day in
thy courts above thousands!   Blessed are they that dwell in
thy house, O Lord: they will praise Thee forever and ever:
They will drink hereafter at the torrent of delight, which,
flowing from the heart of Jesus as its source, inundates from
end to end the everlasting kingdom of God's glory."

THE FOURTH COMMANDMENT.

"*Honor thy father and thy mother, that thou mayest be long-lived upon the land which the Lord thy God will give thee.*" (Exod. xx., 12.)

The principal object of our life in this world is our temporal and eternal happiness. This happiness consists in being united to God and to our neighbor by the virtues of justice and charity. Now, to establish and preserve this union, Almighty God has given us formal precepts of justice and charity. These precepts are contained in the ten commandments. The first three commandments, as they prescribe our duties towards God; that is, adoration, respect, and the santification of the Sabbath, were written on the first tablet of stone. The seven other commandments, as they prescribe our duties of justice and charity towards all our fellow-men, were written on the second tablet of stone.

Now, the first commandment written by the finger of God on the second tablet of stone, prescribes the duties of children towards their parents. It may seem strange that God should have given a special commandment to children to honor their parents. Is it not a natural law, a dictate of good sense, to honor, after God, our greatest benefactors more than any one else? And are not parents the greatest benefactors of children? And yet there are thousands of

8　　　　　[105]

children who have but little or no regard whatever for their parents. It was, therefore, necessary that God should give a special commandment to children to honor their parents.

Now, he who truly honors a person, loves him, fears to displease him, and obeys him with pleasure. By the fourth commandment, therefore, we are obliged to *love, honor* and *obey* our parents in all things that are not sinful.

1. In the first place, we are obliged to *love* our parents. Almighty God commands us to love all men, even our enemies. How much more so does he require us to love those who are so closely allied to us as our parents are, and to whom we are indebted for almost everything that we possess. It is through them that God has given us our very being. At our birth we were more helpless and miserable than any other living creature. At that time our mother, for many months, fed us with the substance of her own body, watched over us by night and by day, lost her own rest to take care of us, and was in continual solicitude about us. She used every expedient to preserve us from harm. She adopted every precaution, by clothing and other means, to shelter us from the inclemency of the seasons, and nothing was left undone to secure us from the least symptom of disease.

Hence, Tobias, when on his death-bed, said to his son Tobias: "My son, thou shalt honor thy mother all the days of her life, for thou must be mindful what and how great perils she suffered for thee." (Tob. iv.)

On the part of the father, what cares and attention for his children! He labors and toils every day for their support. He undergoes sufferings and annoyances to settle them well in the world. He makes many sacrifices that they may be properly educated. His efforts are unceasing in procuring for them respectability and rank. Ah! can we ever make a sufficient return of love to our fathers and mothers, who have loved and do love us so tenderly and constantly? No, says Lenera, a heathen, though we should live a thousand years, we would never be able to make a worthy return for benefits which we have received from our parents.

One day, in 1832, Mgr. Augustine Gruber, Prince Archbishop of Salsburg, in Austria, visited the girls' school of a village in the Tyrol. He addressed himself to one of the children, who might be ten years old, and knew how to count well: "Tell me, my dear child, how much do you think you have already cost your parents?" "I don't know, my lord; they didn't tell me." "Well! let us make this little calculation together. Do you think it cost them 25 centimes every day?" "Oh yes, my lord, that at least; everything is so dear now." "I suppose we may add as much more for your clothes, mendings, books, and other little daily expenses." "You may, my lord; that makes already 50 centimes a day." "And about how many days are there in a month?" "About thirty." "How much does that make, then, at 50 centimes a day?" "That makes 15 francs a month." "And how many months are there in a year?" "There are twelve, my lord." "And twelve months at 15 francs a month, how much does that make at the end of the year?" "My lord, that makes 180 francs." "Very well, my child, and how old are you?" "I am ten years of age, my lord." "Well! can you tell me how much you have already cost your good parents?" "I have already cost them 1,800 francs." "Yes, dear child, you have answered well; but that is not all, for you must add to that the expense of doctors and medicines, journeys, unforeseen expenses, things that you have spoiled or lost, &c. You must add to it all the sufferings, the griefs, the long and fatiguing toils of your father and mother, their good advice, their instructions, the good education they are giving you, &c. All that is not to be repaid by money, but by the love and gratitude of a good heart."—[*Schmid et Belet, Cat. Hist.* ii, 251.]

How should children love their parents?

1, They should be grateful to them, and wish them well from their hearts. 2, They should endeavor to make them happy by their good conduct. 3, They should help them in their necessities, and take care of them in their old age, as well as they are able. 4, They should bear with their faults and weaknesses.

1. As our parents are, after God, our greatest benefactors, our love for them should be a love of gratitude. This love engraves on our hearts the virtue of gratitude, towards our parents; it causes us to feel and acknowledge all the good they have done to us; it excites us to thank them with words full of affection; it makes us wish them well from our heart. This true, sincere love for our parents induces us to add to gratitude of the heart and mouth, that of the hand by giving something to our parents, and even more, if it were possible, than we have received; for to fulfil all the duties of gratitude, we should give something *gratis*, that is, more than we have received, because to give only the same, is to give nothing. If we cannot give them any material assistance because we are poor ourselves, we should at least show them in some way or other how much we sympathize with them in their poverty, afflictions and trials of this life.

The son of a French gentleman in reduced circumstances, was placed at college for his education through the kindness of a friend. It was remarked that for several days after his arrival he partook of nothing at dinner but dry bread and a little broth. His companions kindly pressed him to eat of the meat and vegetables, and also of the fruit which was served at table. He thanked them for their attention, but always declined. This strange behavior came at last to the ears of the president of the college, who sent for him to ask him the reason of it. The young boy at first remained silent, but being encouraged by the kindness of the president, at length said, "It is not because the food is bad, or that I am not hungry, but because I cannot help thinking that my father and mother are now so poor that they have no meat or fruit at dinner as I have, but are often obliged to content themselves with dry bread. I would rather eat as they do, than feast when I know they are hungry and in want." "My good child," replied the president much affected, "you do well to think of your parents. Eat, however, the same as your companions, and I will take care that your parents are provided for, perhaps, better than yourself. The worthy president lost no time in fulfilling his promise. He wrote to the king an account of what had happened, and his Majesty, admiring the noble conduct of the child, granted his father a pension for life.—[*Dict. Hist. de l'Education.*]

2. Heartfelt love for our parents induces us to make them happy by our good conduct, and to give them no unnecessary trouble or pain. '

In 1787, a boy of seven years met with a severe accident at Diegholz, Prussia. He had to undergo a very painful operation; but he uttered not a word of complaint whilst the operation was performed. On being asked why he was so patient, he replied: "My mother is sick, and when she heard of my accident she became still worse. So I concealed my pain that she might not feel worse on my account." Now, when his mother heard how patient her child had been on her account, she experienced so great a joy and consolation that she recovered much sooner than was expected.

3. True, sincere love for our parents induces us to assist them when they are in temporal or spiritual want.

In many countries of Europe there is a bird, called the stork, which is much venerated by the people on account of its love for its parents. When the parent birds grow old and lose their feathers, so that they cannot fly and provide for themselves, the younger birds take care of them. They ward off their enemies, they bring them food, and when danger threatens, they bear them away to a more secure retreat.

What a shame, then, says St. Ambrose, would it not be for children if they were to abandon their parents in their temporal or spiritual wants! Ah! the sad day will yet come when children must part with their parents! What a comfort it will be to them then when they see their parents in the coffin, when they can no longer hear the voice of their father and mother, what a consolation it will be to children when they call to mind that they have always been kind and affectionate to them and assisted them to the best of their power!

St. Cuthman was the son of poor, but pious parents, who lived at Steninges or Estaninges in England. After the death of his father, he spent his whole fortune and all that he gained by the labor of his hands, in supporting his aged mother. At last his mother became so feeble that she could not be left alone. In order to support her he made a handcart in which he took her from door to door to beg for her the necessaries of life. Thus he gave to all children a touching example of true filial love. He died in the odor of sanctity, and after his death God glorified him by many miracles.—[*Butler's Lives of the Saints.*]

There is related in the history of Japan an example worthy the admiration of all, and capable of teaching children how great their love and respect should be for their parents.

Three young men, in the midst of poverty, had a long time labored for the support and comfort of an aged and infirm mother, whom they tenderly loved.

There was, at the time, a band of robbers in the forest, near the city of Meaco. The Emperor of Japan had published, that a certain reward should be paid to the person who should bring within the city any one of the banditti. At the report of this the youngest of the three brothers, of whom we are about to speak, devised a most extraordinary method to procure support for his poor aged parent.

He begged of his brothers to tie him and carry him bound to the city of Meaco, that he might be taken for one of the robbers of the neighboring forest. The brothers were unwilling to comply with this singular proposal. "What do you fear?" said the young man; "do you believe that God will abandon me? and notwithstanding, if I should be put to death, I am very well content to sacrifice my life, provided I can procure assistance to preserve that of my mother."

The two brothers, persuaded by his entreaties, at length consented to his request, and carried him bound to the court of justice, representing him to be one of the robbers from the neighboring forest; he was immediately taken to prison, and the reward was given to the two brothers. But upon taking the last look at their brother, as the prison door closed, they were unable to conceal the tears that rolled from their eyes; this was perceived by one of the officers of the guard, who, suspecting that all was not correct, related it to the judge, who gave him immediate orders to follow the young men at a distance, that he might know the cause of their grief.

No sooner had they returned home, than the mother inquired where they had been. "We have been performing a great day's work," said they; "see how much money we

have earned for your support." "God be praised?" said
the mother; "but where is your brother?" This question
they were unable to answer. "I want to know where he
is," continued the mother; "where did you leave him?
Can't you tell me? O! unhappy creature that I am! You
have not been accustomed to earn so much money in so
short a time; you have, perhaps, come dishonestly by it;
and something has befallen your brother."

The two young men, seeing their mother thus afflicted at
their silence, with much difficulty, yet in the best manner
they were able, recounted the whole affair; the poor mother,
unable to contain her grief, broke out into the most pitiful
cries and lamentations for the loss of her dear son.

At this moment, the officer who had been listening at the
door and heard the whole conversation, entered to the relief
of the afflicted parent. "Take courage," said he, "be comforted, good woman; your son is living and well, no evil
has happened him; the Emperor has been informed of the
whole affair, and admiring the heroic fortitude of your son,
as well as his love for his mother, has given him a fortune,
and allotted also a pension for her during the remainder of
her life."—[*St. Alphonsus, fourth command.*]

One day a gentleman asked his servant: "Why is it that
you do not smoke any more?" "My father," answered the
servant, "is a poor man. So I thought it would be better
for me to give him the twenty cents which I used to spend
every week for tobacco."

As it is a duty of children to assist their parents in their
temporal wants, so it is also a duty of children to assist their
parents in their spiritual wants. Now, parents are in spiritual need in time of sickness, especially if their sickness
lasts long. It is then that they need much patience in order
to bear the sufferings of the body and the afflictions of the

spirit with resignation to the holy will of God. Children, therefore, should ask God to deliver their parents from their sufferings, or to grant to them the grace to bear them with great patience and a holy resignation to the will of God.

St. Gregory went often to church in order to beseech Almighty God to restore his sick father to health, and God was pleased to hear his prayer.

When St. Francis Borgias was at the age of ten years, he prayed to God, with tears in his eyes, to grant health again to his mother who was dangerously ill. His prayer was not heard. His mother died. He felt, however, greatly consoled at the thought that God knew better what was good for him, and that his mother would be better off in heaven. He did, however, never forget his pious mother and her wise and holy counsels which he resolved to follow throughout his life in order to meet her one day in heaven. He began to lead a holy life. He gave himself up to prayer, despised the world, its pleasures and maxims, chose a wise confessor, at whose advice he often received the sacraments. He died in the odor of sanctity in the year 1572. How beautiful and happy must have been the meeting of the mother and son in heaven !

A poor widow, who had been deprived of the use of her limbs, felt the most lively regret at not being able to go to Mass on Sundays. When Sunday came round, she invariably said to her sons : " What a happiness it would be to me if I could go to church and hear Mass ! but I cannot go, for I am old, infirm, and the road is long ;" and as she said these words, the poor woman shed tears and heaved a deep sigh ; then she raised to her lips the cross of her beads, which she was telling with the greatest piety and recollection. Her two sons, who entertained a filial affection towards their old parent, soon contrived to satisfy their mother's pious longings. They attached to her old arm chair two poles, and by this means they carried the poor woman to church. As they entered, for the first time, the road to the church, carrying the old mother in her chair, the people on the road loaded them with their blessings, and even cast flowers on their path. The pastor of the place, hearing of this loving invention of filial love, ascended the pulpit and took for his text these words of Deuteronomy: "Honor thy father and mother, as the Lord thy God has commanded thee." His discourse was full of unction, and produced a thrilling effect upon the congregation. He compared the flowers cast on the path of the two sons, when bearing their mother to church, to the benedictions which God would soon shower down on them.

4. True, sincere love for our parents induces us to bear with their faults and weaknesses and never to expose them to others, but rather cover them from the eyes of the world.

There are many who practise virtue as long as they have no other than their own burden to carry. This practice of virtue proceeds in many, from a desire of avoiding blame and ridicule rather than from a real love of virtue. But to see whether a person possesses true virtue, especially the virtue of true charity—the queen of all virtues, let him be obliged to bear with the weaknesses of his neighbors. This is the best test of true charity.

True, genuine charity proceeds from the heart, and fills the soul with tenderness, condescension, and compassion; it manifests itself exteriorly by grateful manners, and a wisely-tempered demeanor—the fruit of a holy affection.

It is easy to love those who are of an amiable disposition; but to be kind and affable towards those who are ill-humored, irritable and disagreeable is the touchstone of charity. To bear with the imperfections of our neighbor is to possess perfection in a great measure.

Now, who has a greater claim to our charitable forbearance than our parents, especially in their old age? Hence it is that the Holy Ghost says in Holy Scripture, "Son, support the old age of thy father; and grieve him not in his life. And if his understanding fail, have patience with him, and despise him not when thou art in thy strength; for the relieving of the father shall not be forgotten. For good shall be repaid to thee for the sin of thy mother (that is thou shalt be rewarded for bearing with the faults of thy mother). In justice thou shalt be built up, (that is, the filial love which induces thee to be kind to thy parents in spite of the faults of their old age, will draw temporal and spiritual blessings upon thee and thy family), and in the day of affliction thou shalt be remembered (by God and by men) and thy sins shall melt away as the ice in the fair warm weather." (Eccles. iii., 14-17.)

The parents of a certain young man named Joathin were not only poor, but perverse and wicked. Parents who were so bad themselves, were not likely to give their son a pious education; but this son had the happiness of being directed by a holy and zealous confessor, who inspired him with such love and respect for his parents, that he was never found wanting in this duty.

When he was fifteen years of age, his father not being able to support him, ordered him to go to service. Joachim obeyed. He went in search of a place, and he had the happy fortune of being received by a pious and wealthy gentleman named Eugenius. Never was there a servant more affectionate to his master, or a child more attached to his parents than was Joachim, who gave all his wages for their support. Eight years thus went on, at the end of which his sister entered into the marriage-state; his parents, who were then far advanced in life, being left alone, requested him to return. Joachim, without giving himself time to consider on the subject, and desirous to do his duty, left Eugenius, his kind and affectionate master.

The master endeavored to keep him, by promising him more wages, if he would only stay with him. "I had rather show love and respect to my parents," said Joachim, "than receive the highest wages you could give; I can live without your wages, but my parents cannot live without me." "Give yourself no uneasiness on that account," said the master. "I will attend to their support; besides your parents are not entitled to your services; they have loaded you with curses and ill-treatment." "That matters nothing," replied Joachim, "I will never neglect them in their old age. Whatever they may have done, they are still my parents, and I am their child, and I feel what God and nature require of me." "Go, my dear soul," said Eugenius; "God will bless you, for you are an obedient child." Joachim then returned to his parents. It is impossible to conceive what difficulties he had to undergo, in order to support them. And all the recompense that he received for his services and for his love was nothing but injuries and abuse; but he suffered all in silence, and without complaint.

Love and respect so holy united with heroic patience did not remain without reward. Joachim was by means of his virtuous conduct introduced to a pious lady, whom he married and with whom he lived in the fear of God, enjoying the greatest peace. Just before his death, he called his children around him, and thus addressed them: "My dear children, my greatest consolation through life and the greatest that I have at present, is, that I have been kind and respectful to my father and mother. It is to this love and respect that I owe my fortune. I now hope through that kindness which I have ever kept in view for the love of God, that he will now show me mercy. I recommend the same to you; keep God in view, and be kind and affectionate to your mother. If you follow this last advice which I give you, God will never forsake you."

How should children honor their parents?

By always showing them great respect, in word and deed.
2. Children are obliged not only to *love*, but also to *honor* their parents. "Honor thy father in work and word, and all patience." (Ecclus. iii., 9.) A child, therefore, should entertain a great esteem and reverential fear for his parents. "Honor thy father in thy whole heart, and be not unmindful of the sighs of thy mother." (Ecclus. vii.) Our honor and respect for our parents must appear in all our words and in all our behavior; we must speak to them with due respect, pay all deference to them on every occasion, show a regard to what they say and yield to their opinions in all lawful things. We must carefully avoid every action or word which may in any way appear as conveying a slight of them. We must take particular care not to laugh or sneer at their actions or expressions, but overlook their peculiarities, and show respect to them notwithstanding their natural or moral defects. A child who truly respects and honors his parents willingly submits to their correction and listens to their advice.

One evening there was at the house of St. Alphonsus' father a party of ladies and gentlemen, and it happened that one of the domestics showed stupidity in attending to the guests as they arrived. His negligence displeased D. Joseph, the father of St. Alphonsus, who scolded the servant and reproached him with his inattention, and though it was

an involuntary fault, yet D. Joseph did not cease to grumble
at him as he went and came. Alphonsus was sorry for the
man, and said to his father: "What a noise you make about
it, my father; when once you begin you can never end."
This speech displeased D. Joseph, who, being in bad humor
with the servant, was angry that Alphonsus should take his
part, and so far forgot himself as to give his son a blow in
the face. Alphonsus was confused, but said not a word,
and, deeply humbled, withdrew immediately to his room.
The hour of supper came, and as he did not appear, his
mother went to call him, and found him bathed in tears, deploring the want of respect he had shown towards his father.
He confessed how wrong he had been, and begged she would
intercede for him, and obtain forgiveness; accompanied by
his mother, he went to his father and asked his forgiveness.
This single occurrence shows how respectful Alphonsus continued to be towards his father, although he was then old
enough to be one of the first advocates at the Neapolitan bar.
—[*His Life, vol.* 1, *chap.* iv.]

A child who truly honors and respects his parents does
not blush to recognize them in public, however poor they
may be, and however mean be their attire. Should he enjoy
greater wealth and higher honors and dignities in this world,
than his parents, he does not, on that account, fail to show
to them that respect which is always due to them. "Remember thy father and thy mother," says the Holy Ghost,
"even when thou sittest in the midst of great men, lest God
forget thee in their sight, and thou, by the daily custom, be
infatuated and suffer reproach; and wish that thou hadst
not been born, and curse the day of thy nativity. (Ecclus.
xxiii., 18, 19.)

Look at the great King Solomon. The Holy Scripture
tells us that when his mother came to him to ask a favor,

"the King rose up to meet her, he bowed down before her, he caused a throne to be set for her at his right hand. Then the King said to her: 'Ask, my mother, for I will refuse thee nothing.'" (I. Kings, 2-19.)

Note here the filial politeness of Solomon. He rose up as soon as his mother came near him. He went forward to meet her. He bowed to her. He ordered a throne to be set for her, and he placed her at his right hand. He called her by the endearing title "my mother." He had so much respect and love for her, that even before he knew her request, he promised to grant it; "I will not refuse."

Among those who came to congratulate Benedict XI. on his election to the papal throne was also his mother, a widow and washer-woman of Rome. When she was told that her attire was too poor to appear in the papal palace, she went to borrow better clothes from a rich lady, and presented herself in them before her son in order to congratulate him. When the Pope saw her he pretended not to know her, saying: "You are not my mother; for she is no rich and noble lady; she is a poor washer-woman." She then returned home and put on her poor dress, and presented herself again before the Pope. Now it was that the Pope recognized her · as his mother; he received her very kindly and supported her for the remainder of her life.—[*Platus, lib.* 2, *de bono statu relig.*]

The great Sir Thomas More, Lord High Chancellor of England, was remarkable during his youth for his affectionate and dutiful conduct towards his parents. When he had grown up to manhood, and had been raised to the highest dignities of the State by King Henry VIII., he continued to display the same deference and respect towards his aged father, of which he had been so admirable an example when a boy. It is related of him that each morning before taking

his seat in the Chancellor's Court, he was wont to repair,
clad in his robes of office, to the Court of Queen's Bench.
There his father, who was then far advanced in years, sat as
one of the inferior judges; but, though far superior in rank
and office, the Lord High Chancellor of England was seen
each day to come and kneel at the old man's feet to ask his
blessing.   So admirable an exercise of humility and filial
piety drew upon him the choicest blessings of heaven.
When Henry VIII. soon after threw off his obedience to the
Holy See, and impiously declared himself head of the Church
in England, Sir Thomas More firmly resisted every effort
which the king made to draw him into his schism, and by
his fidelity to the faith merited the glorious crown of martyrdom.—[*Life of Sir Thomas More.*]

3. In the third place, children owe *obedience* to their
parents.   Parents hold the place of God in regard to children.   They have their authority from God.   Hence it is
God's will that children should obey their parents.   To obey
our parents is to obey God himself.

"My son," says the Lord, "keep the commandments of
thy father, and forsake not the law" of thy mother.   Bind
them in thy heart continually, and put them about thy neck.
When thou walkest let them go with thee; when thou sleep-
est let them keep thee; and when thou awakest talk with
them; because the commandment is a lamp, and the law a
light, and reproofs of instruction are the way of life."
(Prov. vi., 20-23.)   Children, therefore, should always
remember their duty of obeying their parents; they should
engrave it upon their hearts and live up to it.   It was in the
following words that our Lord exhorted St. Cathaﬁne of
Sienna to be obedient to those who hold his place on earth:
"Remember," said our Lord to this saint, "that the salvation and perfection of my servants consist in their submis-

siveness to my will. The more punctually they obey me, the more they advance in perfection, for by doing my will they unite themselves more and more to me who am Supreme Perfection Itself.

"In order to induce you to practise perfect obedience, my Son became man, and gave you an example of perfect obedience. He was obedient unto death, teaching you by his obedience that your salvation depends altogether on the constant practice of obedience. He said: "Not every one that saith to me, Lord, Lord, shall enter into the kingdom of heaven, but he that doeth the will of my Father, who is in heaven, he shall enter into the kingdom of heaven." (Matt. vii. 21.) He means to say, that no one, whoever he may be, and whatsoever good works he may perform for my name's sake, shall be admitted to the glory of life everlasting, unless he does my will on earth.

He said again: "I came down from heaven not to do my own will, but the will of him that sent me." (John vi., 38); and, "Not my will, but thine be done." (Luke xxii., 42.) "And he went with Mary and Joseph to Nazareth, and was obedient to them." (Luke ii., 51.)

"Now, if you wish to imitate the example of obedience of your Saviour, you must renounce your own will, and seek and do only my will. The more you do this, the more you will please me. I am always with the obedient. My delight is to be with the children of men, to change them, by my grace, into myself, so that they become one with me, by partaking of my perfections, of my peace and of my happiness.

"Now, you will do my will, if you obey those who keep my place for you on earth. Obey them always, and follow their advice. You obey me if you obey them."

This instruction of our Lord on obedience made a deep

9

impression upon St. Catharine. She lived up to it every day of her life and became a great saint.

The saints found but little difficulty in the practice of holy obedience, because they always remembered the obedience which Jesus Christ practised in the whole course of his life, especially in the hour of his death on Mount Calvary. There it was that he gave us the most touching lesson of obedience. There he obeyed all, and he obeyed not only his heavenly Father, but he obeyed even Pilate, the soldiers, the executioners, although they had no power over him. He obeyed even in things most difficult to nature. No sooner was he ordered to lay down on the cross than he prostrated himself on this instrument of our redemption, and presented his hands and feet to be nailed to it. He obeyed in the most perfect manner, without contradiction, without resistance, without appealing to a higher tribunal. He obeyed blindly, promptly and cheerfully, and preferred to lose his life rather than the merit of obedience. Happy those children who imitate the Son of God in this virtue of obedience! Happy those children who always obey their parents punctually and promptly without contradiction, cheerfully without murmuring and complaining, and conscientiously in all lawful things. We read in the life of St. Juliana Veronica that the devil made all possible efforts to induce her to disobey her confessors and superiors. But all that satan effected by tempting this saint to disobedience was that she obeyed still more promptly, cheerfully and conscientiously, and signed her name " Juliana Veronica, daughter of obedience, in spite of the devil." St. Joseph Cupertino used to say that he would die rather than be disobedient.

Now, though God requires children to be obedient to their parents, yet he does not require them to be obedient in all things. He obliges them to be obedient only in lawful things, such as concern their education, their moral conduct, and the family government and order. "Parents," says St. Thomas, "are in their family what a king is in his kingdom." Hence, as subjects are obliged to obey their sovereign in all things concerning the welfare of the kingdom, so also are children obliged to obey their parents in all family concerns which are entirely under their control and management, because parents are the masters of the family, and God has entrusted to them the spiritual welfare of their children. Hence, parents have a right to proscribe for their children such things as are conducive to their spiritual welfare, and forbid such ones as are opposed to it. If parents, therefore, require their children to comply with their religious duties, if they forbid them to associate with certain companions, to frequent certain houses, theatres, places of amusement, games, and the like, children are obliged to obey such orders and prohibitions.

Chateaubriand drifted, in the early days of his life, into skepticism and infidelity, but, moved by the appeal of his dying mother, he returned to the faith of his youth, and, as an evidence of his sincerity, wrote the *Genius of Christianity.* "My religious convictions," he wrote when advanced in life, "were not always so fixed as they are now. Annoyed at what I regarded as the abuses of some institutions, and indignant at the vices of some men, I fell into sophistical and declamatory habits; but Divine Providence graciously deigned to recall me to a sense of my duty." "When my mother was in her seventy-second year," he goes on to say in his Memoires d' Outre Tombe, "she was cast into a frightful prison. In this gloomy abode, whither she had been driven by dire misfortune, she saw several of her children perish about her, and there, too, she ended her life. In her dying moments she called one of my sisters to her side, bidding her to bring me back to the religion in which I had been brought up. It was through my sister that I learned the last wish of my mother. After my mother had passed away, my sister also followed, falling a victim to the rigors of the imprisonment. These two voices, speaking to me from out the grave, the death of the one being the interpreter of the death of the other came with special force upon me. I became a christian. Weeping I believed."

Should parents, however, command a child to do something that is contrary to the laws of God, or to the Evangelical Counsels, the child is bound in conscience to refuse obedience. St. Paul says: "Children, obey your parents in the Lord;" that is, obey your parents in all things that are pleasing to God, but not in such things as are offensive to God.

There is a boy. His father or mother tells him to steal something, or to strike a person, or to set fire to his neighbor's house, or to do anything else that is contrary to the commands of God, is that child bound to obey? By no means; he must positively refuse obedience, for, by obeying such a command, he would become guilty of sin. He must say: "We ought to obey God rather than men." (Acts v., 29.)

There is a young woman. Her parents are not Catholics; but, by the grace of God, she is convinced of the truth of the Catholic religion; she knows that, if she wishes to be saved, she must become a Catholic. She communicates to her parents her desire to join the Catholic Church. Her parents forbid her to do so, and even threaten her with the greatest punishments if she does not renounce her intention of becoming a Catholic. Now, is that child obliged to obey her parents? By no means; she is, on the contrary, bound to refuse obedience, as otherwise she would be lost forever.

There is another child. His parents prevent him from practising the Catholic religion, or even force him to renounce it. Now, must that child obey his parents? By no means ; for, " he who loves father or mother more than me," says Christ, " is not worthy of me."

St. Hermenegild, the son of Leovigild, king of Spain, became a convert to the Catholic faith. When his father, who was addicted to the Arian heresy, heard of it, he became quite enraged, and put his son in a frightful dungeon, where he made him suffer most cruel torments. The holy martyr wrote to his father : " I avow your goodness to me has always been very great. I will preserve, to the last moment of my life, the respect, duty, and tenderness which I owe you. But is it possible that you should wish me to like worldly greatness better than my salvation? I value the crown as nothing. I am ready to lose sceptre and life, too, rather than abandon the divine truth."

The prison was a school of virtue to this great martyr. He clothed himself in sack-cloth, and performed other bodily penances in addition to the hardships of his prison. He offered up to God many fervent prayers to obtain sufficient strength and courage to remain faithful in confessing the truth and dying for it.

The solemnity of Easter being come, the perfidious father sent, in the night, an Arian bishop with the message to his son that, if he received communion from the hand of that prelate, he would be received into favor again. Hermenegild, however, rejected the proposal with indignation, reproaching the messenger with the impiety of his sect, as if he had been at full liberty. When the bishop returned to the Arian king with this account, the furious father, seeing the faith of his son proof against all his endeavors to make him give up the Catholic religion, sent soldiers with orders to kill him. They entered the prison and found the saint fearless and ready to receive the stroke of death. They cleaved his head with an axe, and scattered his brains on the floor.— [*Butler's Lives of the Saints, April* 13.]

There is a young woman. She has no relish for the world. She despises all its vanities. All her joy, all her happiness is in God and his holy service. She hates sin and all the . dangers that lead to it. She avoids them carefully to preserve the peace of her conscience. But her parents are worldly-minded. They are displeased with the spirit of piety of her daughter, and try to undermine it by different means. Must her daughter be obedient to them in this point? By no means. It is, on the contrary, her duty, to cultivate the spirit of piety, without, however, neglecting her work and the duties of charity.

We read in the life of St. Catharine of Sienna that, in her very childhood, the Holy Ghost inspired her with a great desire to lead a holy life. Being powerfully drawn towards God, she despised this world, and all its pleasures and amusements. In her childhood she consecrated her virginity to God by a private vow. Her love of mortification and prayer, and her sentiments of virtue, were such as are not usally found in so tender an age. But God was pleased to put her resolution to a great trial. When she was at the age of twelve years, her parents thought of engaging her in the marriage-state. Catharine, however, besought them most earnestly to allow her to lead a single life; but found them deaf to all her entreaties. She therefore redoubled her prayers and mortifications, being persuaded that her protection must come from God alone.

Her parents, regarding her inclination to solitude and aversion to the world, as unsuitable to the life for which they designed her, endeavored, by different means, to divert her from it. To make her give up her exercises of piety, they deprived her of the little room or cell which they had till then allowed her. They loaded her with the most distracting employments and laid on her all the drudgery of the house, as if she were a person hired into the family for that purpose. Her sisters and other friends persuaded her to join with them in the diversions of the world, saying that virtue is not an enemy to neatness in dress, or to cheerfulness, under which soft names they endeavored to recommend the dangerous liberties of worldly pastimes and vanities. Catharine was prevailed upon by her worldly-minded sister Bonaventura, to dress, for some time, in a manner somewhat more genteel, but she soon repented of her compliance and wept for it during the remainder of her life, as the greatest infidelity of which she had ever been guilty to her heavenly spouse. Her sister Bonaventura, who had induced her to commit this infidelity and endeavored to instill into her heart love for the world and its pleasures, and to make her give up her devotions, was soon after called out of this life. Her death confirmed Catharine in her sentiments of piety and delivered her from one who had done so much to make her worldly-minded. As to the hard labors, humiliations, contempt and the insults heaped upon her by her other relations, they all were to the saint a subject of joy; she received all their railleries with an admirable sweetness and heroic patience. If anything grieved her it was the loss of her dear solitude. But the Holy Ghost taught her to make herself another solitude in her heart. In her admirable Treatise of God's Presence, she says: "Our Lord taught me to build in my soul a private closet, strongly vaulted with the Divine Providence, and to keep myself always close and retired there; he assured me that, by this means, I should find peace and perpetual repose in my soul which no storm or tribulation could disturb or interrupt." Thus, amidst all her occupations she considered herself always as alone with God, to whose presence she kept herself no less attentive than if she had no exterior employment to distract her. (Butler's Lives of the Saints, April 13.) Thus God gave to all children, in this saint, an example to imitate when their worldly-minded parents endeavor to induce them to live up to the spirit of the world.

There is a child, who doubts whether the command of his father or mother is lawful. Is he to obey it? He should seek for light and instruction, if he can; but if it is necessary to act without delay, and if he has neither means nor time to consult and procure information to clear the doubt and settle his conscience, after begging God to enlighten him, he may presume that the command is lawful, because, generally speaking, the parent is better informed than the child, and would not command what is sinful.

There is another case, in which children, as St. Thomas, St. Alphonsus, and all theologians say are not obliged to obey their parents, namely, if their parents unjustly oppose them in the choice of the state of life to which they are called by God; that is, in choosing the *married*, or *single*, or *ecclesiastical* or *religious* state of life. If parents unreasonably endeavor to control their children in marrying, by forcing them to marry a person whom they dislike, or by preventing them from contracting a fitting marriage, then children are not obliged to obey their parents. In such a case, however, children should not be judges for themselves and decide that their parents are unreasonable; they should listen to what their parents have to say, and ask the advice of a prudent confessor before they venture to refuse obedience to them. "Let children also remember," says St. Alphonsus, "that they can rarely be excused from mortal sin, if they contract marriage against the will of their parents, especially if they marry without the knowledge of their parents. From marriages contracted against the consent of parents, arise a thousand evils—disputes, hatred and quarrels." Parents may refuse their consent, if the marriage would be a disgrace to the family and disturb its peace; or, if it would prove highly detrimental to the child, or endanger the loss of religion. Hence, as a general rule, children should not marry without consulting their parents.

It is the duty of parents, says St. Alphonsus, to help and induce their children to become saints. Hence, if children feel called by God to a more perfect state of life and are unjustly prevented by their parents from embracing it, they are not obliged to obey them.

"We have," says St. Thomas Aquinas, "various duties to fulfil towards others according to their rank, merit, and the temporal and spiritual benefits which we receive from them; but God has a claim on our piety, love and gratitude, in preference to all; for he has all perfections in the highest degree, and is the first principle in our existence and preservation. After him come, in order of goodness and generosity, our parents, who have given us birth and education. Hence, filial piety is a special virtue by which we love and serve God before all, and next to him our parents.

"It may seem difficult to reconcile the duties of religion towards God, with those of filial love and respect to our parents. 'If any man come to me, and hate not his father and mother, wife and children, brothers and sisters, he cannot be my disciple.' (Luke xiv., 26.) The Church praises St. James and St. John for having abandoned all—parents and worldly goods, in order to follow Christ. This may seem contrary to the natural principles of filial duties. But religion and piety are two particular virtues which can never be in contradiction with each other, for good cannot be opposed to good, as truth cannot be opposed to truth. If we properly consider our respective duties to God and to our parents, we must be convinced, by the very principles of justice and piety, that we are bound to obey God rather than men. Hence, if parents should throw any obstacle in the way of our salvation, we must abandon them, and always remember that we must be more faithful to God than to them, for he is our eternal Father, and the principal source of our temporal and everlasting happiness. No doubt, children owe love, respect and obedience, and assistance to their parents, and are bound, by divine precept, to observe them faithfully; but, if the fulfilment of these duties according to the wishes of their parents were an impediment to their salvation, children must renounce them, and return to their merciful and eternal Father, in order to merit and obtain life everlasting. But one thing is necessary. 'The friendship of this world is the enemy of God.' (James ii., 4.) "Now, we are to be saved," says St. Alphonsus, "in the state of life to which God has called us. Hence, if a person who is called by God to the religious state, and enters it, he will become a saint; but if he remains in the world to please his parents, he will lead a wicked life and be damned."

Father N. Lancicius, S. J., relates that a certain young man, who was called to the religious life, did not follow his vocation. He went to study at the University of Macerat. There he soon forgot his usual exercises of piety. He no longer frequented the sacraments. Instead of going to church he went to taverns; instead of reading pious books and the lives of the Saints, he read bad novels; instead of keeping the company of pious young men, he visited persons of ill-fame. One night he returned home from such a person. When he came near the convent of that religious order to which he felt called, he was stabbed by a young man. Whilst weltering in his blood he sighed with a broken voice: "Alas! a priest! alas! a priest!" But he breathed forth his poor soul before a priest arrived. In the chronicles of all religious Orders may be read similar melancholy examples of young people who either abandoned the religious life, or, though called to it, did not care to embrace it. Any person, therefore, who is morally sure of being called to a life of perfection, displeases God by renouncing such a divine call.

Irregular affection for parents or kindred is one of those powerful engines used by the devil to undermine religious vocations. St. Jerome fitly calls this affection the ram or warlike instrument to batter down piety and devotion. All those who feel themselves called to the religious life must arm themselves against this great temptation. Let us, then, be firmly convinced, and hold as an infallible maxim that, when once assured of the will of God calling us to the religious state, whatever afterwards occurs to prevent us from following our vocation, must be a temptation of the devil. He tempts all men, but he tempts much more those of whom it it is written: "His food is the elect." It is one of his greatest artifices to conquer by the importunities of those who are especially dear and near to us.

It is, therefore, an undoubted principle of theology that, when parents oppose children in their choice either of the religious or ecclesiastical state, children owe then no obedience to them. Catholic theologians give solid reasons for this.

St. Thomas Aquinas says that, as to the nature of the body, all men are equal among themselves: a servant is not inferior to his master, nor a child to his parent. Hence no

man can reasonably be compelled either to marry or to lead
a single life for other men's or his own father's pleasure.

As to the commandment to honor our parents, we say with
St. Augustine, that we must both honor our parents, and
yet, without any want of piety, may disregard, them, in order to reach the kingdom of heaven, because we honor them
according to their rank and degree, but when that honor becomes an obstacle to the love of God, then we must neglect
it and shake it off.

The power of parents over their children is a participation
of the authority of God, from whom all paternity is derived ;
it is but the power of a deputy or delegate.   Therefore, if
God commands one thing and a parent another, no one can
doubt that the power or jurisdiction of a parent ceases, because it is opposed to the will of him who gave that power.
God, then, is the cause, why it is not lawful for us to obey
our parents, for " who loveth father and mother more than
me," says Christ, " is not worthy of me."   It is better to
incur the displeasure of our parents than that of God.
" Though your mother," says St. Jerome, " should, with
her hair loose about her ears, and tearing her clothes, show
you her breast at which she nursed you ; though your father
lay himself down upon the threshold, pass them by, in order
to hasten to the standard of the cross.   A day will come
when you shall enter the heavenly Jerusalem, crowned like
a man that has been valiant."

When St. Columban was on the point of carrying out his
resolution of entering into religion, his mother threw herself
across the threshold to obstruct his passage, but he courageously stepped over her and hastened to the place of his vocation.

A certain young man, called Theodore, who, as we read
in the life of St. Pachomius, (c. 29) was an only son and

heir to large possessions. He, on a certain festival, prepared a great banquet; on that day God made him feel that
all his riches would profit him nothing at the hour of death.
He then shut himself up in a room and besought the Lord,
with many tears, to make known to him the state which he
ought to choose in order to secure his eternal salvation.
God inspired him to become a religious in the monastery of
Pachomius. He forsook all things, and fled from his family.
His mother went to St. Pachomius with an order from the
emperor to restore her son; but Theodore prayed to God
with so much fervor, that he obtained for his mother the
grace to leave the world and retire also into a convent.

But is it not to have a breast of iron and a heart of stone
to leave parents in this way? It is not, indeed. To be immovable in this, is to be truly pious. If parents believe in
Christ, let them be on the side of their children, when they
fight for Christ; if they do not believe in him, "then let the
dead bury their dead."

To prefer the will of another to the will of God is to offer
a great outrage to our Lord, and what punishment does not
he deserve, who prefers a creature to his creator, darkness
to light, dirt and ashes to heaven? "He is not worthy of
me." Nothing can fall heavier upon man than to be rejected as unworthy of the company of his God.

It is for this reason that many saints, when called by God
to leave the world, quitted the house of their parents without
even making their design known to them; as for instance,
St. Francis Xavier, St. Philip Neri, St. Louis Betrand, St.
Thomas Aquinas. Let me tell you what this great doctor of
the church had to suffer from his kindred for embracing the
religious life. The frequent conversations which Thomas
had with a Dominican Father, a very holy man, filled
his heart with heavenly devotion and comfort, and

inflamed him daily with a more ardent love of God, which
so burned in his breast that at his prayers his countenance
seemed one day, as it were, to dart rays of light, and he
conceived a vehement desire to consecrate himself wholly to
God in that Order. His tutor perceived his inclinations and
informed his father, the Count of Aquino, of the matter, who
omitted neither threats nor promises to defeat such a design.
But the Saint, not listening to flesh and blood in the call of
heaven, demanded with earnestness to be admitted into the
Order, and accordingly received the habit in the Convent of
Naples in 1243, being then seventeen years old. The
Countess Theodora, his mother, being informed of it, set
out for Naples to disengage him, if possible, from that state
of life. Her son, on the first news of her journey, begged
his Superiors to remove him, as they did first, to the Convent of St. Sabina in Rome, and soon after to Paris, out of
the reach of his relations. Two of his brothers, Landulph
and Reynold, commanders in the emperor's army in Tuscany,
by her direction, so well guarded all the roads that he fell
into their hands, near Aquapendente. They endeavored to
pull off his habit, but he resisted them so violently that they
conducted him into the seat of his parents, called Rocca
Secca. The mother, overjoyed at their success, made no
doubt of overcoming her son's resolution. She endeavored
to persuade him that to embrace such an Order, against his
parents' advice, could not be the call of heaven; adding all
manner of reasons, fond caresses, entreaties and tears.
Nature made her eloquent and pathetic. He appeared sensible of her affliction, but his constancy was not to be shaken.
His answers were modest and respectful, but firm. He explained that his resolution was the call of God, and that it
ought, consequently, to take place of all other views as to
the disposition to be made of him even should these views

aim at the service of God in any other way. At last, offended at his unexpected resistance, his mother expressed her displeasure in very angry words, and ordered him to be more closely confined and guarded, and that no one should see him but his two sisters. The reiterated solicitations of the young ladies' were a long and violent assault. They omitted nothing that flesh and blood could inspire on such an occasion, and represented to him the danger of causing the death of his mother by grief. He, on the contrary, spoke to them in so moving a manner, on the contempt of the world, and the love of virtue, that they both yielded to the force of his reasons for quitting the world, and, by his persuasion, devoted themselves to a sincere practice of piety.

This solitude furnished him with the most happy opportunity for holy contemplation and assiduous prayer.

Some time after, his sisters conveyed to him some books, viz: a Bible, Aristotle's logic, and the works of the Master of the Sentences. During this interval his two brothers, Landulph and Reynold, returning home from the army, found their mother in the greatest affliction, and the young novice triumphant in his resolution. They would needs undertake to overcome him, and began their assault by shutting him up in a tower of the castle. They tore in pieces his habit on his back, and after bitter reproaches and dreadful threats, they left him, hoping his confinement, and the mortification which every one strove to give him, would shake his resolution. This not succeeding, the devil suggested to these two young officers a new artifice for diverting him from pursuing his vocation. They secretly introduced one of the most beautiful and most insinuating young strumpets of the country into his chamber, promising her a considerable reward in case she could draw him into sin. She employed all the arms of Satan to succeed in so detestable a design. The

saint, alarmed and affrighted at the danger, profoundly
humbled himself, and cried out to God most earnestly for
his protection; then snatching up a fire-brand struck her
with it, and drove her out of his chamber. After this victory, not moved with pride, but blushing with confusion for
having been so basely assaulted, he fell on his knees and
thanked God for his merciful preservation, consecrated to
him anew his chastity and redoubled his prayers, and the
earnest cry of his heart, with sighs and tears, to obtain the
grace of being always faithful to his promises. Then falling
into a slumber, as the most ancient historians of his life relate, he was visited by two angels, who seemed to gird him
round the waist with a cord so tight that it awaked him, and
made him cry out. His guards ran in, but he kept his secret
to himself. It was only a little before his death that he disclosed this incident to Father Reynold, his confessor, adding
that he had received this favor about thirty years before,
from which time he had never been annoyed with temptations of the flesh; yet he constantly used the utmost caution
and watchfulness against that enemy, as he would otherwise have deserved to forfeit that great grace. One heroic
victory sometimes obtains of God a recompense and triumph
of this kind. Our saint having suffered in silence this imprisonment and persecution upwards of a twelve month, some
say two years, at length, by the remonstrance of Pope Innocent IV., and the emperor Frederick, on account of so many
acts of violence in his regard, both the countess and his
brothers began to relent. The Dominicans of Naples being
informed of this, and that his mother was disposed to con-
nive at measures that might be taken to procure his escape,
they hastened in disguise to Rocca Secca, where his sisters,
knowing the countess no longer opposed his escape, contrived his being let down out of his tower in a basket. He

was received by his brethren in their arms, and carried with joy to Naples. The year following he there made his profession, looking on that day as the happiest of his whole life in which he made a sacrifice of his liberty that he might belong to God alone. But his mother and brothers renewed their complaints to Pope Innocent IV., who sent for Thomas to come to Rome, and examined him on the subject of his vocation to the state of religion, in their presence; and having received entire satisfaction on this head, the Pope admired his virtue, and approved of his choice of that state of life, which from that time he was permitted to pursue in peace.

By following the example of such great Saints, we cannot err, especially if we consider that the Lord showed by miracles that he approved their glorious fight. St. Peter of Alcantara, in going from the house of his mother (to whom he had always paid the strictest obedience since the death of his father), to the monastery in which he was about to become a religious, found his flight impeded by a large river, which he did not know how to cross. He recommended himself to God, and was, in an instant, miraculously transported to the opposite side. So, in a similar case, Stanislas Kostka, when fleeing from his home, without his father's permission, was closely followed by his brother in a carriage, with the object of capturing him; but, just as he was on the point of doing so, the horses stopped suddenly, and could not be made to advance; but, after a short resistance wheeled round and quickly proceeded back to the town. We have also the example of the Blessed Oringa of Valdorno in Tuscany, who, being promised by her parents in marriage to a young man, fled from him to consecrate herself to God; but finding her way stopped by the river Arno, she prayed for a few moments to God, whereupon the waters opened, and rising on each side like two crystal walls, afforded her a dry passage.

10

It is, therefore, not necessary to seek the counsel or the consent of our parents to our compliance with our vocation. The tenth Council of Toledo, in the last chapter, says expressly, that children may become religious without the consent of their parents, provided they are past the age of puberty. These are the words of the Council: "Parents will not devote their children to religion unless they are under fourteen years of age. After this period it is for children to follow their own wishes in this respect, either with the consent of their parents, or according to their own devotion, independently of the direction of parents." The same rule is prescribed in the Council of Tiber (Can. 24), and it is taught by St. Ambrose, St. Jerome, St. Augustine, St. Bernard, St. Thomas, and others, as well as by St. John Chrysostom, who says in his General Thesis, that when parents oppose what regards the spiritual welfare of their children, they must cease to be regarded on that point as parents.

In 1821, Father Charles Nerinckx, the founder of the Loretto Sisters, returned from his trip to Europe. When he had arrived in Baltimore, Md., seven young ladies of Maryland presented themselves as candidates for the Loretto Sisterhood. Among these ladies was a certain Miss Petronella Doran. When she informed her parents that she intended to join the Loretto sisters, she was told by her mother that she should not go. Her parents first scolded her, then coaxed her, cried over her, after pressing her to their bosom, and kissing her with all the affection of the fondest of parents. They tried every means in their power to shake her in her resolution and at the same time pacify her. She was seventeen years of age, was firm in her determination, and could not be overcome. Being, however, so often reminded of all they had done and suffered for her, she, at last, thought within herself: "Yes, I would be ungrateful to leave my good parents thus; and yet my every thought is for Loretto to join those dear, good sisters. But I cannot, I must not go." Her parents scolded and caressed her by turns till eleven o'clock at night, when all retired to rest.

Petronella went to prayer almost heart-broken. She had not been long on her knees when the room was filled with a bright light—to use her own words, "a light ten thousand times brighter than the sun," and she saw three beautiful ladies coming up to her. The middle one was clad with all the brilliancy of heaven. She gazed on the prostrate and penitent lady; then, in a chiding, bitter tone, said: "Yes, you think your mother has done so much for you that you cannot leave her! Look at my son. See, what he has done and suffered for you!" Petronella looked in the direction designated by the finger of the speaker (the Blessed Virgin, of course), and oh the sight! It chills me to write it: Our Lord on the cross, in his bitter agony, his eyes suffused with blood, and looking intently on her, while writhing with pain. Petronella fell prostrate and senseless. She knew not how long she remained thus; but when she recovered all was dark, and she was alone. She rose up, took one dress, wrapped it in a handkerchief, put on her bonnet, went to the room of her parents, and having gained the door, she said in a loud voice: "I am going; good-bye!"

Her parents were not asleep, but they attached no importance to her words. Petronella took the road to the church, walked twenty miles alone through the dark night, reaching the church just at daybreak. She then inquired the way to the house of Miss Eulalia Kelly, who was one of the postulants for the Loretto sisters. She arrived at her house at sunrise, and related her story, at which all were astonished. Eulalia's mother supplied Petronella with all needful clothing and her father took her and Eulalia to Baltimore, and related to Father Nerinckx Petronella's whole history; how she left home for the purpose of going to Loretto, and of her travelling to Baltimore under his special protection. Father Nerinckx was delighted with the narrative and believed every word of it, after having carefully examined Petronella on the subject. He considered her as a fruit already ripe for heaven, a soul in whose beauty the heavenly King was greatly delighted.

While Petronella was at Mr. Kelly's house, one of the children came in, and said Mr. N. Cane was at the front gate. This gentleman was her uncle, and had come on some business. Thinking that he was in search of her, she slipped out at the back door, went to an out-house and concealed herself in some dry flax; nor was she found till after four o'clock, having been in her hiding place over five hours and without her dinner. To the little ones who found her, her first words were: "Is Mr. Cane gone? What did he want? Did he ask for me?' Being now satisfied that he was not in search of her, she went into the house and made her apology for all the anxiety she had caused the family by her absence. The Lord did not permit her parents to look after her for more than six weeks, when she was at Loretto, Ky. When they understood she was really gone, they grieved much for a time, but became reconciled.

When asked if she was not afraid while walking alone in the night, she answered, she was not, for she felt that the Lord had called her, that she was doing his holy will, and that he would protect her.

Her father was an honorable man, a farmer of pretty fair means; and the family were noted for their piety, though they knew nothing of a convent-life, nor of what Almighty God could work in the heart of his chosen ones, and of what he had actually wrought in the soul of their cherished Petronella. Every Sunday half the family were at church; the girls always came fasting, went to confession, to holy communion at the late Mass, and after service (generally one o'clock) they mounted their horses, and rode home for their breakfast, seventeen miles.—[*Life of Rev. Charles Nerinckx, chap.* xxviii.]

A young lady convert went to Loretto, Ky., to school, and soon became very unhappy. She had a perfect dread of becoming a nun, and left the convent lest she should acquire an inclination for the religious state. But as her unhappiness increased at her return into the world, she came back. Unable to conquer her fears, she finally determined to have an interview with Father Nerinckx on the subject, in the hope of obtaining some relief. She told him all and was not a little surprised when Father Nerinckx simply directed her to go to the chapel and say a little prayer. "But, Father, I can't, I won't be a nun!" she exclaimed. "Never mind, my child," replied the priest in a quiet tone, "just go to church; prayer will do you no harm." She went, and scarcely had she knelt down, when all her troubles vanished. Some months later she begged to be received as a member of the community. She became a most exemplary sister, and ended her life by a most edifying death.—[*Life of Rev. Ch. Nerinckx, chap.* xxxi.]

A young lady boarder at Loretto, Ky., had long struggled against the conviction, which forced itself more and more upon her mind that she was called to a religious life. The term of her studies had finally been reached, and a servant had come to take her home to her parents. A powerful struggle between nature and grace now ensued. God's own grace, it is true, was on the one hand; but on the other, the world with all its glittering allurements; the world in which her position and talents would secure for her the admiration of her friends, where the love of a dear mother, who invited her home, awaited her. Should she say farewell to all these, to bury herself, her youth, and all her attainments, within the convent walls, where no admiring eye, no flattering tongue would appreciate her gifts? The conflict was hard, and she was going to take the fatal leap into the world, when a good inspiration came to her: she would go to Father Nerinckx and acquaint him with her struggles. No sooner had she entered his room than the priest spoke in a decided tone: "You have a vocation to the religious life, and you are about to lose it. You are free, my child, to go home or stay. Our Lord offers you the chance to be his now. If you accept it, it will be yours forever. If you go home, you will never return. Your vocation will be taken from you, and given to one who will be more faithful to receive it. You will then be left with only sufficient grace to save your soul. But will you save it? Now, then, do as you please." "Father," she replied, "I will stay. Please write to mother and inform her of my resolution." From that moment her heart was relieved of a great weight. In due time she received the religious habit, and no happier soul can be found within the convent walls than she always was.

It may be asked: "*Is it lawful for a person to embrace the religious life, if his parents are very poor?*" "If the parents of a person," says St. Thomas Aquinas, are in a state of destitution, and absolutely wanted his assistance, he should not abandon them to the mercy of Providence, for that would be tempting God and acting contrary to common justice and charity, as we learn from the reproach which our Lord made to the Pharisees for "making void the commandment of God" by their tradition. (Math. xv., 6.) Our dear Saviour made this reproach to the Pharisees because they maintained that a person might dedicate to God that which he should spend in assisting his parents when they are in necessity. Hence the Church teaches that it is not lawful for a person to dedicate his property or himself to religion, if by so doing he would be unable to fulfil an absolute obligation to assist his parents in extreme necessity; for obedience to God's commands is of higher importance than following counsels of perfection.

"But if his parents have sufficient means to live independently and can get along without his services, he is at full liberty to embrace the religious life even without their consent and approbation; for there is no moral obligation to give them assistance except *in case of absolute necessity.* Once received in a religious house, and having made his profession in a canonical form, he is dead to the world and all other engagements. If, however, his parents have been reduced to extreme indigence and are depending on public charity, he should make some efforts, with the assistance and approbation of his superior, to relieve them. He is confined within the walls of the convent all the rest of his life, and has nothing more to do with the affairs of the world, and with all the joy of his heart often repeats: "All is now for God and my salvation; these I prefer to all the pleasures of this deceitful world."

Again it may be asked, "How long must children obey, love and honor their parents?"

The duty of the children to obey their parents lasts as long as they are under their parents' protection and control. But this duty is greatly modified by circumstances when children are of age and removed from the protection and control of their parents.

But here one may say: "We live in a free country. Man is endowed with the gift of liberty; he is created by God a free agent.   But how can I be free if I am to be submissive to another?" This objection can be made only by him who has conceived a false idea of true liberty.   There are many who think that true liberty consists in doing whatever they please. But they are greatly mistaken.

Man, it is true, is endowed with free-will, which enables him to choose between doing and not doing a thing.   "He" (the just man) says Holy Scripture, "could have transgressed, and hath not transgressed, and could do evil things, and hath not done them." (Eccl. xxxi., 10.)   Free-will also enables a man to choose between doing a thing and doing the opposite.   "Before man is life and death, good and evil ; that which he shall choose shall be given unto him." (Eccl. xv., 18). Now, it is for the merit or demerit of man that God has endowed him with freedom to choose either good or evil.   So that, as St. Augustine says, no human act can be sinful when it does not proceed from a free-will.   "God judged," says this great Doctor, "that his servants would be better if they served him freely."

Indeed, when God made man, he might, by an act of his free will, have decreed that human reason, like the stars, should forever obey him by an unvarying fixed law.   But, as God has his complacency in the homage of our free-will, he made us *free* men, and not puppets, that nod the head and bend the knee as the wires are pulled.   Of everything made by God, it is said in Holy Scripture : "And God saw that it was good."   Man alone did not receive this praise because he has it in his power to become bad ; he is free to choose good or evil, to side with God or the devil, to follow truth or error, light or darkness—to embrace virtue or vice. It is from this two-fold liberty that have risen, from the beginning of the world, two powers, two elements, continually combating each other—the good and the bad : the followers and children of God, and the adherents and friends of the devil.

Now, it is not the followers of the devil, but only the faithful children of God that are truly free, that is, only those who do the will of God in a perfect manner, as St. Augustine says, enjoy true liberty.

Liberty does not consist in being able to commit sin, to follow our passions, and thus go to hell; for, "if, in order to be free, it were necessary to be able to commit sin," says St. Anselm, "God and his angels would have no free-will; but such an assertion would be absurd." God is supreme liberty, and can do all things; yet he cannot sin.

Again, no rational creatures enjoy a greater liberty than the angels and saints in heaven; yet they cannot sin. It is something peculiar to man not to desire anything, or to make efforts to obtain some thing, unless he sees some real or supposed good or happiness in the acquisition of that thing. If it happens that he turns his mind and heart from real happiness, it is because he is seduced by some false good or happiness.

The case of the angels and saints is quite different. They see the Divine Essence in all its splendor and glory. They incessantly contemplate the Sovereign Good, and the universal source of happiness of all created beings. Where could they find something more attractive than God, or how could they choose sin in preference to that divine glory? It is as impossible for them to separate themselves from God by sin as it is for us to deny the first principles of right and wrong.

Their liberty is perfect. The perfection of liberty or free will consists in acting without fear of sinning, as the perfection of the intellect consists in not erring in the conclusions we draw from the first principles. If then the angels and saints in the state of heavenly glory cannot sin, whilst man

unfortunately has the power of sinning, what conclusion can
we draw from this fact? It is that the liberty or free will is
more perfect in the inhabitants of heaven than in us poor
mortals of this world,—a liberty so great and perfect that
they can never abuse it, and consequently are perfectly certain that they can never forfeit their heavenly happiness.

Man, on the contrary, can abuse his liberty and sin.
Now, to be under the power of sin, is no power or mark of
liberty; it is rather a mark of weakness and misery, not of
perfection. To be under the power of sin, implies the possibility of becoming a slave of sin and of the devil. The
more we are under the power of sin, the less free we are;
and, were we to remain under the power of sin and of our
passions, we would necessarily become for all eternity the
vile slaves of the devil in hell.

Ask a man whose heart is set on earthly gain,—ask him
what he thinks of those who renounce all to follow Christ
and purchase heaven; ask him, I say, whether they do
wisely? Certainly, he will answer, they do wisely. Ask
him, again, why he himself does not do what he commends
in others. He will answer: It is because I cannot. Why
can you not? Because avarice will not let me. It is because he is not free; he is not master of himself, nor of
what he possesses. If he is truly master of himself and
of what he has, let him lay it out to his own advantage;
let him exchange earthly for heavenly goods; if he cannot,
let him confess that he is not his own master, but a slave to
his money.

The celebrated Bossuet, Bishop of Meaux, had, out of
affection for Abbe Rance, founder of La Trappe, a beautiful
crib erected at the chapel of the Trappist. It was Christmas-eve. The bishop, pleased with the work, called the
workmen together in order to pay them. They stood before

a covered table. The bishop threw back the cloth and said, with a pleasant smile: "It is Christmas-eve. I have resolved to make each one of you a little present, but I wish you to choose for yourselves. Here is a gold piece, and here is a good book. Now, take whichever you prefer." The first workman immediately took the gold piece without scarcely deigning to look at the book. "I never read much anyhow," said he; "books are of very little use to me." The second workman did the same, remarking that with the gold he could buy a warm coat for the winter. The third man took the gold also, saying that he needed it to buy fuel for the winter.

The fourth workman, the youngest of all, now came. He looked wistfully at the book and then at the gold. At last he said: "My old mother at home is poor and blind. It is true, the money would help her for awhile, but after all it would be soon spent. My mother is pious, and I am sure she would rather have a good book. I can read to her out of it during the long winter evenings. I will take the book for my poor old mother." The bishop was moved to tears as he heard the words of the pious young man. The young man took the book, opened it to see the title, and what was his astonishment to find on the very title-page—six gold pieces! He had thus six times more than his companions, and a good book besides. The other workmen bent their heads, ashamed and vexed at themselves. The bishop now opened each of the three remaining books. Each one contained six bright gold pieces! Oh, how disappointed the greedy workmen felt! "See, my friends," said the bishop, kindly, "I wished to see whether you preferred the goods of earth to the goods of heaven. Three of you, I am sorry to say, have done so. You forgot the words of our Lord and Saviour,—words of living truth: 'Seek first the kingdom

of God and his justice, and all the rest will be given to
you.' (Matt. vi., 23.)   Blessed be the mother that teaches
such principles to her children !   Blessed that Christian who
always remembers and practises this sublime lesson !"   The
three workmen withdrew to meditate on the lesson they had
received, and the virtuous young man knelt down to receive
the bishop's blessing for himself and his mother. (Hungari.)
It is clear that these three greedy young men, by setting
more value on temporal than on spiritual goods, showed that
they were not so free as the other young man, who chose
the spiritual instead of the temporal goods.

We have been created to enjoy the supreme happiness of
God in heaven, on condition that we do the will of God on
earth.   Therefore, the greatness of our liberty is in proportion to the power which we have of willing and of doing what
God commands.   The greater this power of our will is, the
more liberty we enjoy,

, There is one.   He makes the vow of chastity.   What induces him to make this vow is the hope that, by the grace of
God, he will be master of himself, so that he can practise
this virtue.

There is another.   He cannot make this vow.   What prevents him from making it, is the fact that he does not consider himself sufficiently master of himself to be able to keep
the vow.   It is therefore clear that he who makes the vow
has greater power over himself than the other who does not
make it, because he does what he wishes to do, and does
what he believes he ought to do.   But it is precisely in this
that liberty consists.   For the liberty which the other retains
for himself is rather a subjection, nay, even a slavery, than
liberty, because in reality, like a slave, he obeys his passion,
which has the mastery over him, and drags him into sin ; for
he who is overcome is a slave to him who has overcome him

(2 Pet. ii, 19): wherefore, "whosoever sins is a slave of sin" (John viii., 34.) The more, then, the power of sin is lessened in a man, the more the possibility of slavery is lessened, and therefore the more free he becomes; and if this power of sin is entirely taken away in man, his liberty is perfect. "Our liberty," says St. Augustine, "is so much the greater, the less we can sin;" and St. Thomas adds: "He whose liberty is perfect cannot commit sin." St. Alphonsus says the same. (Lib. ii., Tract. Pracamb., n. xxxiii: ed. P. Heilig.)

Now, the grace of God enables us to hate, to detest, and to avoid sin; it strengthens our will to do what God commands, and it inflames our hearts with love for God and everything that gives him pleasure; and thus it lessens in us the power of sin, and thereby increases our liberty, and makes it gradually more perfect.

"Man, after the fall," says St. Augustine, "is undoubtedly no longer free, without grace, either to begin or bring to perfection any act conducive to eternal life. But, by the grace of God, he recovers this liberty; for the strength which he needs to do what is good is granted him by grace through the merits of Jesus Christ. This grace restores his liberty to him, and gives him strength to work out his eternal salvation, without, however, compelling him to do so." (Lib. ii., con. ii., Epist. Pelag., c. 5.)

Now, to be able, by the grace of God, to avoid sin and to do good, is to be truly free; but not to be able to do so, is to be a child of sin and misery, a slave of our passions and of the devil. Good Catholics, who, by the grace of God, believe and practise the truths of the Roman Catholic Church, are the children of light and of true liberty; whilst unbelievers and heretics are the slaves of the darkness of error and their passions, for they do not enjoy the liberty of

the children of God. Hence, when the tyrant said to St.
Agatha, "You are born of noble and illustrious parents.
Why, then, are you not ashamed to follow that low and contemptible life of the Christians?" the holy virgin most wisely
replied : " The most illustrious nobility and liberty is to be
a faithful servant of Christ." Yes, "only he," says St.
Augustine, " is truly free, who does God's will in a perfect
manner ; and who, instead of abusing his liberty to commit
sin, uses it only to do good and please God in all things."
(Tract. 91, in Joan. ; and, L. de Quant. Animæ, c. xxxiv.)

The road of obedience to the will of God in all things
is not a road that leads to slavery and captivity, as the
worldly-minded falsely imagine, from whom the mysteries of
the Kingdom of heaven are hidden ; on the contray, it is the
road of *all those who are truly free*—it is the road of the children of God, to whom it is given to understand the mysteries
of the Kingdom of heaven.

Undoubtedly he is free who does what he himself wills.
Now, a just man, though he obeys the law or authority, does
nevertheless what he wills, because he desires the good
which is commanded, and does it not induced by force of the
outward command, but because he himself wishes to do it.

When a man directs a traveller in his way, no one can say
that he forces him to go that way, because the traveller himself desires to be directed. The just man, in like manner,
desires to be directed by the law of God for his own good
and salvation, therefore freely and cheerfully does all the
good that he has to perform. There cannot then be a better
and more true liberty than that which a just man enjoys ; he
freely chooses and complies with the obligations of obedience
as the true means that leads him to the possession of God.

Children should never lose sight of this all important
truth ; they should never suffer themselves to be deceived by

a false idea of liberty imagining that true liberty consists in thinking, speaking and doing whatever they please, no matter it be right or wrong.

Now, if it is asked, how long children are bound to love and honor their parents, we say that this duty is binding upon children as long as their parents live When God gave the fourth commandment he did not say : " honor thy father and thy mother until you are of age ; no, he says, " honor thy father and thy mother," that is, honor your parents during their whole life, for they are your parents as long as they live. "He that feareth the Lord," says Holy Writ, " honoreth his parents, and will serve them as his masters that brought him into the world. Hence Tobias said to his son : " My son when God shall take my soul, thou shalt bury my body, and thou shalt honor thy mother all the days of her life·" (Tob. iv., 2-4.)

It is especially at the time when parents are very sick and are in danger of death, that children should show their love and affection and high esteem for their parents. It is then that they should do all in their power to provide for the spiritual welfare of their parents' souls. In their last distress, and when eternity is at stake, parents are hardly able to help themselves; and therefore, at that awful moment, more than ever, are they in need of their childrens' assistance.

It is then that children should provide their parents with all things necessary for a happy death. They should send, in due time, for the priest to administer to them the sacraments of Penance, the blessed Eucharist and Extreme Unction. Then after that, children should pray for them, make with them the acts of faith, hope, charity and contrition, recite the Litany of the Saints, read for them good books if they are able to listen to the reading, and often remind them of the merits of Christ and the happiness of heaven. They should, above all, induce them to conform their will to the holy will of God in their last hour. To conform our will to the will of God in accepting death as coming from the hand of God is an act of perfect love of God, which cancels sin and punishment due to it; it is to die with the merit similar to that of martyrdom.

Once, as Monsignor Gindiccioni, bishop of Lucca, was passing through a garden in Rome, he suddely heard the feeble voice of a child utter these words: "My father! repeat the words that I am going to say: 'O my God! I am sorry from the bottom of my heart for having offended Thee because, etc.," and with tender devotion the child went through the act of contrition. Following the sound of the voice, the prelate hastened to the spot whence it proceeded, and found the gardener on one of the trees hanging head downwards, in eminent danger of falling and breaking his neck, his fall being merely arrested by two cross-branches which had caught the unforntunate man by the foot; beneath the tree stood a little boy about eight years old, whose countenance at once expressed grief and courage; he was the gardener's son. The attendants of the bishop released the man, and asking the boy, where he had learned to do so, " in the school", he replied, we were taught to make an act of contrition in danger of death.—[*Life of St. Joseph Callasanctius.*]

The conduct of Joseph towards his father Jacob is a touching example of the manner in which children should respect and honor their parents at all times and especially in their old age. When a child, he respected and loved his father tenderly. When, later in life, he was raised by Pharaoh to the proud dignity of viceroy over all Egypt, he forgot not his father, but when alone with his brothers, and making himself known to them, his first inquiry was about his father. "I am Joseph, your brother," said he; "is my

father yet living? Go, hasten to him, and tell him that his
son Joseph not only lives, but has all the land of Egypt at
his disposal. Go, bring him, be quick, make no delay."
And when Joseph was apprised of his father's coming, he
set off with a becoming retinue to meet him, and proceeded
as far as Gessen. And the moment his father's carriage
came in sight, Joseph got out of his chariot and respectfully
advanced on foot to receive him. As soon as they met,
they rushed into each other's arms, they cordially embraced,
they clung for some time together without being able to utter
a single word. The excess of their joy was too high for
either of them to speak what they felt. They wept, and
their tears best witnessed the glowing sentiments of their
hearts in this unexpected interview. Joseph then conducted
both his father and brothers into the royal city, and, far from
being ashamed of his father, he presented him to King Pharaoh
and ever afterwards treated him with the greatest respect,
love, and tenderness. And when the old man became sick,
and was approaching his last end, Joseph, with his two sons,
set out at once to pay his last duty to his dying father. He
remained by his bed until he breathed his last, and then,
closing the old man's eyes, he threw himself upon the face
of his deceased father, and poured out a torrent of tears.
Then he gave orders to the physicians to embalm the body;
and when the seventy days that Egypt mourned for him were
expired, Joseph made preparations for his father's funeral,
and accompanied his remains to their final resting-place, the
land of Chanaan, and thus fulfilled his father's request.—
[*Genesis.*]

Children should show their love for their parents even
after their death by fulfilling certain obligations which their
parents neglected to comply with in their life-time, and
which they failed even at the hour of death to discharge

11

either for want of time or opportunity, such as cancelling an act of injustice committed by their deceased parents, or removing a scandal to which they had given rise, or paying certain debts left unpaid. Although, by this supplementary satisfaction, the indebtedness as well as the well-deserved punishment cannot be removed, yet, as the venerable Cardinal Bellarmine remarks, the pains which children or the friends of their parents undergo, or the sacrifices which they offer up for their deceased friends, are accepted by the divine Justice in expiation of their faults.

Pope Benedict XIII. relates, in one of his works, the following occurrence, which he had heard from a lay-brother of the Dominican Order. The father of this brother had been accustomed to have his horses shod by a certain blacksmith for several years ; he failed, however, from culpable neglect, to remunerate him for his services. After his death he appeared to a faithful servant, charging him to go to his wife and beg her to discharge this debt, on account of which he was suffering great pains in Purgatory. His wife immediately hastened to discharge not only this, but all other debts of her husband ; after which he appeared to her surrounded with flames, and bound from head to foot with strong cords. "For God's sake," he exclaimed, "loosen these ropes !" Having done so, her husband thanked her for having complied with his request, and told her that he had been obliged to suffer this torment until the debts were paid.

But, if deceased parents, in their last will, left legacies for holy Masses or other pious works to be offered up for the repose of their souls, then it is not only a duty of charity, but also an obligation of the strictest justice for children to execute this will of their deceased parents most punctually and without delay. Those children who neglect to fulfil this duty are guilty of a sacriligious injustice, and incur excommunication according to the decrees of the Church; and although children may afterwards comply with this duty of theirs, yet they will be severely punished by God for having neglected its fulfilment too long

Good, conscientious children detest such a crime, and hold in execration such a want of love for deceased parents; and though their parents should not have left any pious legacies, yet good children will not fail to offer up, for them many fervent prayers, holy communions, alms-deeds, and especially the holy sacrifice of the Mass; they will not fail, on every anniversary of their death, to remember them in their prayers.

In those unhappy days when so many Christians were captured and sold as slaves to the Moors, a society of religious was formed in the Catholic Church to liberate those Christian captives. Numbers of holy men, impelled by divine charity, travelled throughout Europe and collected large sums of money to ransom these unhappy captives. As soon as these good monks had collected a sufficient sum, they sailed over to Africa. It was indeed a touching sight to behold those poor Christian captives as they crowded around the good monks as soon as they landed. Full of hope that they were soon to be delivered, they raised their manacled hands towards the good monks, crying in eager accents: "Welcome, O holy servants of God! Have you brought my ransom at last? Surely, my children have not forgotten me!"

The good religious examines his books. "My friend," says he, "your children send you their love; but they are sorry to say, they cannot help you now; they hope, however, to send your ransom by the next vessel." O God, how bitter, how cruel is the disappointment of those poor parents who must still remain to pine away in dreary captivity! "Ah! ungrateful chil'ren," they cry, "unnatural, heartless children, why do you not make every sacrifice in order to deliver us? Where is all the money we earned for you when we were yet free? Can you not give up those expensive amusements? Can you not sell some of those costly garments, those ornaments of gold and jewels and thus release us from this cruel bondage? Could you understand how much we suffer here, we are sure you would make every effort to release us."

It is thus that the poor abandoned souls of deceased parents complain of their children. The angel of the Lord enters the fiery prison of purgatory. He comes to release a suffering soul for whom alms and prayers and many holy masses have been offered up by his friends on earth. As soon as the angel appears, the souls of deceased parents crowd around him and ask in eager accents: "Ah! angel of God, have our children remembered us? Have they satisfied God's justice for us? Did they not hear the priest speak of our great sufferings? How comes it that they have done nothing?" "Alas! poor unhappy souls!" answers the angel, "your children heard the priest speak of your sufferings. They were touched with compassion, they even shed tears at the thought of your sufferings; they formed the good resolution to go to confession, to offer a holy Mass and communion for you, but they soon forgot all their good resolutions; they are too much buried in the cares and pleasures of the world to think of helping you."

Ah! young man and young woman, can you so soon forget your deceased parents? Can you forget that kind father who toiled for you, that father who passed many a weary day and many sleepless night in trying to make you happy? Now he is suffering; he needs your help, and you forget him. Ah! can you forget that loving mother that bore you, that mother that nursed and suckled you? When you were sick and helpless, that fond mother watched beside your bed through the long dull night; she quenched your feverish thirst; she kissed your burning brow, she prayed, and wept over you in anguish of heart, and now she is suffering the most frightful torments, she thirsts, she hungers for the possession of God, and you can look on and see her suffering and remain indifferent! O! ungrateful children, go kneel beside the grave of your deceased parents; go in spirit to their fiery prison in purgatory and hear their sad wailing; hear how their mournful voices accuse you before God and man. They cry, does the blood of your father, the blood of your mother flow no longer in your veins? Why have you forgotten us so long? We prayed for you so often when you were in danger; will you not now say a prayer for us? We comforted you when you were sick and suffering; will you not now console us in our sufferings? Ah! ungrateful children, it is chiefly on your account that we must suffer here so long. You have been so often the cause of our sins. Our greatest fault was that we loved you too much. Is this, then, the reward of all our love? O Children! if you were to see a stranger fall fainting at your door; if you were to see a poor hungry beg ar asking for bread, you would instantly hasten to his relief; nay, if you were to see a little flower in your garden parched with thirst, you would give a little water to revive it; if you were to see a little bird in the bleak winter pecking at your window for a few crumbs, for a little shelter, you would have pity even on the poor senseless creature. And now it is not a stranger, it is not a dumb senseless creature, no it is your own flesh and blood, it is your father, your mother that crys to you for help! Can you refuse them! Will you not relieve them in their sufferings.

Some time ago, a child came to a priest and said: "Father I have tried hard for some time to save some money. Here

I have a dollar. Please accept it and offer up the holy sacrifice of the Mass for my deceased parents."

God revealed to St. Catharine of Sienna, some time after the death of her parents, that he had bestowed great mercy upon them in the hour of their death, but that his justice had obliged him to condemn them to great pains in purgatory for having made use of different means to divert her from piety and devotion. "However, if you are willing," said our Lord to this saint, "to suffer those pains which I will send upon you in expiation of the temporal punishment of your parents in purgatory, I will deliver them from their pains and torments." Catharine showed herself willing to undergo whatever pains the Lord would deign to inflict upon her, in order to deliver her parents from the burning flames of purgatory. From that very moment God visited her with a very severe head-ache which she had to endure to the end of her life. Thus this holy child showed her love for her parents even after their death in spite of the ill-treatment she had, for sometime, received from them.—[*Life of St. Catharine of Sienna.*]

What blessings are promised to children who faithfully keep the fourth commandment?

God's protection in this life, and eternal happiness in the next.

In Holy Scripture (Eccles. chapter iii) God promises nine blessings to those children who honor their parents:

First. They will be blessed temporally and spiritually. "He that honoreth his mother is as one that layeth up a treasure." (verse 5.)

Second. They will have the happiness of seeing their children growing up in the practice of those filial duties which they themselves exercised towards their own parents.

"He who honoreth his father," says Holy Scripture, "shall have joy in his own children." (verse 6.)

Third. God will hear their prayers, "In the day of his prayer he who honoreth his father, shall be heard." (verse 6)

Fourth. They shall be long-lived. "He that honoreth his father shall enjoy a long life." (verse 7.)

Fifth. They will be blessed as it were with an undying posterity. "The father's blessing establisheth the houses of the children." (verse 11.)

Sixth. They will be highly spoken of and esteemed by everybody. "For the glory of a man is from the honor of his father." (verse 13.)

Seventh. They will be delivered by God from their afflictions. "The relieving of the father shall not be forgotten, for in the day of affliction thou shalt be remembered." (verses 15, 17.)

Eighth. Their sins will be remitted. "Thy sins shall melt away as the ice in fair, warm weather." (verse 17.)

Ninth. They will be blessed by God, and his blessing will remain upon them. "Honor thy father that a blessing may come upon thee from God and his blessing may remain upon thee in the latter end. (verses 9, 10.)

As Gustavus III., King of Sweeden, was one day passing through a village, he noticed a young girl drawing water from a well. Gustavus walked up to her and asked a drink. She immediately gave it to him. "Amiable girl," said the king to her, "if you wish to accompany me to Stockholm, I will procure you a more suitable occupation." "However desirous I may be to better my condition," answered the girl, "I could not for a moment entertain your proposal. My mother is poor, infirm and old, and as there is none to assist and support her but myself, I could not think of leaving her." "Where is your mother?" "In this cabin," replied the

daughter. The king entered the miserable habitation, and
beheld a poor, feeble old woman stretched on a wretched
pallet. Moved at what he saw, the prince said to her:
" Poor woman ! you are to be pitied very much." "I would be
a much greater object of pity," replied the old woman, " were
it not for this good, kind, and generous girl, who, by her attention and care, seeks to prolong my days. May God bless
her and reward her !" she added, and then shed tears.
" Continue to be thus kind to your mother," said Gustavus
to the young girl, presenting her, at the same time, with a
purse, " and I will, in a short time, obtain for you something more. Adieu, dear child ; I am your king." On his
return to Stockholm the monarch conferred on the mother a
pension for life, and after her death it was to revert to the
daughter.

St. Bernardine of Sienna relates that a certain young man
committed great crimes for which he was condemned to die
on the gallows. Now it happened that, whilst he was hanging on the gallows, he appeared to have the hoary head of
old age. It was revealed to the bishop, whilst praying for
him, that this young man would have remained innocent and
become very old, if he had been obedient and respectful to
his parents.

Now, though it is true that God has promised to good
children the goods of this life with long years, yet he often
calls them to himself at an early age, in order to show us,
that the goods of this life are not the final end of man ; for,
of what nature soever they may be, whether long life, health,
wealth, or the like, they are blessings to us only inasmuch
as they contribute towards our salvation and our increase in
virtue. Hence we should wish for them only inasmuch as
they help us to reach eternal life.

2. God foresees the ill use which certain children would

make of the goods of this life. To show them mercy, he removes them from these goods in the days of their innocence and virtue. Thus to cut them off early in life is undoubtedly the greatest blessing he can bestow upon them, because it brings them sooner and securer to their great end —the enjoyment of God himself.

No doubt, it was a most glorious and happy thing for the Holy Innocents to die for Jesus Christ. If they had lived much longer, they would probably have crucified him, as their fathers did. Millions of men are in hell who wish they had died when they were as yet innocent children.

If God, then, calls to himself a child in the days of his innocence, let no one say: "that child is dead." No, that child is not dead; it is living, it is rejoicing with the angels of heaven. How can a mother ever feel sad when she knows that her darling child is so happy! How can this life be dark and dreary to her when she knows that her treasure is safe, when she knows that her angel child is sheltered from the storms and temptations of this wicked world! How proud and happy, on the contrary, must the mother of such a child feel when she reflects that amid the mighty choirs of heaven, amid the silvery voices of unnumbered angels, there is one little voice singing the praises of God; and that little voice is hers; it is all her own. What an honor, what a happiness for a mother to have given to heaven a beautiful little angel! As the bright angels flit to and fro from earth to heaven, they smile upon that mother, they salute her with deep reverence, for she has given them a new companion to increase their joy.

In one of the poorest parts of London there was a cellar, with scarcely any furniture in it. There was nothing but a broken table, a little stool, a bed with a few handfuls of straw and a few rags upon it. A poor woman, whose hus-

band died in Ireland, lived in this cellar with her little
daughter Mary. The woman had become very poor, and her
health was so bad that she could work no more. She
had nothing to live on but what little Mary got by selling
a few matches. But when she became poor she did not neglect her duties to God. She was at Mass every Sunday, and
went to confession and received holy communion every month.

Above all, she took care of her daughter Mary, that she
should not go into bad company; that she should say her
prayers, and go to Mass and catechism, and be good. One
day in the winter the poor woman had been very ill, worse
than usual. She had scarcely had anything to eat all the day
—there was no fire in the grate—the last farthing candle was
burning away. Mary sat by her mother's bedside crying,
for it grieved her much that her poor mother should be so ill,
and have nothing to eat. All at once Mary left her mother,
and went over to the other side of the cellar, and began to
seek for something. She had just remembered that there
were a few match-boxes still remaining, and she thought if
she could sell them, she might buy something for her poor
mother. After searching here and there, she found three or
four boxes. She went back again to the bedside of her
mother with the match-boxes in her hand, and told her
mother what she was going to do, and asked her blessing.
" God bless you, my child," said her mother, in a weak
voice; " I hope I shall see you again."

Mary had a practice of saying the Hail Mary whenever she
went out of the house; and in each street she said either
" My Jesus, I do all for you," or the Hail Mary, or some
little prayer. She prayed fervently that night, for she knew
that if she were to lose her mother, there was nobody on
earth to take care of her. When she got into the street, she
began to cry out: " Matches; very good matches for a

penny." But the snow was falling fast, and the wind blew sharply, and the darkness was coming on quickly. There were few people about to buy her matches; and of those she met, few heard the weak voice of the child, and fewer still paid any attention to it. Mary cried out her matches, till weak, and hungry, and sorrowful, she could cry out no longer, so she sat down on a stone, and began to cry. Then Mary thought of her mother in heaven, and again she said the Hail Mary. She had scarcely finished it when a woman, who was passing by, stopped and asked her why she sat there so late on that cold stone, and crying. "My poor mother," answered Mary, "My poor mother is very ill and has nothing to eat." "Poor child," said the stranger; "take this sixpence, and get something for your mother." Mary was going to thank the stranger, but she was gone. Mary bought some bread in a shop, and then went home as quick as she could. She went carefully down the steps into the cellar, and there she saw her mother lying dead, and a priest kneeling beside her. The priest had given her the last sacraments before she died. But how did the priest come here? The poor woman was dying in cold, and in want, and in darkness. She was alone; there was nobody with her to go and ask the priest to bring to her the greatest of all blessings which can come to a soul which is going out of this world before the judgment-seat of Jesus Christ. But God is good, and he is very good to the poor when they have been good to him. God remembered this poor woman; he remembered how she had always done her best to go to the sacraments, and how she had taken care to bring up her little child in the fear of God. God knew that she was dying, and God said that she should not die without the blessing of the sacraments. But how was this done, for there was no one to bring the priest? Whatever God wishes to be done is sure to be done. At the same hour when the poor woman was dying, it happened that the priest was called to see some one else who was very ill. The priest set off. On his way he passed the cellar where the poor woman was dying. The door which opened on the steps leading down to the cellar happened to be open The night was dark, and it happened that the priest, not seeing the opening, fell down the steps. He found himself in the cellar, and heard a groan in one corner of the cellar, and going over there, he found the poor woman nearly at the point of death. He had with him everything that was necessary. He heard her confession, gave her the holy viaticum, anointed her, and gave her the last blessing; and a few moments after she died! So God is good to those who are faithful to him. This poor woman had not forgotten God during her life, and God did not forget her at her death. She was dying. She wanted a priest to hear her confession. A priest came to hear her confession. But why did he come? Was it because some one brought him? No. Was it because he came of himself? No, for he knew nothing about the poor woman. Did he come by accident? No. Then why did he come? He came because God brought him there. God said, the priest has set off to a sick person, but he shall not go to that person. He shall go to the poor woman who has served me faithfully.

Mary was now a poor, friendless orphan child. An old Catholic woman, out of charity, let the child live in her house. The poor child, however, had there few of the blessings of this world. Her clothes were miserable rags; in her hunger often she had nothing to eat. Little kindness did she meet with from anybody—even the old woman was able to do very little for the orphan, for she was very poor. But there was One above who had been very kind to her. She had lost her father on earth, but she had found a Father in heaven.

God had given his grace to this child; he had filled her soul with many blessed graces. He had made her a good child; and to be good is better than to be rich. Morning and night her child lifted up her hands to heaven, and said: "Our Father, who art in heaven." And he who is the God of orphans heard the orphan's prayer. The poor child got her scanty living by trying to sell a few matches. Often as she went on her weary way, she looked up at the blue sky, and thought how she had a blessed mother in heaven. Many were the Hail Marys this child said during the day; and when she said, "Holy Mary, mother of God, pray for us sinners, now and at the hour of our death," a thought came into her heart, how sweet it would be to die, and go and be with Mary in heaven: God does not forget the poor creatures whom nobody cares about. It is true he waits till the next life to give them their reward. "Blessed are the poor, for theirs is the kingdom of heaven." But still he sometimes sends some little blessing of this world to strengthen the fainting heart. So he made the dogs come and lick the sores of the poor Lazarus. And so he sometimes put into somebody's heart the thought to have pity on this poor child in her hunger, and give her some bread to eat. The ophan never forgot that Almighty God is the giver of all good gifts, and so whenever she got anything to eat, she always made the sign of the cross before and after eating. She never lay her weary head down to sleep at night till she had said her night prayers and examined her conscience; and the last thing she did at night was to fold her arms in a cross, and say: "Jesus, Mary, and Joseph, I give you my heart and my soul." The child went to confession once every month, and perhaps the priest who heard her confessions was the only person in the wide world who knew how much that little child pleased God. She was never absent from Mass on Sundays, and even on

week days she went to Mass as often as she could.   Whenever
she was in the church, and could get an opportunity, she loved
to go and kneel at the rails of the altar of the Blessed Sacrament.   Somehow she had learned, without being taught, how
to say little prayers to Jesus in the Blessed Sacrament.   She
would say : " My Jesus, I believe that thou are present in
the Blessed Sacrament.   I adore thee, O my Jesus—I thank
thee, O my sweet Jesus ; I love thee with all my heart."
How she had learnt these prayers nobody could tell, for she
had never been sent to school ; but she prayed with a great
heart, for greatly did she love Jesus, and she said these
prayers over and over again.

The poor orphan was now about nine years of age.   These
years had been full of sorrows and pains for the poor child.
But these pains did not come to the child by accident.   God
had arranged them all beforehand—before the child was
born—from eternity.   These sorrows were the road, fixed by
God, by which the child was to go to heaven.   God wished
to see whether the child would be good and faithful to him
in all these pains, and if the child was faithful to him, God
intended to give her a great, a very great reward in heaven.
The nine years fixed by God for the child to live were now
finished, and this child had been good and had served her
Creator.   It was a cold winter evening, the snow and the
rain had been falling on the poor child all the day as she went
about trying to sell matches.   She came late to the cottage of
the poor old woman.   She did not feel hungry, although she
had scarcely eaten anything during the whole day ; but she felt
sick and poorly.   Next day she was worse, and she got
worse and worse every day.   At last some neighbor had the
kindness to go and seek a doctor.   The doctor came, and
almost as soon as he had seen the child, he said that she was
dying.   At the moment when the doctor said that the poor

child was going to die, the child's Angel Guardian left her and went away! This was wonderful; for the Angel Guardian had never before left her for a moment in all her life. He had gone with her in all her ways; he had watched over her and taken care of her; he had consoled her when she was hungry and sorrowful. Why then did the Angel leave her just then, when she was dying? Listen and you shall hear. The Angel Guardian went to the church, where Jesus was in the Blessed Sacrament, and kneeling down before Jesus, he spoke thus to him:

"My dear Jesus, the good little child which Thou didst tell me to take care of is dying. Be pleased, O Jesus, to come to the poor child before she dies, and give her your blessing for a happy death."

Now Jesus had not seen the little child in the church for many days, and he knew why the child was not there! He knew very well that the little child was dying, because it was his will that she should die. When the Angel Guardian said this prayer, Jesus turned to the angels—for there are always millions of angels adoring before the Blessed Sacrament—and he said:

"My dear angels, the good little child which 'you have seen so often in the church is going to die, for I want to have her in heaven; but before she dies I will go and give her my blessing for a happy death."

Then the priest came to take the Blessed Sacrament to the dying child, as he always takes it to those who are very ill and dying. Now, just at the moment when the Blessed Sacrament was taken into the room where the child was, a most wonderful thing happened. Jesus spoke—He spoke to the heart of the child, and nobody heard him speak except the child herself. He said these words: "My dear child, I am Jesus whom you love. I want you to die and come to

heaven; and now I have come here to give you my blessing
before you die." That child knew how to answer—to speak
to Jesus—for many and many. a time she had knelt before
Jesus in the Blessed Sacrament and prayed to him. So that
child said these words to Jesus: "O Jesus, God the Son
made man, I believe that you are present in the Blessed Sacrament. Sweet Jesus, I love you; and. now, Jesus, you
know that I am dying, and I want to die for the love of you.
Come, then, my dearest Jesus—give yourself to me, and give
strength to my poor dying heart." Then the priest gave the
Holy Communion to the little child. After that he anointed
the eyes, and ears, and other senses of the child, praying to
God that in his mercy he would forgive whatever sins the
child might have committed by those senses. After each
prayer said along with the anointing, the child answered,
Amen. In the end the priest gave the last blessing of the
Church which is given to the dying, that they may not have
to be punished in purgatory for their sins. This is called
Plenary Indulgence.

The last moments of the little child's life were passing
away—death was not far off. What is called the last agony
came on. It is the struggle between the body and soul,
when the soul begins to leave the body. It is a terrible
sight to see those who are in their last agony. The child's
face became as pale as ashes, big drops of sweat rolled slowly
down it, the eyes moved about as if the child saw something
that frightened her. These were moments of fear, both for
those who stood round the dying child, as well as for the angels above. During those moments all the angels of heaven
were on there knees before the throne of God, they were
praying for the dying child; they said, "O God, have pity
on the poor dying child; do not let the devil come and tempt
her; give her your blessing, O God, to die a happy death; she

believed in you, and hoped in you, and loved you." All was over, the little child was dead. And what do you think happened at the very last moment of her life? Just when she was going to die, with the very last breath that she ever breathed in this world, it said, *Jesus, Mary, and Joseph, I give you my heart and my soul;* and the little child was in heaven at the feet of Jesus, and Jesus was putting a beautiful crown on her head, and that blessed prayer was still, as it were, on the lips of the dead body! And because the soul of the child was in heaven, the angels came down and sang hymns round the lifeless body of the child, for they knew that she would rise again on the last day, bright and shining as the sun.

What should children do if their parents set them a bad example?

They must not follow their bad example, but pray for their conversion.

We have already said that children should assist their parents, not only in their temporal wants, but also in their spiritual necessities. Now, parents are especially in great spiritual want if they are given up to evil habits, such as drunkenness, stealing, neglect of religious duties and the like. In such a case, children, of course, must not imitate the bad example of their parents, but they should remonstrate with them with all possible respect, if they know their temper will bear it, and entreat them most kindly to give up their evil ways and be reconciled to God. If their remonstrance is not successful, they may request some other person whose prudence and authority may be more successful in correcting their parents. They should, moreover, offer up, for the conversion of their parents, many fervent prayers, holy communions, Masses, penances and other good works.

12

A certain young lady, whose father was not a Catholic, entered the convent with the intention to obtain, by her life of self-denial, the gift of the true faith for her father. God heard her prayer, for her father. When on his death-bed, he sent for a Catholic priest, in order that he might be received by him into the Catholic Church and be reconciled to God.

There is a feeling, common to all people, that the prayer of children is all-powerful with God. We know this from the revelation of God himself: "Out of the mouths of infants thou hast perfected praise." (Ps. viii.)

Once the Emperor Henry besieged a certain city for a considerable time. The inhabitants were unwilling to surrender; so he notified them that he would give orders to his soldiers to take the city by assault, and massacre all its inhabitants to a man, even the little children. Alarmed at this proclamation, and seeing no hope left of saving themselves except in moving the Emperor to compassion, the inhabitants of the city had recourse to the following means: They collected all the little children from six to ten years of age, and after having arrayed them in procession, they made them march before the Emperor, and throw themselves on their knees, strike their breasts, and cry aloud in pitiful accents: "*Have pity on us, O Emperor! O Emperor, have pity on us!*" This heart-rending scene affected the Emperor so much, that he could not help weeping himself. He pardoned the inhabitants of the city, and raised the siege immediately.

If the prayer of a child is so powerful with man, it is far more so with God. The prayers of children will sometimes move God, when the prayers of others will not move him.

We read in Holy Scripture that Agar was wandering in the sandy deserts of Arabia with her little boy Ismael. She had with her a bottle of water for the boy, for she could find no water in the deserts. When the water in the bottle was finished, she placed the little boy under one of the trees and went a great way off from him, saying: "I will not see the boy die of thirst." Then she sat down and lifted up her voice, and began to cry for the poor dying boy. Whereupon an angel of God called to Agar from heaven, and said: "What art thou doing, Agar? Fear not, *for God hath heard the voice of the boy.* Arise, take up the boy!" * * And God opened her eyes, and she saw a well of water, and went and filled the bottle, and gave the boy to drink. (Gen. xxi., 17, 18, 19). So God heard the voice, *not of the mother, but of the child,* and he gave them water to drink. Thus does God hear the prayers of children.

In a town called Bethulia the church was one day full of children. What was the cause? Soldiers were on their road to this town to kill the people. The people knew that God hears the prayers of children, for they had read in the Holy Scriptures that "out of the mouths of infants comes forth perfect praise of God." So they made all the children go into the church and bow their heads down to the ground and pray for the people. God heard the prayers of the children. He made the cruel soldiers go away, and the people were saved by the children's prayers.

Dear child, if you have parents who do not lead a good life, God looks to you for their conversion. But what can you do? The good example of a child speaks to the heart of a parent. Then there is prayer—will God turn a deaf ear to the prayer of a child praying for the conversion of its father or mother? No; the Hail Mary which you say every day for their converson, the prayer you say for them each time you hear Mass, the Holy Communions you offer for them, the sighs of your heart, all rise up before God, and are not forgotten by him; and the day will come when God will send down from heaven the grace of conversion into the hearts of your parents.

During one of our missions, a certain child knelt down every night to say three Our Fathers and three Hail Marys for the conversion of his father. One night, towards the end of the mission, when the child was again kneeling down and praying, the father said: "Child, what are you doing there?" "Father," answered the child, "I am praying for your conversion." At that moment the father felt touched by the grace of God. Next day he went to church, made a good confession, and was reconciled with God. Thus it was by the prayer of this good child that God was moved to bestow the grace of conversion upon his father.

Louis Veuillot, editor of *L'Univers*, in Paris, gave the following account of his conversion: "I had been brought up," he said, "in ignorance of the truth, with no respect for religion, and hating the Catholic Church. I had a little child, which was wild, passionate, and stupid. I was cross and severe to the child. Sometimes my wife used to say to me: 'Wait a little; the child will be better when it makes its first Communion.' I did not believe it. However, the child began to go to catechism. From that time it became obedient, respectful, and affectionate. I thought I would go myself to hear the instructions on the catechism, which had made such a wonderful change in my child. I went, and I heard truths which I had never heard before. My feelings towards the child were changed. It was not so much love as respect. I began to feel for the child. I was inferior to it. It was better and wiser than I was. The week for the first Communion was come. There were but five or six days remaining. One morning the child returned from Mass, and came into a room where I was alone. 'Father,' said the child, 'the day of my first Communion is coming. I cannot

go to the altar without asking your blessing, and forgiveness
for all the faults I have committed and the pain I have often
given you. Think well of my faults, and scold me for them
all, that I may commit them no more.' 'My child,' I
answered, 'a father forgives everything.' The child looked
at me with tears in its eyes, and threw its arms round
my neck. 'Father,' said the child again, 'I have something
else to ask you.' I knew well—my conscience told me—
what the child was going to ask; I was afraid, and said:
'Go away now, you can ask me to-morrow.' The poor child
did not know what to say, so it left me, and went sorrow-
fully into its own little room, where it had an altar with an
image of the Blessed Virgin upon it. I felt sorry for what I
had said; so I got up and walked softly on the tips of my
feet to the room-door of my child. The door was a little
open; I looked at the child; it was on its knees before the
Blessed Virgin, *praying with all its heart for its father*.
Truly, at that moment I knew what one must feel at the
sight of an angel. I went back to my room, and leaned my
head on my hands; I was ready to cry. I heard a slight
sound, and raised my eyes—my child was standing before
me; on its face there was fear, with firmness and love.

'Father,' said the child, 'I cannot put off till to-morrow
what I have to ask you—I ask you, on the day of my first
Communion, to come to the Holy Communion along with
mamma and me.' I burst into tears, and threw my arms
around the child's neck, and said: Yes, my child, yes, this
very day you shall take me by the hand and lead me to your
confessor, and say, 'here is father.'" So this good child
also obtained, by its prayer, the grace of conversion for its
father.

In the year 1860, there was a little boy six years old, living
in a large town. He was very sickly. His father was a

drunkard.   One evening he was going home from the children's mission.   When he came home he opened the door, and he saw his father sitting in chair drunk!   The little boy went over to his father and climbed up on his knees.   He joined his hands together and said :   "Father, I want to say something to you."   The father said : "Well, what is it?"   The child said :   "Father, I feel very poorly, and I think I shall die soon.   God is good.   I think when I am dead he will take my soul into heaven."   "Well," said the father, "what then?"   "When I come into heaven," said the child, "I shall be very sorry to do it, but I must go to Almighty God, and tell him that you go to the public-house and ruin us all."   God must have put these words on the tongue of the child!   As soon as the child had spoken, the father did not answer one word, but he quietly took the child off his knees and set him down on the ground.   The father walked out of the house—he went in haste till he came to the chapel.   Next morning he went down on his knees and made his confession.   From that day he never got drunk any more, nor did he ever put his foot in a public-house again.

HOW DO CHILDREN SIN AGAINST THEIR OBLIGATION OF LOVING, HONORING AND OBEYING THEIR PARENTS.

I.   Children sin against *filial love:* 1, When they nourish in their hearts aversion towards their parents, and do not like to speak to them, or to show to them a friendly countenance.

2.   When they bear hatred to their parents.

3.   When they do not willingly listen to what their parents tell them.   If they continue to do so for a considerable time and thus grieve their parents very much, they may become guilty of mortal sin.

4.   Children sin against filial love, when they wish their parents a great evil, or cause them in any other way great

vexation without just reason. The unmerciful brethren of Joseph of Egypt were children of this kind. They sold the well-beloved son of their father to strangers, and said that a wild animal had devoured him.

5. When they take pleasure in thinking of the faults of their parents, when they tell those faults to others who were ignorant of them before, or exaggerate them; in a word, when they, in any way, injure the reputation of their parents. In this case, says St. Alphonsus, children commit a threefold sin, one against the love, another against the respect, and a third one against the justice due to their parents.

6. When they permit their parents to suffer any loss which they could easily prevent.

One of the most melancholy examples of an ungrateful child is that of Absalom, related in Holy Scriptures, in the second Book of Kings, chapter xviii.

Absalom, forgetful of his father's goodness towards him, erected the standard of rebellion against him, forced him to fly from his own city of Jerusalem, and followed him with a powerful army in order to wrest from him the crown. David, seeing that he was pressed closely by his ill-natured son, was obliged to stand and offer him resistance. He called together the few faithful friends he had about him, and prepared to give his son battle. His innate courage prompted him to lead them on in person, but his officers, who knew how much depended on his life, would not suffer him to expose it on the field. He yielded to their reason and gave the command to Joab, with the strictest orders to preserve the life of Absalom. Absalom had taken the field with an army much superior in numbers to that of David. The two armies came to an engagement in the forest of Ephraim. The rebels were defeated with great carnage. Twenty thousand of them remained dead upon the spot; the rest, with Absalom, endeavored to save themselves by flight. The ungrateful son, Absalom, was remarkable for a long flowing head of hair, and being hurried away by the confusion he was then in, rode under a thick spreading oak to avoid his pursuers. His hair became entangled in the boughs, and his mule going on, left him hanging in the air. Some of David's army soon rode up and saw the position of Absalom, but, in accordance with the king's order, no one dared to lift his arm against him. Joab was informed of the situation of Absalom, and he hastened to the spot, and when he arrived he took three lances in his hand and struck them all into the heart of the unhappy and rebellious son, Absalom. Thus miserably perished the disobedient son of a kind father.

Travelers in that country relate that even in our own day Jews, Turks and Christians when passing by Absalom's grave, suddenly stop and take up stones and cast them upon it, saying: "Behold, here lies that unfaithful son who revolted against his father."—[*Schmid's Hist. Catech.*]

7. Children sin against filial love when they neglect to assist their parents in their temporal and spiritual necessities. A certain widow was no longer able to support herself on account of her extreme weakness. She had two daughters who were living out. When she asked assistance of them, one of them said: "I would willingly give you a part of my wages, but then, mother, I could not have anything for myself." The other said: "I, too, mother, would willingly let you have part of my wages, but then I could no longer dress as well as I wish."

In a small town of Germany there lived a good old man who was entirely dependent for support on a son who had been married several years. But alas! this unnatural son, in concert with his wife, finding that *the old father*, as he was not ashamed to call him, was rather burdensome to them, took steps to get him into a hospital so as to have no more trouble with him. The good old man, on leaving the house where he had spent so many happy years, could not help shedding tears ; but his son remained cold and heartless. Some days after, the father sent to ask him, at least, for a pair of sheets, so as to make him a little more comfortable in the hospital. The wicked man took the worst he could find, gave them to his little boy, nine or ten years old, and said to him : " Take these to your grandfather in the hospital, and tell him not to trouble us any more." The little fellow set out, but his father, who watched him, perceived that he stopped a long time behind a pile of faggots at the lower end of the yard. When he came back he asked him what he was doing behind the faggots. " Why, father, I was hiding away one of those bad sheets amongst the faggots, so that some day when you go to the hospital I'll not have to give you one of my good ones." These words were like a thunderbolt to the unhappy father ; he understood his crime, and went himself, without delay, to bring his poor father back from the hospital, and took the greatest care of him till he died, so that his children might one day treat him the same.—[*Schmid et Belet Cat. Hist.* ii, 275.]

One day a certain child saw how his father made a wooden cup. " Father," asked the child, " for whom do you make the cup of wood?" " For your grandfather," replied the father. " Well, then," said the child, " make it nice and strong, in order that I may give it to you when you have grown old."—[*Schmid's Hist. Catech.*]

Whoever makes his father's heart to bleed shall have a child that will avenge the deed.

8. Children sin against filial love, when they wish death to their parents in order to obtain their inheritance or to be no longer obliged to support them.

9. It sometimes happens that parents, during their life-time divide their wealth among their children, on condition that these provide them with certain things. Now, when children do not give these things they sin against filial love.

A rich old man named Conaxa had been so imprudently kind as to divide his wealth between his two sons during his own lifetime. He too soon perceived that they had no longer the same respect for him that they used to have; they were not ashamed even to tell him frequently that he was living too long, and that they considered him a burden. The unhappy old man, in despair at such base conduct on the part of children for whom he had done so much, asked advice of a sincere friend. "You have done very wrong, my dear friend, in acting as you did; nevertheless, there is one way of extricating yourself. Contrive to make your children believe that there are some debts still owing to you. You understand?" Accordingly, some days after, whilst Conaxa was at table with his two sons, a farmer comes in to pay him, and he said, *the remains of an old debt.* It was a big bag of silver lent him by his friend. Conaxa did not seem at all surprised, took the bag, put it away to count over at his leisure, gave the farmer something to drink, and gave not the slightest reason to suspect the trick he was playing. No sooner did his sons find out that he had not divided all his wealth between them than they immediately became as kind and attentive as they had before been harsh and uncivil. Conaxa died some years after, leaving a heavy box, which his greedy heirs hastened to open. What did they find in it? Bags full of stones and pebbles, with a lit-tle note to the following effect: "*I bequeath these stones to stone fathers who divide their wealth amongst their children before their death.*"

Monsignor Abelly mentions (Instr., num. 28) a fact related by Thomas Cantipratensis, and which occurred in his own time. There was a rich man in France, who had an only son, whom he wished to marry a certain lady far superior to him in rank. The parents of the lady consented to the marriage, on the condition that the father of the young man would transfer all his property to the son, and depend on him for his support. The father consented. In the beginning he was treated with great kindness, but after some time, in order to please his wife, the son banished him from his house, and gave him but little assistance. On a certain day on which the son had prepared a great banquet for his friends, the father came to ask relief, but was dismissed with harshness and disrespect. But listen to what happened: As soon as the son sat down to dinner, a toad flew in his face, and took so fast a hold that it could not be removed. He, then repented of the ingratitude with which he had treated his father, and went to the bishop to receive absolution. The bishop enjoined as a penance, that he should go through all the provinces of the kingdom, with his face uncovered, confessing his sins, as an example for other children. Cantipratensis states that the fact was related to him by a father of the Order of St. Dominic, who had seen the unhappy man in Paris, with the toad on his face, and had heard the circumstances from himself.

10. Children sin against filial love when, after the death of their parents, they do not faithfully execute their last will, or delay, without a grievous reason, the execution of it for a considerable time.

11. When they neglect to pray and offer up other good works for the repose of their parents' souls, so that the words of David come true: "Their memory has perished with a noise (Ps. 9) namely, with the noise or sound of the bell announcing their death and funeral.

Thomas Cantipratensis relates that a celebrated warrior of the army of Charlemange left, on his death-bed, his charger, together with saddle and harness, to a nephew, charging him to sell it and apply the proceeds for Masses and pious works, to be offered up for the repose of his soul. His nephew, however, kept the horse for his own use for a long time; but how great was his fright when, one night, the voice of his deceased uncle aroused him from sleep, reproaching him most bitterly for his impiety. "Why," said he, "did you not execute my order? Why did you break your word? You are the cause of my having had to suffer great pains in Purgatory, which I should still be suffering had not the mercy of God remitted part of my temporal punishments. I am now going to enjoy the delights of Paradise; but you must know that, in punishment for your faithlessness, a premature death is awaiting you, and after death you will have to suffer in Purgatory a peculiar chastisement, both that for your own indebtedness to the Divine Justice, and that for mine, which God was pleased to remit." The youth was horror-struck at these words. He repented of his sin, confessed it, and hastily made all possible amends for it; by this means he escaped the eternal, but not the temporal, punishment, for he was soon carried off by a sudden death. (L. II. Apum., 25-53.)

II. Children sin against the *honor and respect* due to parents: 1, When they despise them, give them cross looks, speak to them harshly, or answer them impudently.

2. When they scoff at their advice, mimic them so as to ridicule them.

3. When they utter imprecations against them, or insult them by calling them fools, beasts, drunkards and the like. Such expressions uttered by children in presence of their parents are mortal sins, says St. Alphonsus.

In the Old Law, those who treated their father or mother *contemptuously*, were condemned to death. " He that curseth his father or mother shall die the death." (Exod. xxi., 17.) In our day they are not punished with temporal death, but they are accursed by God, and condemned to eternal death. " He that angereth his mother is accursed of God." (Eccl. iii., 18.)

A young man once cursed his father. The father cursed him. The young man went out and walked along the rail-road track. Blinded and carried away by passion, he neither saw nor heard the cars that came thundering on. He was struck by the engine and killed, and his eyes hung out of the sockets. He was brought home a corpse. " The eye that mocketh at his father and that despiseth the labor of his mother in bearing him, let the ravens of the brooks pick it out, and the young eagles eat it." (Prov. xxx., 17.)

4. But the most crying sin of all, and the worst species of " contempt " of parents, is that of raising the hand against them, and threatening to strike them. " He that striketh his father or mother shall be put to death." (Exod. xxi., 15.)

The son or daughter who is so lost to every feeling of nature as to attempt to lay hands on a parent, ought every day to fear the vengeance of God. If honoring father and mother will obtain for a child a long and happy life in this world, the child that maltreats a parent shall live but for a short time, and shall live in misery and wretchedness. It is told that a certain young man barbarously dragged his father by the feet. When they had reached a certain place, the father said : " My son, you have done enough ; do not drag me any farther ; for I once dragged my father thus far, and in punishment of my sin, God has justly permitted me to be thus dragged by you."

A widow lady of rank, named Alexandrina, had two sons.
The elder, being no more than ten years of age, began
already to use unbecoming language. His mother reprimanded him and said to him: "What, my child, do you use
such expressions in my presence! Have I taught you to
speak in this manner? and although I was so unhappy as
to use such words, you should never pronounce them. Remember that such profane language is spoken only by libertines, wicked people, uneducated and vulgar children."

The child profited by this warning, and never dared afterwards to use an improper word before his mother, but he
continued to speak so with his little companions. The
mother hearing of it said to him: "You no longer speak
improperly before me, but when you are with others you are
not ashamed to scandalize them. My son, have you, then,
lost the fear of God? Do you know that God hears and
sees you everywhere? You dared not speak wickedly before
me, and you continue to do so before God! Remember that
you ought to fear God more than me. He is your Creator,
your first father, and your judge; and it would be better for
you to say a thousand bad words before me, than one before
God. Mend your conduct, my son; for I would rather see
you dead at my feet, than see you pursue such a course. I
forbid you ever to frequent the companions who have taught
you to speak thus." These words made such an impression
on the child's mind that he changed his conduct, and became
submissive to his mother. God rewarded his obedience, for,
having arrived at age, he entered into a religious order,
where he made great progress in learning and virtue.

The second son of Alexandrina had not naturally so good
a disposition as the elder, yet he was more beloved by his
mother; for it often happens that parents are deceived, and
love a wicked child more than he deserves.

Alexandrina reprimanded him, but he laughed at her advice, and notwithstanding her entreaties, continued to visit young libertines, who ruined his mind, spoke only of diversions and pleasures, and inspired him with a hatred of industry, and contempt for his mother. Such company so perverted the heart of this young man, that he lost all respect for his mother, gave himself up to wickedness, impurities, and gambling. His mother wept and warned him of it, but this was not sufficient, it was now too late; she ought to have corrected him in time, or have put him in prison at the commencement of his disorderly conduct.

The young man, disregarding the advice of his mother, visited a young lady, who deceived him, and the more so as she was not his equal. He married her, and brought a lawsuit against his mother, for the property left by his father; but he did not enjoy it long. One day as he went to walk with his new married spouse, he made a false step, fell at the gate of the city, and was bruised under the wheels of a carriage that was passing by. The news was immediately brought to his mother. "O my God!" she cried, "this is the punishment for my son's disregard of me, and for the trouble he has caused me. I pray thee, O Lord! mercifully grant that this unhappy child may at least have time to repent and return to thy favor." The afflicted mother ran to see her son; she had hardly arrived when he expired in her arms, without uttering a word, without confession, and without the Sacrament.

Never forget this example, dear child, and remember that if you cause your parents sorrow, sooner or later you will meet with some unlucky accident. "He is cursed of God," says the Holy Ghost, "who causeth his mother to grieve."

A hermit of the Grand Duchy of Baden, in Germany, if I am not mistaken, was busy one day gathering herbs in a forest.

All at once he hears piteous cries; he runs in the direction of the sounds, and finds lying near a bush, a poor young man who was grievously wounded in the right foot. The hermit raises him up, drags him with much difficulty to his cabin, and dresses his wound. The young man afterwards told his story: "I have been a short time in the service of a rich lord; yesterday, we were riding through the forest where you found me, when my master discovered that he had lost a bag of silver, which he had fastened to his steed; we stopped immediately, and I retraced my steps to seek it; but not finding it, I returned to my master who was waiting for me in great wrath. He was so angry that he accused me of having the bag, and of hiding it in the bushes so as to secure it afterwards. In vain I did declare my innocence, he would not believe me; he even drew his sword and gave me a random blow, that wounded me in the right foot and made me fall to the ground. As for him, he fled with all speed, leaving me in the state in which you found me." "Your story has interested me," said the hermit, "but I pity your fate, because I see you suffer *innocently*." This last word *innocently*, instead of consoling the wounded man, appeared to distress him greatly; he sighed deeply, then burst into tears, his face betraying some strange emotion. "Alas, father, you are wrong in saying that I suffer innocently, for I deserve what has come upon me. Listen to what I am about to tell you. My good mother is still living, and I wish I could see her again, for I am her only son. But what a crime I have committed in her regard! One day we were both riding in a wagon to a neighboring village. On the way we happened to dispute about some trifling matter; I dared to rebel against her, and even carried my fury so far as to throw her out of the wagon with a kick. My poor mother threatened then to give me up to justice, and I, in order to avoid being arrested, took flight and crossed the frontier into a foreign country. Then it was that I entered the service of the nobleman before mentioned, and met with my accident. See now, father, how God punishes me: the foot that is wounded is the very one with which I dared to kick my poor mother!" His story ended, the young man asked the hermit to hear his confession; the man of God healed his body and his soul at once, and, some days after, the penitent son went to throw himself into the arms of his mother, who forgave him with all her heart.—[*Schmid et Belet, Cat. Hist.*, II. 267.]

5. When, after having become rich or elevated in rank, they refuse, through pride or vanity, to acknowledge their parents publicly, to visit them, and receive them at their houses, because they are poor and uneducated.

III. Children sin against filial *obedience:* 1, When they refuse to do what their parents, command, or when they murmur at having to do it.

2. When, in spite of the advice of their parents, they frequent the company of bad people, or suspicious houses, taverns, dances, shows or nightly amusements.

3. When, in spite of their parents' orders, they neglect to hear Mass on Sundays, or feast days of obligation; to go to confession and to assist at the Christian doctrines.

4. When they do not perform what is commanded by their parents for the interest of the family, or when, without a grievous reason, they quit the paternal roof against their parents' will

5. Children who form a particular friendship with a view to marriage, without the knowledge of their parents, are also wanting in deference to parental authority.

To disobey our parents in an important matter is a special sin which we must mention in confession. Thus, for instance,

13

he who in spite of the orders of his parents, does not hear Mass on Sundays, must accuse himself, not only of this sin of omission, but also of having disobeyed his parents.

The sin of disobedience may be mortal or venial according to the degree of resistance or obstinacy accompanying it and according to the importance of the matter. Children often become guilty of acts of disobedience in matters of trifling importance, as, for instance, in commands given by parents without any intention of obliging their children to obey them always and literally. These, and even more serious obligations, when violated through the thoughtlessness and weakness of childhood, are no grievous sins. But when a command is given to a child in such a way that it knows his parents think it a matter of great importance, then it would be a mortal sin wilfully to disobey them without necessity. Such are the commands given by parents, strictly forbidding their children to frequent bad persons, to stay out late at night, and the like.

St. Francis Regis relates the following fact. It occurred in his own family. The Catholics, commanded by Duke de Jayense, besieged Villemare in Languedoc, occupied by the Calvinists. The nobility hastened in crowds to the Catholic camp. The grand uncle of St. Francis Regis had several sons, who were most eager to take part in the fray. The father at last consented to let them go, though very reluctantly, but he insisted that the eldest son should remain with him to console him for the loss of the others. The elder son, however, insisted on going. The father at last flew into a passion and said: "Go, then, since you will not obey me, and may I never see your face again!" The young man set out. Scarcely had he arrived at the camp when the Calvinists made a sally. Young Regis fought bravely till he at last fell dead on the battlefield, and was there buried with the rest of the slain.

Some time after, when peace had been concluded, a poor shepherdess was one day watching her flock near the very spot where Regis was buried. Suddenly the apparition of a soldier, all covered with blood, stood before her. He told her that the body of a certain Regis of Pontconvert, who had been slain in battle, was buried in that spot, and he begged her to request his family to have his corpse removed from this profane place and buried in the consecrated tomb of his ancestors.

The Regis family went to the spot indicated, found the body and brought it to the family tomb, accompanied by the clergy. As soon as the bier approached the paternal mansion, the coffin became all at once so heavy that it was impossible to bring it farther. The people were amazed at this prodigy, but the father understood full well its meaning: "Ah, wretched man that I am!" he cried. "I cursed my boy for his disobedience, and now his very bones are brought here as if to make reparation. O, just and holy God, forgive my son as I forgive him from my heart." Scarcely had he uttered this prayer when the bier became light again, and the body was buried according to the rites of the holy Church. —[*Life of St. Francis Regis.*]

Theophilus Rainaud relates, that on the borders of France and Savoy there was a young nobleman who was disobedient to his widowed mother. She commanded him to be at home at an early hour in the evening, and not to remain out till midnight, as was his habit. He continued to disobey her commands. She one night ordered the doors to be locked. Finding them closed against him, he cried out in a loud voice, but was not heard. He then broke out into injurious language and maledictions against his mother, and, along with his brother and a servant who were with him, he took shelter in a neighboring house.　After having gone to rest, they heard a frightful noise, and saw a hideous looking person entering that part of the room in which the young man lay.　This frightful looking person took the young man by the feet and stretched him on the table, and cut him to pieces with a sabre, and then gave him to be devoured by four horrible dogs.　The brother and servant afterwards made search for his body, but could not find it.　The brother was so terrified at the awful death of this young man that he became a Carthusian, and after a holy life died a holy death.

DUTIES OF THE FAITHFUL TOWARDS THEIR PASTORS, AND OF SUBJECTS TOWARDS CIVIL AUTHORITIES.

1.　When our dear Saviour Jesus Christ was living on earth, he was accused of the worst crimes.　He was accused by the high-priests and the doctors of the law, to whom it belonged to pronounce who was the Messias.　He was accused before an idolatrous judge, in the presence of all the people.　He was treated as a blasphemer, as one possessed by the devil, as a lover of wine, as a destroyer of the Temple, as a seducer of the people, as a rebel, as a seditious man, who gave to himself the title of king, who forbade the payment of tribute to Cæsar, and who wished to destroy the Jewish nation.　If ever infamous calumny was carried to excess, it was undoubtedly in regard to our divine Saviour Jesus Christ, "who knew not sin," who had never uttered a deceitful word, who "did all things well," and who "passed his life in doing good, and healing all kinds of infirmities."

Now, Jesus Christ continues to live in the hierarchy of the Catholic Church—the Pope, the bishops and priests.　He has made a prediction to his apostles and their successors,

which has come true in all ages, and which will be verified
to the end of the world. He said to them: "The servant
is not greater than his lord: if they have persecuted me,
they will also persecute you." (John xv., 20.) This prediction of our Lord Jesus Christ has been especially verified in
our own century. See how the enemies of Jesus Christ
treated our late Holy Father, Pius IX.; see how they mas-
sacred the Archbishop of Paris, and many of his clergy, in
cold blood! *The Pope! the Pope! The Priest! the Priest!*
This has ever been the cry of all the wicked; and what fan-
cies has it not conjured up? Some, when they only hear
the word "Pope" or "priest," turn up their eyes in horror,
and shrink back as if they had suddenly encountered an evil
genius. Others, at the mere sound of the word "Pope" or
"priest," become as rabid as a dog stricken with hydro-
phobia when he sees water. They grind their teeth, they
froth and foam at the mouth, they tremble with rage, and
seem as if they would tear into pieces all the Popes and
priests that have ever lived from Peter to the present
day.

Others shake their heads with an air of majesty, as if they
would say: "How can we get over the Pope—over the
priesthood of the Catholic Church?" The spirit of the
world, the spirit of falsehood and of negation, hates the
Pope, the Vicar of Christ; it hates all our Lord's true ministers, the Catholic bishops and priests, with demoniacal
hatred. Why? Because it hates Christ, whose power as
priest, as teacher and as ruler is invested in the bishops and
priests, and especially in the Pope. As the enemies of
Christ and his holy religion try everywhere to undermine the
power and dignity of the Catholic priesthood, all Catholics
should try to increase in love, respect and obedience towards their pastors; they should respect them and obey

them as they would Jesus Christ, in things especially that relate to the spiritual order; and if necessary they should provide them with the necessaries of life.

All the pastors of the Church have a right to our respect; but we must honor especially the Sovereign Pontiff who is our common father, the Pastor of pastors, the Vicar of Christ; the bishop of our diocese, our parish-priest, and our confessor, because they direct us in the way of salvation. We sin against the respect due to a priest by raillery, back-biting and slander. To injure the character of a priest so much as to render him unable to fulfil the duties of his ministry with advantage to souls is a grievous sin against justice and religion.

There are instances of frightful punishment on record, which Almighty God has inflicted on those who were irreverent to priests. Theodoret, Bishop of Cirus, in Philot, relates that St. James, Bishop of Nissibe, before he was consecrated bishop, went into Persia to visit the Christians of that country. As he passed by a fountain, certain females, who were washing clothes, treated him with great disrespect. The saint raised his eyes to heaven to recommend himself to God, and, by a divine inspiration, cursed the fountain, and it dried up instantly. He then cursed the insolence of the girls. Immediately their hair became quite white, and remained so to the end of their life, as a proof of the respect which is due to priests. Beware, therefore, of ever showing the slightest disrespect to a priest; for, to disrespect the priest is to disrespect Jesus Christ, whose place he takes on earth: "He who despiseth you" (the priest), says Jesus Christ, "despiseth me; and he who thus despises me, despises my heavenly Father, who sent me." Never associate with those who speak against the priests or ridicule them; otherwise, the punishment of Core, Dathan, and

Abiron, will come upon you. Imitate rather the angels and saints in their respect and love for the priesthood.

St. Francis de Sales saw the guardian angel of a young priest whom he had ordained, go in advance to the right of the priest, before his ordination; but, after his ordination. the angel went to the left of the priest and followed him.

The Emperor Constantine the Great held the bishops and priests in such respect, that he would not sit down in the Council of Nice, till after all the bishops had been seated; and, even then, he sat only upon a seat below them all. Wenceslaus, King of Poland, would not even sit down in the presence of a priest. St. Catharine of Sienna, and Mary of Oignies, kissed the ground on which a priest had walked.

St. Francis of Assisium said that, if he saw an angel from heaven and a priest, he would first bow to the priest and then to the angel; for the angel is the friend of God, but the priest holds his place.

2. The duties of subjects towards their temporal Rulers are to respect, honor, and obey them according to the laws so far as these are not contrary to the laws of God and the rights of the Church. St. Paul says: "Let every soul be subject to higher powers; for there is no power but from God, and those that are, are ordained of God. Therefore he that resisteth the power resisteth the ordinance of God. The prince is God's minister for good." (Rom. xiii.) [*See vol. Dignity, Authority and Duties of Parents etc. Chapter* XLII.]

DUTIES OF WARDS, PUPILS SOLDIERS, WORKMEN, AND SERVANTS.

1. The duties of wards towards their guardians are much the same as those of children towards their parents, with the exception, however, of the duty of assisting them.

2. The duties of pupils towards their masters are like those of children towards their parents, at least, as far as regards respect and obedience.

3. Soldiers should respect their officers and obey them in all that concerns military service.

4. Workmen should respect their masters, serve them faithfully and take interest in their concerns.

5. Servants owe to their masters : *justice, obedience* and *respect.*   •

I. *Justice* is a duty which we owe to all men ; it consists in giving to everyone his own. But servants are in a special manner obliged to be just towards their masters for in their case there is either an explicit or implicit contract of fidelity by which they are bound. Hence it is that their masters trust their goods and work to them. "Exhort servants," writes St. Paul, "not to defraud their masters, but to show good fidelty in all things, that they may adorn the doctrine of God our Saviour in all things." (Tim. ii., 9.)

This duty of justice or fidelty obliges servants : 1, Not to wrong their masters in their goods either by stealing, or wasting, or giving them to others. 2, To resist those who try to wrong their masters. 3, To do carefully the work assigned to them by their masters.

II. Servants owe obedience to their masters.

"Servants," says St. Paul, "be obedient to them that are your masters according to the flesh, with fear and trembling in the simplicity of your heart, as to Christ. Not serving to the eye, as it were pleasing men, but, as the servants of Christ, doing the will of God from the heart.

With a good will doing service as to the Lord, and not to men ; knowing that whatsoever good things any man shall do, the same shall he receive from the Lord, whether he be bond or free." (Eph. vi., 5.)

In these words St. Paul tells servants (1) that the obedience they owe to their masters is commanded by God himself; (2) that they should obey in all lawful things; (3) that they should obey without contradiction, in simplicity of heart, as unto Christ himself, and with a good will; (4) that the intention in obeying, should be to do the will of God; (5) that, as a reward for their obedience, they would receive life everlasting.

III. *Servants owe respect to their masters.*

"Whosoever are servants under the yoke," says St. Paul, "let them count their masters worthy of all honor, lest the name of the Lord and his doctrine be blasphemed. But they that have believing masters, let them not despise them, because they are brethren; but serve them the rather because they are faithful and beloved, who are partakers of the benefit." (I. Tim., vi., 1.)

Hence servants are guilty of sin: (1) If they wrong their master in his goods, by taking them for their own use, or by giving them to others, or by carelessly injuring, wasting, or destroying them. (2) If they suffer others to do so, without taking such means as are in their power to prevent them. For, the duty of *fidelity* obliges them to protect their master from these injustices, when they can; either by telling him, or by admonishing the delinquent, or in such other way as prudence shall suggest. A servant who sees strangers, not his fellow-servants, injure his master's goods, and offers no resistance, is bound to make restitution. (3) If they neglect their work; or do it in a bad and insufficient manner; or if they idle away the time for which they are paid; or if they encourage others to do these things.

2. Servants are guilty of sin if they take secret compensation for services which they think are worth more than the wages agreed upon; for Pope Innocent XI. has condemned

the opinion (proposition 37) of those who hold that servants can secretly compensate themselves for services which they think are worth more than the wages agreed upon.

3. If they disobey their masters in lawful things.

4. If they give way to passion and use bad language when they are reproved by their masters.

5. If they reveal certain family secrets which might compromise the honor, reputation, or interests of their masters. Backbiting and calumny on the part of a servant against his master are much more sinful than if directed against another person.

6. A servant is guilty of sin, if he co-operates with the sin of his master, even against his will. He can be excused only in some cases when by refusing obedience, he should suffer a great loss and when his co-operation is not in itself intrinsically bad.

It is not a man's condition, but virtue, that can make him truly great or truly happy. How mean soever a person's station or circumstances may be, the road to true greatness and happiness is open to him; and there is not a servant or slave who ought not to be enkindled with a laudable ambition of arriving at this greatness, which will set him on the same level with the rich and the most powerful. Nay, a servant's condition has generally stronger incitements to holiness, and fewer obstacles and temptations than most others. But for this he must, in the first place, be faithful to God, and ardent in all practices of devotion. Some allege want of time to pray. But their meals, their sleep, their diversions demonstrate that it is not time, but zeal for the divine service that is wanting. What Christian does not blush at his laziness in this duty, when he calls to mind Epictetus's lamp, and Cleanthes's labor, who wrought and earned by night what might maintain him in the study of philosophy by day! Prayer in such a station ought not to trespass upon work, but who cannot, even at his work, raise his mind to God in frequent ejaculations? Also industry, faithfulness, with the most scrupulous exactness, obedience, respect, esteem, and sincere love which a servant owes to a master, with a care of his honor and interest, are duties to God, whose will he does, and whom he honors in proportion to the diligence and order with which he acquits himself of them. Justice, charity, concord, and ready mutual assistance are virtues constantly to be exercised toward fellow-servants, upon which depend the peace, happiness, and good order of the whole family. Patience, meekness, humility, and charity, must be called forth on all occasions, especially under reproofs and injuries, which must always be received in silence, and with sweetness, kindness, and a degree of gratitude when they carry any admonitions with them. Perfect resignation to the will of God, and confidence in his infinite wisdom, power and goodness, must be joined with constant cheerfulness and contentedness in a person's station, which brings servants much greater advantages for happiness, and removes them from danger, hazards, and disappointments, more than is generally considered. Servants who are kept mostly for state, are of all others most exposed to dangers and ruin, and most unhappy; but they must, by devotion and other serious employments, fill up their moments. By such a conduct, a servant, how low soever his condition may appear in the eyes of men, will arise to the truest greatness, attain to present and future happiness, and appear himself dear to God, valuable to man, a most useful member of the republic of the world, and a blessing of the family wherein he lives. The lives of St. Isidore of Madrid, and of St. Zita are evident proofs of what we have just said.

EXAMPLES OF HOLY LABORERS.

1. *St. Isidore of Madrid* —St. Isidore was born at Madrid, of poor but very devout parents, and was christened Isidore from the name of their patron—St. Isidore of Seville. They had not means to procure him learning or a polite education; but, both by word and example, they infused into his tender soul the utmost horror and dread of all sin, and the most vehement ardor for every virtue, and especially for prayer. Good books are a great help to holy meditation; but not in-d'spensably requisite. St. Irenaeus mentions whole nations that believed in Christ, and abounded in exemplary lives, without knowing the use of ink or paper. Many illustrious anchorets knew no other alphabet than that of humility and divine charity. The great St. Anthony himself could not so much as read the Greek or Latin languages: nay, from the words of St. Austin, some doubt whether he could read even his own barbarous Egyptian dialect. Yet in the science of the saints, what philosopher or orator ever attained to the A-B-C of that great man? Learning, if it puffs up the mind, or inspires any secret self-sufficiency, is an impedi-ment to the communications of the Holy Ghost; simplicity and sincere humility being the dispositions which invite him into the soul. By these was Isidore prepared to find him an interior instructor and comforter. His earnestness in seek-ing lessons and instructions of piety made him neglect no opportunity of hearing them; and so much the more tender and the deeper were the impressions which they left in his soul, as his desire was the stronger and the more pure. His patience in bearing all injuries and in overcoming the envy of fellow-servants by cordial kindnesses; his readiness to obey his masters, and in indifferent things to comply with the inclinations of others, and humbly to serve every one, gave him the most complete victory over himself and his

passions. Labor he considered as enjoined him by God in punishment of sin, and for a remedy against it. And he performed his work in a spirit of compunction and penance. Many object that their labors and fatigues leave them little time for the exercises of religion. But Isidore, by directing his attention according to the most holy motives of faith, made his work a most perfect act of religion. He considered it a duty, to God. Therefore he applied himself to it with great diligence and care, in imitation of the angels in heaven, who in all things fulfil the will of God with the greatest readiness and alacrity of devotion. The more humbling and the more painful the labor was, the dearer it was to the saint, being a means the more suitable to tame his flesh, and a more noble part of his penance. With the same spirit that the saints subdued their bodies by toils in their deserts, Isidore embraced his task. He moreover sanctified it by continual prayer. Whilst his hand held the plough, he in his heart conversed with God, with his angel guardian, and the other blessed spirits; sometimes deploring the sins of the world, and his own spiritual miseries, at other times, in the melting words of the royal prophet, raising his desires to the glory of the heavenly Jerusalem. It was chiefly by this perfect spirit of prayer, joined with, or rather engrafted upon a most profound humility and a spirit of mortification, that St. Isidore arrived at so eminent a degree of sanctity as rendered him the admiration of all Spain. In his youth he was retained servant by a gentleman named John de Vargas of Madrid, to till his land and to do his husbandry work. The saint afterwards took a most virtuous woman to wife, named Mary Toribia. After the birth of one child, which died young, the parents, by mutual consent, served God in perfect continency. St. Isidore continued always in the service of the same master. On account of his fidelity, he could say to him as Jacob did to Laban, that to guard and improve his stock, he had often watched the nights, and had suffered the scorching heats of summer, and the cold of winter; and that the stock, which he found small, had been exceedingly increased in his hands. Don John de Vargas, after long experience of the treasure he possessed in the faithful ploughman, treated him as a brother, according to the advice of Ecclesiasticus, "Let a wise servant be as dear to thee as thy own soul." He allowed him the liberty of assisting daily at the public office of the church. On the other side, Isidore was careful, by rising very early, to make his devotions no impediment to his business, nor any encroachment upon what he owed to his master. This being a duty of justice, it would have been a false devotion to have pretended to please God by a neglect of such an obligation; much less did the good servant indulge his compassionate charity to the poor, by relieving them otherwise than out of his own salary. The saint was sensible that in his fidelity, diligence, and assiduous labor consisted, in a great part, the sanctification of his soul; and that his duty to his master was his duty to God. He also inspired his wife with the same confidence in God, the same love of the poor, and the same disengagement from the things of this world; he made her the faithful imitatrix of his virtues, and a partner in his good works. She died in 1175, and is honored in Spain among the saints. Her time-honored veneration was approved by Pope Innocent XII. in 1697. (See Benedict XIV., De Cananiz, 1, 2, c. 24, p. 246.) St. Isidore being seized with the sickness of which he died, foretold his last hour, and prepared himself for it with redoubled fervor, and with most tender devotion, patience, and cheerfulness. The piety with which he received the last sacraments drew tears from all that were present. Repeating inflamed acts of divine love, he expired on the 15th of May, 1170, being near sixty years of age. His death was glorified by miracles. After forty years, his body was removed out of the churchyard into the church of St. Andrew. It has been since placed in the bishop's chapel, and during these five hundred years remains entire and fresh, being honored by a succession of frequent miracles down to this time. The following, among others, is very well attested: Philip III., in his return from Lisbon, was taken so ill at Casarubias del Monte, that his life was despaired of by his physicians. Whereupon the shrine of St. Isidore was ordered to be carried in a solemn procession of the clergy, court, and people of Madrid to the chamber of the sick king. The joint prayers of many prevailed. At the same time the shrine was taken out of the church, the fever left the king; and upon its being brought into his chamber, he was perfectly cured. The year following, the body of the saint was put into a new rich shrine, which cost one thousand six hundred ducats of gold. St. Isidore had been beatified a little before by Paul V., in 1619, at the solicitation of the same king. This solemn canonization was performed at the request of King Philip IV., on the 12th of March, 1622; though the bull was only made public by Benedict XIII.—[*Butler's Lives of the Saints.*]

2. *St. Zita.*—St. Zita was born in the beginning of the thirteenth century, at Montsegradi, a village near Lucca, in Italy. She was brought up with the greatest care, in the fear of God, by her poor virtuous mother, whose early and constant attention to inspire the tender heart of her daughter with religious sentiments seemed to find no obstacles, either from private passions or the general corruption of nature, so easily were they prevented or overcome. Zita had no sooner attained the use of reason, and was capable of knowing and loving God, than her heart was no longer able to relish any

other object, and she seemed never to lose sight of him in
her actions.   Her mother reduced all her instructions to two
short heads, and never had occasion to use any further remonstrance to enforce her lessons than to say: "This is
most pleasing to God; this is the divine will," or, "That
would displease God."   The sweetness and modesty of the
young child charmed every one who saw her.   She spoke
little and was most assiduous at her work, but her business
never seemed to interrupt her prayers.   At twelve years of
age she was put to service in the family of a citizen of Lucca,
called Fantinelli, whose house was contiguous to the church
of St. Frigidian.   She was thoroughly persuaded that labor
is enjoined on all men as a punishment of sin, and as a remedy for the spiritual disorders of their souls: and, far from
ever harboring in her breast the least uneasiness, or express-
ing any sort of complaint under contradictions, poverty and
hardships, and still more from ever entertaining the least
idle, inordinate or worldly desire, she blessed God for plac-
ing her in a position in which she was supplied with the
most effectual means to promote her santification, by the
necessity of employing herself in penitential labor, and of
living in a perpetual conformity and submission of her will
to others.   She was also very sensible of the advantages of
her state, which afforded all necessaries of life, without engaging her in the most anxious cares and violent passions
by which worldly persons who enjoy most plentifully the
goods of fortune are often disturbed; whereby their souls
resemble a troubled sea, always agitated by impetuous
storms, without knowing the sweetness of a true calm.   She
considered her work as an employment assigned her by God,
and as part of her penance; and obeyed her master and mistress in all things, as being placed over her by God.   She
always rose several hours before the rest of the family, and

employed in prayer a considerable part of the time which others gave to sleep. She took care to hear Mass every morning with great devotion, before she was called upon by the duties of her station, in which she employed the whole day with such diligence and fidelity that she seemed to be carried to them on wings, and studied when possible to anticipate them. Notwithstanding her extreme attention to her exterior employments, she acquired a wonderful facility of joining with them almost continual mental prayer, and keeping her soul almost constantly attentive to the divine presence. Who would not imagine that such a person should be esteemed and beloved by all who knew her? Nevertheless, by the appointment of Divine Providence, for her great spiritual advantage, it fell out quite otherwise, and for several years she suffered the harshest trials. Her modesty was called by her fellow-servants simplicity, and want of spirit and sense; and her diligence was judged to have no other spring than affectation and secret pride. Her mistress was a long time extremely prejudiced against her, and her passionate master could not bear her in his sight without transports of rage. It is not to be conceived how much the saint had continually to suffer in this situation. So unjustly despised, overburdened, reviled, and often beaten, she never repined nor lost her patience; but always preserved the same sweetness in her countenance and the same meekness and charity in her heart and words, and abated nothing of her application to her duties. A virtue so constant and so admirable at length overcame jealousy, antipathy, prejudice and malice. Her master and mistress discovered the treasure which their family possessed in the fidelity and example of the humble saint, and the other servants gave due praise to her virtue. Zita feared this prosperity more than adversity, and trembled lest it should be a snare to her soul. But

14

sincere humility preserved her from its dangers, and her behavior, amidst the caresses and respect shown her, continued
the same as when she was ill-treated and held in derision;
she was no less affable, meek and modest; no less devout,
nor less diligent or ready to serve every one. Being made
housekeeper, and seeing her master and mistress commit to
her, with an entire confidence, the government of their family and management of all their affairs, she was most scru-
pulously careful in point of economy, remembering that she
was to give to God an account of the least farthing of what
was intrusted as a depositum in her hands; and, though
head-servant, she never allowed herself the least privilege or
exemptions in her work on that account. She used often to
say to others, that devotion is false if slothful. Hearing a
man-servant speak one immodest word, she was filled with
horror and caused him to be immediately discharged from
the family. With David, she desired to see it composed
only of persons whose approved piety might draw down a
benediction of God upon the whole house, and be a security
to the master for their fidelity and good example. She kept
fast the whole year, and often on bread and water; and took
her rest on the bare floor or on a board. Whenever business
allowed her a little leisure, she spent it in holy prayer and
contemplation in a little retired room in the garret, and at
her work repeated frequently ardent ejaculations of divine
love, with which her soul appeared always inflamed. She
respected her fellow-servants as her superiors. If she was
sent on commissions a mile or two in the greatest storms,
she set out without delay, executed them punctually and returned often almost drowned, without showing any sign of
reluctance or murmuring. By her virtue she gained so great
an ascendant over her master, that a single word would often
suffice to check the greatest transports of his rage; and she

would sometimes cast herself at his feet to appease him in favor of others. She never kept anything for herself but the poor garments which she wore; everything else she gave to the poor. Her master, seeing his goods multiply, as it were, in her hands, gave her ample leave to bestow liberal alms on the poor, which permission she made use of very liberally, but was scrupulous to do nothing without his express authority. If she heard others spoken ill of, she zealously took upon her their defence, and excused their faults. Always when she communicated, and often when she heard Mass, and on other occasions, she melted into sweet tears of divine love; she was often favored with ecstasies during her prayers. In her last sickness she clearly foretold her death, and having prepared herself for her passage by receiving the last sacrament and by ardent sighs of love, she happily expired on the 27th of April, in 1272, being sixty years old. One hundred and fifty miracles wrought in the behalf of such as had recourse to her intercession had been juridically proved. Her body was found entire in 1580, and is kept with great respect in St. Frigidian's church, richly enshrined; her face and hands are exposed to view through a crystal glass. Pope Leo X. granted an office in her honor. The city of Lucca pays a singular veneration to her memory. The solemn decree of her beatification was published by Innocent XII., in 1696, with the confirmation of her immemorial veneration.—[*Butler's Lives of the Saints.*]

THE FIFTH COMMANDMENT.

"Thou shalt not kill."

The object of the first, the second, and the third commandments is to instruct men in their duties of religion and piety towards God, whilst the object of the fourth commandment is to instruct children in the duties towards their parents. Besides these precepts, there are others which instruct every man in the duties of justice towards all his fellow-men. God wishes that we should be united, not only with him, the bountiful source of all blessings in life and eternity, and with our parents, to whom we are indebted for our natural existence; God also wishes that we should be united in the bonds of fellowship with all mankind. Hence it is God's will that we practise, in all things, the moral duties of justice and righteousness towards all our fellow-men. Now, all these duties are contained and positively expressed by God in the other six commandments of the Decalogue.

The first of these commandments, that is, the fifth of the Decalogue, says: *"Thou shalt not kill."*

God alone is the supreme Master of life and death. It is he who has given us our life, and it is he only who has a right to take it, "It is thou, O Lord, that hast power of life and death," says Holy Writ. (Wisd. xvi., 13.)

Now, when God says "Thou shalt not kill," he positively forbids everyone to do, without his authority, any injury to *himself, and to his neighbor in body and soul.*

Our life is a precious gift of God of which we must take reasonable and ordinary care, in order to be able to use it for the intentions of the divine Giver.

I. Hence God forbids us to expose our health or life to danger *without a just reason*. But, if there is a just reason we may expose our life to danger. It is therefore no sin to expose our life to danger from necessity, or for the public good, or for the practice of virtue. It is lawful for a soldier to die rather than quit his post; to spring a mine in order to destroy the enemy of the country, though he foresees that his own life will be lost in the explosion.

It is lawful for a child to give to his father or mother the bread which he himself is in need of.

It is lawful for a person to give up to another the plank which is his only means to save himself from being drowned.

It is lawful to take care of a sick person whose disease is contagious.

It is lawful for a virgin to suffer death rather than the loss of her virtue. It is lawful to practise certain bodily mortifications, although, on account of them, life may be somewhat shortened.

There is a man who is tired of life. However, he has not the least desire to commit suicide. But on learning that it is lawful to expose one's life to the danger of death for the sake of virtue, he goes into a just war, to fight, it is true, for his country, but principally to have an opportunity to lose his life. Is it lawful for him to do so? No; for the simple reason that it is never lawful for any person to wish for what is forbidden by God. If, then, even the desire of one's own death, arising from an unlawful motive is a sin, it is a far greater sin to do purposely something by which such a desire, though only accidentally, is realized.

There are, however, four reasons for which it is lawful to wish for one's own death:

1. We may wish for death in order to get rid of the troubles and hardships of this life, provided we are at the same time ready to bear them patiently and with resignation to the will of God. It is therefore not lawful to desire our own death through anger or impatience.

2. We may wish for our death in order to get out of the danger of offending God grievously.

3. A more perfect reason to wish for death is to get out of the danger of offending God by venial sin.

4. The most perfect motive to wish for death is that of St. Paul when he desired his own death. "I am straitened," he says, "having a desire to be dissolved and to be with Christ." (Phil. i., 23.)

II. The fifth commandment forbids to commit suicide, that is, to take away our own life. We have received from God only the use of our life, and no one is so far master of it that he is ever allowed to take it away whenever it pleases him. The law does not say "Thou shalt not kill thy neighbor," but it absolutely commands, "Thou shalt not kill." He, therefore, who takes away his own life, commits a most hideous crime; for suicide is contrary to the laws and principles of charity, justice and nature. He who takes his own life, most heinously transgresses the law of God who is the Sovereign Master of life and death; he robs him of a portion of his creation, and commits a most frightful outrage against the Lord of heaven and earth. He also commits a great injustice against his parents, friends and society, who contributed towards his support and education, protected him against the dangers of life, and therefore had a claim on his services and gratitude.

The self-murderer is also guilty of an unnatural crime, for

nature inspires every living being with an instinct of self-preservation, and an irresistible impulse to repel all and everything contrary to his life and happiness.

Lastly, he who commits suicide, commits a most shocking crime against his own soul, because he unmercifully launches it into everlasting hell-fire. Hence it is that the Church refuses Christian burial to the wilful self-murderer.

Man, endowed with free-will, can make a good or bad use of it in temporal as well as spiritual matters; but the passage from this world to eternity must depend only on God, who alone has the supreme power and right to fix the time and term of human life.

"If any of the saints," says St. Alphonsus, "have caused their own death," as is related of St. Apollonia, who cast herself into the fire prepared for her by the tyrant, "they have acted from an inspiration of the Holy Ghost, and did not sin. The Donatist heretics voluntarily killed themselves, saying that they died as martyrs. But in this they fell into a foolish error. They died as martyrs of the devil, and lost soul and body." (5th command., No. 4.)

Suicide or self-murder is, generally speaking, the effect of despair, as was the case with the unhappy Judas who in despair hanged himself. Suicide is often the effect of disappointed ambition, or of some other sinful passion, and is in most cases committed by those who have lost the true faith. Hence Professor Morcelli says in his book on suicide in which statistics are compiled from every possible point of view: "The purely Catholic nations, Italy, Spain, and Portugal, stand on the last step of the scale of suicide, while those exclusively or mostly Protestant take the first grade." This, perhaps, might be accounted for on the ground of racial differences, and therefore we quote one further sentence from the same author: "In countries of mixed religions the inclination towards suicide diminishes in direct ratio to the predominence of Catholicism." The frequency of suicides in Catholic States has been reckoned at fifty-eight per million, and in Protestant States at one hundred and ninety."

The folly of suicide is equal to its wickedness, for he who kills himself from pain, disgrace, or any of the ills of life, knows that he thereby casts himself into the flames of hell, which immeasurably surpass all that man can suffer in this world. He flies from temporal coils which soon pass away, and which, if borne with patience, are the source of eternal joy, into the midst of most cruel torments which can never profit him, but which he must needs suffer for endless ages. Can there be a greater folly and madness?

A good means to overcome the temptation of committing suicide is to hear Mass every day, if possible.

Pope Pius II. relates in his works the following: A nobleman of Istria, one of the provinces of Austria, was violently tempted to kill himself; the demon of despair had long urged him to this fatal design; he had even seen himself on the very point of executing it. It came into his head, however, to speak to a friend of his, a learned religious. You may imagine that that pious servant of God consoled him as well as he could; he advised him to have a priest in his castle, and have Mass said every day. "With that," added he, "I will answer for your salvation." The gentleman thus completely overcame the temptation of committing suicide.

Another good means to overcome this temptation is to be kind and charitable to the poor and needy.

Nothing renders life sweeter, more agreeable than the practice of virtue; on the contrary, weariness, disgust and despair are always the bitter fruits of vice. The Abbe Reyre furnishes us with a proof of this in his *Christian anecdotes.* In a city of the south of France, which I think was Nimes, there lived in the last century a rich man who had denied himself none of what are called the sweets of life; and what had all that led him to? Simply to being disgusted with life. He was strongly tempted to kill himself, when, happening to cross the public square of the city, he perceived an inscription placed in golden letters on the front of a hospital. This inscription was as follows:

O THOU FOR WHOM EXISTENCE IS A BURDEN!
SEEK TO DO GOOD!
VIRTUE WILL MAKE THEE LOVE LIFE!

He stops a moment, and remembers that there is in his neighborhood a poor joiner, whose wife died a short time before, leaving several small children. "I am mad," he exclaims, to wish to die and leave my fortune to heirs who could only laugh at me! I will make a worthier use of it." He instantly hastens to the joiner's; adopts all his children, places them at a school, gives them trades, and afterwards establishes them in business, and finally has the consolation of seeing them all become excellent Christians and respectable citizens. He then confessed that he had never experienced more happiness than in occupying himself with that poor family. He lived long and lived happy.—[*Noel, Cat. de Rodez*, V., 229.]

3. The fifth commandment forbids us to endanger our life by intemperance in eating and drinking, dissipation, etc. Hence, "it is a sin," says St. Alphonsus, "to contract wilfully any serious bodily infirmity by eating or drinking to excess, or by leading a dissipated life; for we are bound to preserve life and to avoid the dangers of death."

It is a mortal sin to get drunk wilfully so as to lose the use of one's senses. It is true the privation of reason is not precisely a sin, as St. Thomas says, but the consequence and

punishment of it.   Hence the intoxication which deprives a
man of the use of his senses is no sin, if it was not wilful, as
was the case with Noe, who did not know the strength and
effect of the wine.   Whenever, therefore, intoxication is involuntary, the faults committed in that state of drunkenness
are excusable; but if intoxication is voluntary, the sins committed in that state are inexcusable and sinful.   It is true, a
person in a state of intoxication does not know what he is
doing, but he is not the less answerable for all the sins which
he could foresee he was likely to commit while in that state
of drunkenness; for, as he wilfully exposed himself to that
state, he is supposed to have acted with premeditation, and
is therefore guilty before God and man of all the crimes
which he commits in drunkenness.   Wilful intoxication,
therefore, is a mortal sin.   But even suppose that in wilful
drunkenness there were no other evil than the mere privation of the senses, this evil alone, says St. Alphonsus, is a
mortal sin.

There is nothing more pleasing to God than to be merciful
and to spare.   Therefore the greatest injury that any man
can offer to God is to tie up his hands and to oblige him to
refuse the exercise of his mercy—to tell the Almighty God
that he must not, nay, that he cannot, be merciful.   There
is only one sin and one sinner alone that can do this.   That
one sin is drunkenness; the only man that has the omnipo-
tence of sin, the infernal power to tie the hands of God,
to oblige God to refuse him mercy.   No matter what sin a
man commits, if, in the very act of committing it, the Almighty strikes him, one moment is enough for him to make
an act of contrition, to shed one tear of sorrow, and to save
his soul.   The murderer, even though expiring, his hands
reddened with the blood of his victim, can send forth a
cry for mercy, and by that cry be saved.   The robber, stricken

down in the very midst of his misdeeds, can cry for mercy
on his soul. The impure man, even while he is revelling in
his impurity, if he feels the chilly hand of death laid upon
him and cries out, "God be merciful to me a sinner!" by that
cry he may be saved. The drunkard alone—alone amongst
all sinners—lies there dying in his drunkenness. If all the
priests and all the bishops in the Church of God were there,
they could not give that man pardon or absolution of his
sins, because he is incapable of it—because he is not a man!
Sacraments are for men, let them be ever so sinful—provided that they be men. One might as well absolve the
four-footed beast as lift a priestly hand over the drunkard.
If the Pope of Rome were with him, what could he do for him
while in such a state? The one sin that puts a man outside
the pale of God's mercy is drunkeness. Long as that arm
of God is, it is not long enough to touch with a merciful
hand the sinner who is in the state of drunkenness.

What an accursed vice is not the vice of drinking to excess! But there is one who says: "If I go to bed and
sleep off the bad effects of liquor, am I not in this case free
from sin?" "No," says St. Alphonsus; "if you take as
much liquor as you know will suffice to deprive you of the
use of the senses, you thereby commit sin."

There is another who says: "Father, I often was half
drunk. Is it also a mortal sin to get half drunk?" To get half
drunk is in itself only a venial sin. But it may sometimes
be a mortal sin; for instance, for a father of a family who
often gets half drunk, and thus injures his health and short-
ens his life by slow degrees, or commits other sins, or induces
others to follow his example, or greatly grieves and scandal-
izes his family, whose goods he unreasonably squanders.*

---

*I have shown the great evils of drunkenness in the seventh chapter of
my work, "The Prodigal Son." Not wishing to repeat myself, I refer the
reader to what is said there.

4. The fifth commandment forbids us to grieve and be sad to excess, because excess of grief and sadness undermines health and life itself, especially if it arises from violent passions and self-love, or from insatiable avarice, for these causes of grief and sadness are contrary to the laws of God and nature, and therefore the excess of sadness proceeding from such selfish principles becomes a punishment, to which many fall victims without honor and merit.

When the soul is overwhelmed by excessive grief or sadness, the mental powers are unable to do anything. While the heart is afflicted, the soul is uneasy, and then all mental labor and exertions cease, and the consequence is fatal, often ending as it does in despair or insanity. "As a moth consumeth a garment, and a worm the wood," says Holy Writ, "so doth the sadness of man consumeth the heart. (Prov. xv., 20.) "A sorrowful spirit drieth up the bones." (Prov. xvii., 22.

Excessive sadness is an obstacle to the contemplation of holy things, undermines Christian Charity, prevents the memory and intellect from being active, and shackles the will, the fountain of all our actions; in fact, it is more pernicious to the body than any other passion, for human life depends on the vital movement of the heart, which communicates heat, animation and nourishment to the whole bodily system. The melancholy impression caused by excessive sadness is an obstacle to this life-giving movement, and makes the vital spirits flow back to the region of the heart, where they become morbid, and then ensues a lingering disease or premature death. "For from the sadness and grief of the heart cometh death," says Holy Writ. "So give not up thy heart to sadness, but drive it from thee and remember thy last end." (Eccl. xxxviii., 19, 21.)

Remedies for sadness are tears and sighs, for as they lessen sorrow and grief, they relieve the heart and expand the mind. Hence, persons who cry suffer less from grief or affliction than those whose sorrow remains locked up in the heart.

Sympathy is another powerful remedy to mitigate the bitterness of grief. A compassionate friend alleviates the weight of our affliction by sympathizing with us in our sufferings or misfortune.

But the contemplation of eternal truths is the greatest consolation for an afflicted spirit; and the more pity and wisdom one has, the more joy and happiness he experiences in the meditations of divine truths. Reflections on the vanity of the world, on death, on the immortality of the soul, and on an eternity of glory or punishment, are apt to banish away affliction and tribulation of heart and soul. The splendor of eternal truth infuses so much light and joy into all the faculties of man that he does not feel even the greatest tortures. The holy martyr Tiburtius was condemned to walk barefooted on burning coals. Whilst undergoing this torture he joyously exclaimed: "For the love and glory of Jesus it seems to me that I am walking on flowers."

It may be remarked that a certain sadness which does not exceed the bounds of prudence and moderation is sometimes good for man. It keeps him from many excesses that are often prejudicial to body and soul and gives him more taste for useful studies and moral reflections. "Lord," says the prophet, "they have sought often thee in distress, in tribulation and affliction thy instruction was with them." (Pai. xxvi, 16.)

5. By the fifth commandment God forbids us to commit wilful murder; that is, to take the life of another quite deliberately. If, then, anyone should happen to kill a person accidentally, he would not be guilty of having broken this

commandment, because he had no intention to kill that person. Should a person, however, be engaged in something that might possibly lead to the loss of life of another person, or to some serious injury to anyone, he is strictly bound to take every reasonable care to prevent such loss of life or injury to his neighbor. Hence, it would be a mortal sin for one to fire off a pistol or gun across a frequented public street at the risk of killing or seriously wounding a person who might happen to pass.

In like manner, it would be a mortal sin for a doctor who, from gross ignorance of his medical profession, prescribes a medicine that causes the death of his patient.

Now, there are different grades in *murder*, so that one kind of murder is more grievous than another. There is, first, premeditated or "wilful murder," or that which is designed beforehand in cold blood; and this is the most grievous kind of murder. Of this premeditated or "wilful murder" Cain was guilty when he slew his brother Abel; and so enormous was his crime, that, as God himself tells us, *it cried to heaven for vengeance.* There is again *homicide* or *manslaughter,* which is not intended beforehand, but arises from sudden passion, or from quarreling. This is not so grievous as the first, because it is not attended with such malice. The murder of kings, pastors of the Church, Superiors, and of those in authority, is of a more grievous kind than the murder of others, because their lives are more valuable and necessary. The murder of parents or children, husband or wife, brothers or sisters, or of other relatives, is a crime of peculiar magnitude, and always looked upon with horror and detestation on account of the close relationship with the murderer and the murdered.

There is a kind of murder called *abortion,* which is committed by women in a state of pregnancy, in order to hide their shame, and which is most detestable in the sight of God, and punished even in this life by the severest penalties of the Church. Oh! what an enormous sin it is to cause abortion—to make an infant die without baptism—that is, to cause a soul to be lost for all eternity! What a barbarous remedy, to endeavor to repair the evil of sin committed by a far greater sin! What a great crime are all those guilty of who give or advise pregnant women to take or do anything to procure abortion! 'They murder the soul of the child as well as the body, for by preventing the poor child from being baptized, they exclude it forever from the kingdom of heaven.

There is another kind of murder committed in a *duel*. By a duel is meant a premeditated combat between two or more persons who, on their own private authority, attack each other with murderous weapons in a manner and at a time and place previously agreed upon. Whatever may be said to justify a duel, it is always a great crime in the sight of God; it is even a double crime, since the duellist desires to kill another and exposes his own life. A duel can never be permitted either for the purpose of redeeming one's honor or escaping the imputation of cowardice, or for any other reason.

The Church excommunicates both the duellists themselves and all those persons who take part in their combat as witnesses or otherwise. She declares them to be *infamous*—which title they justly deserve, since they are cowards, not having courage enough to forgive; they are bad citizens, for they violate the laws of society; and they are bad Christians, because they violate the laws of God and his holy Church. Those who are killed in these barbarous conflicts are deprived of the prayers of the Church and also of Christian burial.

Now, to murder any one is a very great sin. It is one of the most grievous injuries we can do to our neighbor—so grievous that it is a matter of surprise how any person can commit so foul a crime. It is a great injury done to God; for it destroys his image, and on this account he strictly avenges it, especially as it is done against his will, and against his express command: "For whosoever shall shed man's blood, his blood shall be shed; for man was made to the image of God." (Gen. ix., 5.) It is an usurpation of an authority which belongs to God alone; for he is the absolute Master of man's life, to whom alone it belongs to take it away, as it is he alone who can bestow it. It is also the greatest injustice of which we can be guilty, because it deprives our neighbor of what is most valuable to him in this world—so valuable that all the riches and all the power of man cannot make due reparation for it.

O, how hateful to God is not the wilful murderer! Even in this life God punishes those who shed blood. David says that they shall not live half the time which God would have given them had they not indulged in revenge. "Bloody and deceitful men shall not live out half their days." (Ps. liv. 24.) The Scripture tells us that, after having murdered his brother Abel, Cain "dwelt as a fugitive on the earth." (Gen. iv., 16.) Such is the chastisement of murderers. After their crime they are always flying away, at one time through fear of the ministers of justice, at another from the relatives of the murdered person. Even the secret murderer seldom remains always unknown, for God almost invariably directs circumstances so as to make him known to his fellow-men, in order that he may be punished even in this life.

St. Meinrad was a young lord of Suabía, in Germany. In the flower of his years he left his illustrious family to commune with God in solitude. The night often found him attentively reading the Sacred Scriptures, an old manuscript copy with golden clasps, which had come down to him from his father. Often, too, he meditated on the virtues, the holiness, the goodness, and the miracles of the Blessed Virgin. He made his vows in the Abbey of Reichenau, situate in the duchy of Baden, and he afterwards left it to take up his abode in a little hermitage on the summit of Mount Etzel. There he spent seven years. The good odor of his virtues reached the depth of the valleys. At first shepherds and wood-cutters came to him, then lords, then noble ladies, then, at last, a multitude of people. This homage was a torment to the holy hermit, who loved only meditation, humility and the solitude of the woods. Hence it was that he secretly quitted his hermitage, taking nothing with him but the statue of the Blessed Virgin, the only ornament of his little chapel. He took refuge in Switzerland, in a forest of the Canton of Schwitz, which bore the characteristic name of the Black or Dark Forest. He there spent peaceful and happy days, and would have reached a good old age if he had not been murdered at the end of thirty-two years by robbers, with whom he had had the charity to share the limpid waters of his spring, and the wild fruits of his forest. But God did not permit this atrocious crime to remain unknown. The murderers had been seen by no one, but they were betrayed by two crows, that harassed them continually even in Zurich. They followed them everywhere with incredible fury; they penetrated even into the city, made their way through the windows of the inn where the murderers had taken refuge, and never left them till they were arrested. The ruffians then confessed their crime, and suffered the extreme penalty of the law. In memory of this singular event, which took place in the year 861, the Abbey of

15

Reichenau, of whose community Saint Meinrad had been a member, placed the figure of two crows in its arms and on its seal. — [*Bollandists Act. Sanc.*, 21st *January*.]

· And though the secret murderer should not be found out, yet he will be unceasingly pursued by his own conscience. We read (Map. pamon. Istorie, tom. ii.) that Constans II., after having put to death his brother Theodosius, thought he saw the murdered brother by his side, holding in the hand a cup filled with blood, and that he heard, him say, " *Drink brother, drink.*" Horror-struck by the vision, Constans wandered through the world, always full of terror, until his miserable death.

A certain robber killed a child. After having committed the murder, he imagined that he saw the child before him, and heard him cry out, "Barbarous wretch, why have you murdered me?" This apparition continued for nine years. At length the robber, being unable to bear the reproof any longer, voluntarily confessed his crime before the judge, and was executed.—[*Prat. spir.* chap. clxvi.]

There are, however, three cases in which it is lawful to take the life of another, namely :—

1. In a *just war*. Kings and rulers of States have certain rights to maintain for the maintenance of which it is lawful for them to have recourse even to arms when all other means fail; and their subjects are not only justified, but even bound to assist their sovereign in carrying on a *just* war. In such a war, and even in a war when its justice appears doubtful, it is lawful for subjects to kill enemies if they are commanded by their own sovereign to do so.

2. It is also lawful to take the life of another in self-defence, or in defence of another's life, chastity, or property of great value when unjustly attacked. · As it is lawful for a

nation to take up arms in defence of its rights, or in resistance to the unjust encroachments or demands of another, so, also, it is lawful for any person to take the life of any unjust aggressor in defence of his own. In such a case every one is allowed to prefer his temporal life to the spiritual life of his unjust aggressor. However, it must be remembered that in defending our own life, or chastity or property of great value, we are not allowed to go beyond the limits of a just defence; that is to say, we are not allowed to do more harm to an unjust aggressor than is necessary to protect ourselves from harm, nor is it allowed to strike him before or after the time of his attack. He must have first attacked or shown his intention of attacking us before we have a right to wound him; if, for instance, we see him loading his pistol or drawing his sword, we are then allowed to defend ourselves. This is the doctrine of all theologians. It is taught by St. Thomas (2, 2, qu. 64, a. 7), by St. Alphonsus (fifth commandment, No. 7).

3. In the execution of a just sentence of death. In the same way as each one may defend himself when unjustly attacked, so may society defend itself against the crimes of any of its members. The well-being of a State, and the protection of its rights from acts of violence are entrusted to its supreme ruler, and in the exercise of his authority he may punish, even with death, those who are guilty of very great crimes. For though God is the master of life and death, kings and rulers act as his ministers in the punishment of criminals. Hence it is lawful for any one who acts in the name of his sovereign, and with his sanction, to carry out the sentence of death; but it would be wrong for him to execute the criminal on his own responsibility, even though he were certain of his crime, because those alone who exercise supreme dominion, or to whom special authority has

been given, are the representatives of God in the execution
of his justice.

With these three exceptions, it is not lawful for us to take
away human life. Hence it would be wrong to put to death
those who have become a burden to society—who, for instance, are hopelessly mad, or mortally wounded, or who are
reduced to such a state of infirmity or suffering that they are
weary of existence. Hence, too, it would be wrong to kill
persons in order to save them from torture or disgrace. It
would be wrong also to put an innocent man to death to preserve the lives of many others, or to kill an unborn child to
save the life of the mother, because we are never allowed to
do evil that good may come out of it.

6. The fifth commandment forbids not only wilful murder, but also everything that leads to it, as quarreling,
abusive words, fighting, hatred, anger, revenge. Quarreling
means idle, noisy disputes, warm contentions, and rude
strifes. All these are forbidden by this commandment, because they are, of their own nature, injurious to our neighbor's person as well as to our own, for by them the mind is
displeased and vexed, and anger and hatred are excited.
They also tend to murder, for it is well known from experience that many murders have sprung from quarreling. "As
the vapor of a chimney," says the book of Ecclesiasticus,
" and the smoke of the fire goeth up before the fire ; so also
injurious words, and reproaches, and threats before blood."
(Ecclus. xxii., 30.) Quarreling is a rock which we should
carefully avoid, for it is a source of much mischief. We
ought, therefore, not quarrel with others upon any consideration, for it is a wicked and pernicious quality, and the
mark of a weak and vulgar mind ; as the wise man says :
" The lips of a fool intermeddle with strife, and his mouth
provoketh quarrels." (Prov. xviii., 6.) If it should happen

that any one *quarrels* with you, even when you give no occasion on your part, endeavor to behave discreetly, not permitting yourself to be carried away by the passion of anger. Strive to appease your neighbor with mildness, according to the advice of the wise man : "A mild answer breaketh wrath, but a harsh word stirreth up fury." (Prov. xv., 1.) Show, in a quiet, gentle manner, that you have done him no wrong, or if you have offended, excuse yourself mildly. If he be not then pacified, withdraw from him, to let his anger cool.

One day St. Alphonsus was requested by his companions to play with them a certain game. He excused himself on the plea of not knowing the game. His companions, however, urged him so much that at last he consented. Fortune favored him. He won the game thirty times. This success made his companions jealous, and one, older than he, began to quarrel, and said in a rage, " It was you who did not know the game, was it?" adding in his rage a very indecent word. Alphonsus reddened when he heard it, and with an air of severity turned towards his companions, and said : "How is this, shall God be offended for the sake of a few pence? Take back your money," and throwing on the ground what he had won, he left his companions with a holy indignation.—[*Life of St. Alphonsus, chap.* ii.]

7. Next to the sin of quarreling comes that of *injurious words*, for seldom does a quarrel take place without abusive words or rude and insulting nick-names being bandied to and fro. Indeed it is the bad habit of calling names which often leads to quarreling and fighting, for he who is insulted soon retorts, and the passions being aroused, angry words are quickly followed by blows. Our Blessed Lord, in his sermon on the Mount, speaks of this sin in very severe terms, telling us that all abusive names are forbidden by the fifth commandment, and are worthy of the severest

punishment. "You have heard," says he, "that it was said to them of old, *Thou shalt not kill, and whoever shall kill shall be in danger of the judgment.* But I say to you, that whosoever is angry with his brother shall be in danger of the judgment. And whosoever shall say to his brother, *Raca*, shall be in danger of the council. And whosoever shall say, *Thou fool*, shall be in danger of hell fire." (Matt. v., 21, 22.) From these words we see that injurious names, if they are such as to be a very grievous insult to the person we address, may even amount to the guilt of mortal sin which is punished with the eternal fire of hell. Thus, among the Jews, to call a person a *fool* was considered the greatest insult you could offer him, and was therefore a great crime. Among us it is not looked upon in the same light, nor would it usually amount to the guilt of grievous sin, unless it were spoken to a parent or superior.

8. *Anger* is likewise forbidden by the fifth commandment. Anger is a feeling of displeasure at some real or supposed injury, with a desire of punishing the offender. Anger is called in the catechism one of the seven deadly sins, because it is a sin which, if not checked in time, is sure to bring death to the soul. It does not follow, however, that anger is always a mortal sin. Sometimes it is only a venial sin, and sometimes it is no sin at all. Hence St. Paul says, "Be angry and sin not. Let not the sun go down upon your anger." (Eph. iv., 26.)

How can a person be angry and not be guilty of sin?

Let us suppose that one of your companions has hit you a blow in the face. You feel very angry, and you cannot help feeling angry at first, for the blow has hurt you. There is no sin so far, because it is only natural for us, being made of flesh and blood, and not of wood or stone, to feel angry when we are hurt. But the next moment your Guardian Angel whispers to you to bear the blow patiently for the love of Jesus, who for us was buffeted and struck upon the face, yet bore it like a meek and gentle lamb without opening his mouth. Immediately you try to check your angry feelings, you say a little prayer in your heart, to our Blessed Lord, and speak good-naturedly or do a kind turn to the one who struck you. Here you have done exactly what the Apostle tells you, you have been angry and yet you have not sinned; On the contrary, you have gained a victory over yourself and over the devil, and have merited a great reward here-after.

Now let us suppose that you have acted quite differently. The blow has put you in a passion, and you have not tried to overcome it. You speak angrily to the one who struck you, you call him names, you try to hit him back. You do not wish to do him great harm, but to hurt him a little as he has hurt you. In this case you have been angry and sinned, but your sin is a venial sin, and not a mortal one.

But perhaps the blow you have received has put you in a very great passion indeed, because you did not try at all to check or control your temper. You call your companion the worst names you can think of, and blinded by rage you seize whatever is at hand to strike or throw at him, careless what injury you do him, as long as you can only revenge yourself. In this case there is great reason to fear that your anger will amount to the guilt of mortal sin.

Thus you see how anger may be either a mortal sin, a venial sin, or no sin at all, according to the manner in which we indulge or resist it.

Anger, when it is not checked, is the fruitful source of innumerable crimes. Quarreling and fighting, cursing and swearing, revenge and hatred, bloodshed and even murder, are often the terrible consequences of this detestable passion. Hence we cannot guard against it too carefully, or fight against it to earnestly. For anger is like a viper, which, if we cherish it in our bosom, may at any time turn against us and inflict a mortal wound. So does our passion, if we are in the habit of indulging it, often hurry us, when we least think of it, into the most frightful crimes. Moreover, it is the cause of great misery and unhappiness, for the passionate man is a torment to himself and a torment to every one about him. He is not, indeed, fit for the company of men, for he is no longer a reasonable being, but is guided like a brute beast only by the blind impulse of his rage. No wonder that he is an object of ridicule to every one about him, and is shunned and avoided by all that know him. Have you ever seen a man in a fit of passion? His eyes start from their sockets, his cheeks become pale and livid, his face ugly and deformed, so that you would hardly know him. He shouts at the top of his voice like a madman; he stamps on the ground; it is dangerous for any one to come near him, for he knows not what he strikes at, and is sometimes so foolish as to break and destroy all that he lays his hands on. Finally, he generally ends by a passionate fit of crying. Can you imagine a more pitiable creature?

9. Fighting is also forbidden by the fifth commandment. By fighting is meant a sanguinary encounter between two or more, in which blows are dealt, either by the hands, sticks, or other dangerous weapons. *Fights* occur often at fairs, and are generally to be traced to the drinking of exciting liquors. We should always hold in the greatest horror those brutal affrays, for besides the great offence offered to God by them, there is scarcely anything that lowers man, and brings him down to the level of the brute beasts, as fighting. Those engaged in such affrays, by their turbulence and sanguinary

acts, are like so many enraged animals. If, as our Lord says, *any one who is angry with his brother will be guilty of the judgment*, what guilt must those not incur who attack their brother with brutal blows? Ah, how much it is to be deplored that we should so often be witnesses of those savage encounters among Christians! And what is chiefly to be lamented is, that these *fights* often take place between persons the most closely united, and who should have no feelings towards one another but those of kindness and love. We often see the brother fighting with the brother, the husband fighting with his wife, and friends the most intimate fighting in the most cruel manner with one another. Oh, who can recount the many scandals and frightful consequences of those fights, brawls, and dissensions?

10. Hatred, too, is forbidden by the fifth commandment. Hatred is, of all other sins, the one most opposed to Christian charity. Charity teaches us to love our neighbor as ourselves, whereas hatred leads us to abhor and detest our neighbor; it makes us feel sorry at his happiness, and glad at his misfortune. He that has given himself up to this detestable sin no longer knows peace or happiness. The object of his hatred is ever before his mind, his heart is full of rancor and bitterness, and he becomes gloomy, restless and miserable.

The sin of hatred is, moreover, most heinous in the sight of God, who is a God of love, and who, though he meets with so many injuries and outrages from his ungrateful creatures, loves them all, as the Holy Scripture says, and hates nothing of those things which he has made. (Wisd. xi., 25.) In this he teaches us to follow his own divine example, bidding us to love our neighbor and even our enemies for his sake. Without this love we cannot please God; all our works of piety or virtue, our prayers, our Communions, our fasts, our almsdeeds, our mortifications, will not avail us if we cherish in our hearts feelings of hatred against our fellow-men.   Hence the holy Apostle St. John says, "If any man say 'I love God,' and hateth his brother, he is a liar ; for he that loveth not his brother whom he seeth, how can he love God whom he seeth not?" (I. John, iv., 20.)   And in other places the same Apostle, to show us the evil and the terrible consequences of the sin of hatred, compares it to the heinous crime of wilful murder.   "Whosoever hateth his brother," he says, "is a murderer;" (I. John, iii., 15 ;) that is, he is a murderer in his heart, since his hatred, if not checked, will lead him to that sin, or at least to desire and rejoice at his neighbor's death.

Notice, however, that there is a great difference between *hating* and simply *disliking* a person.   To dislike another is not always a sin, for we cannot help disliking those, for ex-ample, who are proud, selfish, or quarrelsome.   But then we must not give way to our dislike, or show it by our black looks or by any unkind word or action.   On the contrary, we must try to check it, to put away uncharitable thoughts and suspicions, and to speak to and act towards those whom we dislike with charity and kindness.   If we find that, instead of resisting, we indulge our dislike, that we are often brooding over it, and taking every opportunity of showing it, let us redouble our efforts and pray earnestly to God to enable us to overcome these dangerous feelings, which, if not checked, will sooner or later lead us to the grievous crime of hatred.

Be then always on your guard to suppress the feeling of anger as soon as it arises within your breast; but should it sometimes get the start before you were able to crush it, en-deavor to return quickly to yourself and to calm down your mind and be especially careful not to say or do anything whilst your mind is in a state of excitement.

One day a young nobleman became enraged at an offence which he imagined was offered him by St. Francis de Sales. After having given vent to his anger by creating a great noise and disturbance in front of the holy prelate's house, he went, at last, to his room. There, he reviled the saintly bishop by every disgraceful expression that rage could suggest. Looking mildly at his abuser, who stood before him foaming with anger, St. Francis answered not a single word. The young nobleman considered this silence as a mark of contempt, became still more enraged, and gave full vent to his passion. The bishop continued calm and silent. When the bold intruder had withdrawn, a witness of the scene asked the holy man how he had been able to keep silence on such a provoking occasion. " My friend," was the answer, " my tongue and I have made an inviolable contract with each other, agreeing that whilst I am under the influence of excited feelings I will never utter a word. The excitement over, it is free to say what it pleases. How could I have better taught this young nobleman to speak kindly and properly than by being silent? And by what means could I have sooner and more easily subdued his anger, than by silence? After the lapse of a few hours he will regret his behavior and come to beg my pardon. Should he not do so, I will beg his, and this from my heart. Ought we not to be merciful to a poor fellow-creature, who is such a slave to passion? If God were to strike us dead when we are in the heat of passion, what would we think? It is an acknowledged fact, that no one ever regretted being silent, while many often feel remorse for having spoken."

" We ought to be patient with one another," he used to say ; the most courageous persons are those who know how to bear with the weaknesses of their fellow-men. This forbearance of imperfections is, in a great measure, perfection itself; it is one of the best means to practise Christian charity. It is not difficult to love those who are of an amiable and attractive disposition; but to love those who are irritable, ill-humored, and obstinate, is the touch-stone of charity.

11. Another sin, forbidden by the fifth commandment, is the sin *revenge*. Revenge is the desire or act of returning evil for evil. When we earnestly and deliberately think of returning evil for evil, we are guilty of revengeful thoughts, and if we really do the evil to our neighbor in his body or property, we are guilty of revengeful actions. When we go to confession, and are guilty of the sin, we must tell the priest in what way we are guilty, that is, whether we only desired revenge, or whether we really took revenge.

Revenge is very sinful, and is condemned in the most emphatic terms by Jesus Christ. He tells us that so far from taking revenge on our enemies, we must even love them: "I say to you, love your enemies; do good to them that hate you." (Matt. v., 44.) And he forbids revenge in such a manner, that he will not pardon our sins except we lay it aside altogether: "If you will not forgive men, neither will your Father forgive you your offences." (Matt. vi., 15.) You must not, then, take revenge or wish any ill to those who injured you; but, on the contrary, you must desire their good, and act kindly towards them, when their necessities require this.

You may say, it is difficult to do an act of this kind towards those who injure you. Yes, it is difficult; but God requires this at your hands. Will you say that it is hard not to take *revenge?* But remember that if you *revenge* yourself on your neighbor, God will be revenged on you, and will not forgive you for your offences. You must confess that you have been guilty of many offences against God, and have often provoked his anger, but that you hope for pardon. But will you seek for revenge for a single offence offered to you, and at the same. time expect pardon from God for the many offences which you yourself have committed against him? In so doing do you not act inconsistently? We must, then, either renounce God and our eternal salvation, or we must pardon injuries, lay aside all thoughts of revenge and return good for evil.

St. Frances de Sales relates that, when he was studying in the city of Padna, the students of the university indulged in the dangerous and wicked practice of parading the public streets at night time, armed with swords. Whomsoever they met they questioned as to his name and business, and if he refused to reply, they drew their swords upon him. On one occasion it happened that a certain student, meeting one of his companions whom he did not recognize, put to him the usual question, and, on his refusal to reply, stabbed him to the heart. Fearing the consequences, the murderer immediately took refuge in the house of a widow, whose son was an intimate friend, and, confessing what had been done, begged of her to conceal him in some secret place until the matter was hushed up. The good woman consented, and conducted him to a private room; but what was her grief and astonishment when, a few moments after, her own son was carried home, a bleeding corpse! She at once perceived that the youth whom she had secreted was his murderer, and running to the place where he lay hid, she asked him what her son had done that he should treat him so cruelly. The student, little thinking that it was his friend whom he had slain, was almost beside himself with grief, and, instead of begging for mercy, besought her to deliver him up to the officers of justice, that he might atone for his crime with his life. The poor mother, however, being very charitable, would not hear of it. "No," said she, "I do not wish to avenge my son's death with your blood. All I ask of you is that you should repent of your sin, and promise to change your life." The young man readily promised, and shortly after she furnished him with all that he required, and assisted him to escape beyond the reach of pursuit. This act of mercy was so pleasing to God, that he permitted the soul of the deceased youth to appear to the mother, and assure her that thereby she had procured his release from purgatory, where he would otherwise have been long detained.—[*Life of St. Frar.eis de Sales.**]

12. The fifth commandment forbids us to injure our neighbor in his soul by giving him *scandal or bad example.* The word *scandal,* in its original acceptation, means a rock or stone, or any other obstacle which, laid on the road, will cause passers-by to stumble. Scandal, in its now received sense, means any word, or action, or omission which is either evil in itself or has the appearance of evil, and is, on that account, to our neighbor the occasion of falling into sin. Bad words or actions, therefore, are not scandals if they are heard or seen by such persons as cannot be induced by them to commit sin.

"It must needs be," says our Lord, "that scandals come." (Matt. xviii., 7.) Our divine Saviour means to say: "Men are, in general, so strongly inclined to evil and make so little efforts to resist their evil passions that they will naturally give scandal; yet for that they are not excused from sin, because giving scandal is an act of the free will of man. When a physician sees a man addicted to continual intemperance, he can say in truth: "that man must needs ruin his health," meaning to say that, if the intemperate man does not change his manner of living, his intemperance will necessarily make

---

*See "Greatest and First Commar dment," p. 63, etc.

him fall into a bad state of health. In like manner, says
our Lord, scandals must necessarily be in the world, if men
do not make serious efforts to overcome their evil inclinations.   Perfect Christians never give nor take scandals, because they always adhere to virtue in spite of all scandals.

Now, scandal is twofold—*direct* or *indirect*. Scandal is
direct when a person deliberately intends to induce others to
commit sin.   Scandal is *indirect* when, without intending to
lead others into sin, or wishing to do so, we say or do anything evil which is calculated to be an occasion of sin to
them.

There are also two other kinds of scandal—the *scandal of
the weak* and *pharisaical scandal*. A person is guilty of *scandal of the weak* when, without having any design of drawing
others into sin, he does an indifferent or even a good act, which
weak brethren—that is, ignorant and ill-instructed people—
are scandalized at seeing, and thence take occasion to sin.
Thus if a person, for a just reason, has permission to eat
flesh-meat on Friday, and is seen eating it by an ignorant person, who, not knowing that he has permission, says, "If
this person eat flesh-meat, why may not I?" He then follows the example he sees, and without any cause or permission eats flesh-meat, and therefore sins.

When one foresees that weak, ignorant people will probably be scandalized at what he does (though that thing be
indifferent in itself), and will be induced to commit sin, he is
obliged, by the law of charity, either to abstain altogether
from doing what will produce such evil effects, or to use whatever precautions in order to prevent them.   A young woman,
for instance, knows that, by going to the garden, she gives,
to a dissolute young man, an occasion of bad thoughts and
desires.   In such a case she is obliged not to go to such a

place, provided she can stay away without great inconvenience.   But how long is she under such an obligation?   Must
she never go to such a place?   By no means; she is obliged
to stay away from such a place only as long as Christian
prudence requires; for to stay away forever would be too
great an inconvenience, to which she is not obliged by charity to submit.

St. Paul, in his epistle to the Corinthians, is very clear on
this point: "Wherefore if meat (that is, if my eating flesh)
scandalize my brother, I will never eat flesh, lest I should
scandalize my brother." (1 Cor. viii., 13.) Our Saviour
himself performed a miracle that he might be able to pay the
tax demanded of him, though he was not bound to pay it,
and assigned this reason: "That we may not scandalize
them." (Matt. xvii., 26.) Oh, what a reproach does this
example of Jesus Christ and St. Paul convey to many of us,
who, when we see our brother scandalized at what we do,
say: "What do I care? That is his affair and not mine.
I am doing no harm; let him look to it."

Pharisaical scandal is the scandal taken by those who,
without reason, but through the malicious and evil disposition of their own hearts, are scandalized at even the good
they see in others—putting the worst construction upon what
they see and hear.   It is called *pharisaical* because the Pharisees took scandal at Christ himself.   And all those who envy
others, because they see them more pious and devout than
they themselves are, follow the example of the Pharisees.
The occasions of this sort of scandal we are not bound to
avoid, because it is not true scandal.   We should never be
hindred from the performance of our duty on account of that
peculiar scandal.   And in this we follow the example of our
Lord, when his disciples told him that the Pharisees were
scandalized at some truth he had said, answered them:

"Let them alone, they are blind and leaders of the blind; and if the blind lead the blind, both shall fall into the pit." (Matt. xv., 14.)

The worst kind of scandal is malicious scandal, and is committed principally by the following persons :

1. By those who by smooth speeches and alluring words, or by an immodest dress and carriage, entice others to sin, or teach them the evil they knew not before, or engage them in dangerous diversons and conversations—too often occurring among young people—which are the great means by which impurity, drunkenness, and gaming are promoted.

2. By those who ridicule and laugh at others on account of their piety and virtue. This is the most crying sin of scandal, for it is one of the chief instruments that the devil makes use of to advance his cause, and to destroy religion and piety.

3. By those who receive young persons of different sexes into houses at night for the purpose of drinking, or dancing, or gaming, for this is the source of innumerable crimes.

4. By parents who speak obscene words, or pronounce blasphemies and curses in the presence of their children ; or bring into their houses, among their daughters, young men who are in love with them.

5. By those who tell to another what they heard said against him by another person, and thus give rise to hatred, discord, and quarrels. Persons who are guilty of this particular scandal are called *tale-bearers*. Their conduct is highly offensive to God, and on the last day they must render a strict account of the sinful consequences of their *tale-bearing*.

6. The sin of scandal is committed by the authors of bad books, songs, pamphlets, novels, story-papers, newspapers, etc., which are contrary to religion and morality.

7. By those who spread abroad or give such bad writings to others to read.

16

8. By those who introduce an unchristian or godless system of education.

9. By those who approve of and support, by word or deed, such a system of education.

10. By those artists who paint or carve indecent pictures or statues.

11. By those superiors who give bad example, or do not hinder evil, as they are in duty bound to do.

Now, the sin of scandal is more or less great according to the evil effects which it produces. To induce a person to commit a venial sin is a scandal which is but a venial sin. But to cause a person to commit a mortal sin is a scandal and is a most grievous sin, because by it we murder the soul of our neighbor, and outrage Jesus Christ. Scandal deprives our neighbor of the life of grace—the life of the soul. And as the soul is more precious than the body, the death of the soul is more dreadful and fatal than the death of the body; and as the murder of the body cries to heaven for vengeance, how great must be the cry to heaven of the murder of the soul! You have a great horror of murder—you would feel indignant and humbled at being suspected of so black a crime; but the crime of scandal is not merely the murder of the body, but the murder of the very soul—far more precious than the body. On this account it is that our Saviour denounces in words so strong the sin of scandal. In St. Matthew he says: "But he that shall scandalize one of these little ones that believe in me, it were better for him that a millstone should be hanged about his neck, and that he should be drowned in the depth of the sea." (Matt. xviii., 6.) What hope of life can the man entertain who is cast into the sea with a millstone about his neck?

Scandal outrages Jesus Christ, because it robs him of those souls for which he shed the last drop of his precious blood—it defeats, in a manner, the ends for which Jesus Christ came on earth. Our Lord came on earth to seek out those who had strayed, and to save those who had perished; but the man of *scandal* destroys the souls for which Jesus suffered and died. By *scandal* we are adversaries and opposers of our Redeemer, for we espouse the interests of the devil in opposition to Jesus Christ. "Woe to the world on account of scandals," says our Lord; "woe to the man by whom scandal cometh." (Matt. xviii., 7.) And again, he says, addressing the Pharisees: "Woe to you, scribes and Pharisees, hypocrites; because you shut the kingdom of heaven against men; for you go not in yourselves, and those that are going in you suffer not to enter." (Matt. xxiii., 13.) St. Chrysostum writes that the Lord is more inclined to show mercy to those who commit other more grievous sins, than to those who are guilty of the sin of scandal. Ah! think, and think often, of the great injury you do to another when you draw him into sin, either by words or deeds, persuasion or bad example. •

Oh scandalous soul! what has the Son of God, your holy Redeemer done to you that you should persecute him? What has your neighbor done that you seek his eternal ruin?• What have the holy angels done that you should grieve them? Has the devil been so great a benefactor to you that you thus earnestly endeavor to satisfy all his wishes? Can it be that the piety of your neighbor provokes you to malice? Do you seek his ruin only that you may triumph over innocence? Have you not sins enough of your own to account for, without loading yourself with the sins of others? Do you not fear that they will fasten a millstone about your neck, which will precipitate you into the depths of hell, for having scandalized one or many of his little ones? And what, think you, will be your sentence at the tribunal of Christ, after

having scandalized the great ones as well as the little ones,
men and women, the rich and the poor, the good and the
bad? How will you fare in hell, where you shall have as
many souls to torment you as you have caused to be damned,
and where all the scandals you have given, in defiance of
heaven, shall fall like thunderbolts on your head?

Some years ago there lived in one of the villages of France
two young men, who disedified the whole neighborhood by
their wicked and dissolute conduct. The curé of the parish,
finding that his good advice and repeated warnings were
treated by them with contempt, addressed himself to their
parents, hoping that they would assist him by their authority
to bring their sons to a sense of their duty. Instead of doing
so, however, they blamed him for interfering unnecessarily in
the concerns of their families, and insolently told him that
they knew how to bring up their children without his advice.
The good priest meekly replied, that whoever despised the
advice of his pastor was guilty of an act of contempt against
God himself, which certainly would not remain unpunished.

The next day, which was Sunday, was spent as usual by
the young men at the public house, where they openly boasted
of their insolence to their pastor, and declared that they set
him at defiance. Meanwhile a dreadful thunder storm gathered in the air, and, bursting over the village, filled every
one with terror and consternation. The two young libertines, accompanied by two other youths, ran to the church
tower to sound the consecrated bells, as is usual in Catholic
countries on such occasions. While they were thus engaged,
a dreadful peal of thunder resounded through the air immediately above their heads, which filled them with such alarm
that they all hastily ran down the steps of the tower to seek
some place of greater security. A vivid flash of lightning,
however, entering at the same moment by the loopholes of

the tower, passed down the stairs as if in pursuit of the fugitives. Descending in a zigzag form, it struck and killed on the spot the second and the fourth of the company, who were the two libertines; their two companions escaped without injury. The lightning then descended into the church where the people had begun to assemble, and picking out the mother of one of the youths, dashed her violently against the wall. This awful judgment of God produced the deepest impression upon the guilty parents, who came to the curé with tears in their eyes to beg pardon for the disrespect they had shown him.

The author of *Bibliotheca of Pastors* (page 120) relates, that a boy, having associated with a dissolute young man, was scandalized by his bad example, and lost his innocence. On the following morning the boy went to the house of his companion, that they might, as usual, go to school together. The father of this wicked young man went to the room in which he slept, to reprove him for his sloth. But on opening the door, he was driven back by a frightful spectre. The mother ran to the window, and saw her unhappy son dead on the bed, black as a coal, and covered with marks of fire. The parents learned from the boy the scandal which had been given to him on the previous day, and thus perceived the cause of the vengeance inflicted on their unhappy son.

Is there, then, no hope of salvation for him who has been guilty of the sin of scandal to others? Yes; the mercy of God is infinite; but he who has given scandal must do great penance, and must unceasingly ask pardon of God; he must also repair the scandal by giving good example, by frequenting the sacraments, and leading a life of piety. Fearing that he had given scandal by dissuading a person from a religious vocation, St. Raymond left the world and became a religious of the order of St. Dominic.

A good Christian may sometimes be mistaken, he may even scandalize others without meaning to do so; but, as soon as he perceives the scandal he has given, he makes it a duty to repair it, disavowing and condemning his error. Thus it was that several Christian soldiers comported themselves, who had been insidiously led by Julian the Apostate into his apostacy. It was customary, on certain occasions, for the emperors, seated on their throne in pompous array, to give money to the troops with their own hands. In one of those ceremonies, which took place about 361, Julian had an altar placed beside him, with a brasier and incense, and each soldier was required to throw a little incense on the fire, before receiving his present. They were given to understand that it was only the renewal of an ancient custom, of no importance whatever. Most of them did not perceive the stratagem prepared for them; but, on being reproached with what they had done, they gave the liveliest proofs of repentance, ran through the streets and squares crying aloud: "We are still Christians; be it known unto all. O Jesus Christ! Our adorable Saviour, we have not renounced thee! If our hand was surprised, our heart had no share in it!" They were courageous enough to go and cast the money they had received at the feet of the emperor, telling him aloud: "Reserve your gifts for those who accept them on so shameful conditions; to us, they are far more odious than death. Cut off our hands, which have been defiled, cut short the thread of our life, immolate us to Jesus Christ, our divine Master, whom you have made us betray against our will." What a lesson, or rather what a reproach for the apostates of our times, who, very far from repairing the scandal they have given, renew it every day by persevering in their apostacy! —[*Reyre, Anec. Chret.*, 26.]

13.   Finally, as it is a sin to injure our neighbor in body

and soul, so it is a sin to wish evil to him. Hence, all imprecations of any grievous evil to another, when accompanied
with a desire of the evil, are mortal sins. It is not necessary that the desire should last for a long time. To sin mortally, it is enough that you for a moment deliberately wish
death or any other grievous evil to a neighbor. Banish,
then, forever from your mouth these accursed imprecations,
and accustom yourself to say, *God make you a saint; God
bless you.* And when any person addresses you in a tone of
anger, adopt the great remedy taught by the Holy Ghost.
" A mild answer breaketh wrath." (Prov. xv., 1.) Answer
with sweetness, *Have compassion on me; have patience with
me; excuse me, I did not perceive the evil I was doing;* and
you shall soon calm the anger of the person, and he will offer
you no further offence. If a person say to you, *I wish you
were dead*; let your answer be, *And I wish to see you happy
and in good health.* Thus you will extinguish his fury. But
when you feel angry, it is better to remain silent, and not to
speak at all; for passion will make certain answers appear
necessary; but when it shall have subsided, you will see that
you have said what you ought not to have said, and that you
have committed many venial and perhaps even mortal sins.
When an insult is offered to you, recommend yourself immediately to God; and if a thought of resentment arises in
your heart, think of the offences you have offered to God.
He has suffered so much from you and yet he has borne with
you so long. Is it, then, too much for you to suffer patiently
an offence from your neighbor for God's sake?

It is a strange, I might almost say an amusing thing, to
see how ingenious saints are in doing good, or avoiding evil.
I will tell you how one of them revenged himself, it was the
blessed Peter Fourrier, who was pastor of Mattaincourt, in
Vosges, at the beginning of the seventeenth century. There

was in his parish a wicked man who had seduced a young woman and led her into sin. A good confession made to the Saint opened the eyes of this poor sinner, and she was sincerely converted. Enraged at this change, which he had not the courage to imitate, her seducer discharged all his fury on the pious pastor. He waited for him one day at the church door, began to abuse him and dared to strike him with his fist. That did not last long, however, for the children, coming out from catechism, and venerating their pastor, attacked the insolent ruffian and quickly drove him away. Many persons ran after him, and he would have been hardly dealt with were it not for the ingenious device of the Blessed Peter. He goes to the church in all haste and begins to ring the bell, as if a fire had broken out somewhere. Hearing the alarm-bell, all the people run towards the church, asking " What is the matter?" The good pastor ascends the pulpit, relates his stratagem, and winds up by saying: " My dear brethren, let us pray for this poor lost soul, it has much need of our prayers." In this way he kept them in church for half an hour, and his enemy had time to escape. God did not fail to reward his servant for this act of charity, so ingenious ; on the following morning, the criminal came to throw himself at the feet of the pastor of Mattaincourt, made a general confession, repaired the scandal he had given, and led ever after an exemplary life.—[*Chapia, Life of Blessed Peter Fourrier.*]

The year 1832 was sadly signalized in Paris by scenes of disorder, which were the effect of the unhappy revolution of 1830 ; but it was still more marked by the horrors of the cholera, which then made its first appearance in France. One day Sister St. Mary was going into the charity hospital, when she was rudely insulted by a working-man, who followed and abused her, and would even have struck her if some one had not prevented him. The good Sister knew only how to pardon and pray. Some days passed. In the beginning of the month of April, hundreds of cholera patients were crowded into the wards of the hospital, mingled with the dead bodies of those who daily expired. One morning a new patient was brought in, whose condition appeared desperate. "*No more room*," was the abrupt answer of the person charged with the reception of patients; "*doctors and nurses can attend no more*." But Sister St. Mary was there; she recognized the patient, and exclaimed: "I will take charge of him—I will find for him a corner somewhere. Do not refuse him; I will tend him myself." She immediately enters on her task, and, without neglecting the other patients, she attends to this one with the most assiduous care. At the end of eight days the man was in a state of convalescence; but one morning he missed from his bedside the good Sister St. Mary, his benefactress. "Alas!" he was told, "she took the cholera herself, and died during the night." In fact, the good Sister had died attending the wretch who had insulted her some days before: she had recognized him, and revenged herself on him after the manner of Saints. She died on the 8th of April, 1832.—[*Guillois, Nouvelle Explic. du Cat.*, 167.]

Behold how true Christians take revenge!

GETHSEMANI ABBEY,
GETHSEMANI, P. O. KY.

THE SIXTH COMMANDMENT.

" Thou shalt not commit adultery."

The greatest injury which our neighbor can suffer next to the loss of life, is unfaithfulness in a husband or wife. Hence it is, that the prohibition of adultery follows immediately after the prohibition of murder. By forbidding adultery, God forbids every kind of carnal sin. Holy Writ mentions several kinds, namely: adultery, fornication, sacrilege, incest, and sins against nature.

When a married man breaks the sixth commandment either with a married or unmarried woman; or when an unmarried man breaks the sixth commandment with a married woman, their sin of impurity is called *Adultery.*

When a single, unmarried man breaks the sixth commandment with a single, unmarried woman, their sin of impurity is called *Fornication.*

When persons sin against the sixth commandment in a place consecrated to the worship of God; or when persons sin against the sixth commandment who have made the vow of chastity, either solemnly or privately, their sin of impurity is called *Sacrilege.*

The peculiar malice of this sin consists in the abuse of what is sacred and devoted to God; for by the solemn or private vow of chastity which persons make, they consecrate the purity of their souls and bodies to God. But if after such an engagement, they prove unfaithful to the promise they have made, they abuse and defile what is consecrated

[242]

to God; and in this they commit a great crime over and above that of impurity.

When a person sins against the sixth commandment with another who is within the four forbidden degrees of either consanguinity or affinity, their sin of impurity is called *Incest;* and the nearer the kindred or relationship, the greater the crime.

The last species of impurity are *sins against nature;* so called, says St. Augustine, because by such wickedness human nature cannot be propagated. Of these there are several sorts, and some greater than others.

When a person sins with himself, or with another person of his own sex, against the sixth commandment, their sin of impurity is called a sin *against nature.*

When a person lowers himself so far as to gratify his impure passion with a brute, his sin of impurity is a most atrocious crime against nature, and is called *Beastiality.*

These sins are so detestable in the sight of God that, as Holy Scripture says, they call loud for the revenging hand of God.

Each one of these sins is a particular species of the sin of impurity. Hence, when one goes to confession and is guilty of any of these sins, it is not enough to say, "I have sinned against the sixth commandment;" he must also confess the species of sin committed, namely, whether it was the sin of adultery, or of fornication, or of sacrilege, or of incest, or of a sin of the flesh with himself or a person of the same sex, or some other thing.

Now, it is not only these most shameful actions that the sixth commandment forbids, it also forbids all wilful immodest looks, words, and everything that leads to impurity.

All immodest looks are forbidden by the sixth commandment. The senses are the avenues or gates of the soul, and on that account we must carefully keep them closed against everything impure. We should especially have a guard over our eyes, because it is through the eyes that sinful objects seek to introduce themselves into the soul; for the sight is the quickest of all the senses, and makes, above all others, the most sudden, the deepest, and the strongest impression upon the heart. Innumerable souls have perished by one single glance of the eye. "Gaze not upon the maiden," says the wise man, "lest her beauty be a stumbling-block to thee." (Eccl. ix., 5.) And Christ declares: "Whosoever looketh on a woman to lust after her, hath already committed adultery with her in his heart." (Matt. v., 28.) Upon which words, St. Chrysostom, preaching on the crime of assisting at stage entertainments, spoke thus to his flock: "But you will say, what, if I do not look to lust? And how will you be able to persuade me of this? For he who will not refrain from a look, how will he be able to remain free from a wound in the soul? Is your body a stone? Is it iron? You are encompassed with flesh; I say, with human flesh, which is more easily kindled from concupiscence than straw catches the flame. Are you more virtuous and strong than so many great and stout men, who have perished by a single glance of the eye?" You should never stop to look at immodest statues or pictures, or at any persons who may be immodestly dressed; for if you do, you will soon find that evil thoughts will arise in your mind. Whenever it happens that your eyes encounter naked statues or pictures, turn them aside immediately, and have recourse to God by prayer, that you may not enter into temptation. We read in the life of St. Louis Gonzaga, that he never looked at women; even in speaking to his mother, he kept his eyes cast down upon the ground.

Immodest words are also strictly forbidden by the sixth

commandment. Of all the artifices which the devil uses to destroy souls, there is not one more effectual than immodest words and impure discourses. Thousands of souls have been damned by immodest and impure discourses. And yet, alas! we pronounce them daily and hourly without dread or the fear of God. Some there are who fix no limits to this diabolical language, but allow the most filthy and obscene expressions to issue from their lips, to the great ruin of children, and of all those who hear them. Others there are who distil this poison more covertly, and, consequently, more effectually; and they are those who speak words of double meaning. St. John Chrysostom calls both one and the other *the tongues of the devil.* And so they are. As God has his apostles and his preachers, who are called *men of God*, the devil has his apostles and preachers, who do his work by means of the foul and filthy language they speak. Some may say that they have no bad intention when they speak these words, and that they make use of them only to amuse others. You have no bad intention! Think you, that you will be excused on that account? St. Paul tells us that no improper word should ever proceed from our mouth: "But now lay you also all away . . . . filthy speech out of your mouth." (Coloss. iii., 8.) When very young, St. Bernadine used to blush as often as he heard an immodest word; hence, his companions were careful never to use improper language in his presence. Such was the horror which St. Stanislaus felt at obscene conversation, that on hearing an immodest word he swooned away, and lost the use of his senses.

But you may say that you speak such words only to amuse your companions. Amusement! Ah! can obscene words and filthy speech be an amusement to a Christian, whose conversation, as St. Paul says, should be in heaven? Should the tongue, on which the body of Jesus Christ has so often reposed, be the vehicle of obscene discourses? You wish to amuse yourselves in outraging the God of holiness! Amuse yourselves! But recollect, if you repent not, that God will one day *laugh and mock* at you in turn, when you must appear before his tribunal, to be judged and condemned to eternal flames for your filthy and obscene language: " I also will laugh in your destruction, and will mock." (Prov. i., 26.) Oh! how great is the evil caused by immodest language! One obscene word may be the cause of the perdition of all who hear it. Many examples, says St. John Chrysostom, can be counted of young boys and young girls, who, from being angels of purity and innocence, became devils by listening to immodest words! Never, then, pronounce immodest words or words of double meaning ; for by so doing you shall sully the purity of your own souls, and wound by your scandal the souls of those who listen to you.

And everything that leads to impurity is forbidden by the sixth commandment. *Kisses, touches* of the hand, and the like liberties, with danger of impure delight, are strictly forbidden by the sixth commandment. Kisses and touches of the hand are extremely dangerous, and among adult young persons, at least, if frequent or long-continued, are always mortal sins. St. Basil compares them to red-hot iron, the touch of which cannot but raise blisters on the flesh.

Intemperance in eating or drinking is forbidden ; for it is impossible to preserve chastity, especially in youth, if persons be not temperate and abstemious. The heat of blood which boils up in that age, excites them very much to sensual pleasures ; but when it is assisted by exterior causes, as spirituous liquors and good cheer, it blazes out. St. Jerome, in his epistle to Euria, says, that " Mount Etna, and Mount Vesuvius, and Mount Olympus, which so often exhale fire and flames, do not burn with greater heat than the marrow of young people, when they are inflamed with wine and delicious meat."

Frequent interviews or familiar conversation with persons of another sex is contrary to chastity, and extremely dangerous. It is during these interviews that the virtue of young persons is utterly lost; and often, after it has been preserved from other dangers, it is then deplorably shipwrecked. Impure love enters but too easily into young minds; but when it is assisted by the presence of the object, it is inflamed beyond all imagination. For this reason the wise man gives us this important admonition: "I found a woman to be more bitter than death; she is the huntsman's noose, her heart is a net, her hands are fetters; the man who loves God will escape her." (Ecclus. vii., 27.) The holy Fathers often repeat this lesson, and in the strongest language denounce indiscreet familiarities with women. "Trust not to your former success," says St. Jerome, in his epistle to Nepotian, "for thou art neither stronger than Samson, nor more holy than David, nor wiser than Solomon. Never forget that a woman banished the first man from paradise. Never be alone with a woman." Indiscreet freedoms, caresses, and demonstrations of friendship, and other such-like fondness, too common among young persons, are most destructive of virtue and purity, and are, as St. Jerome calls them, "the forerunners of the ruin of chastity." Carefully avoid, then, all these things, so contrary to chastity, for they are the most ordinary causes of impurity. Fly them as the plague of your souls, if you desire to be freed from their pernicious consequences—the certain ruin of the purity of your souls.

Immodest songs, discourses, novels, comedies, and plays,

are also forbidden by the sixth commandment, and it is
sinful to join in them.

Immodest songs and discourses are forbidden in the sixth
commandment. Of immodest discourses and words we have
already spoken, and have shown the great injury they cause
to souls both of those who speak them and those who listen
to them. Immodest songs are even more dangerous than
immodest words, for they kindle more promptly in the heart
the fire of impure love. Many there are whose lives were
pure and innocent, until, hearing impure songs, they took
the fatal resolution of committing impurity, and soon fell
from one abyss of crime into another! We every day witness the frightful consequences of immodest songs. What
is the ordinary subject of these songs? Is it not illicit love
or gallantry? Do we not find in the greater number of these
immodest songs expressions, if not openly obscene, at least
covertly so—protestations of sensual love and the like? But
are not songs of this nature very apt to excite wicked and
impure thoughts? The Fathers of the Church have written
in the strongest language against immodest songs. St. Cle-
ment of Alexandria says that we should never take part in
those profane love songs, but leave obscene productions to
drunkards and immoral women.

All immodest novels are also contrary to the sixth commandment. By *novels* are meant those books which treat of
extraordinary and fictitious adventures, and which are in
most cases filled with stories of sensual love. There are
many of these works openly obscene, but the greater number have their poison concealed under a fair and modest exterior. They are not openly lewd, but they are more dangerous on that account, because *novels* openly obscene, as
they professedly teach wickedness, easily create an aversion
to them in those souls which have some shame and conscience

left; but the covertly immodest *novels*, not seeming to be directly bad, attract the mind by their fair discourses; and, by the agreeableness of the subject, delight the sense and inflame the heart with impure love.

Avoid all such *novels* and books, as inventions which the devil has found out to destroy you. Bad books, like bad company, are the ruin of young persons. Bad books are the poison of the soul. You can scarcely ever read them without a mortal sin. In every country on the earth there are thousands of young people daily and hourly perishing under the horrible, the frightful curse of bad books and immodest novels. When a passion for *novel* and romance reading has gained on young persons, business and everything else serious are neglected, and the mind becomes poisoned with impure, filthy images. See what bad *novels* did for St. Teresa, who was, even in her childhood, a saint. "It happened," she says, "that there were some novels and romances in our house. I began to read them, and I gave myself up entirely to this reading. Then I forgot my duties, and thought only of these novels, and I fell into many sins." If you have any of these *novels* or tales, keep them not. Do not rest content with a resolution not to read them, but part with them at once, for if you do not, curiosity will tempt you and overcome you in the end. Say not that these novels are well composed, that they are beautifully written, and that from reading them you learn to speak well, and obtain a great deal of information. I shall answer you in the words of St. Augustin, that "all this is but a false pretext by which you deceive yourself, for by these wicked books we learn not to speak well, but only to become wicked and commit vice with less restraint." (Book II. Confessions.)

Immodest comedies are also forbidden by the sixth commandment. Comedies and other representations of that sort

17

are extremely dangerous, because vice is often represented
in such plays in the most seductive form, while virtue is often
held up in the most odious colors.   In comedies and plays
there is invariably something that is hurtful to modesty,
either in the sentiments spoken, or in the dress and attitudes
of the players.   Many a soul has been ruined by attending
at theatres, for in those places it was that their virtue was
shaken for the first time, and those who knew not vice before, after they had visited the theatres and beheld immodest
comedies represented, became profligate and debauched.
"It is at plays," says St. Jerome, "that we see fulfilled
the prophecy of Jeremias: *Death enters through the windows
of our soul*," that is, through the eyes and ears.

The Church has ever exhorted her children to keep away
from plays, and has exerted herself in every way to turn
them aside from such exhibitions.   St. Augustin relates that
a certain lady having gone into the theatre, was immediately
possessed by the devil.   The devil was commanded, in the
name of Jesus Christ, to say why he had entered that person, since she was a Christian.   He answered that the theatre was his house.

Immodest dressing is a violation of the sixth commandment.   When young women dress immodestly they are guilty
of scandal, for they cause the ruin of many souls.   Tertullian,
in speaking of women who dress immodestly, says: " You
are at the devil's gate ; you are a deserter from the flock of
Christ.   You ruined those whom the devil dared not attack;
you have seduced man, the image of God.   Such are the effects of your meretricious attire."—[*De Cultu Feminarum.*

" A lady of high rank," says St. Jerome, "married to
Hymentius, the uncle of the virgin Eustochium, was prevailed upon to dress her hair and put on her richest attire to
conquer the virgin's virtue and the mother's care, when be-

hold, she was visited that very night by an angel, threatening her in angry terms: Hadst thou the imprudence to prefer thy husband's desire to the law of Christ? Were thy
sacrilegious hands employed to lay snares for the virgin?
Those hands shall now wither, and thou shalt be taught by
excruciating pains the heniousness of thy crime. Five
months were scarcely elapsed when she made a miserable
end, and sunk into hell flames." (St. Jerome, L. 2, Ep. 7.)

In his "Introduction to a Devout Life," St. Francis de
Sales gives the following advice with regard to the manner
in which young persons should dress: "Be neat, *Philothea*;
let nothing hang loose about you, or be ill put on; but then
avoid all affectation, vanity, curiosity or levity in your dress;
keep yourself always, as much as possible, on the side of
plainness and modesty, which, without doubt, is the greatest
ornament of beauty, and the best excuse for the want of it.
For my part, I would have my devout people, whether men
or women, the best clad of the company, but the least pompous and affected. I would have them adorned with grace-
fulness, decency and dignity; in a word, I wish that each
one should dress according to his condition and state."

Nightly interviews and parties lead to the sin of impurity.
The Holy Ghost tells us that, "he who sins, loves darkness
and hates the light," because darkness is more favorable to
the designs of the devil. It is this that makes the night parties of both sexes so fatal and destructive to youth. Licen-
tiousness and immoral discourses are often tolerated in public parties, and on that account they are productive of greater
scandal. In private houses criminal attachments are formed,
indecent familiarities are permitted, and the conversation is
generally filled with indecent jests and lascivious expressions, and very rarely indeed does a young man or a young
woman leave such parties as innocent as they entered them.

Young persons who have the fear of God strongly impress ed
on their hearts will avoid these nightly assemblies. As long
as they are under the eyes of their parents, a mother or
guardian, they are safe; but if, trusting to their own guidance, they go to those night parties, the enemy of their salvation will certainly surprise them. It is ordinarily at such
places that young persons lose the fear of God, and give the
death blow to their chastity. The young man who frequents
such places, will in a short time experience a great revolution within himself; he will become rebellious, disobedient,
indecent and abandoned. A young woman, however virtuous she may be, if she frequents such places, will soon lose
all respect for her parents, will become haughty, capricious
and puffed up with vanity, regardless either of piety or modesty. These are commonly the effects that follow from
nightly assemblies, without mentioning the many sins and
criminal desires that sully the soul.

HIDEOUSNESS AND ENORMITY OF IMPURITY.

Every wilful and deliberate consent to the carnal pleasure
of impurity, whether it be *in thought, word,* or *action,* is a
mortal sin, as is evident from the voice of conscience—from
the declarations of Holy Scripture,—from the punishments
of this vice,—and from its effects on the sinner.

1. *From the voice of conscience:*—

The law of nature, written in every man's heart—the
voice of conscience—tells him that it is a sin to defile his
soul and body by the shameful vice of impurity. Every
one is born with a natural sense of modesty. A certain
feeling of shame restrains the heart, as yet unsullied, from
every thought, word, and action. The honest blood rushes
from the pure heart and mantles the flushing cheek whenever anything immodest is spoken of or hinted at. The

voice of conscience warns every one before he commits the shameful deed. And when at last, after long and fearful struggles, a pure man has unhappily consented to sin, his feelings of shame, of agony, and remorse torture and crucify him.

Where is the man who does not feel and know for certain that the vice of impurity defiles and dishonors him? Where is the man who, after having committed the foul deed, does not feel degraded in his own eyes—whose conscience does not torture and reproach him? Where is the man who, after having gratified his vile passion, does not feel how empty and drear his heart is—how poor and wretched this sin has made him?

The libertine seeks the most secret nook, the darkest night, to cover and conceal his infamy. He strives to hide the blush of shame beneath the fall of darkness and secrecy. He whispers into the ear of his unhappy victim, "No one sees us;" but he forgets that there is an Eye that sees all, that there is One before whom the darkest night is as the broad light of day. Why does he act thus? It is because his own conscience condemns his foul actions.

Among the old heathen tribes in Germany and Gaul, if a young girl lost her innocence, her father had the power to put her to death, and thus wash away the stain of dishonor from his family. St. Boniface tells us, in a letter to King Ethelbald of Mercia, that it was a custom and law among the Saxons that if a girl dishonored her family or a woman proved faithless to her husband, the unhappy wretch was forced to take a rope and hang herself. Her infamous body was then cut down and burned. The villain that had ruined the unhappy creature was then dragged to the spot and hanged like a dog over the smoking ashes of her whom he had ruined. In other places, whenever a woman fell into sin, all the women of the place gathered around the guilty one, drove her from place to place, and scourged her till at last she fell bleeding and exhausted to the ground.

Another ancient law decrees that "if a woman prove faithless to her husband, both she and her seducer shall be dragged to the place of execution. There a grave is dug seven feet long and seven feet deep, and filled with sharp thorns. The guilty pair are tied together and hurled into the grave. A long, sharp stake is then driven through their yet living bodies, the earth is then heaped over them, and they are left there to perish."

Why is it that we find even among heathens so severe punishments inflicted upon the impure? It is because they know by the light of reason how heinous and shameful a crime the sin of impurity is.

"What!" said a priest to a bad Catholic, "you have been living with this woman for these eighteen years without ever marrying her, and you mean to tell me that that is not wrong?"

"Yes, sir! I have done nothing wrong. I am an honest man. I have never stolen, never killed any one. In my youth I wished to have a little enjoyment and that is surely nothing wrong. Besides I did not force this woman. Why did she allow herself to be deceived?"

"Well, let us change the subject. Are these all the children you have?"

"O no, sir, our oldest girl Seraphine is not here."

"Ah! I should like very much to see her. How old is she?"

"O, she is about twelve. She can sew very well. She goes to the Sisters' school. She is high in her class. O she is a good girl."

"I see that your boys are fine, healthy looking children. Is Seraphine just as good looking as the rest?"

"Good looking! I tell you, sir, she is the best looking in the whole house, and yet there are eighteen families living in this tenement."

"Well, my good man, in a few years Seraphine will be a fine grown up young lady. She will be your pride and your consolation. Now, what would you say if some young man would lead her astray as you have done to her mother?"

"What would I say!" shrieked the man in a furious tone. "I would not say anything. I would kill the wretch who would dare touch my daughter."

"Yes, but according to what you told me yourself a few minutes ago, there could be nothing wrong in all that. The young fellow would nevertheless be an honest man, since he had neither robbed or murdered any one, but only wished to enjoy himself."

"I tell you," shrieked the man, "I would murder the villain!"

"Then, my friend, you must condemn yourself. Your own wife was no doubt the child of some good honest man, and you have—"

The poor wretch burst into tears and seized the hand of the priest.

"Pardon me, father," he cried, "I was lying when I spoke as I did. You must not think that I am quite as bad as I pretended."

The poor man was so struck by the sight of his crime in all its hideous enormity that he actually fell sick, and had the fever for several days. He was entirely converted and was thankful ever afterwards to the good friend who had opened his eyes.

What is it that gives the young man, and especially the young woman, their freshness, their beauty, their lovliness? Is it not innocence, purity of heart, stainless virginity? This heavenly virtue casts around them a halo of glory that nothing else can give.

But if this lustre is once lost, if the lily of purity once withers and dies, what can replace it? That young woman, with all her beauty, with all her finery, is but an ornamented corpse, a gilded tomb wreathed with flowers; without all fair, but within full of mould and stench and rottenness. Of what avail are all her ornaments, her silks and satins, her gold and precious stones, if she has lost the greatest ornament of all—her virtue? All these are but the symbols, the fit ornaments, of a chaste and noble heart. On those who have lost their innocence they are but a glaring mockery, the remembrance of what their wearer once was and might have been. Away, then, with costly trappings—the price, perhaps, of lost honor; they are but the flimsy tinsel that covers a vile and degraded heart.

2. *From the declarations of Holy Scripture* it is evident that the vice of impurity is a most grievous sin. Our Blessed Redeemer tells us that "evil thoughts, adulteries, fornications, etc., are the things that *defile a man*." (Matt. xv., 19.) Frequently, in Scripture, the Almighty expresses his hatred of these sins by calling them "*detestable things*," "*abominations*." "Every soul," says he, "that shall commit any of these abominations, shall perish from the midst of his people." (Levit. xviii., 29.)

"Your bodies," says St. Paul, "are the living temples of the Holy Ghost." What a crime it is to profane the church, to dishonor the sacred chalice or ciborium! But how much more enormous is the sin of a Christian who dishonors his soul and body by the sin of impurity! If it be a sacrilege to profane the material temple of God, the lifeless vases consecrated to his service, how much greater is the crime of him who profanes the living temple of God; how much greater is the crime of him who defiles his soul and body, which are consecrated to God by the most intimate union with him!

Let us be mindful of our dignity. Our soul was made the image of God in creation and to the likeness of God in baptism. The vice of impurity especially defiles and dishonors the soul and degrades it to the likeness of the brute.

"Your bodies," says St. Paul, "are members of the body of Christ." Your body has become intimately united with Jesus Christ in baptism, but more especially in Holy Communion. You can say with truth, especially after having received Holy Communion, that the blood of a God flows in your veins. What an unspeakable honor! Men boast of their ancestry. They are proud of royal blood and the blood of heroes. How great, then, is the honor of a Christian in whose veins flows the blood of the King of kings—the blood of God! What a burning shame, then, what a horrible sacrilege, is it for a Christian to defile his body and soul by the foul vice of impurity! By committing that sin he dishonors Jesus Christ. He causes Jesus, the God of purity, to serve him in his sins. He takes the members of the body of Jesus Christ, as the Apostle assures us, and makes of them the members of a harlot. (1 Cor. vi., 15.) This crime, as St. Paul the Apostle assures us, is so great that it should not be even named among Christians. Now, if it be forbidden even to name this sin, what must it be to commit it? "Do not err," says St. Paul; "neither fornicators, nor adulterers, nor the effeminate shall possess the kingdom of God." (1 Cor. vi., 9.) "Whatsoever sin you name," says St. Isidore, "you shall find nothing equal to this crime." (Tom. Orat. xxi.) Indeed "there is nothing more vile or degrading," says St. Jerome, "than to allow one's self to be conquered by the flesh." In the lives of the ancient Fathers it is related (Part ii. c. viii.) that a certain hermit, being once favored with the company of an angel, met on his way the fetid carcass of a dog. The angel gave no sign of displeasure at the stench which it exhaled. They afterwards met a young man elegantly dressed and highly perfumed. The angel stopped his nostrils. Being asked by the hermit why he did so, he answered that the young man, on account of the vice of impurity in which he indulged, sent forth a far more intolerable stench than the putrid dog which they had passed.

8. *From the punishment of the vice of impurity* its great hideousness and enormity are also manifest. The terrible judgments which have been executed upon mankind on account of the vice of impurity, clearly show that it must be very displeasing to God. For, being infinitely just, God never inflicts upon any sins more punishment than they deserve; but being infinitely merciful, he may inflict much less. Now, he has executed the most severe vengeance upon this vice. For—

First, When "all flesh had corrupted its way upon the earth," by yielding to the vice, God said: "I will destroy man, whom I have created, from the face of the earth; from man even to beasts; for it repenteth me that I have made them." (Gen. vi., 1 to 13.) And, in accordance with this terrible threat, he covered the earth with a universal deluge, which destroyed the whole human race, except Noe and his family. (Gen. vii., 21, 22, 23.)

Second, When the inhabitants of Sodom, and of the neighboring cities, gave themselves up to sins of the flesh, their crimes were so grievous that Scripture says *they cried to heaven for vengeance!* And, in his anger, God showered down fire and brimstone from heaven, and destroyed them all, except Lot and his family. (Gen. xix., 24, 25.)

Third, Onan, for defiling the marriage-bed, was struck dead, "because (says the Scripture) he did a detestable thing." (Gen. xxxviii., 10.)

Fourth, Four-and-twenty thousand of the Israelites were on one occasion put to death by God's command for crimes which they had committed against the sixth commandment; *i. e.* for adultry and fornication. (Numb. xxv., 1-9.)

Fifth, Sins against this commandment exclude those who die guilty of them from the kingdom of heaven, and condemn them to everlasting torments. "The works of the flesh are manifest, which are fornication, uncleanness, immodesty, luxury; . . . of which I foretell you, that they who do such things shall not obtain the kingdom of God." (Gal. v. 19, 21.) "But (Almighty God delares) the *abominable* . . . shall have their portion in the pool burning with fire and brimstone, which is the second death." (Apoc. xxi., 8.)

At the present day we see more severe temporal punishments inflicted on this than on any other sin. Go into the hospitals, and listen to the shrieks of so many young persons of both sexes. Ask them why they are obliged to submit to the severest treatment and to the most painful operations, and they will tell you that it is on account of the sins of impurity. At the first glance, the impure man presents an aspect of languor, weakness and thinness. His countenance is pale, sunken, flabby, often leaden, or more or less livid, with a dark circle around the sunken eyes, which are dull, and lowered or averted. His physiognomy is sad and spiritless; his voice feeble and hoarse. There are dry cough, oppression, panting and fatigue on the least exertion; palpitations, dimness of sight, dizziness, trembling, painful cramps, convulsive movements like epilepsy; pains in the limbs or at the back of the head, in the spine, breast or stomach; great weakness in the back; sometimes lethargy; at other times slow, consumptive fever, digestive derangements, nausea, vomiting, loss of appetite or progressive emaciation. Sometimes the body is bent, and often there are all the appearances of pulmonary consumption, or the characteristics of decrepitude joined to the habits and pretensions of youth. What a wretched and degraded being such a man becomes! He bends under the weight of his crime and infamy, dragging in darkness a remnant of material and animal life. Unhappy man! He has sinned against God, against nature, against himself. He has violated the laws of the Creator. He has disfigured the image of God in his own person, and has changed it into that of the beast. He has sunk lower than the brute, and, like the brute, looks only upon the ground. His dull and stupid glance can no longer raise itself toward heaven. He no longer dares to lift his brow, already stamped with the seal of reprobation. He descends little by little into death, and a convulsive crisis comes at last violently to close this strange and horrible drama.—[*Dr. Debreyne.*

But while the physical symptoms are so grave, the moral degradation goes even farther. The impure man, the desecrator of his own body, gradually loses his moral faculties; he becomes dull, silly, listless, embarrassed, sad, effeminate, in his exterior; he becomes indolent, averse to and incapable of all intellectual exertion; he is destitute of all presence of mind; he is discountenanced, troubled, uneasy, whenever he finds himself in company; he is taken by surprise and even alarmed if required simply to reply to a child's question; his feeble soul succumbs to the lightest task; his memory daily losing more and more, he is unable to comprehend the most common things or to connect the simplest ideas. The greatest means and the brightest talents are soon exhausted; knowledge previously acquired is forgotten; the most exquisite intelligence becomes naught,and no longer bears fruit; all the vivacity, all the pride, all the qualities of the spirit disappear; the power of the imagination are at an end for them; pleasure no longer fawns upon them; but, in revenge, all that is trouble and misfortune in the world seems the portion of the impure fellow. Inquietude, dismay, fear, which are his only affections, banish every agreeable sensation from his mind. That last crisis of melancholy and the most frightful suggestions of despair commonly end in hastening the death of the unfortunate man, or else he falls into complete apathy, and sinks below those brutes which have the least instinct, retaining only the figure of his race. It even frequently happens that the most complete folly and frenzy are manifest from the first.—[*Dr. Gottlieb Wogel.*]

One day a young man spoke to me about one of his companions who had lost his mind. I told him that many a young man nowadays loses his mind on account of self-abuse. He then avowed that he, too, had lost his mind for some time, and was taken to the mad-house; God permitted him to recover his mind that he might repent. But he soon after relapsed and was again taken to the mad-house. The overseer told one of my friends that two-thirds of the inmates had become insane in consequence of the shameful sin of self-abuse. Such, then, is the physical degredation of the impure man—of the desecrator of his own body. If these evils are not always visible, yet they are all present, and will show themselves in proportion as the vice of impurity is practised.

Not all offenders, it is true, are visited so severely as above described. Perhaps even a small proportion of the whole number die in this manner; yet in this comparatively small minority those who persist in the practice will, sooner or later, surely be included. Let no one delude himself with the false assumption that he can be exempt from the universal law. There can be no possible exemption. Those who persist will surely die the death most horrible of all deaths; while the very individuals who seem to escape are those who most surely carry their punishment for the remainder of their lives, never live to attain old age, and frequently fall victims to some chronic disease, the germs of which they owe to this detestable vice. "Thou hast cast me off behind thy back," says the Lord; "bear thou also thy wickedness and thy fornications." (Ezech. xxiii., 35.)

Dr. Tissot relates that a young man from Montpelier, a student of medicine, died from excess of the crime of impurity. The idea of his crime so agitated his mind that he died in a kind of despair, believing that he saw hell open at his side to receive him.

L. D., a watchmaker, had been virtuous and healthy until the age of seventeen. At that time he delivered himself to the vice of impurity, which he committed three times a day. In less than one year he began to experience great weakness after each criminal act. This warning was not sufficient to drive him from the danger. His soul, already wholly delivered to sin, was no longer capable of other ideas, and the repetition of the crime became every day more frequent, until he found himself in a condition which led him to be apprehensive of death. Wise too late, the evil had made such progress that he could not be cured. He soon suffered from habitual spasms, which often seized him without apparent cause, and in so violent a manner that, during the paroxysm, which sometimes lasted fifteen hours, and never less than eight, he experienced in the back of the neck such violent pains that he commonly raised, not cries merely, but howls, and it was impossible for him, during all this time, to swallow either liquids or solids. His voice became hoarse;

he entirely lost his strength. Obliged to abandon his profession, overwhelmed with misery, he languished almost without relief for several months. A trace of memory, which had nearly vanished, only served to remind him incessantly of the causes of his misfortune and to, increase his remorse. He was less a living being than a corpse, groaning upon the straw, emaciated, pale, filthy, exhaling an infectious odor, almost incapable of any movement. Often a pale and watery blood issued from the nose, and a constant slime flowed from the mouth. Like a pig, he wallowed in his own abominable filth. Bleared, troubled, and dull, he had no longer the faculty of motion. His pulse was extremely low and rapid; his breathing very difficult; his emaciation excessive, except at the feet, which commenced to become dropsical. The disorder of his mind was just as frightful. Without memory; incapable of connecting two phrases; without reflection; without inquietude as to his fate; with no other sentiment than that of pain; a being far below the brute; a spectacle of which it is impossible to conceive the horror, one would with difficulty recognize that he had formerly belonged to the human species. He died at the end of some weeks (June 17, 1857), dropsical from head to foot.

What has already been said regards the temporal punishment inflicted in this life on sins against chastity. But what shall the punishment be in the next? You say that God has pity on this sin. But St. Remigius says that few Christian adults are saved, and that the rest are damned for sins of impurity. And father Segneri says that three-fourths of the reprobates are damned for this vice. The hatred which God bears to sins against purity is great beyond measure. If a lady finds her plate soiled, she is disgusted and cannot eat. Now, with what disgust and indignation must God, who is purity itself, behold the impurities by which his law is violated! He loves purity with an infinite love, and consequently he bears an infinite hatred to the sensuality which the lewd, voluptuous man calls a small evil. We may rest assured that, as pride has filled hell with fallen angels, so impurity fills it with the souls of men.

A young student, a model of piety, and who frequented the sacraments, was one morning going to Mass. He met two of his schoolmates, who invited and forced him to breakfast with them in a saloon. He refused; but he was in a manner forced to consent. He took some wine with them; very little at first, but soon liked it, and took more. It began to rise to his head. At this moment his eyes fell on one of the waiting girls. He yielded to the temptation, and was stabbed in the very act of sin. His two companions, terrified, quitted the world, and led lives of rigor and penance in a monastery.

About six years ago, a young man came to one of the Redemptorist Fathers in New York, and said: "Father, be kind enough to hear my confession without delay. I have been so unfortunate as to scandalize a young woman. She died in the very act of sin. A while ago she appeared to me all on fire, and said that she was damned, and that I was the cause of her damnation, of her everlasting torments. I tremble all over, and fear I may die in the same manner." The same father was one day called to assist a dying man in a house of ill-fame. But he went in vain. The impure man was dead and judged. He died in the very act of sin. The same punishment was inflicted about two years ago on some young people in one of the New England States. They were found dead in the corn-field in the act of sin.

One day, the Fathers of the Mission of St. Vincent gave a retreat in their house at Florence to a gentleman who had lived in criminal intercourse with a woman who died before making her peace with God. While this gentleman, in the bitterness of his repentance, was imploring the divine mercy for the companion of his guilt, she appeared to him, and said: "Do not pray for me, for I am damned;" after which, to convince him of the reality of her apparition, she placed her hand on the table before which he was kneeling in prayer, and the part which she touched received the burnt impress of her hand. This table is still preserved in Naples. —[*Life of St. Alphonsus.*]

The impure may say that the sin of impurity is but a small evil. But at the hour of death they will not say so. Every sin of impurity shall then show itself such as it really is—a monster of hell. Much less will they say so before the judgment-seat of Jesus Christ, who will tell them what his apostle has always told them: "No fornicator or unclean hath inheritance in the kingdom of God." The man who has lived like a brute cannot sit among the angels. Common sense, the voice of conscience, Holy Scripture, the Fathers of the Church, all the saints, even all the devils, tell him so.

From the evil effects of the vice of impurity, its enormity is clearly shown.

"In no sin," says St. Thomas, "does the devil delight so much as in the sins against chastity." (i. ii. q. 73, a. 3.) The reason why the devil takes so much delight in this vice is because it is difficult for a person who is addicted to it to be delivered from it. And why? Because this sin so blinds the sinner that he commits it oftener than any other sin. A blasphemer only blasphemes when he is drunk or provoked to anger. The assassin, whose trade is to murder others, does not, at the most, commit more than eight or ten homicides. But the unchaste are guilty of an unceasing torrent of sins, by thoughts, by words, by looks, by complacencies,

18

and by touches, so that when they go to confession they find it impossible to tell the number of sins they have committed against chastity. Even in their sleep the devil represents to them obscene objects, that on awakening they may take delight in them; and, being the slaves of the .devil, they obey him, and give consent to his evil suggestions. "There is," says St. Thomas, "no sinner so ready to offend God as the votary of lust is" on every occasion that occurs to him. To other sins, such as blasphemy, murder and slander, men are not prone; but to this vice of impurity nature inclines them, and therefore it is so easy to contract the habit. How many foundlings, abortions, infanticides, may one count every day in our large cities! How few young couples come with pure hearts to the altar! How many lost creatures earn a livlihood by a life of infamy! How many houses of shame! How many so-called fashionable houses of assignation in every city—houses of infamy not only for the hoary sinners, but even for young and thoughtless children!

What forms the favorite topic of conversation in company, in the cars, on the boats, in the tavern, in the streets, in the market-place, in the ball-room, in the theatre? Is it not the shameful vice of impurity?

What constitutes the interest of the great majority of the novels, magazines, weeklies, that fill our libraries, that are to be found in the hands of every one from the young school Miss to the venerable old maid? Is it not sensual love? Is it not impurity?

Which dances are the most popular? Are they not the obscene, impure round dances? How many a young girl will tell you that she will not give up these forbidden dances, even if she had to burn in hell for it!

Which are the most popular plays in the theatre? What plays are those that always draw crowded houses, while the churches are often empty? Are they not the most immodest plays that hell itself could invent—plays wherein lost creatures sell their modesty to make a paltry living?

What class of pictures are to be found in those weekly papers? What kind of photographs and statues in the windows of so many stores? Are they not usually the most indecent?

Another reason why the devil delights so much in seeing men commit the sin of impurity is that it is the fruitful source of many other sins. The impure man is, to a certain degree, guilty of idolatry—of giving to some creature the love and honor which is due to God alone.

Is not that impure man guilty of idolatry who loves the frail, erring creature of his passion to such a degree that for her sake he willingly sacrifices his health, his honor, his hope of heaven, and God himself? Does he not love that creature more than God? And is not that idolatry?

The impure man is guilty of perjury. Impurity leads to perjury. Is not the young woman who protests solemnly to her parents that she keeps no dangerous company; is not that vain woman who protests again and again to her husband that she receives no dangerous visits, guilty of perjury when they call God to bear witness to their innocence, though they know in their inmost hearts that they are not innocent? How many false oaths has not that young man taken; how often has he solemnly sworn to the unhappy victim of his passion that he would never abandon her; and how quickly has that solemn promise been broken as soon as his brutal passions were gratified?

Impurity leads to sacrilege. Who are those that make bad confessions? Who are those that conceal their sins in confession, and make so many sacrilegious communions? They are, generally, those who have been guilty of the crime of impurity. They are ashamed to confess their

secret crimes. They will not reveal to their confessor the
dangerous company they keep, the sinful liberties they permit, the shameful thoughts and desires that they nourish in
their hearts. They never mention to the confessor the wicked
books that they read, the immodest conversation in which
they indulge. And even if they do mention any sin of this
kind, they never tell the whole truth; they cover and lessen
the sin; so that their confession is worthless, and they leave
the confessional with the curse of God and the sin of sacrilege on their soul. Oh! how many of these souls are lost
forever. How many are now burning in hell who were led
astray by the demon of impurity, and who afterwards had
not the courage to open their hearts sincerely, to tell every
thing honestly to their confessor!

Impurity leads to theft. A young man filches from his
employer; he keeps back part of his wages, that he may have
the means to spend the night in those haunts of sin and
shame which are the very hot-beds of hell. The young
woman steals from her parents in order to buy some finery
which she thinks will make her more captivating in the eyes
of others. A husband and a father squanders his means and
ruins his family in order to gratify the vanity of some infamous woman who has gained those affections which alone
belong to his lawful wife. To gratify his passion he is even
cruel to his family.

A certain man kept a mistress in the house. His wife
knew it, but bore the insult patiently, in order to prevent
greater evils. One day the servant came to the good lady
with tears in her eyes. "What is the matter? Why do
you weep?" asked the good woman. "Ah!" answered the
servant, "your husband has sent me to take the keys of the
house from you. He says that henceforth this young woman
in the house is to be my mistress." The lady grew pale, her

heart pierced by this last crowning insult, went to the "mistress" and ordered her to quit the house instantly. The husband heard of the difficulty. He told his wife if she did not beg pardon on her knees of the mistress, he would send her and her child a thousand miles away, where they would never see him again. And the poor mother had to obey.

Impurity leads to cruelty and hardness of heart. There lived some years ago in the city of Vienna a young widow. She had an only child—a little girl about six years of age, named Lena. Soon after the death of her husband this young widow began to receive the visits of a young man of the neighborhood. By and by the visits became more frequent, their friendship ripened into intimacy, and wicked tongues were not wanting to whisper suspicions that this innocent friendship would end in shame. The young widow felt the shame of her unhappy position very keenly; but she was blinded by her passions, and would not give up the young man's company. She urged him frequently to save her from shame by an honorable marriage; but he steadily refused. "I cannot marry a woman with a family," he said; "it would only bring trouble." At last the woman, who had now given herself up entirely to the devil, formed the horrible resolution to do away with her child, and thus set aside every obstacle to the wished-for union. In the house in which she lived there was a deep, dark cellar. One day the unhappy woman took her little daughter by the hand, led her down into this damp, gloomy dungeon, and said, in a harsh tone: "Here, Lena, remain here until I come back for you." The poor innocent child began to cry, but the unnatural mother hurried away, and closed the heavy door behind her. Two days passed. The mother hoped now that her little child was dead. In the darkness of the night she stole down to the cellar, slowly opened the door, and

called out: "Lena, are you there?" The sad, plaintive
voice of the little child was heard: "Ah! mamma, mamma,
give me a piece of bread." But the mother turned away and
closed the heavy door once more. Another day passed by.
The mother spent it in the company of her wicked companion, gratifying her sinful passions; and the poor helpless
child remained pining away with hunger in her gloomy prison.
Once more the wretched woman went down to the cellar.
This time she expected for certain that the child would be
dead. She opened the door and called again, "Lena, are
you there?" Again the sad, moaning voice of the child was
heard crying in feeble tones: "O mamma, mamma! a piece
of bread." The unnatural mother turned away; her heart
trembled not with compassion—the impure heart has no compassion—but with fear lest she should be found out. She
trembled with rage that her child was not yet dead. She
now waited several days, and when she went to the cellar
once more the child was dead! She took the poor dead
child to her room and dressed it for burial. Early the next
morning the neighbors were aroused by loud wailing and
lamenting in the house of the young widow. They hastened
to her room; they found her crying and shrieking and acting
as if she were beside herself with grief. There lay the dead
child, pale and cold. It was dressed in white; a wreath of
flowers was placed upon its breast. No one suspected anything of the foul, unnatural murder. Next day the child
was buried. All the little playmates of Lena formed a procession and accompanied the body to the grave. The body
of the dead child was now lowered into the grave; the first
handful of earth was thrown upon the coffin; the priest then
knelt down with all those present and recited the customary
prayers. Every heart was touched—every eye filled with
tears. There was one heart, however, that remained cold

and unmoved; it was the heart of the mother. She was now free. She could now gratify her sinful passions without restraint; there was no longer any fear of detection. The secret deed was locked up securely in her heart. But oh! terrible justice of God! when the priest recited the "Our Father," and came to the words, "Give us this day our daily bread," the sad, plaintive cry of her dying child rang in the ears of the mother; a wild feeling of terror and remorse seized her, and she fell senseless to the ground. She came to herself again, but she had lost her reason and became a raving maniac. And now, with a wild, unnatural laugh, she related to the horror-stricken bystanders the full particulars of the murder of her child.

Impurity leads to jealousy, murder and suicide. George Bauman, one of the principals of the public schools of Williamsburg. N. Y., and Anna McNamara, both Catholics, met frequently for nine months in a house of assignation in Elizabeth street, in New York. Bauman at last shot her, and then himself, in that infamous house. Their bodies were taken to the Morgue, near Bellevue Hospital, where they were laid out in coffins side by side. The face of the unhappy murderer looked as if he had died in the most horrible agony.

About four years ago, Catherine Lenan, a virtuous and handsome young girl, left her home in the County Cork and came to this country, where she soon obtained employment as a domestic servant, her last place being in Longwood, near Brookline, Mass. She was a careful and industrious girl, and those who employed her became attached to her. There were few or none of those near her whom she had known in Ireland; she had only one relative in this country, who lived at a distance from her. Thrown upon herself, she naturally wanted to form new acquaintances and make new friends; and we soon find her, in company with another girl, walking from her employer's house on every evening she could spare, and visiting a saloon or drinking-house, kept by Irish people, where she had become acquainted with several young men. In taking this walk on the night of Tuesday, Oct. 24, poor Kate Lenan was waylaid on the road by some miscreant, yet unknown, and brutally outraged and murdered.

The third reason why the devil takes peculiar delight in the vice of impurity is because this sin involves the malice of scandal. Other sins, such as blasphemy, perjury, and murder, excite horror in those who witness them; but this sin easily excites and draws others to commit it, or at least to commit it with less horror. Ignorance of evil is a part of innocence, and the best rampart of virtue. Those who have never seen evil done think not of seeing it. They will entertain a horror of it unless they see it committed and excused by others. One is ashamed to practise virtue among the wicked, and to be innocent among the guilty. How many have received their first lessons in immorality or crime from the hostler, or the cook, or the nurse; while a single night with a strange bedfellow may initiate a boy in mysteries to which he had else remained a stranger. This last danger is greatly increased if the casual room-mate be by a few years his senior; for the power of mischief possessed by the older boy is increased in proportion to his size and his experience. An impure boy or girl is sure to corrupt the smaller ones whenever a safe opportunity presents itself, and thus children of six and twelve fall victims to those who are older than themselves.

The fourth reason why the devil rejoices so much in seeing one commit the sin of impurity, is because it blinds the sinner to such an extent as not to allow him to see the injury which he offers to God, nor the miserable state in which he lives and sleeps. Like "the sow wallowing in the mire," the impure are immersed in their own filth, so that they are not sensible of the malice of their actions, and therefore they neither feel nor abhor the stench 'of their impurities, which excite disgust and horror in all others. By this sin they lose the light of God, which shines in the hearts of all his children, so that they may not stray from the narrow path that leads to heaven. But suddenly this light of the soul is extinguished by the sin of impurity, and the impure are left in utter darkness. Their sins degrade and dim their understanding more than does any other vice. They have eyes and see not, they have ears and hear not, they have reason and understand not. If the unchaste are deprived of light, and no longer see the evil which they do, how can they detest it and amend their lives? The prophet says that, being blinded by their own mire, they do not even think of returning to God. Their impurities take away from them all knowledge of God. "They will not set their thoughts to return to their God, for the spirit of fornication is in the midst of them, and they have not known the Lord." (Osee v., 4.) Yes, this sin, if often repeated, will become a habit, and this habit will become strengthened and deeply rooted in the soul by repeated falls till it finally attains to a degree of malice that is truly devilish.

Whoever has arrived at this degree of sin is possessed by a hardened, unyielding determination to commit sin—a determination which neither warnings nor threats, neither punishments nor favors, can change. Shrouded in impenetrable darkness, in insolent defiance of God and man, the rays of divine light cannot penetrate this heart. The unhappy man is separated from God. The wounds of his conscience have become encrusted so that he can no longer feel any remorse, and at last he reaches such a depth of wickedness that it is almost impossible for him to become either better or worse.

By lust the devil triumphs over the entire man—over his body and over his soul—over his memory, by filling it with unchaste thoughts and making him take pleasure in them; over his intellect, by making him desire occasions of committing sin; over his will, by making it love its impurities as his last end, and as if there were no God. Hell governs him, hell dwells in him; he is already, one may say, a victim doomed to the flames, an agent and slave of the devil. What Jesus said of Judas may be said of him: "One of you is a devil. There is one among you, and it were better for him that he had never been born."

A certain person was so much addicted to the vice of impurity as to commit the most atrocious crimes no longer through weakness, but out of sheer hatred of God. Her accomplice died suddenly in the very act of a most abominable sin of impurity, and afterwards appeared to her enveloped in fire and flames. From that time forward she felt within her, as it were, a burning so intense that she imagined herself in hell, and kept uttering the most horrible cries of despair. This happened in 1858 in a city of Pennsylvania.

There stood once in the middle of Jerusalem a beautiful temple. It was adorned with silver, and gold, and precious stones. It was the work of many kings, and the wonder of ages. In an unhappy hour a torch was cast by a soldier's hand into this beautiful temple. It caught fire, the flames gained apace, and soon the glorious temple was a heap of smouldering ruins. Jews and Romans, the friends and the stranger, made every effort to save the temple, but their efforts were of no avail.

What a sad image this temple is of the soul that has been

ruined by the vice of impurity! A single spark of impure fire is cast into the pure soul which is the temple of the living God. The spark is soon fanned into a flame—the hellish flame increases and gains full mastery over the soul—the friends and relations of the deluded creature may speak to her—the priest of God may warn her—heaven and earth may strive to save her; but in vain. The impure fire, the flame of impure love, burns on—it burns to the very verge of the grave, to the very brink of hell, where the worm never dieth and the fire never quenches.

This vice when habitual clings so firmly to nature that the desire for carnal pleasures becomes insatiable, and will cease only when the unhappy man who indulges in it is cast into the fire of hell. " O hellish fire!—lust, whose fuel is gluttony, whose sparks are brief conversations, whose end is hell." The unchaste become like the vulture that waits to be killed by the fowler, rather than abandon the rottenness of the dead bodies on which it feeds.

Some years ago a gentleman of rank and education forgot himself so far as to keep in his house a young woman of loose character. His friends, his relatives, and even the priest of God, advised and begged him again and again to give up that wicked girl. But it was all in vain. His only answer was: "I cannot, I cannot." At last he fell sick, and his illness became so dangerous that he was at the point of death. The good priest now came to see him. He saluted the dying man, and spoke kindly to him, in order to win his confidence. " My dear friend," said the priest, "your illness is dangerous, it is true, but you are young yet and have a strong constitution, and we may hope that you will recover. But, at all events, it would do you no harm to make your peace with God like a good Christian." " Ah! Father," said the dying man, " I know that I am in great danger. It is true I have led a very wicked life, but I now wish to amend. I wish to die a good death. Tell me, then, what I must do?". The priest was overjoyed to see him in such a good disposition. "Well," said the priest, "since you desire to die a good death, you must prepare yourself by a good confession." "Oh! most willingly," was the reply. "Are there any debts that you have not paid?" asked the priest before he commenced to hear his confession. "I have paid them all," answered the sick man. "Have you never defrauded your neighbor or injured him in his good name or property?" "Yes, but I have made restitution." "Have you no ill-will against any of your neighbors?" "I had, but I have forgiven them all." "Are you willing to ask pardon of all those whom you may have offended?" "Yes, I humbly ask pardon." "Do you wish, then, to receive the last sacraments?" "I desire it with all my heart." "Well, then," said the priest, "since you desire to receive the last sacraments, you know you must put away every obstacle to the grace of God—you must send away this wicked girl from your house; she is a constant occasion of sin to you still. You must send her away." "O Father!" said the dying man, "what do you mean? Send away that girl! Oh! I cannot do that." "What is that?" said the priest, amazed. "You cannot? Why can you not? Do you not know that you must do so if you wish to save your soul?" "Father, I cannot, I cannot." "But you are at the point of death. In a few moments more you will be forced to leave her. Why not send her away now of your own free will?" "I cannot do it, indeed I cannot." "Oh!" cried the priest, drawing forth his crucifix, "look at this crucifix. Our Redeemer, your Lord, suffered and died for you. He shed his heart's blood for you. Will you not make this slight sacrifice to please him? Oh! look upon his wounds; see his blessed head crowned with thorns—can you refuse him? For the love of Jesus, have pity on your poor soul. Will you not send away that wicked woman, at least for the love of Jesus Christ?" "Father, I have already told you that I cannot do it." "But if you do not send her away, I cannot give you the sacraments." "No matter, I cannot do it." "You will be excluded from the kingdom of heaven." "Well, I cannot help it." "You will die excommunicated; you cannot be buried in consecrated ground; you will be thrown aside like a dog?" "I cannot help it." "But you will be condemned to the everlasting flames of hell." "Well, I cannot help it." "In the name of God, be reasonable. Is it not better to send away this wicked woman than to lose soul and body, heaven, and God himself?" "I cannot send her away." The dying man then beckoned to the wretched woman, who was standing at some distance from him, and wept. As soon as she drew near, he threw his arms around her neck, and in a voice which trembled with weakness and passion, he cried: "Ah! you have been my joy during life; you shall be my joy in death and throughout all eternity." These were his last words. In that same instant he breathed forth his soul, and died in the very act of sin.

Oh! how difficult it is for a person who has contracted the habit of this vice to amend his life and return sincerely to God!

MEANS TO PRESERVE CHASTITY.
(According to St. Alphonsus.)

The ermine is an animal which is sometimes covered with a fur of spotless white. This animal is said to be so sensitive to the purity of its color that it pines away and dies of grief when it beholds its color stained in any way. Whether this little story is true or not, it shows us how greatly we should esteem the purity of the soul and how carefully we should watch over that unspeakable treasure, in order that we may never lose it. Now to watch over this treasure of the soul is to make use of the proper means to preserve it.

For those, says St. Alphonsus, who find it too difficult to keep the sixth commandment, or who are in great danger of falling into sin against it, God has, as St. Paul says, instituted matrimony as a remedy. "But if they do not contain themselves, let them marry; for it is better to marry than to be burnt." (I. Cor., vii., 9.) "*But, father*," some may say, "*marriage is a great burden*." Who denies it? But have you heard the words of the apostle? It is better to marry, and to bear this great burden, than to burn forever in hell. But do not imagine that, for those who are unwilling or unable to marry, there is no other means but marriage by which they may preserve chastity.

Now, what are these means?

The first is to humble ourselves constantly before God. The Lord chastises the pride of some by permitting them to fall into a sin against chastity. It is necessary, then, to be humble, and to distrust, altogether, our own strength. David confessed that he had fallen into sin in consequence of not having been humble, and of having, perhaps, trusted too much in himself. "Before I was humbled, I offended." (Ps. cxviii., 67.) We must, then, be always afraid of ourselves, and trust that God will preserve us from sin.

The second means is to have recourse to God for help as soon as we are assailed by temptation against purity. When an impure image is presented to the mind, we must immediately endeavor to turn our thoughts to God, or to something which is indifferent. But the best rule is, immediately to invoke the names of Jesus and Mary, and to continue to invoke them until the temptation ceases, or at least until it becomes weak. When the temptation is violent, it is useful to renew our purpose of never consenting to any sin, saying, "*My God, I wish to die rather than offend you.*" And then let us ask aid: "*My Jesus, assist me; Mary, pray for me.*" The names of Jesus and Mary have special power to banish the temptations of the devil.

The third means is to frequent the sacraments of Penance and Eucharist. It is very useful to disclose unchaste temptations to your confessor. St. Philip Neri says that a *temptation disclosed is half conquered.* And should a person have the misfortune to fall into a sin against purity, let him go to confession immediately. By ordering him, whenever he fell into sin, to confess it immediately, St. Philip Neri freed a young man from this sin. The Holy Communion has great efficacy in giving strength to conquer temptations against chastity. The most holy sacrament is called " wine springing forth virgins." (Zach. ix., 17.) The wine is converted into the blood of Jesus Christ by the words of consecration. Earthly wine is injurious to chastity ; but the celestial wine preserves it.

In Ferrara, there lived a man who, in his youth, was very much molested with temptations of the flesh to which he very often gave consent, and thus committed many mortal sins. To free himself from this wretched state he determined to marry ; but his wife died very soon and he was again in danger. He was not disposed to marry again ; yet, to remain a widower was, he thought, to expose himself anew to his former temptations. In this emergency he consulted a good friend and received the advice to go frequently to confession and holy communion. He followed this advice, and soon experienced such extraordinary effects of the sacrament that he could not help exclaiming : "O, why did I not sooner meet with such a friend ! Most certainly I would not have

committed so many abominable sins of impurity had I more
frequently received this sacrament which *maketh virgins.*"
—[*Baldesanus in Stim. Virt.* i., c. 6.]

The fourth means is devotion to Mary, the Mother of God,
who is called the *virgin of virgins*—Sancta virgo virginum.
How many young men have, by devotion to the Blessed Virgin, preserved themselves pure and chaste as angels ! Father
Segneri relates, that a young man, so polluted with the vice
of impurity that his confessor could not absolve him, went
one day to confession to a Father of the Society of Jesus.
The Father dismissed him, and told him to say every morning the *Hail Mary* three times in honor of the purity of the
Blessed Virgin, in order to obtain, through her intercession, the grace to be delivered from the bad habit. After
several years the young man returned to the same Father,
but had scarcely a venial sin to confess ; when he had finished
his confession he said to the confessor : "Father, do you
know me? I am the person whom you could not absolve
some years ago, on account of my sins against purity ; but by
saying the *Hail Mary* three times every morning, I have, by
the grace of God, got rid of the bad habit." He gave leave
to the confessor to state the fact in general terms from the
pulpit. A soldier who was on terms of criminal intimacy
with a woman, heard the story told in a sermon. He began
to say the *Hail Mary* three times, and was freed from the habit
of sin. One day the devil tempted him to go to the house
of the female in order to convert her. But what happened?
When he was on the point of entering the house, he felt
himself driven back by some invisible but powerful hand
and carried to a considerable distance. He thus became
more and more convinced of the protection of the Blessed
Virgin Mary. Had he entered the house, he would probably
have relapsed in consequence of being exposed to the prox-

imate occasion of sin. Let each one practise this little devotion of saying the *Hail Mary* three times in honor of the Blessed Virgin, adding, after each *Hail Mary*, "*Through your pure and immaculate conception, O Mary, obtain for me purity and sancity of body and soul.*"

The fifth means, which is the most necessary for avoiding sins against chastity, is to fly from dangerous occasions. Generally speaking, the first of all the means of preserving yourself always chaste, is to avoid the occasion of sin. The means are, to frequent the sacraments, to have recourse to God in temptations, to be devoted to the Blessed Virgin; but the first of all is to avoid the occasions of sin. "And your strength," says Isaias, "shall be as the ashes of tow . . . . and there shall be none to quench it." (Isa. i., 81.) Our strength is like the strength of tow thrown into the fire; it is instantly burnt and consumed. Would it not be a miracle if tow cast into the fire did not burn? It would also be a miracle if we exposed ourselves to the occasion and did not fall. According to St. Bernardine of Sienna, it is a greater miracle not to fall in the occasion of sin, than to raise a dead man to life. St. Philip Neri used to say that, in the warfare of the flesh, cowards, that is, they who fly from occasions, are always victorious. You say, *I hope that God will assist me.* But God says, "He that loveth the danger shall perish in it." (Eccl. iii., 27.) God does not assist those who, without necessity, expose themselves wilfully to the occasion of sin. (*I here refer the reader to what I have said on the occasion of sin and the necessity of avoiding it, in my work "The Sacraments of the Holy Eucharist and Penance," p. 380 to 412.*)

I must, however, add here a plain instruction on improper dancing, and refute the objections of its advocates, as there are many who, for want of better knowledge, are unwilling

19

to believe that the improper dance is an occasion of sin for the young.

IMPROPER DANCING.

Good sense tells us that man must have his repose, his recreation, his pleasures—he must have his repose after the fatigue of a task well done ; his recreation after occupation ; his true pleasure in which is intermingled the remembrance of duties well accomplished.

Good sense also tells us that any one who, instead of using pleasure worthily, uses his life unworthily by abusing pleasures ; who, instead of partaking of them, gives himself up to them ; reverses the order of reason and of nature, and greatly deserves to meet with weariness at every step. He looks upon life as if it were a game. He forgets that man is not here to lead an idle life, but to be active and to gain merit.

Good sense again tells us that such pleasures and amusements as endanger our spiritual welfare, are altogether unworthy of man, and still more unworthy of a Christian. The improper dance, especially the waltz in its different shapes and with its modern improvements is one of such amusements. I do not wish to defile these pages with a description of such dances. Suffice it to say that they are occasions to most lascivious looks, very obscene words and improper actions.

If we consider dancing as a mere exercise, it undoubtedly appears quite ridiculous. What, in fact, can be more laughable than to see dancers advance, fall back, bend the body, throw it back again, and whirl around like birds struck on the head ? If music had not lent the charm of its harmony to cover the folly and absurdity of dancing with an appearance of sense and propriety, and if people could only see the movements of dancers performed in silence, they could not help exclaiming with the greatest Roman orator, Cicero, that

" He who dances must be drunk or mad"—(*Nemo fere saltat sobrius, nisi insanus.*)

What can be more repugnant to the taste of people of sense than the motions, the gestures and the jumps made in the dance? Louis Vivez, preceptor of Charles V., says that some Spaniards who visited France were so frightened at seeing women dance that they ran away, *believing them laboring under some extraordinary madness.*

If the exercise which dancing affords was the sole object of those who frequent the ball room and the dance house, if it afforded them only the innocent pleasure which men can procure in the absence of women, and women in the absence of men, it would not exist long; to abolish it, it would suffice to make it the object of our ridicule, and compel young men and young women to dance separately, without seeing or speaking to each other. There are many who would never go to the dance house if they did not expect to accompany thither, or did not hope to find there, the object of their passion.

But we must not examine the mere external form of dancing; we must consider its aim and consequences. We see, then that it comprises an infinite number of dangers which are natural to it, which we cannot separate from it, without abolishing the whole form. It is almost always the rock on which innocence is wrecked; it is the *tomb* of modesty, the theatre of all worldly passions, and the triumph of them all. We can easily see that it is a collection of all that is most dangerous to our salvation, and an assemblage of all temptations; that everything in it is injurious or poisonous; company, objects, conversations, occasions, the music—all concur to seduce the mind and heart, and to stifle in them every sentiment of piety.

Hence it is that even some of the pagans, according to

Aemilius Probus, thought that the dance should be reckoned among vicious things.—"Scimus saltare etiam in vitiis poni."

Cato accused Murena, a Roman consul, of having danced in Asia. Cicero, in his eloquent pleading in favor of the latter, took care not to justify him if he had danced, but he firmly denied the fact. What he said in this respect is remarkable. "If Murena has danced, O Cato," exclaimed this great orator, "the accusation you bring against him is strong and grave; but if he has not danced, it is an extreme outrage you do him. To render credible what you advance against him, you should consider first and show us to what vices he whom you accuse must have been subject; *for no one sober is ever found to dance, unless he be a fool.*"

"Blush!" exclaims hereupon Cardinal Bellarmine; "a pagan has thought more sanely than you, and a pagan will condemn you on the judgment day; mere natural knowledge put this pagan in a condition to teach us that dancing is only fit for drunkards and fools. And you who are children of God and enlightened by the celestial knowledge of the Gospel—you, among whom such absurdities ought not even to be mentioned—you have the folly to give yourselves up to dances, even on the most solemn and sacred days!"

I have just given you the opinion of a sensible pagan about dances. Let me now give you the opinion of a French courtier. When M. de Rognette, Bishop of Antun, France, was about to give to his people an instruction on dancing, he thought it advisable to consult, on this subject, a man who, by his character and condition of life, would be far from condemning such a diversion; he consulted the Count of Bussy-Rabutin, so famous for his wit and irregularities. "I have always been of opinion," said the Count, "that balls are dangerous. Reason and experience make me condemn them. Although the teaching of the Church concerning dancing is rather severe, yet I think that the opinion of a courtier on this point ought to be of greater weight. I know there are persons who run less danger in these places than others; nevertheless, the most passionate are excited in them. They are usually young people who compose these balls, who are almost unable to resist temptation in private; and how can they resist it where the most beautiful objects—brilliant lights, violins, and the agitation of the dance—would enkindle passions in anchorites? Old people who would go to balls would be ridiculed for doing so against their conscience, and young people, to whom propriety permits this, must not only act against conscience, but expose themselves to great dangers. Therefore I maintain, that no one calling himself a Christian should go to the balls or dances of our age; and I believe that clergymen would do right to oblige parents and masters to keep their children and servants from balls and dances." It is not a priest who speaks here, but it is a man of the world, a courtier; his testimony has the more weight since he is more interested to speak entirely different. It is only the force of truth which compels him to condemn so sternly the ball and dance.

It cannot be questioned, says Madame Leprince de Beaumont, that of all the desires that rule the heart of women, that of pleasing is the most ardent; it is this desire which produces in them love of dress, jealousy, and vanity. But at balls this desire acquires new strength. It leads them to envy the lot of persons of their own sex, whom they see better dressed, or better dancers, than themselves; it makes them hate those whose society is more courted or sought after; in a word, this desire makes them sow discord among men, who often, in order to satisfy the vanity of a contemptible

woman, quarrel and fight among themselves, and kill one another in duels.

If women were sincere, they would agree that the desire of
pleasing and being preferred to others, rather than any thing
else, brings them to the ball room. But among the great
number of men whom they try to attract, there are always
some who attract them in turn, and please them too much.
As these women badly conceal the impression made on them
by young men, the latter profit by it, by holding tender and
impassioned discourses with them, the poison of which they
swallow with a relish that they cannot always hide. If the
effects of this passion are not seen immediately, they are not
the less real or the less frightful.

As young persons of both sexes are at all times and in
all places occasions of sin to one another, it is especially at
the dance that the occasion is most dangerous, the peril most
imminent, and most difficult to be shunned.   In the perilous
occasions with which the world is filled, people are not
always incited to sin by all their senses at once. If their
mind is troubled by thoughts contrary to chastity, the heart
does not feel at the same instant the fatal impressions. If
their ears are sometimes flattered by tender discourses or immodest songs, their eyes are not always struck at the same
time by the presence of seductive objects, so that if they are
urged on to sin by one sense, the others can at least hinder
them from yielding to the temptation ; but in the dance young
people are incited to sin by all their senses together.   The
senses are so many channels which the devil uses to pour, all
at once, into their souls the poison which lust begets. Whilst
their eyes are dazzled by the splendor and pomp displayed by
the vanity of those composing these worldly assemblies, per-
fumes and odoriferous essences please the smell ; their heart
is a prey to the charms of all those seductive objects placed

before them; their ears are pleased by the poisoned sweetness of licentious conversations that are being held, and by
the harmony of voluptuous music, which seems to communicate to the objects assembled a new life and new attractions,
in order to seduce them more easily, and entirely enslave
their already softened and enervated hearts. As, while cel-
brating in the sanctuary the benefits of the Creator, music
inflames the coldest heart with the fire of divine love,—as on
the field of battle it communicates to the most timid an in-
domitable courage,—so also in the dance, by inflaming the
heart with impure love, it fills it with lust, and strengthens
this lust after it has been allowed to enter. If to all these
dangers which beset young people in these pernicious assemblies, we add those which the tumult and agitation that reign
in them, and the immodesty which every one tries to show in
his looks and by his deportment, naturally produce, we shall
be forced to confess that it is almost impossible for young
persons to resist long the attractions to lust, in a place where
everything inspires it; we must say that these diversions cause
the love of the world and of creatures to enter sweetly and
agreeably into the hearts of the dancers, and banish the love
of God and of religious duties. Horrible corruption ensues,
whose vapor clouds their minds, extinguishes the light of
faith, and gives rise to irreligion and atheism; for *from impurity to impiety there is but one step!* When once you have
fallen into this infamous passion, you have a thousand difficulties to surmount in your way back to virtue. If the acute
remorse of a disturbed conscience may force you to shun
crime for a moment, habit, which always rules, and the pleasures that you imagine are to be found in it, soon lead you
back to your old course of life, and prevent repentance, without which there is no possibility of gaining salvation. When
man has reached this degree of corruption, he cannot bear the

thought of a just God, into whose hands he must fall after death; he wishes to smother those importunate qualms of conscience which trouble and imbitter the pleasures which he loves, and which he is unwilling to sacrifice. He endeavors to persuade himself that there is no God, and consequently no hell; he sleeps in this foolish security, and is awaked only by the *heat of eternal flames.*

I ask, now, if we have not good reasons to say with the holy doctors and most famed theologians, that dancing is an infectious *sink of jealousy, rivalry, buffoonery, raillery, quarrels, obscenity,* and *impiety,* a *school* of *vice,* where one learns the art of *corrupting himself and of corrupting others?* What virtue so strong as to be able to appear in the dance without running the risk of fading in the pestilential air exhaled from it?

If a religious woman should forget herself so far as to appear at a ball, would not such levity and imprudence give rise to the most malignant reflections? "If this person," most men would say, "does not conceal a corrupt heart disposed to deliver itself up to the most shameful disorder under affected modesty, she will soon find that it is impossible to throw herself into the bosom of corruption, and the most seductive temptations, without being infected; she may have been a chaste dove, she will soon have all the malice of the impure serpent." Would you not blame a woman who, having communicated in the morning, would go in the evening to a dancing party? Could you hesitate to say that she had gone to receive her Creator in the sanctuary only to be able to despise him, trample him under her feet, and sacrifice him to the devil? Can expressions strong enough be found to express the indignation we feel at the indignity offered to God?

If it is acknowledged by every one that balls are dangerous and criminal for a religious person, or for one who has received the bread of life, can they be innocent and without danger for one who loves them passionately, who frequents them with all the vain show of worldly pomp, with that air of levity which characterizes the professional dancer, who has little or no love of God, little fear of offending him, little anxiety for her salvation? Is it not evident that a giddy, careless young woman runs more danger in such places than a holy soul, that is opposed to vanity and worldly follies, and deeply endowed with the love of God? Will not the blow which wounds the one undoubtedly kill the other?

Whoever knows the true value and delicacy of chastity, that a too lascivious look, a simple desire, will destroy it, and is aware of the violence of the passions that conspire against it, will agree that it is not possible to go to dances and balls without exposing this virtue to the greatest dangers; that people never leave them without either having lost it or weakened it considerably. But if dancing is dangerous for every one, it is especially so for young people, whose passions are most unruly and most destructive, as they take very little pains to restrain them.

What should one do in order to restrain his passions? He should avoid the occasions which make them spring up, and refuse them the fuel which keeps them burning; but these are means which young persons do not wish to use. They know that nothing is more apt to for strengthen their passions than the frequenting of these worldly assemblies, where everything glitters, where everything seduces; this consideration does not prevent them from frequenting them whenever an occasion is offered; and, far from seeking to shun the seduction which they encounter there, they find no greater pleasure than when they give themselves up to it without reserve. Going forth from these haunts of lewdness, says St. Anthony, a thousand bad thoughts follow them step by step; they feel that their imagination takes them back to the scenes of their immodest pleasures. The objects which they have seen, the conversations they have heard, the embraces that they have received and returned, come into their head, seduce their heart, and fill them with the desire of returning; and, *in fact*, they return as often as possible. The excessive passion that they conceive for these foolish joys strips them even of a thought of avoiding them, makes them forget their most important duties, inspires them with disgust for the practice of piety, with a sacrilegious contempt for religion and its holy truths, a monstrous indifference for their salvation; it hardens their heart, and leads them to despair. Such are the sad fruits of dancing, and of the sins which it occasions. Ought we any longer to be astonished at the terrible maledictions launched forth against the daughters of sin and the vanity of their dress? They, as well as those who imitate them in this practice, invented by the devil, are threatened with becoming the prey and laughing-stock of the conqueror, and with all the horrors which war and captivity bring with them. (Isaiah iii.)

What should we do to restrain our passions? We should employ watching, prayer, mortification, and penance; but young people regard these virtues as strangers to their age. Watching requires us to avoid sin and its occasions. Young people ought, therefore, to avoid the dance, which is generally an occasion of sin to them, and which exposes them to many dangers, a single one of which would suffice to destroy their virtue. Diana, daughter of Jacob and Lia, impelled by an indiscreet curiosity, wished to go, on a festival day, to the town of Sichem, to see the customs of the women of the country, and how they appeared in public. God, to punish her curiosity, and to give a warning to posterity, that young women could not avoid with too much caution all occasions of sin, permitted the son of Hemor, king of that country, to see, and conceive for her a violent passion, of which she became the unfortunate victim. He protected Sarah and Rebecca, ancestors of Diana, because they were not curious about these things; but he did not protect Diana, because she exposed herself to a danger that she ought to have shunned. It is thus that God abandons young persons who go to balls with intentions far worse than this young Israelite had. If he strengthens them against temptations which they try to avoid, but which, nevertheless, they experience, he withdraws his support from them when they seek to fall into temptation by choice. "*He that loveth danger*," says our Saviour, "*shall perish in it;*" we love it when we do not shun it; we love it far more when we seek it. All is danger in the dance: is it not to wish your own ruin to go to it? If chastity cannot be preserved without God's grace, if God gives his grace only to those who pray for it sincerely, can we be supposed to ask for it sincerely, or can we hope to obtain it, when we are disposed to go to the ball? When we ask his grace, what attention could he be supposed to pay to our request? What grace can that young woman expect who loves the pomps of Satan which she has solemnly renounced in baptism, who wishes to follow those customs of a perverse world which he has a thousand times cursed? If God would grant her any favor in such a case, would it not be that of avoiding dangerous amusements? Therefore, when she is disposed to frequent the dance, she takes care not to ask such grace from God, for she would be very sorry to obtain it. Can we be astonished, then, to see reigning in towns and places where this abuse has taken root, a crowd of disorders unknown elsewhere?

The only precaution that we can take in order to avoid the snares of the impure spirit, is to keep away from balls and dances ; for if St. Jerome, St. Arsenius, St. Benedict, St. Francis, and so many other holy hermits, in their deserts, removed from every occasion of sin, were obliged to mortify themselves, by painful works and continual fasting, to throw themselves among briers and thorns, to plunge themselves into the snow and into frozen ponds, lying there entire nights in order to resist their rebellious flesh, worn out by perpetual mortification, how shall it be possible for young people, without strength and without experience, to resist the demon of impurity in assemblies where all is capable of inflaming the most icy hearts, of exciting the most shameful passions of a corrupt body, and of adding fuel to the devouring flame in young minds so easily mastered by their rising passions? How can people walk amid the flames of such a fire without being burned?

If improper dances are criminal at all times, they are particularly so on Sundays and holy-days of obligation, which are especially consecrated to the service of the Lord. How do licentious dances agree with the worship of God? Who will be foolish enough to believe that the dancers serves and glorifies God? It would be better, says St. Augustine, to sow or to plough on the days of the Lord.

A second circumstance which renders dances more dangerous and criminal, is when they are held at night. Everyone knows that darkness, being an enemy of modesty and a friend of crime, emboldens the most timid to execute the criminal projects which they have formed. How many persons permit and receive, under favor of darkness, criminal liberties which they would not dare to countenance in daylight, through a remnant of modesty or fear of men! Nothing is more opposite to this rule of St. Paul than night dances: " *Walk soberly and modestly as in the daylight.*" (Rom. xiii. 13.)

A third circumstance which makes dances more culpable, is when they are attended by persons disguised; if the darkness of the night gives more boldness for committing wicked deeds, this boldness is naturally increased when we are confident of being unknown under a mask or other disguise. But the most dangerous manner of being disguised is when the dress of a different sex is assumed. God forbade his people in the strongest terms to do so; this prohibition regards Christians as well as Jews, and is far more binding on us, who, living under the law of grace, are obliged to greater holiness. "A woman," says the Lord, "shall not assume the dress of a man, nor a man the dress of a woman; the one that does so is abominable in the sight of God." (Deut. xxii., 5.) In fact, how many sins does not this change of dress occasion! A woman by changing her dress strips herself of modesty and chastity, which are the ornaments of her sex; and a man by assuming the dress of a woman, gives us reason to fear that he is effeminate and licentious, and feigns a change of nature which is abominable before God.

A fourth circumstance, rendering dances especially criminal, is when they are held on fasting days, and particularly during the holy season of Lent, which ought to be exclusively devoted to mortification, to weeping and grief. It is for this reason that the church has denied us our usual food. All that is mournful or afflicting is joined to fasting now, as well as when sackcloth, ashes and tears were its accompaniments among the Jews; and as it is an expression of the grief of the church, in the season when she lost her divine Spouse, conformably to these words of Jesus Christ: "The friends of the bridegroom do not mourn while the bridegroom is with them; the time will come when the bridegroom will be taken away, and then they will fast," (Matt. ix.), we see that mourning and fasting ought to be characteristic of the days on

which the church mourns the death and absence of her divine
Spouse. She has always interdicted, and still interdicts,
even innocent sports during this holy time, because they do
not become the solemn mourning obligatory on all Christians.
But by holding these dangerous amusements at all times, we
withdraw from the divine authority of the Church, which regards rebellious Christians as heathens and publicans. To
do this is in a manner to rejoice with Satan at the death of
Jesus Christ.

What we have said in general about dancing is confirmed
in the Holy Scriptures, in the writings of the Holy Fathers,
and of theologians most renowned for their piety and learning.

The Holy Ghost tells us that a female dancer should be
avoided because she is a very dangerous person. "Use not
much the company of her that is a dancer, and hearken not to
her, lest thou perish by the force of her charms; for the conversation of these women burns as fire." (Eccles. ix., 4.) In
these words the Holy Ghost forbids us not only to be in the
company of female dancers, and to look attentively at them,
to converse with them, for fear that we may perish by the
power of their charms, and be consumed by the fire of their corrupt conversations. He adds, "Tarry not among women; for
from garments cometh a moth, and from woman the iniquity
of man" (Eccles. xlii., 12–14); that is to say, as the moth
which is engendered in the garments is not perceived till the
evil is done, so also the spiritual evil, which springs from
conversations too frequent and too familiar with those of the
other sex, is not perceived at first, because it is still concealed in the thoughts and desires; but it is not slow to manifest itself in actions. It is for this reason that he adds, that
a man who injures you, and thereby gives you an occasion
for exercising your patience and temper, is better than a

woman who serves you, and who, by her engaging manners, inspiring you with love for her, and causing you to fall into sin, becomes your confusion and shame.

Again the Holy Ghost says to every one of us: "Gaze not upon a maiden, lest her beauty be a stumbling block to thee; turn away thy face from a woman dressed up, and gaze not about upon another's beauty, for many have perished by the beauty of a woman, and thereby lust is enkindled as a fire." (Eccles. ix., 5, 8, 9.) Now, if the Holy Ghost forbids us to look on a woman dressed up and fickle in her desires, and commands us not to gaze upon a maiden, is it not evident that he more strictly forbids balls, because it is at balls that numbers of giddy women and fickle maidens are assembled and occupied only in displaying their charms, in order to attract the attention of young men and enkindle their criminal passions.

If all Christians would wish to act like holy Job—set a guard on their eyes to prevent them from too attentively regarding a maiden, for fear that her beauty might be their ruin—it would not be possible to observe this in dances, since they cannot frequent them without gazing on those with whom they dance; for this is the first lesson which the teachers of this dangerous amusement inculcate to their unfortunate pupils.

Again the Holy Ghost says: "Hast thou daughters? Show not thy countenance gay towards them." (Eccles. vii., 26.)

By showing undue affection for his daughter, says the Holy Ghost, the father teaches her by his example to be rather free with persons of the other sex, and lose that fear and modesty which become the female sex. Let the behavior of a father be kind towards his daughter, but grave at the same time. It will do for her if her mother is loving and

affectionate to her.   The daughter should not wish her father
to be over-indulgent and over-affectionate towards her.   Now
I ask :

Can any one dance, especially with those of the opposite
sex, without taking with them liberties infinitely more culpable
than those the Holy Ghost here forbids?   Is it not to free
impurity from the shame which concealed it, to manifest it
before the eyes of a crowd of spectators, who are so much
infected with it themselves as to applaud its ravages?   Can
we not say that the *waltz*, which, in the opinion of even the
most careless men, can destroy the most rigid virtue, strengthens the corruption which it creates?   That it is a violent passion, which kills on the spot the soul of young women and
men, and sends them to the horrible flames of hell?

"Love not the world," says St. John, "nor the things of
the world.   If any man love the world, the charity of the
Father is not in him.   For all that is in the world is the
concupiscence of the flesh, and the concupiscence of the eyes,
and the pride of life, which is not of the Father, but of the
world." (I. Ep. ii., 16.)   If concupiscence is not of God,
then all that strengthens is not of God, but of the world.
Now, nothing is more fit for creating and strengthening concupiscence than lascivious dances, which are so much frequented at the present day.   Dances are, therefore, not of
God, but of the world, which could not invent a more dangerous diversion, nor one more fit for seducing and destroying souls.   Those who love these diversions passionately do
not belong to Jesus Christ, whose maxims are contrary to
those of the world, and whose whole life was a manifest condemnation of such amusements as the dance.

God has permitted many strong in virtue to be destroyed
there before you, in order to teach the weak that the surest
way to avoid the evil is to shun its occasions.   We are not

more holy than David, wiser than Solomon, or stronger than Samson ; we know how great a number has been destroyed by frequenting the dance house or ball room and their occasions. The sight of Bethsabee made David commit adultery ; Samson's love for Dalila caused him to lose his strength, and put him in the power of his enemies ; the strange women whom Solomon loved corrupted his heart, and led him into idolatry. Who does not tremble at the thought of these frightful examples? "If your right eye and your right hand scandalize you," says Jesus Christ, "pull out that eye, cut off that hand, and cast them far from you." (Mark ix.) It is evident that our Saviour, in saying the right hand and the right eye, wished us to understand that we should sacrifice our dearest and most precious possessions or loves in order to avoid sin. In adding that we should throw away this eye or this hand far from us, he means that we cannot avoid too much that which leads us into sin, which is the only earthly evil. As reserve in conversation, in looks, and in manners, is the only protection of chastity, a Christian, who wishes to preserve this virtue, must banish forever the thought of going to balls or dances, where it is impossible to have this reserve.

With St. Ephrem, I demand, now, of the most zealous partisans of dancing, how they will prove "that it is allowed to dance." What single one of the prophets has said so? What Gospel authorizes it? In what Epistle of the apostles is there a single word in its favor? To permit such a diversion to Christians, we must brand the law, the prophets, the writings of the apostles and evangelists, as full of errors ; but if all the words of these holy books are true and inspired by God, as they really are, it is incontestable that Christians are prohibited from frequenting or enjoying the amusements of which we speak. "Yes, there is no safety for modesty,"

20

says St. Ambrose, "where this precious virtue has every-thing to fear from the attractions of pleasure."

" Young women who love the dance," says St. Basil, "lose the fear of God, and despise the flames of hell; far from pondering, in retirement, on that terrible day when the heavens will be opened and when the Sovereign Judge of the living and the dead will descend to render to every one according to his works; far from endeavoring to purify their hearts from every bad thought, and effacing by their tears the sins they have committed, they shake off the yoke of the Lord, they trample under foot his holy law, they cast off the veil with which decency requires them to be covered; they expose themselves, without shame, to the eyes of men; they assume an impudent look, laugh immoderately, and act as becomes neither their age nor sex; they conduct them-selves like those in transports of madness, and excite by their behavior the passions of young men." (*Hom. Inebrio-sos.*) Whether they act with the intention of exciting irreg-ular passions, or do not, they are not the less culpable, for the evil is produced in either case. " It is by her dancing," exclaims St. John Chrysostom, "that the daughter of Herodias captivated the heart of Herod, who had the folly to promise, as a reward for it, to give her whatever she should ask; and she had the cruelty to demand from him the head of St. John the Baptist. It is the devil," he continues, " who made her dance so gracefully, and who made Herod fall into his snares; for he is always present where there is a dance; it is in such amusements that he is most pleased, and where he has the greatest ease in destroying souls. If dancing at the present day does not cause the death of St. John the Baptist, as that of the daughter of Herodias did, it causes a death far more sorrowful to the members of Jesus Christ. Those who dance now do not demand that the head of the holy precursor be

brought to them on a dish, but they ask, for the devil, the
souls of those present. If no daughter of Herodias appears
in the dances of our times, the devil, in whose form, as it
were, she then danced, is the spirit of them, and leads captive the souls of his dupes who frequent them." "This
spirit of darkness," says St. Augustin, "takes, as the occasion may require, different forms to attack Christians. He
had taken the form of a furious lion, when he incited infidel
princes to murder them on scaffolds, burn them at the stake,
and torture them on the rack; after the persecutions, he took
the form of a serpent, which endeavors to seduce and deceive
them." "As he cannot exercise his cruelty on their body,
he destroys their souls by dances and lust; and the better to
use his mortal poison, he conceals himself and slips under
the leaves of worldly pleasures," says the learned Gerson.
"With what address does he not deceive you," says St.
Ephriam, "and persuade you to do evil instead of good; to
leave off dancing to-day in order to return to it to-morrow;
to be to-day fervent Christians, to-morrow pagans, impious
wretches, apostates, enemies of God! Do not deceive yourself; you cannot serve two masters at once; we cannot serve
God and dance with the devil. Remember that the Saviour
has said, 'Woe to you who are in joy, for one day you will
be in affliction and tears.'" "Why do you try so much
to procure pleasures? A slight cold may put an end to
them; a single hour can separate you forever from those
with whom you are accustomed to dance. In a single hour
those feet which God has given you to walk modestly, and
which you use so ill, may be immovable, stretched out stiff
in death. Then all those who have been your companions in
these diversions will abandon you. No one will be nearer to
you now than the demons whom you have obeyed, and who
await the consent of the Saviour to carry your wretched soul

into hell; for you cannot expect to rejoice with angels in heaven after having diverted yourself with demons on earth," says St. Peter Chrysologus.

"The devil," says Tertullian, "leads people no longer to the temples of idols, but to the ball, where one sees living statues, living idols, who try with all their charms to seduce the heart, and make it apostatize." If we find Christians in these profane assemblies, it is a mark that they are no longer true Christians; for can that which wounded the conscience of the primitive Christians be permitted to those of our days? Is not our holy religion as invariable in its morality as in its dogmas?

"The dance," says St. Charles, "is an ingenious invention for corrupting morals; it is the cause of bad thoughts, impure expressions, of adulteries, of the most shameful acts of impurity, of quarrels and murders; it turns away many persons from their religious duties, from prayer, holy reading, and makes them inattentive to the instructions of which they stand in extreme need. One cannot go there," continues this holy archbishop, "without frequently and grievously offending God. Can any one desire his salvation, and expose himself to so many and so great evils, which are the unhappy fruits of dancing?" [*Actes des Conciles de Milan.*]

St. Anthony, Archbishop of Florence, says that those who deliver themselves up to the fatal diversion of dancing travel on the road to hell, and will arrive there unexpectedly at some future day where the road ends. By their very act of dancing they declare themselves enemies of Jesus Christ; for they act in opposition to the commandments and sacraments which he has instituted for the sanctification of sinners. First, they go against baptism, because they violate the solemn promises they made at it to renounce the devil, all his pomps and all his works. Can one dance without following Satan, who directs it, without being attached to his pomps, or without doing his works which are sins? They act against confirmation, because, after having been marked by the seal of Jesus Christ, they dishonor him by indecent postures and gestures of the body in the dance, and show thereby that they glory in bearing the seal and character of the devil, from whom everything immodest comes. They sin against penance, because they put obstacles in the way of repentance and the sorrow which they should have for going to the dance house, or having been at the dance; they act contrary to the sacrament of the Eucharist, because, after having received Jesus Christ, they go to crucify him again in these worldly assemblies; they act against the sacrament of marriage, because the dance gives rise to thoughts and desires contrary to conjugal fidelity.

"O if some one could open your eyes to see the immense number of demons mixed up with the dancers?" says Cardinal Bellarmine; "O if some one could make you perceive with what zeal those demons attend to the men and women assembled at the dance, with what art they try to make passion for women spring up in the hearts of men, and for men in the hearts of women, the sparks, or rather the flames, of impure love, in order to make their heart a furnace of concupiscence! O if you could see how these malicious spirits rejoice at the sight of those whom they have led into sin, far from being so anxious to be present at balls and dances, you would shun them with horror.

"Avoid the society of those impure spirits who incessantly try to enkindle in the hearts of those around them the fire of lust. A young man cannot dance with a young woman without feeling the sparks of an impure flame. If adultery and fornication are sins, the dance must consequently be so, since it leads to them."—[*Bellarm. Sermon.*]

"In fact, there is nothing in dances that does not exceed the bounds of modesty," says Petrarch* ; "they present a spectacle which cannot but displease chaste eyes ; the action of the hands, the movements of the feet, the immodesty and impudence of the looks, show that there is some internal disorder in the soul ; the least marks often show that there is something hidden in the heart. The motions of the body, the manner of being seated or reposing, the gestures, the laugh, the gait, the conversations, are so many signs by which we can tell what is passing in the soul. Those who have any love for modesty ought to allow nothing effeminate to appear in their manner, and ought not to love a diversion which leads, in the end, to impurity ; for while dancing we think less about the present pleasure than what we expect to come ; the freedom that one gives to his hands, to his eyes, to his tongue ; the immodesty of the songs, the darkness, dispel the restraint which modesty inspires, and gives loose rein to the passions. Take away impurity, and you will have destroyed dances. It is the levity of our mind that makes the body so light, and gives it the power of making the motions necessary for dancing ; so that it is properly to the dance that the words of holy David can be applied : "The wicked walk in a circle, of which the devil himself is the center." (Ps. 11, 9.)

As to the theologians most renowned for their learning, they are notoriously of one mind, not only as to the principles in this matter, but also to their application. Father Gory, an eminent theologian of the Society of Jesus, does not scruple in his Moral Theology to class among indecent dances forbidden under pain of mortal sin, according to the common opinion of theologians, the modern dances, called Waltz, Polka, Gallop and others of the same kind.

---

*Des Remedes contre la Bonne et la Mauvaise Fortune, 24·h dialogue

"It is self-evident," says this Father, "that dances rendered improper by the indecency of the costumes, *the manner of dancing*, or by words, jests, or songs are forbidden under pain of mortal sin. Among such dances, *according to the common opinion of theologians*, must be numbered the modern dances, vulgarly called the waltz, the polka, the gallop and others of the same kind."

In the Second Plenary Council of Baltimore, all the American Bishops declare that "they consider it to be their duty to warn their people against those fashionable dances which, as at present carried on, are revolting to every feeling of delicacy and propriety, and are fraught with the greatest danger to morals;" and to all those priests who have the care of souls, they say in their four hundred and seventy-second decree: "Let them attack and boldly condemn immodest dances, which are becoming more and more common every day. Let them admonish the faithful how much they sin, not only against God, but against society, against their family and against themselves, who take part in these dances, or at least seem to countenance them by their presence. Let them teach parents particularly of how grievous a judgment they become guilty if they expose their young sons and daughters to the danger of losing purity and innocence of mind by allowing them to be thus entrapped in the snares of the devil."

Soon after the Council, Archbishop Martin John Spalding enacted, in the Diocesan Synod, the following statute: "As the Fathers of the Second Plenary Council of Baltimore, in their pastoral letter to the people, wholly condemn those dances which are commonly called waltzes and round dances, we decree that they are not to be taught nor to be tolerated in the colleges, academies and schools of the diocese, even for the sake of recreation, among persons of the same sex."

Indeed, you cannot find one Pastoral, one doctrinal declaration of any kind from any Catholic Bishop explicitly containing a judgment opposed to what has been said about indecent dances; nay, it would be difficult to find a man of the world who would dare conscientiously to sign a declaration absolving from any stain of immodesty the unhappy family of these modern waltzers. No one would dare do it, so general is the contrary opinion among all men of sense.

St. Eloi, Bishop of Noyon, preached one day in a parish near Noyon, and strongly condemned dances, because they were the cause of great disorders to the inhabitants. The latter, not being able to suffer themselves to be deprived of the amusements which their forefathers practiced, and which they held from time immemorial, disobeyed the Bishop, and resolved to kill him if he spoke any more of them. Their threats did not intimidate the holy pastor, who burned with the desire of shedding his blood for his flock, and who longed for the glory of becoming a martyr. The following year he preached, on the anniversary of the former day, on the same subject, with still more vehemence than before. His zeal was met with insults and outrages; the people talked of massacring him; but the veneration of his sanctity was so great that no one dared raise his hand to strike the holy man. St. Eloi, seeing that his exhortations did not produce the desired effects, "gave," through excommunication, the most obstinate and hardened "to the devil, to mortify their flesh, that their soul might be saved on the day of the Lord." These are the words of St. Paul, pronouncing excommunication against the incestuous Corinthian. There were more than fifty servants of Archambaud, mayor of the palace, who immediately found themselves in the power of the devil, and taught others by their example to fear the judgments of God, in those of his ministers. Their pains and humiliations lasted a whole year. The holy Bishop cured them only on the following festival, after having received their submission and that of all the inhabitants.—[*Baillet and Godescard, Life of St. Eloi.*]

ANSWERS TO OBJECTIONS.

1. There are certain persons who, in order to justify dancing, cite the example of David before the ark of the Lord.

If they give the name of dance to the action of David in this circumstance, they must at least avow that it was not a dance like any of those we speak of. " This holy king did not dance through love of pleasure," says St. Ambrose, " but through a spirit of religion; not to strengthen his passions, but to make his love for God more evident and public, and to publish his gratitude to him for his benefits, who was now crowning his wishes; not to make himself be admired by the spectators, but to humble and abase himself before God, in whose sight all are as nothing." Can we compare the dances of our times with that of David? Do people go to dances to humble themselves before the Lord, to give homage to his greatness and majesty, to manifest their gratitude to him for all his liberality? Do people sing holy songs, that elevate the soul in our modern dance houses and ball rooms? On the contrary, do we not hear licentious airs and dissolute songs, which plunge the soul into the filth of sin, and inspire it with love for creatures? Are not men and women mixed up together in those hells? Are there not discourses and liberties permitted, the very mention of which make modesty blush? It is foolish, then, to pretend to authorize dancing, where there is not a thought of God permitted, by quoting the example of David, whose dance expressed the sentiments of the most lively gratitude and the most perfect piety towards his Creator.

2. Some again will say, I grant that public dances are dangerous, but I do not see the same danger in private dances.

Holy Scripture, the Fathers and the best theologians of the Church make no difference between public and private dances; they teach unanimously that they are equally dangerous, because they expose one to the same dangers, the same occasions to sin; they are sometimes even more dangerous than public dances. In a public assembly a young woman fears all eyes. She knows that all present observe everything, and that a gesture, a glance may become the object of severe criticism; but in private assemblies she is not so much reserved, because she is less afraid of unfavorable criticism. Rest assured that hundreds of young women who have come to ruin owe their disasters to attending night parties, balls, and dancing soirées.

If parents would only attend some of these devilish institutions for corrupting the morals of young girls, they would as soon cut their daughters' throats as to allow them to frequent those villainous places. If a young girl attends one of these night festivals the chances are that after the heat of the dance she drinks some beer, or perhaps something stronger, until she forgets all moral restraints, and too often becomes a victim of her own folly. In order to illustrate the evil influences of such associations, we would relate a case coming under our own knowledge:

A young man and his sister who were fond of social amusements one night in a certain garden formed the acquaintance of a very accomplished, gentlemanly young fellow and "his sister." They were captivated with each other's society, and soon the brothers and sisters changed partners. The new and fascinating acquaintances were nothing more than swindlers and worse. The result was that the young man became so infatuated with the siren ways of his charmer that he robbed his employers to keep her in money, and is to-day in Sing Sing, while his amiable sister became a victim to the seductive wiles of her new friend, and in mercy the grave hides her shame. What will parents who allow their daughters or even sons to frequent such places say to this? It may be gratifying to their vanity to read in the columns of the devil's organ the announcement that Miss Blank dressed in silk and satin and was admired by all the guests, and was waited upon by the handsome Mr. Sparkle. The devil gloats over their floolish delight, for he knows too well that for this poor enjoyment Miss Blank has bartered her eternal salvation.

3. But if young people are not allowed to dance, they may do worse.

A greater evil does not excuse a less; we cannot even approve of the smallest, since we are commanded to avoid all. Would it not be the height of folly to believe one's self authorized to commit a slight fault because a great one is forbidden, or to commit a great one because a small one is condemned? To think or act thus shows that your eyes are shut to the truth, and that you are determined to commit evil on every favorable occasion.

4. There are certain parents who say that if their daughters go to dances they will get married sooner or more advantageously.

It is great folly to imagine that by going to dances wealthy acquaintances will be formed and marriages more readily accomplished.

If a young woman be mild, modest, diligent, obedient to her parents, regular in her conduct, the fame of her virtues will draw her from oblivion, and make her known enough; she will obtain the respect and esteem of honest men, who will never speak of her but with praise. Even the worldly, in whose eyes she has no fault than that of not participating in their foolish pleasures, cannot but feel a sentiment of respect and esteem for her, on account of her virtues. If a young man who prefers libertinism to virtue, does not seek her acquaintance, ought she to be afflicted thereat? Ought she not, on the contrary, to be glad that she shall not have as husband a young man who probably would render her unhappy, and whose perverted example and wicked discourse would end perhaps in perverting herself? Is it not a happiness that a libertine of this sort avoids her, and leaves her in peace in her father's house?

But if he is a good man and well instructed, who prefers virtue to vice, he will be happy to obtain for a wife such a virtuous young woman. They will be, as the Holy Ghost says, "the recompense of each other's merits." (Prov. xxix.) If the fear of offending God hinders this maiden from appearing at these profane assemblies, her good Father in heaven, who is never conquered in generosity, will not permit so praiseworthy a motive to be an obstacle to her happiness. "Seek first the kingdom of heaven, and all else shall be added over and above." In fact, if God takes care of a poor sparrow, if he wishes not a single hair of our head to fall without his permission, can he remain indifferent in regard to a young woman who, in order to serve him, avoids these profane dances? What can he refuse this beloved child, who is entirely devoted to him, and who, by her faithful discharge of her duties, renders herself worthy of his love? He will send her from afar, as he did to Sarah, a Tobias who will render her happy.

You, young woman, who, in order to be sought in marriage, do not omit any opportunity to appear at dances, who appear so giddy, so free in your manner, and who permit all sorts of liberties from young men, do not think that this is the way by which you will best succeed. Are you then so little acquainted with the world as not to see that this young man who takes these liberties would be very sorry to have you for a wife? He wishes to divert himself and pass his time with you; but the thought never once enters his head of uniting his lot to yours. Do you think that any man of good sense would prefer a flirting, giddy woman, a dancer by profession, to a young woman of sober, modest, and decent disposition, who leads a Christian life in retirement? Undoubtedly he will take pleasure in dancing with you, but at heart he will not esteem you—he will despise you; he will regard you as a woman without restraint and of very equivocal virtue. He will easily imagine that you are not more modest with others than with himself, and that you would be far more foolish than now if you were once engaged in the bonds of marriage.

" There is lying in this grave," said a sexton to a missionary, pointing out the grave of one lately buried, " a young woman about eighteen years of age. She had a practice of going to the dancing houses. One evening in the dancing house she picked up with a Protestant young man; they danced and talked together. The time passed on and it was getting late. The Protestant young man asked her if she would marry him. She was silent for a few moments. She remembered very well she had often heard the priest say it is a very bad thing for Catholics to marry Protestants, or those of any other religion—that God does not bless these marriages. No matter, she answered 'Yes'—she promised to marry him. They do not think about these things in dancing houses. Before the marriage the young man made many fine promises; how she should go to Mass every Sunday, and he would go with her, and the children should be christened by the priest, and brought up Catholics, and very likely, he said, he would become a Catholic himself. This marriage took place—a dancing house marriage! She was married to the Protestant young man. It was a bright sunshiny morning, the morning of the marriage, but there were dark clouds not very far off. The Protestant young man behaved pretty well to her for a few months. At last the dark cloud came. The Protestant young man came home one day to his dinner. He sat down at the table and began to eat. The meat was not to his liking. There was a sulky anger on his face. At length he stood up on his feet, holding the knife clenched in his hand, fury and rage flashing from his eyes. He cursed his wife and said : ‘ You Popish beast, I will stick you with th's knife, and take every drop of Popish blood out of you !’ The wife turned deadly pale ; she fell off the chair ; her senses were gone with the fright. She recovered her senses again, but it was only to live for a day or two. She died of the shock which the fright had given her ! And now, your reverence,” said the sexton, “ she lies buried under this wall, where the ivy grows, and it is just a year since she was married. So ended the dancing house marriage.”

.5. Some will say that balls in high society which are frequented only by the rich and those who are well educated do not offer these occasions of sin you speak of ; the surveillance that one has over the other banishes all kinds of disorder.

At the present time men, in what it is universally agreed to call good society, allow themselves to say incredible things to women. You will not, I know, attempt to deny it. And why is this?

They dare venture on *saying* much, because they are permitted to *do* much.

They dare venture so far in their speech, because they are permitted to go so far in their acts. Do not be scandalized! It is not simply familiarity, but it is audacity which is the fruit of these dances. These men do not feel themselves bound to treat with too scrupulous a respect those who do not respect themselves sufficiently. All the exterior polish of the world will never prevent things from being what they are.

A conscientious Christian, therefore, does not dance round dances even in good society.

Miss Sherman, the daughter of the Commanding General of the United States Army, and holding a conspicuous place in the highest society of Washington, never would dance any of the round dances. When Prince Albert visited that city there was great rivalry among the ladies for the honor of being his partner in the dance. Miss Sherman was the chosen one; but with a moral courage greater than that of the soldier upon the field of battle, while hundreds of envious female eyes were gazing at her, she declined to waltz, even at the invitation of a prince who may one day be King of Great Britain. The Prince, instead of being offended, had the good sense to honor the young lady for her rigid adhesion to the virtuous principles in which she had been educated by her pious mother. He invited her again when the music admitted of the plain square dances. She now accepted the invitation. The Prince afterwards remarked that of all the ladies he had seen in America, he esteemed and honored Miss Sherman most. And, as a memento of his high appreciation, he sent her from England an elegant piece of jewelry. God, who seems to have raised up this young girl from the capital of the country to give a lesson of Christian modesty to all her sex, rewarded her moreover by a wedding more brilliant than that of the daughter of the President himself, and moved the Khedive of Egypt to make her a more magnificent bridal present than any other lady in this country ever received.

As to the surveillance that one has over the other, let me ask, can it extend to the heart? Does it protect the soul from the poisoned arrows which the seductive objects assembled hurl at it? Does it render the heart insensible to the attraction of these girls and women who display themselves in a gaudy dress to receive the homage and sacrilegious incense of adoring fools? Does this surveillance repress bad thoughts, and the consent given to them from the heart? or does it prevent the mind from consenting in secret to the indulgence of the thoughts which the dance created?

If fear hinders a young man from manifesting his feelings, his soul is not the less free from bad desires, nor less seduced by the beauty of a young woman, as the heart of Holofernes was captivated by the beauty of Judith, and that of a Sichemite prince by the charms of Dina.

I say the same thing of the presence of parents; if it hinders their children from extreme excesses, it is unable to prevent the too subtile poison of impurity from penetrating into their hearts by their eyes and ears, to repress thoughts and desires; desires of the flesh which escape the most clear-sighted. What use is it to appear pure in the eyes of men, if one is not so in the eyes of *him who examines the heart and reins, and whose observation nothing can escape?*

6. "But," cries the fair dancer, "you must remember that no lady will permit herself to be introduced to or accept as a partner any but a gentleman, who she is sure will treat her with becoming respect."

I will not ask what your definition of a "gentleman" is—whether the most courteous and urbane of men may not be a most desperate and profligate man at heart. The attitude, motions and contact, etc., are the same in any case. Let your partner be the crême de la crême of all that is respectable and eligible in society, you cannot perform with him the waltz, in its various shapes of "Dip," "Glide," "Saratoga," "German," and what not—the King of Dances "with all the modern improvements," and remain a respectable lady.

Nor are even the square dances any longer left as a refuge for the more modest; for to such a pitch has the passion for their public sexual intimacy come that the waltz is now inseparably wedded to the quadrille. It may be said that every arrangement of the dance looks to an "equitable" distribution of each lady's favors.

But if it even be supposed that a lady can waltz virtuously, it is sure that in that case she cannot dance *well.* And what a pitiful spectacle, surely, is that of a lady trying "how not to do it"—converting her natural grace into clumsiness in order that she may do an indecent thing decently and remain " *Warm, but not wanton; dazzled, but not blind.*"

How then can even the most ardent lovers of the dance be blind to its impurity? Is there one so-called respectable woman among them who would submit to be painted or photographed in the attitude she assumes while dancing the latest variety of dance—even though her partner in the picture, instead of being a stranger just met for the first time, were her most intimate friend—aye, even though he were her husband? Not one of them would submit to be thus depicted. But if some maiden could be persuaded, what a pleasing family picture it would be for the husband and children to gaze upon in later years! Had I such a one to illustrate this book with, the success of its wide circulation would be most sure with the simple drawback of the author being held amenable to an offended law for issuing obscene pictures.

21

814 THE SIXTH COMMANDMENT.

7. "You imagine dangers," says another one, "which do not exist. You are frightened at shadows. I am accustomed to these amusements; they do not make the least impression on me."

I answer, you cannot spoil an old egg.

O all ye holy hermits and penitents, throw away your coarse sackcloth, leave your dreary deserts, cease your fasts and your vigils, come back into our cities; clothe yourselves with purple and fine linen; feast sumptuously and enjoy the good things of this life. The age of innocence has returned to earth. The lion may now lie down with the lamb, and the child may play with the fangs of the serpent. Come, I will show you the grandest miracle you ever beheld. See our young men and young women. They are well dressed, well nourished, brought up in ease and luxury. They can whirl in the giddy dance, and speak love to eye, and listen to voluptuous music, and take moonlight strolls, and receive affectionate embraces, and sit for hours alone together at night, and read the most insidious romances, and yet they never do anything wrong; no, they have not a single bad thought. Come down then from your pedestal, O Angelic St. Aloysius; that innocent model young man will take your place; and you, O Saint Virgin Rose, make room to that impeccable young girl! Let her be placed in your niche, with her snow-white ball dress, fit emblem of the snow-white purity of her soul! It is true, that ball dress is of very frail texture, but don't whisper a word about its frailty lest some wicked tongue be tempted to make some comparison between it and the wearer's virtue!

But let me ask those persons who say that whilst at dances they never experienced the bad effects generally attributed to dancing—let me ask them: Do you watch sufficiently over your hearts to perceive all the evil that is working in

them? Did you fear sin enough, you would be alarmed at
what leads to it. You think you have escaped all the dangers of dancing if you avoid such external thoughts as are
gross and revolting in the eyes of everybody. You look
upon immodest thoughts and desires arising on such occasions, as light faults to which the Lord, as you imagine, pays
no attention.

Nevertheless, it is bad thoughts and desires, and internal
consent which we give to them, that form, in reality, sin ;
for a wicked action, which we could not prevent, to which
we did not willingly expose ourselves, and to which we did
not consent, does not sully the soul which has had no part
in it, and consequently is no sin ; but bad thoughts and bad
desires blacken the soul, kill it, and make it fit for eternal
chastisements in hell. If a young woman looks on a young
man *to lust after him*, she has already committed sin in her
heart ; if, according to the divine oracle, it is the same with
respect to a young man looking at a woman, how many sins
of thoughts and desires do young persons of both sexes commit at dances, although they do not commit a single wicked
action !

Nevertheless, I will suppose for a moment, what I have
much difficulty to believe, that people never have suffered
any spiritual damage from merely frequenting dances ; supposing this, I say with St. John Chrysostom (Homil, xxxiii.
in Math.), is it not certainly a great loss and injury to your
soul and salvation, to employ so ill a time of which all the
moments are infinitely precious to you, and to make it a subject of scandal to others? For when leaving these diversions, though even yourself have not been injured by them,
are you not guilty of inspiring others, by your example, with
a greater love for these dangerous pleasures? On this account all the disorders which spring up in regard to others,

weaker than you, recoil on your head; for since if no one
would frequent dance houses, there would be no dances, it
follows, that being a mere looker-on is as bad as to participate in the amusement, because our presence makes dancing
to be kept up, and the spectators will go to hell as well as
those who sin by joining in the amusement. Therefore, even
though you could dance without injuring your chastity, still
you would deserve severe punishment for having contributed
to the ruin of others by your bad example. Certainly, however chaste you may be, you will be much more so by avoiding these dangerous pleasures.

Ah, when the cup of pleasure is full and foaming, it fills,
indeed, those who drink it with a wild delicious joy; but at
the bottom of the cup, the dregs are bitter as gall, and their
poison burns in the brain as with the fire of hell. When the
young girl, who has spent the night in unbecoming dances,
awakes from her slumber, in broad daylight, ah, God, what
ails her then? Her heart is stung by remorse. A deadly
weariness possesses her; her heart cries aloud in her anguish.
Ah! last night, it was so happy, and now! O how utterly
miserable! An unutterable sadness devours me; I can only
weep and suffer and weep. Whither shall I turn? Where
shall I find relief? A burning thirst for happiness consumes
me. How shall I appease it? The spectral voice of conscience upbraids me in my sadness. It tells me that the
pleasures of the ball room are vain and fleeting; they pass
and leave the heart an empty arid desert. In vain I seek
new pleasure; in vain I fly to the dance; vainly I drain the
cup of pleasure; I find but dregs at the bottom, and they
burn in the brain like the fire of hell!

The immortal soul is too noble, too sublime, to be satiated
with the husks of swine. All the pleasure that earth can
give will never satisfy the human heart. There is in it a

void that God alone can fill. After you have tasted of all earth's pleasures, there remains to you but the empty solitude of a weary heart.

Let us, then, not argue uselessly; let us not imagine vain excuses or defences which have no weight before God. Our greatest defence is in avoiding this furnace of Babylon, and flying, like the chaste Joseph, the Egyptian seducer, when, to escape her wiles and hands, it becomes necessary to abandon all, even our clothes. By doing so we shall procure true and solid pleasures by peace of conscience, which will no longer be troubled by remorse; we shall spend in this world a pure and chaste life, and obtain in heaven life eternal by the grace and goodness of our Lord Jesus Christ.

8. There are others who, in order to justify dancing, appeal to the authority of St. Francis de Sales; they allege that this great saint and doctor of the Church is not opposed to balls and parties.

St. Francis de Sales was too enlightened to teach anything contrary to good sense and the doctrine of the Fathers of the Church. In the 33d and 84th chapters of his *Introduction to a Devout Life*, he shows the danger and poison of dances and proposes the most pressing motives to dissuade Christians from taking any part in them. He says in the first place "that balls and parties are in their nature indifferent; but then the manner in which they are carried on renders them extremely destructive, as the soul is endangered by them." Now, St. Francis de Sales never said that it was permitted to love danger, and voluntarily to expose one's self to it.

He adds, "What makes these recreations so susceptible of mischief is, that being generally carried on in the darkness and obscurity of night, it is by no means surpising that several vicious circumstances should obtain easy admittance,

since the subject is of itself so susceptible of evil. The ama-
teurs of these diversions, by sitting up late at night, disable
themselves from discharging their duty to God on the morning of the day following. Is it not then a kind of madness
to exchange the day for night, light for darkness, and good
works for criminal fooleries? Everyone strives to carry the
most vanity to the ball ; and vanity is so congenial to the
growth of evil affections and dangerous familiarities, that
both are the natural consequences of such amusements."
Such are the reflections of a saint; are they those of a person who approves of dancing?

"I have the same opinion of dances," continues St. Francis, "as physicians have of mush-rooms; as the best of
them, in their opinion, are good for nothing; so I tell you,
the best ordered balls are good for nothing. Mush-rooms
attract the infection and poison of serpents that approach
them; so also nocturnal meetings ordinarily attract the reigning vices and sins together; viz: quarrels, envy, scoffing, and
wanton loves; and as these exercises open the pores of the
bodies of those who use them, so they also open the pores of
their hearts, and expose them to tne danger of some serpent
taking the advantage to breathe some loose words or lascivious suggestions into the ear, or of some basilisk casting an
impure look, or wanton glance of love into the heart, which
being thus opened is easily seized upon and poisoned."
Such is the doctrine taught by St. Francis de Sales. Can
any person say that such language authorizes balls and
parties?

"These idle recreations," adds the great saint, "chase
away the spirit of devotion, and leave the soul in a languish-
ing condition; they cool the fervor of charity, and excite a
thousand evil affections in the soul. It is for this reason,"
continues the holy bishop, "that they ought never to be per-

mitted, and not even in necessity, without the greatest precaution."

Remark, attentively, these last words, and understand well their meaning, for he spoke in this manner for fear that the world or some false teacher would lead you into some error, or snare; for this great saint knew well that there were certain inevitable dangers in the world, according to the words of our Saviour, who, seeing the corruption of the world, said: *It must needs be that scandals come;* even the virtuous themselves would be sometimes obliged to bear testimony to them. The holy bishop, therefore, through charity for virtuous souls, thought it his duty to caution them on those dangerous occasions, when they would at times find themselves, as it were, necessitated to engage in the like recreations.

But of what case of necessity does he speak? He himself explains it: "It is," says he, "upon an occasion when you cannot absolutely refuse; when prudence and discretion demand your compliance with a company. But such occasions are extremely rare," says the holy prelate; "that is to say, it seldom happens that one is ever so necessitated, because he ought to dread, foresee and shun such occasions. If you love such dangers, and if you engage in them when you can conveniently avoid them, then they are voluntary, and you are guilty before God for having exposed yourself; for, according to the Holy Ghost, *he who loves danger shall perish in it.*

If you should find yourself, without any fault of yours, present at a ball or dance, and that you could not *absolutely* leave the company, then conduct yourself on the dangerous occasion with much discretion, bearing in mind the wise precaution that St. Francis lays down. "If you must eat mushrooms," says he, "highly season them, and eat but sparingly of them, otherwise their malignancy becomes a poison." In like manner, if you find yourself necessitated to dance, dance but little, and let all the circumstances be seasoned by the remembrance of God's holy presence ; let it be done to please him only, and do it with great modesty.   It is necessary that when you find yourself, as it were by necessity, at an assembly where such amusements are carried on, to make use of some salutary reflections to guard yourself against the dangerous impressions that such vain pleasures are apt to make upon the heart.

"The following," says St. Francis, "are the reflections you ought to make " :

1.   " Consider that during the time you are dancing, innumerable souls are burning in the flames of hell, for the sins they had committed in dancing or were occasioned by their dances.   2.   That many religious and devout persons of both sexes are at the very time prostrate before God, bewailing their sins, while you are at the ball.   3.   That whilst you are dancing millions of souls depart out of this world in great anguish, and that thousands of thousands of men and women then suffer great pains in their beds, in hospitals, in the streets, by the gout or burning fevers ; and do you not think that you shall one day groan as they do, whilst others shall dance as you did.   4.   That our Blessed Saviour, his Virgin Mother, and angels and saints behold you at the ball. 5.   That, in fine, while you are there, time is passing away, death is advancing, and that very soon it will hasten you to the judgment seat of God."

We are not obliged to use much precaution in doing what is innocent in it itself ; so that when we perceive so great and pious a man as was St. Francis de Sales exacting such precautions for balls and such amusements, it evidently proves that he considered such diversions unlawful, or dangerous, and we ought to do every thing we possibly can to shun them.

If any were permitted to attend dances, it would not be those who love and cherish them; inconstant and dissipated persons, who have but little or no love for God, or who do not fear to offend him; dances, according to the instructions of the great saint, will be pernicious to them. Pious souls, enemies to the vanities and follies of the world, and those endeared to God by ardent love, have less danger to fear than others. Such was St. Elizabeth, Queen of Hungary, who, though obliged at times to attend the assemblies of profane amusements, departed from them with her heart filled with greater devotion. Such was also Queen Esther, who was indispensably bound to ornament herself with great pomp, to appear on certain occasions with the king: yet she detested from her heart the pompous appearance of her vain dress, and united herself more intimately to her God.

Everything contributes to the santification of souls who sincerely love God. What to others would be dangerous or evil, they convert into a blessing. They anxiously preserve the grace of God, the fire of divine love, while others lose both; like great fires, says St. Francis de Sales, which are increased by the winds, whilst smaller ones are extinguished.

Thus you see the opinion of a holy bishop concerning dances and balls, in which you may observe that he has not made a solitary remark upon masquerades, for he considers it unnecessary in addressing Christians to advert to such unlawful amusements; because there is no sensible Christian who does not see that such abuses are not only unbecoming their condition, but every one of common sense. If paganism itself condemned such disorders, with how much greater reason does religion forbid and prohibit them.

9. In such matters, you say to yourself, one is apt to be too severe, when not oneself is a man of the world.

Experience engenders a broader toleration. Priests render heavy that yoke which our Lord proclaimed light.

To this objection Cardinal Dechamps of Mechlin, Belgium, replies as follows:

" Set your mind at rest on this point. We are not so ignorant of the world as you imagine, and we know with certitude the law which must be obeyed by all. Besides there are two worlds: the inner and the outer; the visible world and the world of the conscience. Granted that you are men more of the outer world than we are, you will at least allow that we are men more of the world of conscience than you are; and it is not your world, but ours which God will judge.

" As to the law which governs this world, and according to which it will be judged, it is none of our making. We are not legislators.

" The Church herself has but the power to make laws in order to enforce the observance of the law of God. She is but the organ of God, and her teaching is but the echo of the divine law, echo divinely faithful, living and life giving though it be, according to the promises of Jesus Christ, verified by the experience of nineteen centuries.

" She has ever condemned a pharisaical spirit, jansenism and rigorism, and all those hypocritical doctrines which would put upon the shoulders of the faithful burdens which God has not imposed. But at the same time she has ever rejected latitudinarian doctrines of those accommodating moralists whose worldly prudence finds reasons and excuses for all; or at least motives for authorizing, by a cowardly silence, the most manifest abuses, which would be rejected with horror by Christian consciences, if only their good inspirations were seconded.

" You ask of what abuses we speak, and if we allude to those modern dances, which have become a subject of *offence* in all that portion of society which still desires to remain Christian?

"Yes, these are the abuses to which we allude. But you will say, have you no hesitation in qualifying them thus? Will you have the goodness to remember that we do not enter the pulpit (*Cathedra veritatis*) to preach our own thoughts, to seek an unknown truth; but that we teach what we know: *Græci sapientiam quaerunt, nos autem praedicamus.*

"We know, thank God, that none may transform their *opinion* into *law;* and that such temerity, culpable in any case, would here become profanation. But we also know that none may transform *law* into *opinion.*

"The moral law relating to dancing is not in Christian society and in the Catholic Church an enigma which each may solve for himself, or to which he may give any interpretation he thinks proper. There exist on this point of moral law certain principles, universally taught, and which may be rejected by none, seeing that they are those of the wisest, the holiest, and the most authentic organs of the Church herself.

"But in order to remove any pretext for misapprehension, we will single out from among the voices, to which the Church bids us listen, those of two learned theologians, two saintly Bishops and Doctors of the Church accused of laxity by the rigorists of the last century, so careful were they to impose no burden of uncertain obligation on the faithful. 'Dances,' according to St. Alphonso di Liguorio, 'are not in themselves sinful. *Secundum se non sunt malæ, nec actus libidinis, sed lætitiae*; but they become so if they are performed with a bad intention, or in a manner capable of exciting our passions, or those of others, *nisi malo fine fiant, aut cum periculo alios aut seipsum incitandi ad libidinem, vel cum aliâ circumstantiâ malâ.* When the Fathers condemn dancing, they

speak of indecent dances, and of the abuse of dancing;
*Quando sancti Patres eas interdum valde reprehendunt,
loquuntur de turpibus, et de earum abusu.* (Lib. 4, Tract. 4,
No. 429. *Theol. moral.*)

"'With regard to dances,' writes St. Francis de Sales,
'I say what doctors say of mushrooms: the best are good
for nothing; and I say that the best balls are scarcely good
for much; if, however, you will eat mushrooms, take care to
have them well dressed. If circumstances render it obligatory for you to go to balls, be careful of your dances. How
so? See that they are modest, dignified, and have a pure
intention. The doctors say of mushrooms that we should
eat of them sparingly and rarely, for however well cooked
an excess in quantity is mortal. On the same principle I
say, dance little and rarely, lest you run the risk of becoming attached to dancing.

"After dancing," adds the saint, "you must nourish
yourself with certain good and holy thoughts, which will
prevent the dangerous impression this vain pleasure might
leave in your minds."

You see, the most condescending of sages, the gentlest of
men, the great and learned Bishop of Geneva, raised up as
it were by Providence to serve as a guide to the multitude
the most deeply engaged in the world, permits dancing only
on conditions of the manner being modest, and this pleasure
being rare, moderate, and undertaken with a good intention.
Now I ask you: is society in general, are you in particular,
faithful to these conditions, required by the most tolerant of
saints? Instead of dancing little and seldom, do you not
dance much and often? The moderation which, as you have
just heard, is indispensible, is it not sacrificed by you to that
excess which constitutes the life of pleasure, and which saps
the sources of piety, charity, and Christian earnestness?

But is moderation alone sacrificed? Two answers, we are convinced, will arise—one on the lips, the other in the heart. The lips will say: No, there is no excess; sermons are not to be taken literally. St. Francis de Sales is too severe for our day. *Little, rarely, moderately,* all this betrays the style of the "good old days;" it doesn't do for us. After all, we must do like the rest of the world.

But the truth, which human respect will banish from the lips, will be avowed in the heart; and we shall be forced to acknowledge two vices needing reformation: The *quantity* and the *quality.* The excess in quantity we have sufficiently demonstrated, the quality we have only hinted at, and we confess the repugnance we feel to define it more clearly. We find no modest expressions in which to say what you *do;* we blush to describe what you do not blush to execute.

We will content ourselves with listening to the "world" itself, and thus we will hear its defence before judging it. A very clever author, M. Boulay, who most certainly does not sin by an excessive severity, speaks as follows in a work entitled *Réforme de la danse des salons:* "Have we alone cast a glance of uneasiness on the dances of the modern ball-room; are we the first to raise the doubt? Surely not, and we shall perhaps find ourselves in very good company. If we were to recall all we have heard on this subject, we should only be regarded as a very feeble echo of protestations, which become daily more numerous and more general."

After a historical sketch of the different dances which have turn by turn scandalized and demoralized society, he adds:

"These dances, of foreign origin, are not adapted either to our character or to our usages; they shock our eyes, if we only for a moment consider them seriously; they wound our most delicate susceptibilities, if we examine them from that point of view, and as delay would only entail greater abuses, we must put a stop to them at once.   In a word, their condemnation, pronounced already in every mind, may be expressed simply thus :   'They are not proper.' "

The author of *l' Histoire de la société francaise pendant le Directoire*, describes with still greater truth the waltz, introduced into France by the despicable women who then ruled society.   You deserve to hear this definition since you do not scruple to practise it.   Do not be shocked ; what you dare to show to all eyes may well reach your ears.   And yet we hesitate again from this act of justice which we owe ourselves and you ; and once more we blush to *say* what you do not blush to *do*.   Thus we spoke in our sermon ; but what we refrained from saying in the sanctuary we have not the same scruple to write here.   It is surely the least we can do, to put before your eyes what you expose also to all eyes, and it becomes a duty for us to take away from you all the right to accuse us of exaggeration and to defend thus what morality condemns.   Hear then a man of the world :   " These women must have a dance *abandonnée* . . . they grant more than their smile, more than their look, more than their hand ; it is a reel, voluptuous and intimate, in which the couple wedded by the rhythm of the dance, breast to breast, whirl round, locked in each others arms ;   mothers are afraid to scold, husbands to pass for jealous, women become tops, and the modern waltz begins in these days of utter license its immodest reign in the degenerate ball-rooms of a degenerate France."

But as we live in America, it may be better to give the opinion of an American dancing-master, and of an American author on this subject :

Professor James Welch, a dancing-master, interviewed in the Philadelphia *Press*, declared that "never in his ten year's experience in teaching the art of dancing was the waltz so immodest, vulgar and generally demoralizing as it is at present. "Ten or fifteen years ago the waltz was not so objectionable as at present," said Mr. Welch. "Dances of to-day come into altogether too close contact. In the old time a gentleman merely touched a lady's waist, at the same time holding her right hand in his left. Now he throws his arms clear around her form, pulls her closely to him, as though fearful of losing her, brings his face into actual contact with her cheek, and, in a word, hugs her. Such action is altogether too familiar, but still custom and society sanction it, and, instead of improvement for the better, we see, year after year, a marked advance in the improprieties of the dance. In the old days the waltz was comparatively modest; now it is just the reverse, and the waltz is calculated to do more injury to the young than many of the vices that are preached against from the pulpit and deeply deplored in private life. I have made it my practice for years to attend balls and parties in order to keep pace in my teaching with the popular demand. I have no hesitation in saying that I attribute much of the vice and immorality now prevailing to the insidious influence of the waltz. This may seem an overstraining of the point, but it is my honest conviction. I tell you that in the higher circles young ladies at parties and balls are absolutely hugged by men who were altogether unknown to them before the music for the waltz began to inspire the toes of the dancers. Is this a pleasant sight to contemplate? I have seen couples so closely interlocked that the face of the man was actually in contact with that of the girl in his arms. I have seen kisses interchanged amid the whirl of the maddening waltz.

"There are six (?) dances now in vogue that involve the hugging principle of the waltz," he says. "They are the

plain waltz, which was introduced by the Germans (who seldom, by the way, take part in square dances); the glide, a
very fashionable and pretty dance; the redowa, which has
held its own for many generations of dancers; the Danish
(half march and half waltz), and the three-step galop."

This description, given by a man who ought to know, is
exact. It is not the work of an extremist who, in his zeal,
imagines more than he sees, and lets his indignation run
away with him. It is not given by a priest who never saw
a "round" dance and who takes the testimony of others.
It is not open to the objection which some young people
make to strictures on their favorite art, that they are too
severe. It is not too severe. It is taken from life; and any
person who cares so little for his reputation as to venture to
attend a party where "round" dancing is permitted, may
verify it. During a long-drawn-out dance called the "German," or cotillion, which sometimes lasts three hours, the
young woman changes her partners many times, and is
"hugged" by every man in the "set."

To this testimony of a dancing-master we add that of Wm.
Herman, author of "The Dance of Death." In his little
book he says: "I have repeatedly declared, and I now do
so again, that the waltz has grown to be a purely sexual
enjoyment. That I may not be supposed to stand alone in
this assertion, I will quote the words of a worthy clergyman.
He writes: 'The dance consists substantially of a system
of means, contrived with more than human ingenuity, to excite the instincts of sex to action, however subtile and disguised at the moment, in its sequel the most bestial and degrading. It is a usage that regularly titillates and tantalizes
an animal appetite as insatiable as hunger, more cruel than
revenge.'

"Gail Hamilton, in a contribution to an Eastern journal,

says: 'The thing in its very nature is unclean and cannot be washed. The very *pose* of the parties suggests impurity.'

"That the waltz has been the acknowledged avenue to destruction for great multitudes, is a truth burnt into the hearts of thousands of downcast fathers and broken-hearted mothers; and the husbands are legion who can look upon hearths deserted and homes left desolate by wives and daughters who have been led captive by this magnificent burst of harmony and laying on of hands. One of our ablest writers says: 'It is a war on home, it is a war on physical health, it is a war on man's moral nature; this is the broad avenue through which thousands press into the brothel.'

"The dancing hall is the nursery of the divorce court, the training ship of prostitution, the graduating school of infamy, it is the abomination that maketh desolation.

"Does the scandal end all in the ball-room, or, as Byron says, may we not marvel, '*If nothing follows all this palming work* (and who does feel himself constrained to believe that), *something does follow at a fitter time?*'

"Picture to yourself the condition to which a young girl is reduced by the time that her carriage is announced. All the baser instincts of her nature are aroused — to use the words of Erasmus, she has 'a pound of passion to an ounce of reason.' Is she not now in a fit state to fall an easy prey to the destroyer? to pay for the sweetness of 'stolen waters' and the pleasantness of bread 'eaten in secret?'

"The comedy ends in tragedy. When the man is himself and the woman herself; when their dream of love is over, they come at last to despise each other. With George Herwich, they say: *Wir haben lang genug geliebt und wollen endlich hassen.*

"They now despise each other. She sets no value on his flattering praises. He no longer cares for her good opinion

22

The wine of woman's approval has gone stale, and the sunshine of man's admiration is darkened in her eyes."

And you ask after this if the dignity of woman is not sacrificed in these modern dances! If you are still tempted to deny it, I appeal to all true mothers. Tell me, Christian mothers, if the day that, conquered by *human respect*, you yielded to the torrent, you did not suffer to see your daughters given up to such pleasures as these? And you, young maidens, tell me, did not that natural modesty of yours, the gift of God, given you to be at the same time your protection and that of society, did it not for a long time protest within you before being silenced! Since you have not preserved intact this safeguard of public morals, you have also forfeited the right to feel these words too severe: "We complain of the decadence of society, of the predominance of sensuality. To prevent this decadence, this sensuality, it was necessary for woman never to have renounced that respect which was her due, never to have consented to become the occasions of corruption for Christian youth, at the very threshold of their life in the world."

You hear the witness of men of the world; it is time to turn to the judgment of men of God, and convince ourselves that the bishops of our day make use of the same language as St. Francis de Sales, and that the organs of the Holy Church have but one voice, to repeat the law of him that sent them.

"We are tempted to ask ourselves," exclaims the Cardinal de Bonald, Archbishop of Lyons, "when in one of these assemblies, if we are not in the midst of a pagan festival. In vain we seek for decency, modesty, nay for simple propriety, and we know not where to repose our eyes in this reunion of disgraceful nudities, this confusion of *wanton* and effeminate dances. No! this is no assembly of Christians;

we dare not say what it is. If we are accused of exaggeration, we ask in our turn, if these new dances, devoid of that dignity with which our ancestors pursued this recreation, are not invented for putting at their ease the worst feelings of a corrupt heart! Where, after these corrupting dances, is the heart, where the imagination of that young girl who had preserved until then her affections so pure, her sentiments so chaste? And the young man, at the age of the war of passions, how can he escape uninjured from these trials so perilous for his virtue? Sensuality has entered by every pore; its dangerous emotions have sown disorder in the heart, and he will no longer seek elsewhere but in disorder, that joy which before he found in the calm of the senses, and internal peace.

"We are no longer surprised that these modern dances have passed from our large towns to the humblest village. Hell could not but be glad to propagate rapidly this source of so many disorders, this spark, cause of conflagrations, which have cost so many, but tardy, tears. We add that we have no hesitation in saying that the heads of families, who have not sufficient courage to oppose in their own homes the abuses of which we complain, are unfaithful to their mission here on earth; they are the accomplices of this corruption of morals, which begins to know no limit, and which ravages our youth more cruelly than those epidemic scourges, which in a few days fill so many graves."

It is on the same subject that the illustrious Archbishop of Arras, Mgr. Parisis, does not hesitate to tell his clergy, when speaking of these modern dances, "that towards those young people of both sexes who practise them habitually, charity demands an inflexible firmness."

Mgr. Bauvier, an extensive writer who, weighed down with years and infirmities, died at Rome at the time of the dogmatic definition of the Immaculate Conception, does not scruple to declare : *Interesse choreis graviter inhonestis ratione nuditatum, modi saltandi . . . est peccatum mortale : hinc saltatio germanica vulgo dicta* Waltz *numquam permitti potest:* "The act of being present in a ball seriously indecent by reason of the dress, or of the manner of dancing, is a mortal sin ; consequently the German dance called the *waltz* can never be permitted.

When such enlightened bishops, whose voices are in harmony with those of the saints and sages the most authoritative in the Church Universal, assert without hesitation that waltzing can *never* be permitted, because morally sinful, will you have the temerity to declare the absolute creditude of the exact opposite, and will you not allow that dignity, decency, and even propriety, are strangely compromised in your ball-rooms?

And it is you, Christian mothers, who allow the virtue of your sons, the modesty of your daughters, to be thus put in question !

We do not go so far as to say that the latter are always the knowing accomplices of these much to be regretted abuses. But what we refuse to say of the daughter in general, we say of the mothers, who give up their daughters to these undignified dances. Yes, the great culprits are the parents, who can, doubtless, if they will, recall the ball-room to other fashions.

Let the heads of one or two families co-operate, let them insist upon their daughters being firm, and very soon the power of good example will crush the evil, and the liberty of true dignity will be accorded to those women who desire it.

10. "But we cannot help thinking that you are too severe towards us. You judge our pleasures with an excessive severity."

Severity! Do you know what severity is in this matter? If
you wish to know it, read Bourdaloue. Peruse the sermons of
this great theologian, and you will find not an exaggerated
(God forbid that we should speak so presumptuously of the
wise and famous Jesuit), but you will find a severe doctrine;
you will see, for example, balls and theatres ranked without
distinction, among forbidden pleasures. "In a word," he
asks, "balls and theatres, are they permitted or forbidden?"

"Some, enlightened by true wisdom, the wisdom of the
Gospel, condemn them; others, deceived by the false light
of a carnal prudence, justify them, or attempt the task.

"For me, dear brethren, were I not of a profession which
of itself forbids me these pleasures; if, like you, I had to
come to a decision on this head, it seems to me that at the
first glance, the simple diversity of opinion would alone be
sufficient to decide me to renounce them. For why, I should
argue, risk my peace of conscience in so vain a matter, and
for a thing I can so easily give up? On one hand I am told
that these amusements are sinful, on the other that they are
innocent; one thing is clear then, that at least they are
doubtful, and since those who maintain their sinfulness are
the most exact in their life, the most attached to their duties,
the most enlightened in the knowledge of God's law, is it
not wiser, is it not surer to follow their advice and not to
risk my salvation? This would be my conclusion, and it
would undoubtedly be the most sensible and the most reasonable. But this is *not* all, and there are stronger considera-
tions to determine me. What would be the course *I* should
pursue? I should question those whom God has given me
to be my teachers in the faith, the Fathers of the Church,
*Interroga Patrem tuum, et annuntiabit tibi; majores tuos, et
dicent tibi.*" (Deut. xxxij., 7.)

Further on he continues: "Say not that this was the

334   THE SIXTH COMMANDMENT.

moral law of one only of these great men; no, in this matter
all are agreed, they have but one voice, often the self same
expressions. Say not that such was their opinion in one
age and not in another; no, they succeed each other century
after century, and in each century they renew the same prohibition, profess the same maxims, pronounce the same decisions.

"Say not that these are the ethics of weak-minded and un-
learned men of narrow views, timid and precipitate in their
judgments; no, over and above the holiness which makes
them venerable, we know that they were men of the greatest
genius; we are in possession of their works, we see the sublimity of their wisdom, the penetration of their ta' n   the
depth, the breadth of their erudition. Say not that these
were maxims of perfection and simple counsels; you have
but to weigh their expressions, and to take them in their
obvious sense; on what subject do they speak more precisely?
Of what do they more earnestly make us fear the fatal consequences? To what do they give the force of a precept more
plainly? Say not that these maxims were founded on peculiar
or exceptional circumstances; no, I have already called your
attention to the fact that they give no other reasons than we
do; they had no others to give; what they said against the
theatre and the worldly assemblies, that same say we, and
all they say we have an equal right to say to you. Finally,
say not that they spoke for certain characters and dispositions; no, they make no distinction of conditions or tempera-
ments or dispositions; they spoke to Christians like you, and
alike to all."

Bourdaloue, you see, leaning on reason and tradition, condemns, in the name of true wisdom, all dancing as well as
theatres, and declares their defenders deceived by a false tolerance. We have felt ourselves justified in being less severe

than the illustrious Jesuit; we have ventured to follow St. Alphonsus Liguori, and make distinctions. We desire to go as far in the way of condescension as it is possible for us to go, and to say with the most tolerant of sages, St. Francis de Sales, that balls, always dangerous, may however be permitted under certain conditions; that is to say, if the dancing be modest, indulged in moderately, rarely and with a good intention.

These are our principles. Who will venture to find them too severe? And now, how did we make the applications of these incontestable principles?

We first invoked the admissions of men of the world and the judgments of men of God. To the admissions of the world, we opposed its excuses, it is true; but the latter cannot be allowed the same weight as the former, because the accused is always more trustworthy in his admissions than in his excuses. As for the judgments of men of God, we refrained from following, like Bourdaloue, a continuous chain of authorities in each century, particularly quoting the Fathers, proving as he does, that what they say is applicable to the case in point; no, in order to prevent any possible miscarriage of justice, we have simply completed this chain by contemporary and competent authorities. Recall, I beg (to mention only one), the words of Mgr. de Bonald.

What conclusion did we draw from these judgments? When such authorities assert that these dances are *certainly* sinful, how dare you maintain that their lawfulness is not even *doubtful?* Be sincere and allow that it would be impossible to stretch moderation further, without adulterating i with a latitudinarianism evidently contrary to reason and to Christian doctrine.

It is then incontestable that decency, dignity and propriety are, to say the least, *compromised* in these dances. And is

not this too much, far too much for Christian women? Alas!
it is even too much for those who are not Christians; for the
instinct of modesty and reserve is a gift which God gives to
all women, to be in their hands the safeguard of morals public and private. Religion here, as elsewhere, does but stim-
ulate and aid the natural law. Who among you would dare
to say, to sign, to publish the assertion that these modern
dances are proper, modest and dignified? Not one of you!
In dancing then, therefore, you commit a breach of propriety,
modesty and dignity.

11. "Some," continues the learned Prelate, "go so far
as to call ridiculous the idea of bringing into the pulpit a
question purely sacramental, the solution of which depends
upon the particular disposition of each. It is, they say, a
question thoroughly relative, a question for the confessional."

These words contain a great error and a little maliciousness. A great error; for the question of these modern dances
is not *merely* relative and sacramental, but one of public
decency and Christian dignity. A little malice, for by pro-
claiming this question purely relative to the personal disposition of each, they insinuate that the young women who are
decided to give up these dances as unworthy of them, are
not equal in virtue to those who intend to continue to dance
them.

To the question then of modesty is added that of scandal?
Doubtless; and it is distinctly what we showed when we
said: forget not the words of the great moralist holy Church
bids us listen to: "dances to be tolerated must be such as
excite neither our passions nor those of others."

It is then doubly false to say that this question is simply
personal and relative: First, because it is a question of sin
against modesty, Christian dignity and public decency; this
is certain. Second, because there is also the question of

participating in the sins of others by actions which "compromise the innocent and rejoice the vicious," who cannot be avoided in society any more than the others. We willingly, however, admit, what is evident to all eyes, that if this question be not exclusively sacramental, it is *also* an object of confession, since immodesty and scandal offend God and our neighbor, and, we will add, calling your particular attention to this point, that if these are an object of *confession* they must also be the object of contrition and a *firm resolution for the future*, the three essential and indivisible parts of a good confession, and in this case, as always, it is true to say: "As the confession, so the absolution."

We said that there is a certain maliciousness in insinuating the exclusively relative character of this question, but it merits a harder name; it is an artifice and a very contemptible one. It is an attempt to dishonor the most worthy and the most courageous, and to award the prize of virtue to the most frivolous and the most cowardly.

We prefer, told us certain good mothers, seeing our daughters whirl round in these improper waltzes, because they are then less struck by the immodest attitudes which are its essential conditions. You see, these poor mothers admit that their daughters are to others the painful and immodest picture that they are glad to hide from the eyes of their daughters themselves.

12. Others say: "If *we* refuse to dance these dances, men will dance them with women unworthy of their notice. But it is precisely by leaving these dances to those who *are* worthy of them that you will put an end to them in good society." Would you resemble these women in order to deliver the slaves of sensuality from the desire to descend lower?

13. Here again is another style of excuse: "It is *his*

opinion," some say; "opinion in which all priests do not
agree; he is not more infallible than another." Doubtless,
and it is because we are as liable to err as another, that we
preach, thank God, neither our opinions nor those of others.
We have said before that we are not legislators and that we
should have reproached ourselves with having deeply sinned,
should we dare impose on others obligations not certainly
imposed by moral law; but the doctrines which we have
transcribed in the very words of St. Alphonsus and St. Francis, these elementary precepts of Christian morals, are not
opinions; they are certain principles, universally taught;
they are uncontested, and the application we made of them
will not be less so. Tell me, where is the preacher who
would dare to say that the modern waltz fulfils the condition
of St. Francis, and is modest or dignified, and that it offends
the moral law in nothing? No, all without exception are
agreed, and proclaim unanimously the necessity of the reform
of these scandalous abuses.

14. Again it is said: "If the author of *L' Histoire de
la Société francaise,* if the Lecturer of Notre-Dame, have
truly and exactly described modern waltz, these dances are
evidently unfit for good society and are really immoral.
"But is this description exact? Is it true that the dancers, breast to breast, breath to breath, whirl round locked in
each others arms?" Is it true that they indulge in "a
sensual whirl . . . inattitudes, postures and embraces,
which rejoice the vicious and compromise the innocent?"
(Pere Felix.)

Is not the picture overdrawn? As an answer, I will in the
first place repeat a conversation, or rather a little discussion
at which I was present. A lady of title, ignoring my opinion
on the abuse in question, brought me her daughter, whose
conscience she considered needlessly alarmed.

She lived in hopes of tranquilizing her by my counsels. Exasperated at length by the blind, ambitious tenderness of her mother, this young girl, more noble, I mean more grandly Christian than her mother, put to her this question: May I ask of you, mamma, what made you beg of me to give up that bouquet (the ornament in question was the *bouquet de luxe*, then very generally worn at the waist in front) ; was it not, • as you yourself said, because it was too soon crumpled and even flattened? The mother blushed, and no word on my part was necessary to complete her defeat.

I left no stone unturned to assure myself of the reality of this fact, and I affirm that all the witnesses, ocular and more than ocular, to whom I applied, assured me unanimously that it was morally impossible, under the different styles of dancing met with in a ball, to avoid the result above mentioned.

Besides it is not only the actual contact, but also the positions and attitudes inherent to these dances, devoid as they are of all modesty, dignity and decency, which render them always *materially* sensual dances, and in a host of cases *formally* so also. I say as much of the pressure which they require. Doubtless all partners do not permit it to the same extent, since it is one of the conditions of these boisterous and romping dances, and then again is one always at liberty to choose one's partners? Are we not generally, on the contrary, obliged to accept them? But we repeat, it is not only the fault of this or that dancer, but the nature of these dances themselves which necessitates these positions, which no one will seriously deny, and which all mothers will admit as freely as that good lady who artlessly exclaimed: "Dear me! what a thing music is! How we should cry out if we saw our daughters in the arms of young men, *without the music*." Once again then we ask, do not such attitudes offend decency, even without that pressure which is ordinarily inevitable?

I can easily believe that for a great many the attention which they are forced to give to the dance, diverts their attention from what they are doing, but they do it not a whit the less for that, and how long, I beg, has a thoroughly free action ceased to be immoral by the sole reason that the attention which it requires diverts the attention from perceiving its immorality? Listen to the avowals and to the counsels, as significant as the avowals of the lady author (the Comtesse de Bassanville) of the work entitled: *La science du monde.*

"Formerly, not only young girls were not allowed to waltz, but even young married women waltzed very little, and this was but seemly . . . But since one must march with the age, *even when it makes a false step*, I will say a word on modern dances, at the same time repeating that were I mother or husband, I would never tolerate them, either for my daughter or my wife. . . . In the Polka-Mazurka a lady who throws herself too much forward or who on the other hand leans too much on the arm of her partner, transgresses not only good breeding, but even decency; the same holds good for the gentleman who holds his partner too close. . . . The *instant* the lady stops dancing her partner must withdraw the arm that is round her waist. . . . If the lady express the wish to sit down, it would show an utter want of good breeding, to urge her to continue, for either she is tired, or else she thinks: *you do not dance properly!*"

Was I not right in saying that the counsels of the world were as significant as its avowals? When a lady begs to leave off because "her partner does not dance properly," it is too late, the thing is done; and if the gentleman must withdraw his arm from around the lady's waist the *instant* she stops dancing is it not clearly because such an attitude if prolonged but an instant, would be highly improper? Why then does it fail to be so during the whole time the dance

lasts, when more than at any other time it is so difficult, nay,
morally impossible to follow the counsel; not to bend too
much forward nor lean too much on your partner's arm, etc.?
The author adds very truly: "in square dances at any rate
every one is his own master," whereas in round dances
every one is more or less dependent on his partner. The
gentleman is often far from scrupulous in observing the caution " not to hold his partner too close " and the lady herself
does not generally stop for such a trifle, either because she
would blush to show that she remarked it, or because, daughter of Eve as she is, she is, like all her sisters of the great
family, not always displeased to " march with the age *even
when it makes a false step.*" The expression is witty, but it
is not Christian, the author feels it, since she almost redeems
it by that other phrase which is better: " were I mother or
husband I would never tolerate them, either for my daughter
or my wife. " Once more then, these counsels of the world
are they not as significant as its avowals, and do they not
fully justify the energetic words of Father Felix?

But after all you say: is this action a proximate occasion
for mortal sin, and is this occasion absolute or relative, the
whole question is there. I really beg your pardon, but there
you give proof of having entirely forgotten what we have already established and you deserve to have it repeated.
There is not all the question.

This action is not *only* the *occasion* of a fault, but it is in
itself, *in se*, a fault more or less grave, it is at the same time
a cooperation in a fault, more or less grave, of another, and
in the still greater faults, which this action may be the occasion of for him, and lastly it is, relatively, the occasion of
still greater personal faults. Am I not right in saying that
it is a fault in itself? Is it not a fault, a real sin, reprehensible from a moral point of view, to put oneself in positions

such as those so courageously stigmatised by Father Felix ?
Is not this fault composed of a double element : first, immodesty, second, bad example, more or less pernicious, in proportion to the higher rank and the better reputation of the persons
who give it ?   Is not this action a cooperation in a fault precisely similar for another ?   Here then are two certain faults
viz :   An immodest action, and the cooperation in the immodest action of another, and these faults are absolute, not
relative.   Besides these two faults, this action may be the
proximate occasion of sin, first for yourself, secondly for
another.

And I beg of you to remark that the cooperation is in this
case as proximate as it can well be, since the action which
constitutes it does not only lead to the sin, but is in itself
a part of it.   But even in cases where the cooperation in
another's sin is only *material*, that is to say, when the action
which constitutes it, is in itself indifferent, the more proximate, the more immediate this occasion is, the more important, the more serious must the motive be, which prompts this
action.   And what important reason is there I pray in this
case ?

But again, is it simply a question of a barely material
cooperation ?   Not at all, but of a cooperation in greater
faults by actions, less guilty, but nevertheless reprehensible,
and of which not the guilt, but the *degree* of guilt only is
doubtful.   It is a question of an action which constitutes in
itself a part of the abuse which it causes ; you can then no
longer maintain that the whole question resolves itself into a
personal and relative occasion of sin.

And need I add that you unintentionally shirk the question when you say : " I can quite believe that these dances
rejoice the vicious, they rejoice at less, they are rejoiced to
be able to give their arm to a lady, to sit beside her or even

to be in her society, *a fortiori* then to waltz with her; truly *a fortiori!* Yet none would consider it the fault of the lady to remain beside such a person, at table for instance, or in a quadrille." Evidently none could impute a fault great or small, but there is neither parity nor even analogy between these cases. In the case you propose, where is the improper attitude, the cooperation, at any rate material, in the sin of others, where is the bad example!

In round dances on the contrary there is the impropriety of the attitude, the cooperation in another's sin and the bad example. Such comparisons are but loop holes.

It is again shirking the question to raise a lament over other abuses when one refuses to recognize this one. The excess of luxurious extravagance is a great evil, indecency in dress is a positive scandal; but these round dances which permit the young people of both sexes attitudes and contacts which are less than modest, are also a sad abuse, nay, I fear not to say that they are even greater than the others, because two persons participate in it.

It is true, and I have already expressly admitted the fact all dancers do not participate formally in the abuse, that is to say with a consciousness of their fault, and thus *post factum*, these must be judged according to their ignorance or their good faith. But, with the exception of those cases, in which charity permits, or counsels us to leave a person in his good faith, it is an absolute duty, and a duty which grows in importance when one is questioned by persons whose position renders their example peculiarly contagious, to show them the scandal they give and also their proximate cooperation in the sin of others. Let us bear in mind these incontestable truths: first, Good faith, springing from involuntary ignorance, does sometimes excuse from venial or even from mortal sin. Second, There are cases in which prudence and

Christian charity permit or counsel us to leave a person in his good faith.   Third, Should he ask *to* be enlightened, or if, without asking, he ought to be enlightened, because of the pernicious influence of his example, *ne licitum judicetur ab aliis quod impune ab his exerceri animadvertitur*, *S. Alphonsus in praxi Confess*. c. i. § 2. No. 9, it is a duty to show him the fault he commits.   I cannot then admit the possibility of those to whom God has confided the guidance of souls, taking under their protection the bad cause of the modern waltz, which would be the case if, as you assure me, they formally tolerate it for those who desire to lead a Christian life.   On the contrary I think with the Bishop of Ghent, when from the pulpit of his Cathedral he addressed these words to his flock :   " I say with sorrow that for some years the fever of pleasure compels Christian mothers to conduct their daughters to assemblies where they permit them to take part in immodest dances.   These same persons make a profession of earnestness in religion, and they are devoted to the frequent reception of the sacraments.   They have consulted their director of conscience, they say.   We cannot believe it.   A director of conscience cannot tolerate such abuses, he would cooperate, by a culpable indulgence in the scandal these persons give, and he would have to answer for it before Almighty God. "

But you will say, "Is there in this case a question of mortal sin?"   I answer by an interrogation.   Suppose that the question of mortal sin *in se* appears to you doubtful ; it seems to you that, as these almost unavoidable contacts and attitudes—though they are a cooperation evidently more than material in the faults of partners whom a person is not free to choose, are a kind of scandal, yet, in your opinion this cooperation, this scandal does not constitute, *ex genere suo*, matter sufficient for a mortal sin : you will at least admit that, even in this hypothesis, the fault, though venial in itself, tends by a very inclined plane to overstep the frontier between mortal and venial sin ?

Does not St. Alphonsus, the master of all really prudent *Probabilists*, say expressly that it is unlawful to expose oneself or one's neighbor to a *probable* fall into mortal sin, and that to incur such a danger it requires a just cause or a real necessity? And if we may not follow a probable opinion with the risk of injuring our neighbor's temporal interests, how much less is this allowable when our own or our neighbor's eternal interests are in peril ? For then in point of fact it is the fall alone which is uncertain, whereas the danger is certain.

Leaving then out of the question the proximate occasion of mortal sin, I ask, what is the degree of culpability of a young girl who, knowing what young men for the most part are, joins with them in dances which involve attitudes which are for them at any rate the probable proximate occasion of mortal sin?

Second, I ask: can the public and avowed commission of sin, mortal or venial, against decency, be tolerated in Christian families, in Christian women, in a society that desires to remain Christian?

I confidently await your answers, in the name of morality good sense, and good taste.

This brings me to the question which closes your letter. You ask me if the instructions of St. Francis de Sales on this matter are not addressed more to persons striving after perfection than those who walk in the paths of an ordinary Christian's life?

St. Francis, my good Sir, wrote works for *both* these classes; but his *Introduction* in spite of the old fashioned word "devout life, *vie devote*," is evidently destined for

23

those who desire to lead Christian lives in the world. Glance at the headings of the chapters of this little masterpiece, and you will have no doubt of this. The chapter I quote from would alone suffice to prove it. Is it, I ask, to souls especially devoted to holy living, and to good works, or to those who desire to live Christianly in the world, that it is necessary to teach how to dance properly?

And again the moderation and the modesty which the Saint requires are evidently obligatory for all.

It is asked again, " If I apply to every kind of waltz, the *nunquam permitti potest* (it can never be permitted) of the theology of Mgr. Bouvier, and the strictness of Father Gury and you dwell upon this point adding " Would this apply to a waltz from which all the disadvantages of these new dances had been eliminated ?"

"Allow me, my dear sir, to make my answer more practical than your question.

"I have nothing to say against any *possible* round dances, because it is not the rotary movement particularly that would ever put them in opposition with morality. I have nothing to do with waltz *in abstracto*, but with the real waltz *in concreto*, that is to say such as that described as : " a voluptuous reel in which a couple whirl around locked in each others arms. " (M. de Goncourte.)

This definition of the author of *French Society under the Directory* refers to the waltz in general ; it refers then *a fortiori* to modern waltzes, which have aggravated what was blamable in the older ones. In case you should deny the considerable modification the waltz has undergone of late years, I refer you to the *Dictionnaire des Arts* of M. Bouillet of the *Institute de France* ; but I rely on your eye-sight and on your memory. You have not forgotten the general surprise that the apparition of these new waltzes produced in the ball rooms of 1840, for you at that time related to me the indignant exclamation then in every mouth, of a certain magistrate notorious nevertheless for his tolerance, moreover you admit implicitly this modification when you seem to plead the cause of the old waltzes. I say when you *seem* to do so, for you yourself allow that, in times gone by, every one united in considering it the least proper, the least decent of all dances, and that the majority of women of rank considered it unworthy of them and left it to the giddiest, you will then excuse me from entering more profoundly into this question of ancient history, and you will suffer me to keep to the more practical and palpable question of contemporary history. In conclusion then, nothing in my pamphlet is opposed to what you say of *possible*, or what I may call : metaphysical round dances, and on the other hand nothing in your letter is opposed to what my pamphlet says of *actual*, and *existing* round dances, since you require, as a *sine qua non*, and they should be stripped of just what constitutes their being ; that is to say that they should not be what they are ; you would have done better then, to have expressed your idea in the words of Father Gury quoted in my last letter ; you observe he simply states that these are the opinions generally accepted by theologians, and I ought perhaps to accuse myself of an excessive moderation for asking my readers to doubt only as to the gravity of the fault, and consequently not to suffer the habitual commission of sin, be it mortal or venial, in their ball rooms."

There-are others again who, in order to justify dancing appeal to custom which has established dances everywhere ; they invoke the pretended necessities of their position ; they must do like the rest of the world ; they are pleased to think that the more extensively dancing is established, the less dangerous it becomes.

> "Custom does often reason overrule,
> And only serves for reason to the fool."

"Woe-creating torrent of custom," exclaims St. Augustine, "where are all those who resist thee? Shall we then never see thee dried up? How long wilt thou sweep the unfortunate children of Adam into that deep, stormy sea, from which even those who hold to the wood of the Saviour's cross have difficulty to save themselves? How many sins would be excusable, if custom were a lawful excuse! Blasphemy, theft, impurity, adultery, could not be crimes any longer, because there have always been many blasphemers, thieves, libertines, and adulterers. What would become of the law of God, if custom, which is often contrary to it, were the rule of conduct? Follow not the multitude in doing evil, says Jesus Christ; the many go by the broad road that leads to hell." "A bad custom," says Tertullian, "is established by ignorance and libertinism against truth and God, who is truth itself. For this reason, no space of time, no authority of men, no national privileges, have been able to render a custom legitimate which has not justice or truth as its foundation."

It was almost a universal custom among the Israelites to adore the golden calf of Jeroboam, king of Israel; but Tobias alone, of all the others, went to Jerusalem to adore the Lord in his temple. This custom, so opposed to the law of God, made then no impression on the mind or heart of the young Tobias. Why should custom sway us? Do we not owe to God the same fidelity as this holy man? Is it more lawful for us than for him to fall away from virtue, by following a custom which is contrary to God's law?

Here we may claim with the poet :—

> "Vice is a monster of so frightful mien,
> As to be hated, needs but to be seen,
> Yet seen too oft, familiar with her face,
> We first endure, then pity, then embrace."

Let us remember that Jesus Christ does not say, "I am the fashion, the custom, the usage," but "I am the way, the Truth and the Life;" he will judge us not according to the laws of fashion, but according to the precepts of the Gospel.

But are charity balls, and round dances at charity picnics objectionable, where the priest is present and permits them?

Bishop Lefevere, the zealous and learned bishop of Detroit, in his pastoral (Oct. 1850,) thus addresses the clergy and laity, in relation to an abuse prevailing in his, as well as in several other cities, where excursions, etc., are availed of to raise money for good and charitable objects :—

"To our age is reserved the honor of adding to the dictionary of our language the word 'charity-ball,' and of teaching that what dishonors God, blasphemes our religion, and places a stumbling-block for a multitude of souls, who find in both spiritual and temporal ruin, can be right, and even praiseworthy, on account of that relief which it may afford to the poor, &c.; in other words, that the end justifies the means, however criminal they may be in themselves, or in the circumstances attending them. You are well persuaded and we loudly proclaim it, that you must give alms according to the precepts of our Lord; but remember well that this God, infinitely wise, cannot be indifferent to the manner in which you acquit yourself of this work of charity, in order that it may answer his design, and be meritorious to you.

"For in order that any work whatever may be truly good, it does not suffice that it should be good under a certain relation, or in some of the circumstances attending it, but it must be good in every relation—in its objects, which should be proportioned to the act; in its end and in its circumstances, which should all be in harmony with the act itself; in fine, in its intention, which should be nothing else than the goodness of the act. If one of these conditions be wanting, it not only ceases to be good, but it becomes vicious and detestable in the eyes of God—becomes a sin.

" After this, can we imagine that God will receive as righteous and meritorious an act of so-called charity, through this instrumentality of balls and dances, with all the dangerous and criminal circumstances that, especially in our days, accompany them? Is not this to overturn all the rules of Christian morality, and to insult God by pretending to perform an action agreeable to him, while we make use of the means which he has himself forbidden; which the church, ever guided by the Holy Spirit, condemns; and of which even men of the world avow the fatal consequences from their own experience, and which pagans, despite the laxity of their morals, have marked with infamy ? "

Under the title of " Charity-Balls, " we read the following in the *Semaine religieuse*, of the Diocese of Cambrai : " We have been cursorily reading some of the sermons of Mgr. Obrè, auxiliary Bishop of Beauvais, and have met with these strong thoughts, expressed in a striking manner, which cut themselves into the minds of the listeners in ineffaceable lines. After the lapse of twenty-five years, he was agreeably surprised to hear one of his listeners say :—

" 'Monseigneur' (he was then a prelate), 'I have never forgotten what you said one day in a charity sermon at the Cathedral.'

" 'And what was it, Mademoiselle ?'

" 'Oh, it was a long time ago' (it was on January 14, 1840, a date marked in the journal of the pious Christian). 'You spoke of alms, and of the strange and profane custom of giving balls for charitable purposes.' 'But can we not,' you asked, 'unite pleasure and charity? and will not an amiable philanthropy permit playing and dancing for the profit of the poor? Certainly not ; the Church has never approved of this manner of giving; alms, to gain merit, ought to be the gift of a pure heart, and not of impiety; now, in the eyes of religion, it is impious to corrupt an excellent work by forbidden pleasures, of which it becomes the fruit. Do not alms kicked at the poor become an insult to those who receive them, and works of evil for those who give them?"— [*L. Univers.*]

Is it not wickedness then in any man to use the name of heaven-born charity as a cloak "to cover a multitude of sins." (Com. Pl. Balt. II.)

As to the presence of the priest at round dances on the occasion of charity picnics, who permits such dances, I have but little to say. I know that priests, who may not only witness but take part with seculars in other permitted amusements — in a game of cards for instance — are forbidden to countenance and encourage this. Pope Benedict XIV., in his *Casus Conscientiæ*, teaches, that a priest who would play the music—on a piano for instance—for a dance at the home of a friend, or who would go to a ball, though he should be there only as a spectator, should be suspended—that is, be deprived, under the pain of mortal sin, of the right to say Mass and administer the Sacraments; and in the Archdiocese over which the Pope presided when he was Cardinal suspension, to be incurred *ipso facto*, was the penalty in each of these cases.

19. To enjoy dancing undisturbed, some people appeal to the authority of their confessor, saying: "My confessor allows me to dance; he does not oppose it, at least he does not say anything against it."

I can hardly believe that your confessor should allow you to go to such dances as are unbecoming by the indecency of the costumes, or the manner of dancing, or by words, jests or songs, as, for instance, the waltz, the polka, the gallop.

For every confessor knows that he cannot approve of what is condemned by the Fathers and Doctors of the Church, and by the best and most learned theologians. If all physicians decided that a certain article of food was poisonous, would it not be rejected with horror by all?

Every confessor knows that if he were to favor such dances, he would belong to the number of those of whom Holy Scripture says: "Woe to you who call evil good, and good evil." (Par. v., 2.) He knows that if he should say nothing against them, his silence would mean approval, and that approval would mean participation in guilt, and he would be one of those of whom our Lord says: "Let them alone, they are blind and the leaders of the blind. And if the blind lead the blind, both fall into the pit." (Matt. xv., 14.) He knows that these dances are very often proximate occasions of mortal sin, and constitute always in themselves (*in se*) as immodest dances, at least a venial sin; he knows that to those for whom they are an immediate occasion of sin, they must be forbidden under pain of a refusal of absolution, and that to all they must be shown to be, what they are in fact, unworthy of any one truly animated with the spirit of Christianity; he knows that it is his duty to explain to those who are in earnest in spiritual matters, or even devoted to frequent communion, such a practice of piety is incompatible with the deliberate commission of venial sin.

Lastly, your confessor knows that if he does not comply with this duty of his, our Lord says to him: "Son of man, I have made thee a watchman to the house of Israel, and thou shalt hear the word out of my mouth and shalt tell it to them from me. If when I say to the wicked, thou shalt surely die, thou declare it not to him nor speak to him, that he may be converted from his wicked way and live; the same wicked man shall die in his iniquity, but I will require his blood at thy hand. But if thou give warning to the wicked and he be not converted from his wickedness and from his evil way, he indeed shall die in his iniquity, but *thou hast delivered thy soul.*" (Ez. iij., 16, 19.) How can I, then, believe that your confessor allows you what he is bound in conscience to condemn?

However, it is true that false prophets are never wanting, and our divine Saviour has warned us of them. It is also true that there are many Christians who do not like to hear such truths as put a check on their passions. "There shall be a time when they will not endure sound doctrine, but according to their own desires they will heap to themselves teachers having itching ears, *ad sua desideria coacervabunt sibi magistros,* etc. (ii. Tim. iv. 8.)

Achab, King of Israel, was unwilling to listen to the only true prophet who had the courage to speak the truth. He preferred to listen to the false prophets who concealed it from him through complacency, and thus engaged him in an enterprise which cost him his life. Is not this the unfortunate disposition of many Christians who, secretly enemies of truth which combats their vices and errors, consult only those who may give a favorable response to their passions? Do they not deserve to be deceived, like Achab? "Because men have not received nor loved truth," says St. Paul, "God will send them a spirit of error, so that they will believe a lie, in order that all who have not believed truth, and who have consented to iniquity, may be condemned." (Thess. xi.)

Any one who is not blind cannot help seeing the truth of what we have said. If he is blind, it is a curse upon him; for God has withdrawn the light of his grace and the delicate perceptions which grace gives to the conscience.

THE SEVENTH COMMANDMENT.

" Thou shalt not steal."

We have seen that God, by the fifth commandment, protects our life, and by the sixth the honor and reputation of
the family. Now, by the seventh commandment, he wishes
to protect us in the just possession of our other temporal
goods. Hence he forbids every one to steal, or to be unjust
to any one of his fellow-men.

From the beginning God impressed upon man the principles of justice, the notions of right and wrong. Hence it is
that the voice of reason tells every one not to violate the
principles of justice. "Whatever you would have men to
do to you, do you that to them," says the Lord (Matt. vii.,
12) ; that is to say, as you wish others to be just to you in
all things, so be you also just to them in everything. And
"What thou hatest to be done to thee by another, see that
thou do it not to another at any time." (Tob. iv., 16.) By
these two principles of justice it is easy to know when we
are just or unjust towards our neighbor.

We call a thing *right* or *just* when it is well adapted to
what it is applied and exactly united thereto. In the same
manner right or justice establishes a certain union, a degree
of mutual harmony between two or more individuals. For
instance you agree with me to pay me so much for my work,
or for what I have sold you. In this case and in similar
ones my right is to receive what is due to me, and your duty
is to pay me what you owe. Thus justice imposes a strict

[354]

obligation of right on the one side and of duty on the other.

Now, right is twofold—natural and positive. The right which proceeds from the general laws of nature is called *natural right*. The right which proceeds from a special contract conformable to the law and custom of the country, is called *positive* right.

Natural justice or right is immutable and universal for all men, because it is founded on divine law. Positive right, however, is variable according to times, places, circumstances, and events.

Natural right, though immutable, is nevertheless, in particular cases, liable to certain modifications. Natural right, for instance, obliges me to return to another what he lends to me or what he intrusts to my care; but if he becomes insane or a dangerous enemy to the country, then natural right does not oblige me to return it to him whilst he is in that state of mind.

A thing is said to be legally right when once established by law, which gives it the character of positive right. But if a legal right is opposed to natural justice or right, it is not obligatory; for instance, if it sanctions robbery, adultery or other crimes repugnant to natural right, it is null and void, because it is contrary to divine justice and to the laws of nature and humanity. Hence God says through his prophet, Isaias: "Woe to them that make wicked laws, and when they write injustice." (Chapt. x., 1.)

We are *just*, then, when our will is always inclined to give every one his right or due. A man is just to himself when he does nothing contrary to his temporal and eternal happiness; and he is just towards others if he gives them all that they are naturally and legally entitled to.

Justice establishes equality between individuals on the one side, and the community of which we are members on the other. Hence the distinction of "*commutative*" and "*distributive*" justice.

Commutative justice establishes the rights in affairs of private persons. Distributive justice establishes the rights between the community and each of its members. By this right each member receives from the State or community his part of the public or common goods in proportion to his rank and merit.

To violate the principles of commutative or distributive justice is to break the seventh commandment. Now this commandment is broken:

First, By taking or injuring unjustly what belongs to another; and,

Second, By keeping unjustly what belongs to another.

For the sake of clearness we arrange the various sins of injustice under these two heads:

I. Persons become guilty of taking unjustly what belongs to another:

First. By *theft*. What is theft? Theft consists in taking what *belongs* to another, without a *just cause*, and *against the owner's will*. To commit, then, the sin of theft it is necessary first that what is taken must *belong* to another. Hence it is no theft to make a man restore to the right owner a thing which he possesses unjustly.

Second. To commit the sin of theft it is also necessary that what is taken from another is taken without *just cause*. Hence, when a person is in extreme necessity, that is, in proximate danger of death or of a most grievous evil, it is no sin for him to take from another, even against his will, as much as is necessary to free himself from that proximate danger.

But a person who is only in a grievous necessity has no right to take what belongs to another without the owner's consent, as appears from the condemnation of the 86th proposition by Innocent XI. With regard to compensation, no one can make it to himself, unless the debt is certain, and even most certain, and unless he has no other means of obtaining what is due to him. Hence a servant cannot make to himself occult compensation for services which he judges to be deserving of more wages than he has received. To assert that he can make such compensation has been condemned by Innocent XI. (Prop. damn. 87).

Third. To commit the sin of theft it is also necessary that what is taken from another must be taken against *his will.* Hence it is no theft to take from another with his consent, what belongs to him; according to a certain principle of right which says : " *Scienti et volenti non fit injuria,* " that is, no injury is done to him who knows it and is willing to undergo it. An act of injustice supposes two persons, one who commits it, and another who suffers it. Now, if the sufferer of it freely consents to suffer it, he is no longer a passive, but rather the active and free agent of his misfortune. He, therefore, who wishes for bad luck, must have it and has to blame no one else for it than himself.

Now, there is the *public* theft when things are stolen from the commonwealth or public treasury and the *private* theft between man and man.

. Of public *theft* those are guilty who misapply the public funds, or turn them to their own private uses; who acknowledge not all they have received, or charge the public with what they have not expended. Guardians of the poor, executors of last wills, and all those who have the trust or charge of what belongs to others, are guilty of public *theft,* if they fraudulently retain any of the money that passes through their hands. They are also guilty of public theft, who, holding any public office, take bribes, and administer their office unjustly and unfaithfully.

Thus a judge is guilty of public theft, if he receives bribes, or wilfully causes by unnecessary delay, greater expense, or passes an unjust sentence. A lawyer is guilty of public theft, if he neglects the interests of his client, or encourages him to begin or continue a lawsuit which he easily foresees will be lost, or which he knows is unjust. A witness becomes guilty of public theft, if he causes another to suffer a loss by giving false witness, or by concealing part of the truth; in a word, any one is more or less guilty of public theft, who makes use of the law to keep or obtain possession of what belongs to another, or who, by vexatious lawsuits, either keeps another out of the possession of his due or unjustly involves him in the expense of establishing his right. It would be too tedious to mention the variety of ways and means by which lawyers, executors, trustees, guardians, and all such as are in public offices, commit injustice and render themselves guilty of public *theft*. Those who practise these unwarrantable ways are sensible of the wrong and injustice they perpetrate, and need not be informed that by their proceedings they violate the seventh commandment.

Of *private* thefts are guilty:

(a) Those persons who steal from the rich to give to the poor, under the pretence of alms.

(b) Those who steal from the rich and wealthy, under the plea that such rich persons want not what is taken, that they will not miss it, or that they will be made no poorer by the money or value taken. This, says the Catechism of the Council of Trent, is only a wicked pretence.

(c) Those children who take the goods of their parents without their knowledge and consent, as also those servants who take secretly goods of their masters.

(d.) Those who take a considerable quantity by small repeated thefts from the same or different persons, etc.—

2. *By fraud.* There is another way of taking unjustly the goods of our neighbor, namely, by fraud and deceit.

Merchants, traders, and storekeepers become guilty of injustice when in dealing they use false weights or measures; or when they give bad merchandise for good; or when, availing themselves of the wants or ignorance of others, they sell too dear, or, when they make a monopoly of any article of trade, that is, when they purchase all the goods of a particular kind, in order that they may sell at an excessive price. Thus they rob the public in the hour of distress. The sin of injustice may also be committed by bodies or companies; thus, if all the members of the same profession or trade combine amongst themselves to sell their merchandise only at an excessive price, they are all guilty of a criminal monopoly.

3. *By neglecting or performing badly a duty for which we are paid.* Laborers and mechanics become guilty of injustice when they do not employ in the service of their masters the stipulated time, or when they do their work badly; or when, through their own fault, the goods of their masters of which they have charge, are either lost or damaged.

4. *By usury.* By usury is meant the exaction of gain or interest without any just title, for any thing lent, the thing lent still remaining the property of the lender. It can, of course, never be wrong for us when we lend money or any other kind of goods to protect ourselves against any real or probable loss. Hence it is lawful to receive interest as compensation, (a) when the lender loses by lending or is deprived of a lawful profit which his money, had he not lent it, would secure for him. To illustrate. I am about to lay out my money in trade or land, which will produce for me a certain lawful revenue; you ask this money; to please you, I

. lend it you; by this I am deprived of my profit in trade or land, you are the cause of this loss, I tell you so before I lend the money; simple justice then requires that you should compensate me for this loss; and to prevent disputes, the government of the country regulates the rate of interest to be given on such occasions. Again, I am about to pay a debt, principal and interest, which I owe a creditor; you desire me to give you the loan of this money; if I lend it you, my account in interest and principal will run on and increase; by lending my money to you, I suffer this loss; and hence justice requires you should return with my loan a full compensation for what I have lost, if I have informed you of this before making the loan.

(b)   It is lawful to take interest for a loan when the lender runs the risk of losing the sum lent, and may be put to expense in the recovery of it; for, as St. Liguori says (de Sept. decalogi præcepto), a *certain* sum is more valuable than a *doubtful* sum, and this is confirmed by the decision of the Council of Lateran, sess. 10, and by a declaration of the Sacred Council de Propaganda Fide, confirmed by Innocent X., in which it is declared that we may receive interest for a loan, on the ground that there is a probable risk that the loan may be lost.   It is lawful also to derive profit from moneys put into legal public funds, societies or companies, for in all these cases we retain the dominion of such moneys; whereas, when we lend money, we voluntarily strip ourselves of that dominion, and retain only the right to exact what we lent; to the borrower belongs the profits arising from the loan, as to him also belongs the loss if he sustains any either in capital or profit.

The simple reason, then, why the damage we sustain or the gain we lose or the risk we run in lending money justifies us to take interest, is because it is but just that he who causes any damage should repair it, and that our good will in lending should not be made prejudicial to ourselves (St. Thom., ii., 2, Quest. 78, a. 1.) ; and a probable risk is a probable loss, for which we should receive compensation.

(c) It is now the general opinion of theologians that if none of these reasons exist, a moderate interest allowed by custom and the law of the country may be taken with a safe conscience as long as the Church does not teach the contrary.

The rate of interest which may be lawfully taken is in proportion to the risk incurred. But if it is more than a just and fair compensation, or if, where no such risk exists, it is more than is allowed by the general practice and the laws of the country, we have no just claim to the excess.

5. *By rapine or robbery.* If what belongs to another is taken by force it is called rapine or robbery. Of this sin of rapine those are guilty who oppress the orphans, the widow, or the poor, and take advantage of their unprotected position and necessities to squeeze money from them. This is the most detestable kind of *rapine* in the sight of God ; and in Holy Writ he denounces woes and calamities against all those guilty of it. Those who attack and rob persons on the highway, or plunder the houses or farm-yards of others, despite every opposition and remonstrance, are also guilty of *rapine;* and so, too, are those who abuse their power and authority to deprive others unjustly of their goods and possessions, as Jezebel did to Naboth, as we read in the Book of Kings. Of such persons the Scriptures speak in the severest terms : " The bread of the needy is the life of the poor ; he that defraudeth them thereof is a man of blood. He that taketh away thy bread gotten by sweat is like him that killeth his neighbor." (Ecclus. xxxiv., 25.)

6. *By unjust destruction of our neighbor's goods.* To

24

damage or destroy unjustly the property of our neighbor is another way of becoming guilty of the sin of injustice. For example, those who set fire to the possessions of another or cause to their neighbor any loss by depriving him unjustly of his character and good name, are answerable for the loss they have caused him.

II. So far we have seen some of the ways by which what belongs to another is unjustly taken. Let us now see some of the ways in which persons become guilty of injustice by *keeping unjustly* what belongs to another.

Now, persons keep unjustly what belongs to another :

1. When they refuse to give back what they have taken from another or what has been intrusted to their care.

2. When they refuse to pay their just debts contracted for services or goods which they purchased ; they are bound to pay their debts as soon as they are due, and if, by unjust neglect or delay, they cause a loss to their creditors, they are also answerable for such loss.

3. When they take no means to find the owners of the things which they have found. When things lost fall into our hands we are obliged to take reasonable care to find the right owner. By neglecting to do so we become guilty of injustice, because we keep unjustly what belongs to another.

4. When they buy or receive things which they know have been stolen. Only the real owner of a thing has a right to dispose of it. He, therefore, who buys or receives anything from one who has no right to sell it or give it away, becomes a partaker in his injustice.

5. When they prevent another from obtaining what is due to him in justice, or when by fraudulent means, by force or by calumnies they prevent him from obtaining a present or legacy not due to him in justice.

Finally, it may be remarked that all those are guilty of

injustice who assist any one in stealing or cheating or robbing or keeping unjustly another's goods. "Those also," says St. Alphonsus, "are also guilty of injustice who do not pay to their pastors what they owe them."

THE SIN OF THEFT.

Theft is contrary to the principles and virtue of justice, which consists in giving every one his due.

Theft is also contrary to charity, which obliges us to love our neighbor and wish him well in all things; but the thief, instead of loving his neighbor or wishing him well, does him a material injury by taking unjustly what belongs to him.

Theft, moreover, is a violation of the rights of society, for no society could possibly exisit if thefts were frequently committed to the disadvantage of its members.

Now, though theft is a sin of injustice, yet its guilt is only in proportion to the value of the thing stolen, or the amount of injury done to another. To determine, then, whether a theft is a mortal sin, we must take into account, not only the value of the thing stolen, but also the circumstances of the person to whom the thing stolen belongs, and also the circumstances of time and place. St. Alphonsus Liguori, who wrote on this subject in the last century, when money was of greater value than it is now, lays down as a rule that to steal a sum of three dollars is a mortal sin. Other theologians say that it is a mortal sin to steal the quantity of a day-laborer's wages, for one day from any person, either in money or in its equivalent.

Under the name of stealing is comprehended all manner of cheating in weight, measure, or reckoning; all wilful waste, or embezzling other persons' goods, and the like, with all manner of cheating whatever, to the value, I say, of a day-laborer's wages for one day, or thereabouts.

However, it is hardly possible to establish an absolute and invariable rule in this matter. The faithful, therefore, must leave such decisions to the judgment of the confessor, whose duty it is to weigh all the circumstances of the case.

It is true a much less quantity, under certain circumstances may be a mortal sin, where the theft is from a person who is very poor, or in great want, or when a greater damage follows from a small theft; as, for example, where one steals a workman's tools, whereby he loses a day's work, or the like.

Hence it is generally agreed that we cannot lessen the fault in proportion to the riches of the person from whom we steal or whose goods we misspend; for those who have much, have much to do with it, and, doubtless, have as just a title to every cent they have as any of those have who are much poorer; and, therefore, we act contrary to justice, whenever we take, misspend, embezzle, or dispose of what belongs to them without their order or consent.

It is, then, certain that every considerable theft is a mortal sin, even though the whole amount was taken only in small quantities, and not missed by the owner, because small sums make up large amounts.

It is also certain that small thefts and frauds which are often repeated with the intention to take a considerable sum, are mortal sins, because each of these small thefts is committed with such an intention as is a mortal sin; for the will of stealing a large quantity is a mortal sin, says St. Thomas. "Neither thieves, nor the covetous.... nor extortioners, shall possess the kingdom of God." (1 Cor. vi. 10.)

Now, of mortal sin are guilty not only those who steal or cheat considerably, but also all those who withhold from another a considerable amount of property to which he is entitled; as, for instance, a rich man, who neglects to pay to servants, to laborers and mechanics, their wages. Many of the rich have but little scruple about this sin of injustice. If the poor man does not receive in due time what he has earned in the sweat of his brow, he is compelled to buy on credit the things he needs for himself and his family, and consequently is charged a higher price. This is for him a great loss, for which the rich man is responsible. "The bread of the needy is the life of the poor; he that defraudeth them thereof is a man of blood." (Eccl. xxxiv. 25.) They who defraud or neglect to pay the poor man, take away his life; for he lives by the work of his hands. St. James says that the wages due to the laborer, and not paid him, cry to God for vengeance against him who withholds them. "Behold the hire of the laborers. . . . . which by fraud has been kept back by you, crieth; and the cry of them hath entered into the ears of the Lord of Sabaoth." (St. James v. 4.) The Holy Ghost exhorts us to pay before night (that is, as soon as we can) what we owe to the poor. "But thou shalt pay him the price of his labor on the same day, before the going down of the sun, because he is poor." (Deut. xxiv. 15.) You say, *I will pay him to-morrow*; and in the meantime he is dying of hunger. Jusuranno, the son of Luderic, count of Flanders, in a time of scarcity, deferred to pay for a basket of fruit which he had purchased from a poor woman; in consequence of the delay, three of her sons died of hunger. In punishment of this crime the count commanded the head of his son to be cut off. This fact is related by Verme. (*Catech.*, 11.) "*Pudeat*," says Cassiodorus, "*illis tollere quibus jubemur offerre.*" We should be ashamed to defraud the poor, whom we are bound to relieve.

Some years ago, a holy priest, Matthew a Bascio, gave a mission. A Vienice gentleman of the place invited the missionary to dinner. The good priest accepted the invitation.

This gentleman had grown rich by injustice; he defrauded and oppressed the poor whenever it was in his power. Many of the leading gentlemen of the place were also present. Before they sat down to dinner the priest blessed the food, and see! in an instant everything on the table was tinged with blood. The priest then took a loaf of bread in his hands and squeezed it and instantly red drops of blood gushed forth and fell upon the ground! Then turning to the dishonest man, he said in a voice of thunder: "See here, dishonest man! See here the blood of the poor, see here the blood of the widow and orphan whom you have wronged. Their blood cries out to heaven against you for vengeance." With these words he walked out of the room leaving the host and the assembled guests pale and trembling with horror.

"Those also," says St. Alphonsus, "are condemned to hell who do not pay pious legacies left by their ancestors. The poor souls remain in the fires of purgatory, and are silent. The Masses are not celebrated, nor are the alms dispensed. O, what calamities fall on so many families as a punishment for not paying pious legacies."

"What shall we say of lay administrators? To those we may apply the words of David: 'They eat the sacrifices of the dead. . . and destruction was multiplied among them.' (Ps. 105, 28-29.) *They eat the sacrifices of the dead*; they spend in banquets and drunken feasts, the revenues left by the deceased for Masses. and for other pious works. And what are the consequences? '*Destruction is multiplied among them.*' Destruction follows on destruction,—fathers, sons, grandsons, great-grandsons, whole families are damned. Such are the consequences."

Usury, so frequent in modern times, is also a mortal sin; it is a pernicious system of robbery and replete with all kinds of fraud, extortion, and imposition. It is strictly prohibited by many formal precepts of the Old and the New Testament, and condemned by several Councils of the Church. It is a destructive, detestable traffic on the accidental wants of persons in public or private business. It is the fruit of insatiable avarice, a moral plague of society, and irreparable ruin to thousands. Banks and public establishments authorized by the government of the country, and conducted by men of honor and respectability, can lend and borrow money at lawful interest, and this is even necessary for the general welfare of society; but the unlawful practice of usury which is contrary to common justice is nothing less than public robbery. Usurers are like quack doctors who kill numbers, and by chance cure but very few. So that even they who lend them money are guilty of sin; for they act like those who lend fire-arms to a madman, or to a gang of robbers for the destruction of honest, industrious people. "Let the public usurer remember," says St. Alphonsus, "that, by a decree of the Council of Lateran (*Clemen. unic. de Usur.*) they are excommunicated, forbidden to receive the body of Christ, and after death are to be deprived of Christian burial. Let it also be remembered that sometimes usury is not manifest, but is palliated by being taken under some other pretext; the gain received must be restored. Alas! how many poor souls go to hell on account of this accursed usury! If any one feel a scruple on this point, let him confess it immediately, and apply a remedy, now that he has time; for, if he dies with this scruple, he will go to hell, where he will be no longer able to repair the evil. A certain virtuous young man became a monk. While in the monastry he saw his father and brother damned for the usury which they had practised, and heard one of them cursing the other. The afflicted religious asked if he could give them any relief.

They answered, no; for out of hell there is no redemption. (*Mattoil*, lib. vi. ex. 10.)

In the fourteenth century, a terrible famine having broken out at Rimini, in Italy, the exorbitant price of grain threw desolation among the inhabitants. It was only a certain usurer that rejoiced, because his granaries were full. Nevertheless, although the corn was already beyond all price, he refused to sell his, hoping that it would rise still higher; and in order to escape importunities he even retired to the country. Every day he went to walk on the high road, and never failed to ask the people coming from the town how corn was selling. When told that it was still going up, he heaved a compassionate sigh, but laughed within himself. But it happened that two wealthy inhabitants of Rimini having bought enormous quantities of grain in Apulia, in the kingdom of Naples, in order to provide for the necessity of the moment, the corn fell at a single stroke to half the price. The usurer, who proposed to return that very day to the town, to profit by the misery of his townsmen, inquired, as usual, of the passers-by, what was the price of corn. What was his surprise to see joyous troops of villagers coming along, driving before them asses loaded with corn. "What has happened?" he asked, trembling with anxiety. "Thanks be to God!" cried all the peasants at once, "corn is down one-half this morning!" "*Down one-half?*" slowly repeated the astonished usurer. He ran to the city, people met him, saluted him, bid him good morning, but to all these attentions he could only reply with these words, slowly articulated: "*Down one-half?*" On reaching his home his wife and children could get no other answer from him. He took to his bed, his ghastly countenance giving rise to serious alarm. They ran for a doctor, who arrived in all haste, and asked him what was the matter with him. "*Down* one-half?" murmured the unhappy man. A priest arrived, wanted to hear his confession, spoke to him of trusting in the mercy of God. "*Down one-half?*" repeated the dying man whom every one regarded as stricken with madness. His condition became worse and worse; medicine and care were alike ineffectual, and the infamous usurer expired articulating for the last time the words that seemed to be the warrant of divine justice: "*Down one-half?*"—[*Schmid et Belet, Cat. Hist.* II. 411.]

Theft a *sacrilege* under certain circumstances.

It is also a mortal sin to steal something that is consecrated to the service of God; because this sin is not only the sin of theft, but also that of *sacrilege*.

Robbery. Again, it is a mortal sin to take by *force* what belongs to another. Robbery or plunder, which is a public, violent act, dangerous to both person and property, is contrary to common justice, public order, civilization and the safety of society. It is a greater sin than theft, because it adds insult and outrage to the violence of the act committed against honest, industrious people.

Robbers, thieves, usurers, extortioners, or persons who are too covetous, are often taken in their own snares. That often happens to them as a particular punishment of God for the sins of their injustice.

A certain merchant, who was travelling through a forest with a quantity of jewels and gold and silver ornaments, was attacked by a party of banditti, who stripped him of all he possessed and beat him severely. Having done so they carried off into their cave the treasure which they had stolen, and sent the youngest of their number into the neighboring town to buy wine and provisions.

During his absence the two robbers said to each other: "Why should we be obliged to share all this treasure with

that boy? As soon as he returns let us make an end of him."
Meanwhile their young companion thought within himself as
he journeyed to the town, "What a grand thing it would be
if all that gold and silver belonged to me! And why should
it not? For I can easily poison my two comrades and take
it all for myself." Accordingly when he had reached the
town and bought the provisions, he purchased some poison
and put it into the wine; he then set out on his return.

No sooner had he reached the cave than his two companions set upon him and murdered him with their daggers.
They then ate heartily and drank the poisoned wine. In a
short time they died amid agonies of pain, and the dead
bodies of the three were soon after discovered beside the
treasure, which was restored to the rightful owner.

RESTITUTION.

By the seventh commandment God commands us, not
only not to commit acts of injustice, but he also commands
us to pay our lawful debts.

A debt means anything that is due to others. If we have
at any time borrowed money or purchased goods, we are
bound by the seventh commandment to return the money
borrowed and to pay for the goods purchased, and that at
the time fixed on between the lender or seller and ourselves.
It would be a violation of every law of probity and justice
not to pay our lawful debts when it is in our power to do so;
for to refuse to pay what we owe is to wrong another of what
is justly due to him. To delay paying debts when due, and
when the creditor needs them, is unjustly to retain what
belongs to another, is the cause of the owner being put to
great loss and inconvenience for want of his own, and is
frequently the source of the ruin of merchants and traders.
But if, after having contracted debts, we find it impossible

to pay them, what should we do? All unnecessary expenses should be avoided—we should live in the most economical way, and labor unceasingly to improve our means, so that we may be enabled to discharge those debts which we have contracted. "Render, therefore," says St. Paul, "to all men their dues." (Rom. xiii., 7.)

Moreover, the seventh commandment strictly obliges us to give every one what belongs to him. Every one, therefore, who has unjustly in his possession the goods which he knows belong to another, is bound by every law, divine and human, to restore them. Injustice or fraud is a violation of the rights of others which cannot be repaired except by an equivalent restitution. The obligation of restitution is dictated by the law of nature and the positive law of God. The law of nature, written in the heart of every one of us, by the very fact of forbidding us to take unjustly what belongs to another, commands us to restore, what belongs not to us, to the rightful owner.

To this law of nature, impressed on the heart of man from the beginning, God added also his positive law to restore ill-gotten goods and repair the damage unjustly done to another. "He who has taken away anything by stealth, shall make good the loss to the owner." (Exod. xxii., 12.) This positive law of God is so strictly binding in conscience that neither the sin of injustice nor any other sin will be forgiven unless we are willing to repair the injustice we have committed.

In the book of Ezechiel we read: "And if that wicked man restore the pledge, and render what he had robbed, and walk in the commandments of life, and do no unjust thing, he shall surely live, and shall not die." (Ezech. xxxiii., 15.) Here life is promised to such as are guilty of the sins of injustice, but it is upon condition that they not only do penance

for them, but likewise do justice by returning what they
have wrongfully in their possession, or what they unjustly
withhold from others. On these, and only on these terms,
the prophet assures them of the pardon of their sins. And
this stands to reason ; for if a real repentance is necessary for
the pardon of our sins—as certainly it is—satisfaction is,
without doubt, necessary. But how can there be a real will
to repent of the evil we have done, where there is not a real
will to satisfy for it as far as we are able? How can any
one be sorry for the injustice he has committed, whilst he
still designs to continue the injustice? How can he have a
regret in his heart for having injured another in his property, when he has no mind to repair the injury?

In order to obtain forgiveness of sin, says St. Thomas,
we must strictly observe the laws of equity ; and therefore,
adds the saint, to obtain pardon of sin, we must restore if
we possibly can, that which we have unjustly taken ; for
without this restitution there can be no real conversion, nor
any hope of obtaining pardon from God. Yes, we may strike
our breasts and call on the Lord for forgiveness ; we may
groan with sorrow at the feet of God's minister ; we may
confess with tears in our eyes ; still all this will be of no
avail, if we retain unjustly the property of our neighbor. If
we restore not ill-gotten goods, our sighs and tears and prayers will be a mere mockery ; there is no real sorrow for sin,
but a hypocritical, fruitless sorrow.

For this reason it has been always the constant practice
of the church to refuse absolution and the holy sacraments
to thieves, robbers, usurers, extortioners, unjust dealers, re-
ceivers, accomplices, and usurpers of other men's goods, unless they both renounce their wicked practices, and make
restitution for their past injustices. Unless this be done by
them, they cannot be supposed to be true Gospel penitents,

or to have a real regret for their past sins. Their conversion is but a mere phantom; for as St. Augustine says, in his letter to Macedonius, where there is injustice no forgiveness can be had from God. "They are the worst sort of men," says the Saint, "whom you mentioned to me; they reap no benefit from the healing sacrament of penance; for where injustice is the sin, if what is taken away be not restored in itself, or its equivalent, there is only a pretence of repentance, but not a real repentance; for there is no forgiveness to be had where restitution is not made." (Epist. 153.)

Finally, all nations agree in this positive law of restitution, a law so advantageous to human society that, were it punctually observed, it would change the face of the world and secure every one in his right and property. It would preserve the poor from the oppression of the rich, and the simple and unwary from the knavery of designing men. It would also guard the rich from the private attempts of the poor and needy; and protect the industrious from the pilfering of lazy drones, who knavishly live upon the labors of others. Thus all would, with security, enjoy what God has pleased to give them, and right would be a sufficient protection against all wrong.

"Some," says St. Alphonsus, "who have acquired property by unlawful, dishonest means, look upon restitution when imposed by a confessor, as a very severe penance. But it is not a penance; it is a duty imposed by justice, from which neither the confessor, nor the bishop, nor the Pope can dispense.

Let us now see how the duty of justice imposes the obligation of restitution:

First, Upon those who are in unjust possession of their neighbor's property *without the help of others;* and

Second, Upon those who are in possession of their neighbor's property *by the help of others.*

I. There is a man named Anderson. He obtained possession of a certain amount of property without any dishonesty on his part; it was given to him by mistake, or he took it because he thought it belonged to him. Now after some time, he begins for good reasons, to doubt as to whether that portion of the property is really his own. From that moment he is bound in conscience to investigate the matter in order to find out for certain whether he or some one else is the rightful owner of that part of the property. If after a diligent investigation, he finds out for certain that not he but Mr. Barr is the rightful owner of that property, he is bound to restore to Mr. Barr that portion of the property, or its value. He is, however, not bound to compensate Mr. Barr for the loss sustained during the time he was deprived of that part of the property. On the contrary, if he, Mr. Anderson, had expenses in taking care of it, or incurs expenses in restoring it, he is entitled to have the amount of those expenses refunded by Mr. Barr. But if Mr. Anderson consumed Mr. Barr's goods during the time of his sincere belief that those goods were his own, and has not become richer by the use of them, he is under no obligation to restore their value to Mr. Barr. But if Mr. Anderson became richer by consuming Mr. Barr's goods, he is bound to restore to Mr. Barr as much as he is made richer by the consumption of them, that is to say, Mr. Anderson must restore to Mr. Barr what he has saved up by the use of Mr. Barr's goods and what still remains of them in his own property and should have been spent, had he not used Mr. Barr's property.

Another, Mr. Anderson knows that he has obtained possession of a certain portion of property by dishonest means; he stole it, or received it from one who he knows had no right to it. In this case Mr. Anderson is obliged to restore, at his own expense not only the ill-gotten property, but also to indemnify the owner for all the losses caused, even accidentally, by his injustice.

Again, Mr. Anderson set accidentally fire to Mr. Barr's house. He did all in his power to extinguish it; but in spite of all his efforts to extinguish the fire considerable damage was done to Mr. Barr's house. Now, as Mr. Anderson had not the least intention to damage Mr. Barr's property by fire, he is not guilty before God of the sin of injustice, and where there is no sin of injustice, there is no obligation of restitution; and where the sin of injustice is but venial, the obligation of restitution is not binding under pain of mortal sin. Hence Mr. Anderson is not bound in conscience to repair the damage caused by fire to Mr. Barr.

Again, if any one has committed a real act of injustice, but did not foresee its serious consequences or the extent of the damage done, he is only so far bound in conscience to make restitution as he is guilty before God, or in other words, he is answerable only for such consequences as he could foresee at the time he committed the act of injustice. Let us, for instance, suppose that Mr. Anderson, out of revenge, throws into the fire a valuable book belonging to Mr. Barr, containing a twenty-dollar note, of which he (Mr. Anderson) is not aware. Now, Mr. Anderson, in this case, is bound in conscience to restore to Mr. Barr only the value of the book itself, but not the twenty dollars, because he is innocent in the loss of the twenty dollars.

These remarks apply simply to the obligations of conscience, and are quite independent of what the civil law might enforce, and should any such case be brought before the civil court, its decision must be respected.

II. Let us now see how far the seventh commandment

binds those who have obtained possession by the help of others.

When several persons together, suppose Andrew, Bernard, Cyrillus and David, have committed an act of injustice, then he, suppose Andrew, who is in possession of the thing stolen or its value, is first bound to make the restitution; but if he neglects to do so, the other accomplices, Bernard, Cyrillus and David, must make restitution.

If the property stolen was divided among the accomplices, each one is bound in the first place to return to the owner the part he received; but if all refuse to make restitution, each one is bound to repair the whole loss.

If the person or persons who have secured to themselves the whole benefit of the theft, refuse to make restitution, or if there has been simply an unjust destruction of property, under what obligation are the accomplices in this case? If they had an equal share in the damage done, they are all bound to an equal share in making restitution; and should any of them be unable or unwilling to restore his part, the others are bound to restore it for him.

However, if they acted under the guidance of some one who planned the whole affair, or who got the accomplices together and by command, counsel or persuasion caused them to commit the act of injustice, the obligation of restitution rests whole and entire on him alone in the first place, because the whole act of injustice is principally owing to him. But if he is unable or unwilling to repair the loss, the obligation of restitution rests upon his companions in the crime in proportion to the share which they had in committing the act of injustice, and if they fail to comply with this duty, each one is bound to repair the whole loss.

If any one of the accomplices has repaired the entire loss, none of them is any longer under any obligation to the person whose property they stole or injured, but they are obliged to compensate the one who restored the full amount.

To put the principles in a clearer light:

Suppose Andrew, by command, counsel or persuasion, induces Bernard, Cyrillus and David to steal a sum of money belonging to William. With the assistance of Cyrillus and David, Bernard secures all the money and uses it for his own benefit. Which of them is bound to make the restitution? In the first place Bernard is bound to restore the whole amount, because he is in possession of the stolen property. Secondly, if Bernard fails to comply with his duty, the obligation of restitution rests upon Andrew, who, too, in this case is bound to restore the full amount of the theft, because the whole loss caused to William is principally owing to Andrew. Thirdly, if both Andrew and Bernard refuse to make restitution, the obligation rests on Cyrillus and David; and if either of them is unable or unwilling to comply with his duty, the other is bound to restore the full amount. Now, let us suppose that David restores the full amount to William, then the other accomplices are no longer under any obligation to William; but Bernard is still bound to restore the full amount to David, and if Bernard fails to do this, the full obligation falls upon Andrew; and if both Bernard and Andrew fail to comply with their obligation, Cyrillus is bound to pay half the amount of the theft to David.

If, however, Andrew's command, counsel or persuasion are not the efficient cause of the injury, then, though he sins, he is not bound to restitution. To be bound to make restitution, the injury must in every case be not only intended, but also inflicted; in other words, counsel, consent or persuasion do not oblige any one to make restitution unless they are the efficient cause of the injustice done.

25

ANSWERS TO OBJECTIONS.

There is one who says: "Father, I am willing to make restitution, but I am quite poor at present. What must I do?"

If you are really unable to make restitution at present, if you and your family have hardly enough for your daily support, you are excused from sin, says St. Alphonsus. It will do for you to have the sincere intention to restore the ill-gotten goods as soon as you are able, and to restore as much as it will be in your power to restore. If you are unable to restore all that belongs to your neighbor, you are bound to restore at least as much as you are able. And in order to be able to put your intention into execution, you must curtail the expenses of your family, make sacrifices of comfort and ease, suffer inconveniences, and submit to privations from time to time. You have, for instance, to make a restitution of fifty dollars. Try to save a dollar every week, and at the end of the year you will be able to restore all.

But you say, "I shall never be able to restore all I owe" In this case, it will do to restore as much as you can and whenever you can.

There is another. He says: "If I make restitution, what will become of my children?"

And if you do not restore the ill-gotten goods, what will become of you and your children? Do you not thus expose yourself and your children to the imminent danger of going to hell? And will you be foolish enough to go to hell for the sake of your family?

Peter de Palude relates that a certain father of a family who was very rich, but whose riches were obtained unjustly, had contracted a dangerous malady. He was well aware that his malady would prove fatal, yet he could not be induced to restore his ill-gotten property. Whenever he was spoken to on the subject. he immediately answered: "What should become of my three sons? They would be wretched forever." A priest who had heard of this circumstance determined to bring the dying man to a sense of his duty, and for this purpose had recourse to the following ingenious artifice: "If," said he to the sick man, "you wish to recover from your malady, you must procure a little of the fat of human flesh, extracted by fire, and have it applied to your body. It will be no easy matter to procure it, but perhaps a large sum of money may induce some person to put his hands for some minutes in a fire to have a little fat extracted from it." The sick man replied that it would be impossible to procure, even for the largest sum of money, what he deemed necessary for his cure. "Have you not children?" said the priest; "send to them, and make known your desire of obtaining the remedy." The sick man had three sons, the matter was proposed to each of them in turn, but none of them would submit to the pain of fire for the recovery of their father. The priest then said to the sick man: "Is it not the greatest folly on your part to ruin both your soul and body, and cast them into hell to burn forever, through regard for your children, who, to save your life, would not consent to endure for a quarter of an hour the pain of an earthly fire?" This circumstance touched the sick man. "I have done wrong," said he, "but my eyes are now opened to my injustices." He then restored all that he owed, and compensated for all the losses others suffered through his means.

What an excess of folly to go to hell in order to leave your children comfortable! Listen to what one day happened to a certain father of a family, who had burdened his conscience by taking the property of others in order to assist his children. At his death he called for a lawyer, in order to make his will. As soon as the lawyer arrived, the dying man said: *" Write the following bequests: I leave my soul to the devil."* The family began to exclaim, *" O Jesus, Jesus, the poor man is delirious!"* He replied: *" I am not delirious, I am not delirious; lawyer, write; I leave my soul to the devils, that they may carry it to hell, in punishment of the thefts I have committed. I also leave to the devils the soul of my wife, who has encouraged me to steal, that she might indulge her vanity. I also leave to the devils my children, who have been the cause of my thefts."* The confessor who heard his confession during life, and who was then assisting him, exhorted him not to despair, but to have confidence in God. The dying man concluded his will, saying: *" I also leave to the devil my confessor, because during life he always absolved me, and did not oblige me to make restitution."*—[*Ardia Inst. Tom. ii. Ins. 48, n. 8.*]

In the life of the venerable Father Louis la Nuza, a celebrated missionary in Sicily, who died in 1656, we read that having gone to pay a visit of charity to a gentleman laboring under a serious malady, he was told that the gentleman possessed the property of others to a large amount. He exhorted him to make restitution. The gentleman answered: *"If I make restitution my son will not be able to live like his equals."* Father Louis entreated and conjured him not to expose his soul to certain damnation; but the gentleman remained obstinate. On the following morning, as the father was walking on a solitary road, he met four black men conducting a man bound on a beast of burden. He asked where they were carrying the miserable man. They answered: *"To fire."* The father looked at the man, and saw that he was the man who obstinately refused to make restitution. He afterwards went into the city, and was informed that the unhappy gentleman had just expired. Behold the end of those who refuse to make restitution, in order to leave their children in affluence.

One day St. Anthony of Padua was giving a mission in the city of Florence. During the mission a rich miser died. The relations of the deceased invited St. Anthony to preach the funeral sermon. The Saint accepted the invitation. He first prayed for a while, and during his prayers God revealed to him that this rich man was damned on account of his sins of injustice. St. Anthony then ascended the pulpit and as the text of his discourse, he quoted the words of our Saviour: "Where thy treasure is there is also thy heart." He explained these words very forcibly, and to the astonishment of those present, he applied them to the rich man who had just died. "Yes," cried he in a voice of thunder, "this rich man has died and he is buried in hell. If you doubt my words, hasten to his house and throw open the chest in which that unjust man kept his gold. Look into it and you will find there his heart still fresh and warm in the midst of his money. You shall find, that though his body lies in the grave, his heart is where his treasure is." At these words, the friends and relatives of the deceased rich man rushed out of the church; they hastened to his residence; they opened the chest, and to their horror they saw there a human heart still reeking and warm in the midst of these ill-gotten gains.

> Curs'd merchandise! where life is sold,
> And avarice consents to starve for gold.

There is another. He says: "Father, I am willing to make restitution. But I cannot restore those goods to the rightful owner without exposing my character. And I do not see how one should be obliged to reveal his own crimes and expose himself to public censure."

Your case is not so difficult as you think. You can

restore ill-gotten goods secretly and without compromising yourself. Any prudent confessor can suggest a way in which restitution can be made to the proper party without betrayal of the guilty one.

Suppose, for instance, Andrew owes something in justice to Bernard, but cannot give it to him without compromising himself. Now, it will often happen that Bernard needs something of the same value. In this case Andrew can send the equivalent as a present to Bernard.

Again, a storekeeper has for some time given short weight or measure. Now, if the same customers continue to deal with him, he may easily make restitution by allowing them a little more than just weight. Thus there are many ways in which ill-gotten goods or their value may be restored without making the thief known to the owner of the goods or to other persons.

"But, Father, can I not fulfil my obligation of restitution by getting Masses said for the sum I owe, or by giving it for pious uses?" No; suppose you had already distributed in alms the sum you owe, your obligation of restitution would not be cancelled, as long as you know the rightful owner or heir of the ill-gotten property. What the owner, in your case, wants is his property which you have taken, and not your Masses or other good works for it.

There is another. He says, "Father, some time ago I bought some goods; but at the same time I had good reasons to believe that they were stolen. Now, as I paid for them, am I not justified to keep them?"

You say you knew that those goods were stolen. How, then can you keep them? You did wrong in buying them. You must now restore them, for every one must get his own. "But, Father, if I had not bought them, another would have purchased them." Do not allow yourself to be deceived by the devil. If another had bought them, not you, but he would be obliged to restore them. But as you have bought them, not another, it is you that are obliged to restore them, for the simple reason that those goods do still belong to him from whom they were stolen.

There is another. He says, "Father, I found a purse containing two hundred dollars. As I do not know the owner may I not keep it?"

It would be a great delusion to think that whatever we find we can keep. The goods lost by another are still his goods; for he is unwilling to give up all claim to them. Hence, if they are found, they must be restored to him. "Justice," says St. Augustine, "obliges us so strictly to return the property of another when found, that if we restore it not, we are as guilty as if we had stolen it." What you have found, and not restored, you have, as it were, stolen. If the owner cannot be found, or if he has no heir, the value must be given to the poor, or for some charitable object. This rule applies also to all those who have in their possession property which belongs to another whose residence cannot be found, or if dead, whose heir is unknown. "If the person to whom a restitution is to be made is dead, it must be made to his lawful heirs. If he is absent and his residence known, it must be transmitted to him as soon as possible. If he has no lawful heirs, or if his residence cannot be found out, the amount of the restitution must, for his sake, be distributed among the poor or given to some charitable institution. This rule now generally carried out in practice, is in accordance with justice and probably also with the intention of the owner of the property lost, or unjustly taken or retained.

A poor Chinese Christian found in one of the streets of Pekin a purse containing twenty pieces of gold. He looked around, hoping to find a claimant; and thinking it might have fallen from a gentleman on horseback, who had just passed, he ran after him and asked him if he had lost anything.   The gentleman searched his pockets, and missing his purse, replied in a tremulous voice: "Yes, I have lost my purse containing twenty pieces of gold!" "Be not disturbed," said the poor man, "here it is with the twenty pieces."   The gentleman, recovering from his alarm, could not but admire so noble an action, in a man of humble condition.   "But who are you?" said he; "what is your name?—where do you live?" "It matters little," said the poor man, "for you to know who I am; it is sufficient to tell you that I am a Christian; one of those who make profession of observing the law of the Gospel, which forbids, not only to steal the goods of others, but even to keep what may be found by chance, when the owner may be found."   The gentleman was so struck with the purity of Christian morality, that he went immediately to the church of the Christians, in order to receive instructions in the mysteries of our religion.—[*Letteres Edifiantes.*]

There is another who keeps the property of his neighbor and wishes to make restitution; but says, "When I am dying I will speak about it."

Do you, then, wish to make restitution when you cannot take the property with you?   When a person, says St. Alphonsus, is able to make restitution and defers it for a notable time, he is guilty of mortal sin, though he should have the intention of making the restitution.   He is excused from mortal sin if he defers the restitution for a short time, for ten or fifteen days, but no longer.   And should his creditor suffer a loss on account of this short delay, he is bound to repair the loss; for it is certain that a thief is bound to compensate the owner for all the damage done him by the theft.

He who is able to make restitution and will not make it immediately cannot be absolved. For most persons find it very difficult to make restitution; and therefore he who, though able, does not make it immediately, is in danger of not making it at all. A certain gentleman stole and retained a hundred pieces of gold. He went to confession and was required by his confessor to make restitution, and perhaps under pain of being refused absolution. "*Father*," said he to the confessor, "*I shall make restitution as soon as I return home.*" But he did not fulfil his promise; he frequently made similar promises, but afterwards violated them. The confessor said to him: "If you wish to receive absolution, go home and bring me the stolen property; otherwise, I shall not absolve you." He went home and brought back the money. The confessor said, "*Give it to me.*" He replied, "*Father, stretch out your hand and take it.*" Thus he made restitution. From this fact, you may learn how improbable it is that a person who was absolved before he made restitution will afterwards restore what belongs to others. It is certain that unless he makes restitution he can never obtain the pardon of his sins. "For this reason," says St. Alphonsus, "no sin is more dangerous to the soul than the sin of theft. Other sins are forgiven if we are sincerely sorry for them and confess them; but how great soever our sorrow for the sin of theft may be; how sincerely soever we may confess it, and how great soever the penances may be that we perform for it, this sin will not be pardoned by God unless we make restitution when we are able to do so."

Unhappy the man who keeps in his possession the property of another; for he will hardly make restitution, and will probably be damned.

One who had for many years been guilty of unjust practices being at last at the point of death, sent for a confessor

to administer to him the last sacrament. The confessor told
him that the first step to be taken was the restitution of
property, as his goods had been unjustly acquired. "I cannot resolve on doing what you require; I cannot do it,"
replied the unfortunate man, and in a few moments after he
expired. How awful a death! How much it should cause
those to tremble who have acquired the goods which they
possess by fraud and injustice.—[*Catechime de L'Empire.*]

I repeat, unhappy the man who keeps the property of
another! Will he ever in this life have comfort in the enjoyment of the goods of others? No; for he shall be continually tortured by remorse of conscience. A certain robber
stole an ox from St. Medard; the ox had a bell suspended
from its neck. The robber brought the ox to his house, and
though the ox remained motionless, the bell never ceased to
ring. The night came; fearing that he should be detected
the robber stuffed the bell with hay; but it still continued to
ring. What did he then do? He took the bell off the ox,
and shut it up in a chest; but the bell did not cease to ring.
At last the robber, filled with fear, took the ox and restored
it to St. Medard, and the ringing ceased. Let us make the
application to ourselves. He who keeps the goods of another
has within himself a bell, which rings unceasingly and says:
"*Unless you make restitution you shall be damned.*" Go,
then, and find peace in the midst of such continual remorse.

The prophet of the Lord says that when our neighbor's
property enters unjustly into our house, a curse enters with
it at the same time. "This is the curse that goeth over the
face of the earth . . . It shall come to the house of the
thief . . . and shall consume it." (Zach. v., 3.) "He,
therefore," says St. Gregory, " who possesses wealth unjustly, shall lose even his own riches which he has justly
acquired, as a punishment for his injustice."

THE EIGHTH COMMANDMENT.

"Thou shalt not bear false witness against thy neighbor."

Did you ever reflect on the power that is in a word? To utter a word requires but little effort on your part. Only one breath is sufficient to waft it from your lips to the ears of your listener; but when once uttered, it is past recall. It reveals the secret motives and thoughts of your heart.

Your word may have been a cheerful, pleasant, loving word, proceeding from a heart full of kindness, which, like sweet music struck the listening ear, which will ever respond in strains of love and harmony. Your word may, perhaps, have been a word of sympathy or encouragement, uttered in tenderest accents, so that it scattered the clouds of despair, and diffused sunshine into the heart well nigh crushed beneath its burden of woe.

Perhaps your word was an unkind one, harshly spoken, and accompanied by a cold, chilling look which cast a gloomy shadow over some loving, sensitive heart. Your word was perhaps one of malice, envy, or deceit, and enkindled a bitter feeling of resentment which will live on and on while memory lives.

Ah! Your word might have been a thoughtless one, spoken in an unguarded moment; but it left its impression and may be remembered long after your voice is hushed and you are sleeping in the grave.

Words may seem but little things to us, but they possess a power beyond calculation; they swiftly .fly from us to

others, and, though we scarcely give them a passing thought
their spirit lives; though they are as fleeting as the breath
that bore them, their power for good or evil is as enduring as
the heart they reach.   Hence St. James, the apostle, says
that the tongue of man though but a little member, is the
cause of many great evils.   We have already explained several of these evils, such as false teaching, cursing, swearing,
blaspheming, immodest words, etc.; besides these, there are
many other sins of the tongue, namely, all such words as
tend to ruin the character and destroy the good name of our
fellow-men.   It is of these sins of the tongue that we now
come to speak in the explanation of the eighth commandment, — "*Thou shalt not bear false witness against they
neighbor.*"

This commandment is given us by God to regulate our
words.   It forbids:

1. *False testimony.*   A false testimony is to affirm a
thing, upon word or oath, to be true, when we know or believe it to be false; or to declare a thing to be false, which we
know or think to be true; and this, whether it be by word of
mouth or by writing, by signs, or any kind of behavior
whereby one can discover our meaning.

To appear as a witness in open court before a judge or
magistrate appointed to administer justice, and there to
affirm what is not true, or to tell as true what we know to be
untrue, that is also what we understand by false testimony,
or false evidence.

False testimony is a grievous breach of the eighth commandment, and being so is a grievous sin.   Our Lord speaks
in the strongest terms of false testimony.   In the book of
Proverbs he says: "A man that bears false witness against
his neighbor is as a dart, a sword, and a sharp arrow, whereby
he ruins his neighbor, and kills his own soul." (Proverbs

xxv. 18.) And again in the same book, he says: "A false witness shall not go unpunished, and he that speaks lies shall perish." (xix.) Yes, indeed, they shall not go without punishment, for though they escape punishment in this world, they shall not escape it in the world to come. Though they may impose on men in this world by their knavery and deceit, all their tricks will be of no avail when they shall appear before God, to render an account of their false testimony.

If one bears false witness in an open court, where a man's life is at stake, he commits two grievous sins, the sin of perjury and the sin of murder, and thus he commits an offence against God and man. He is guilty of a great offence against God, for he abuses his holy name, and calls on him to witness his villany. He is guilty of an offence against man, and that of the greatest kind, because he endeavors to take away his life wrongfully. When a man's life has been taken away by false testimony, it is not the judge that condemns, nor the hangman that executes, but it is the *false witness* that murders him. The judge is allowed to follow the testimony of the legal witnesses; and the hangman is not obliged to weigh the merits of the case, but to do his duty. The whole guilt and crime, therefore, of the murder falls upon the false witness.

Again, if a man bears false testimony in defence of a criminal, and out of friendship preserves a murderer from the gallows, he is equally guilty of a great offence against God, and of inflicting an injury on the public, by letting loose a villain, and turning him again on the world. He may say I have concealed the truth that *my neighbor might not be injured*. This excuse is not sufficient, because when asked by lawful authority, you are bound to tell what you know, though it should be the cause of loss to your neighbor. This is a just loss, for the public good requires that malefactors should be punished, but they cannot be punished if witnesses do not depose to what they know.

Those that bear false testimony in trials of less importance than life, such as trials regarding estates, money, damages, or the like, are also guilty of a great offence against God, for they commit perjury — as witnesses are not allowed to give testimony till they are sworn. They are also guilty of all damages they occasion their neighbor, by their false testimony, if hè has a just title or right on his side; and their crime is more or less grievous in proportion to the damage of which they have been the cause.

Those who bear false testimony, do it through fear or love, or interest. . False testimony is given through *fear* when the witness is intimidated by those who have influence over him, or by those on whom he depends. False testimony is given out of *love*, when a friend or relative is connected with the case to be tried, and that we wish to oblige him. False testimony is given out of *interest*, when we receive a bribe—a sum of money for our unjust service. But persons, who, in giving false testimony, are influenced by one or the other of these motives, are far from being gainers by their bargain. Those who, in the first place bear false witness out of *fear*, show that they fear men more than God, and that they prefer the countenance of the great of this world to the laws of Christ. But on the last day of judgment, they shall find how great their error was, and how baneful to them was that preference. Those who bear false testimony out of *love* and affection for a friend, show a mistaken, not a real love for the friend, for, to love him thus, is to love him for his ruin; for what else can it be, whilst he lives in the usurpation of what belongs to others?

Those, in fine, who bear false testimony out of *interest*, give a clear proof that they prefer temporal before eternal;

because for a little unjust gain they choose to lose everlasting wealth, and condemn themselves to eternal woes—the consequence of such a loss. For, as we have said before, they must repair all the damage they have occasioned, as far as they are able, or they must lay aside every hope of seeing the face of God, or sharing in the happiness of the saints in heaven; and must have no other expectation than that of being cast hereafter into eternal darkness and of being chained in eternal flames. One or the other must certainly be their lot, or rather their choice; for, where injustice is at the bottom of the crime, forgiveness is not to be had, if restitution be not made.

All those who bear false testimony against their neighbor may, indeed, bear the name of Christians, but certainly they cannot believe in Christ and his promises and rewards; for, surely they cannot hope to please a righteous God by wronging their neighbor, nor can they expect on the last day a crown of *justice* for having lived and died in the ways of *injustice.* No; such a blessing they cannot expect, for they well know that the blessing of God, belongs only to the just according to the words of Christ himself: "Blessed are they that hunger and thirst after justice, for they shall have their fill."—(Matt. v. 6.)

False testimony or perjury has been at all times severely punished by the law of God, and also by human laws. In the law which Almighty God gave to Moses, a false witness who is found to be so, is ordered to be condemned to the same punishment that the person falsely accused would have suffered, had he been really guilty of the charge brought against him. "And when after most diligent search, they shall find that the false witness hath told a lie against his brother: they shall render to him, as he meant to do his brother." (Deut. xix. 19.)

Several nations have punished this crime with death. The Romans formerly cast those guilty of false testimony from the Tarpeian Mount, as a terror to others. The church in her ancient canons, excommunicates false witnesses, and forbids them communion to their death because, says the great council of Arles, the Scripture says: "A false testimony ought not to be unpunished." (Deut. xix. 19.)

If, you should at any time be called on to give evidence in a court of Justice, never swerve in the least from the truth, no matter what may be the consequence. Tell exactly the truth, declare what you know and in the manner you know it, with sincerity and candor. Let neither hatred, nor love, nor pity, nor fear, nor hope of base gain—let neither entreaties, nor menaces, ever induce you to bear false testimony, for it is a grievous sin against the eighth commandment.

2. *Lies.* To *lie* is to tell to another what we believe to be untrue with the intention to deceive him. The nature of a lie, therefore, consists in the intention of deceiving our neighbor. Hence, one may tell what is perfectly true, and yet tell a lie, if he intends to deceive him by what he tells; or, he may tell what is not true, and yet not tell a lie, because he has no intention to deceive his neighbor by what he tells him.

Suppose Andrew tells Bernard to-day that he intends to leave to-morrow for Europe, without having, however, the least intention of doing so. In this case Andrew told a lie, even though next day he leaves for Europe, for some reason that he was not aware of at the time when he told Bernard that he would go to Europe next day. But suppose that Andrew told Bernard he would not leave next day for Europe, and had at the time really the intention not to depart, yet for some reason occurring afterwards, was induced to set out, he, in this case, did not tell a lie.

There are three kinds of lies and some much worse than others. There is, *first*, the *jocose lie*, which is injurious to nobody, and is told out of mirth or sport, and only to please those present for a moment, without prejudicing any. Of this kind of lie was that of Sarah, when she said she did not laugh, when she really did so, as we read in the eighteenth chapter in the book of Genesis. There is, *secondly*, the *officious lie*, which hurts none, and is told because it is profitable to some. The lie of the Egyptian midwives to Pharaoh was a lie of this kind; because it was told to save the male infants of the Israelites from being murdered, as we read in the first chapter of the book of Exodus. There is, *thirdly*, the *malicious lie*, which is injurious to God and is prejudicial to our neighbor. Of this kind of lie was the lie of the devil to Eve, when he said to her, in order to induce her to eat the forbidden fruit: "You shall not die." (Gen. iii., 4.)

Every lie, of its own nature, is a sin, because it is contrary to the truth, and on that account offensive to God, who, being truth itself, necessarily hates all lying and duplicity. It is sinful, too, because it is injurious to our neighbor, for, by telling a lie, we deceive him.

That *lies* are offensive to God clearly follows from his sacred word, for all lies, without exception, are there strictly forbidden. In the book of Leviticus we read: "You shall not *lie*, neither shall any man deceive his neighbor." (Lev. xix., 11.) And in the book of Ecclesiasticus it is said: "Be not willing to make *any manner* of lie, for the custom thereof is not good." (Ecclus. vii., 14.) St. Paul, in his epistle to the Ephesians, strongly urges the avoiding of all lies: "Wherefore putting away lying, speak ye the truth every one with his neighbor." (Eph. iv., 25.) And in the book of Revelations St. John thus speaks of liars: "Without are . . . sorcerers . . . and murderers, and

26

servers of idols, and every one that loveth and maketh a lie." (Rev. xxii., 15.)   From these and several other texts of Scripture it clearly follows that all lies, without exception, are forbidden.

As every lie is a sin, it can never be lawful to tell a lie, not even for the best of motives ; for, as St. Paul says, it is never allowed to do evil that good may come from it. (Rom. iii., 8.)   Hence it would not be lawful to tell a lie even for the purpose of escaping death, or of saving mankind from hell.

Our Saviour tells us that lies are from the devil ; that the devil is the master and father of lies :   " When he speaketh a lie, he speaketh of his own, for he is a liar and the father thereof." (John viii., 44.)

Liars are, therefore, hateful to God, and are also contempt- ible in the eyes of men.   For, together with being offensive to God, there is such a meanness in telling a lie that no person of honor will be guilty of it.   Such is the contempt in which liars are held even by worldly persons, that the greatest insult which can be offered to a man is to call him a *liar*.   He may patiently allow himself to be called a drunk- ard, a wrangler, a brawler, or any other opprobrious name, but when branded a liar, he is no longer patient, but pas- sionately resents what he considers the greatest insult that could be offered to him.   The character of a liar is every- where hated, and the imputation of being a liar is considered as a stain of the deepest hue by every one who has a regard for honesty and morality.   No greater reproach can a man lie under than to be reputed a liar.   And such is the idea that the world entertains of this vice that few characters are considered more despicable than liars.

The vice of lying is subversive of social intercourse, and is opposed to God's beneficent design in conferring the gift of speech ; for what would become of society if lying were tolerated ? How could we contrive to live with persons whose promises and words we could not believe ?

Were we about to transact business with an *untruthful* person, we should be continually embarrassed, for no precaution could preserve us from being deceived and over-reached. A lying person will become a cheat and deceiver in his behavior, double in his words, unfaithful in his promises, a hypocrite in his manners, a dissembler in his actions, a flatterer, and faint-hearted when he should speak the truth ; bold and shameless to affirm lies, impudent to maintain them as certain truths ; a swearer, a detractor, mistrustful of every one ; for, as he is accustomed to lie, he believes that others always speak false. A mind addicted to lying will easily be so in things of moment, and consequently involved in heinous sins.

Hence St. Francis de Sales was right in saying that " we can hardly tell an untruth, be it ever so little, without injury to our neighbor ; it will always do harm either to him who utters it or to others ; it wounds truth and straightforwardness of the heart. Whoever lies, were it only in fun, shows that his heart is not sincere, but that he speaks with *a double heart* (Ps. 11) ; and we are told in Holy Writ that " *the Lord will destroy deceitful lips*," and is not he deceitful who tells a lie ? "

St. Andrew Avelino was sent in early life to Naples, to study civil and canon law. Being promoted there to the degree of doctor in laws, and to the dignity of the priesthood, he began to plead such causes in the ecclesiastical court as the canons allow clergymen to undertake. This employment, however, engrossed his thoughts, dissipated his mind too much, and insensibly weakened his affection for holy meditation and prayer. A fault into which he fell, opened his eyes and made him see the precipice which lay before him. Once in pleading a cause in a matter, indeed which was of no weight, a lie escaped him, for which, upon reading these words of Holy Scripture: *The mouth that lieth killeth the soul*, he was struck with so great a remorse and deep compunction, that he resolved immediately to renounce his profession, and to give himself up entirely to a penitential life and to the spiritual care of souls. This he did with so great ardor that his whole conduct was a model of perfect virtue, and in the year 1556 he became a member of the order of the Theatins.—[*Albert Butler.*]

There are few vices more hurtful than the habit of lying. For this reason Holy Scripture says: "Be not willing to make any manner of lie, for the custom thereof is not good." (Ecclus. vii., 14.) That is, according to the expression of the Scripture, the custom is very bad.

Now, though every lie is sinful, because it is opposed to truth, and expressly forbidden by the word of God, yet every lie is not a *mortal* sin, because every lie is not a grievous breach of the love of God, nor does it deprive us of sanctifying grace. On that account, a *jocose* or *officious* lie is only a venial sin; it does not offend God grievously nor injure our neighbor seriously.

A lie is a *mortal* sin when, besides being contrary to truth, it is also opposed to any of those virtues which are necessary to salvation, such as faith, hope, charity, justice and religion, or when it is attended with scandal or confirmed with an oath. Of this sort of lie it is that the Scriptures speak when they tell us that "lying lips are an abomination to the Lord." (Prov. xii., 22.); and that "The mouth that lieth killeth the soul." (Wis. 1., 11.) Hence every lie against the truth revealed by Jesus Christ is a mortal sin and against faith; and every lie which seriously injures our neighbor, either in his person, goods or reputation, is also a mortal sin, because it is contrary to justice and charity. Putiphar's wife, in telling a lie in reference to Joseph, sinned mortally, because she injured him in his reputation and good name.

A lie attended with great scandal to others is also a mortal sin, because by that lie people are led into sin and are induced to think lightly of the commands of God.

Mental restrictions. Mental restriction or equivocation, *properly such*, is the act of a person who, in his own mind, puts a sense on the words he says, contrary to or different from their plain, natural and usual meaning; and which the hearers cannot possibly perceive, and have no grounds or occasion to suspect. Mental restrictions and equivocations of this nature are lies, and therefore never allowed, because they are always sinful; and the Catholic Church has declared them altogether unlawful. If they be used when one is upon his oath, they are perjury, and therefore never can be lawful for any end whatsoever, especially when one is called upon by public authority to declare the truth.

Mental restrictions and equivocations, *not properly such*, are effected when the words used have either in themselves or from circumstances two natural and plain significations, and the speaker uses them in one sense and the hearer takes them in another; or when they have both a literal and spiritual meaning, as when our Saviour said of St. John the Baptist, that "he was Elias," and St. John himself said: "I am not Elias." Mental restrictions and equivocations of this nature are not sinful and unlawful, for, if in such cases the hearers be deceived, it is their own fault, and the speaker is not guilty of lying.

Although lying is never lawful, yet we are not always obliged to make the truth known. Thus, instead of answering a question directly, you may answer it evasively, provided you do not tell a falsehood. I find an example of this kind in the life of St. Athanasius, who was so long persecuted by the Arians. One day, having been compelled to fly in all haste, he entered a boat which he found on the banks of the Nile, and went up the river towards the Thebaid. The person sent to kill him, hearing of his escape, pursued him as fast as he could; but he was outstripped by a friend of Athanasius, who apprised the saint that he was closely pursued. His companion then advised him to make for the desert. He, on the contrary, turned his boat to go down again to Alexandria, whence he came, " to show," he said, " that he who protects us is mightier than those who persecute us." All he then did was to conceal himself at the bottom of the bark. They soon met the boat in which was the persecutor, who asked them if Athanasius was far off, or if it was long since they left him. Guessing the Saint's intention in ordering the bark to be turned, the people in his boat simply answered: " He is not very far away, and you can easily overtake him if you wish." Hearing this, the other passed on and continued his pursuit. You may easily understand that he did not find the holy patriarch. It was thus that the great St. Athanasius, without having recourse to falsehood, but simply by means of an evasive though true reply, escaped from the hands of his enemies.—[*Schmid et Belet, Cat.'Hist.*, II., 449.]

When St. Thomas, Archbishop of Canterbury, in England, was persecuted unjustly by King Henry II., his sovereign, he was several times obliged to fly and conceal himself. He took refuge once in a hermitage near Sempringham, where he remained three whole years. During that time he walked always on foot, clothed as a monk, and bearing the name of *Brother Christian*. Nevertheless, being unaccustomed to travel in such a toilsome way, he had much to suffer, especially during a cold and rainy autumn. One day, overcome by fatigue, he threw himself on the ground and said to those who accompanied him: "I can go no farther; try to procure me a little nourishment, else I cannot walk." They brought him a wretched horse, without either bridle or saddle, laid their cloaks on the animal's back, and placed the Archbishop thereon, though with great difficulty. In this sorry plight they journeyed on for some time, when they saw approaching at full speed some armed men, who addressed themselves directly to St. Thomas, and said abruptly: "Are not you the Archbishop of Canterbury, whom we have been long seeking?" "My friends," he replied, "judge for yourselves; is this the equipage of an Archbishop?" They did not recognize him and put no further questions. Thus, by a very simple word, he got out of his difficulty, without offending God.—[*Schmid et Belet*, *Cat. Hist.* II., 452.

Hypocrisy. Hypocrisy is also a kind of lie; it consists in putting on the appearance of virtue in order to gain the esteem of men. A liar deceives his neighbor by his words; a hypocrite deceives him by his actions; he feigns to be what he is not; he pretends to virtues which he does not possess; he acts in such a way as to make his fellow-men believe that he is better and holier than he really is, in order thus to deceive them. The true hypocrite, therefore, cares not to be good and virtuous; he only cares to appear and pass as such before men.

By exterior good works he tries to conceal his wicked intentions and actions. He plays the saint, and is a devil. The Scribes and Pharisees, who lived at the time when our divine Redeemer lived on earth, were full of hypocrisy. Hence it was that he never spared them in his sermons. He pronounced on them and all hypocrites a very severe judgment. "Woe to you Scribes and Pharisees, hypocrites! You are like the whited sepulchres which outwardly appear to men beautiful, but within are full of dead men's bones and of all filthiness. So you also outwardly appear to men just, but inwardly you are full of hypocrisy and iniquity. (Matt. xxiii. 27-28.)

. Hypocrisy may be a mortal or a venial sin. It is a mortal sin when one tries to obtain something that is grievously wrong. Judas kissed our dear Saviour. He pretented to be his friend; but his kiss was that of a hypocrite; it was a mortal sin, because, by it he betrayed his divine Master.

Hypocrisy is a venial sin when, by it one tries to obtain what is not grievously wrong. A poor person, for instance, pretends to be poorer than he really is, or prays a little more fervently in order to obtain a larger alms. As such an intention of a beggar is not a grievous sin, his hypocrisy is but a venial sin.

Hypocrisy is always detestable even when it is but a venial sin. The hypocrite seeks not God's glory, but his own. He wishes to be praised and honored for what he does not possess. He is hateful to God and man.

There are many hypocrites everywhere. How many false devotees are there not, who, under the beautiful appearance of piety, are devoid of truth and charity, and who, while they converse like angels, live like devils. How many are thus not who unjustly possess ill-gotten goods, or commit adultery, child-murder, and other crimes secretly, and then, in order not to be suspected as thieves, adulterers, etc., put on the cloak of piety—they say many prayers, go often to confession and holy communion, join pious sodalities, speak in a most edifying manner, etc. — and all this, I say, to cover their secret crimes.

The worst kinds of hypocrites are those who, under the

cloak of charity or devotion, try to lead men away from God that they may join the army of Antichrist. See, what Freemasonry does to make Catholics join their diabolical society. By means of bad Catholics who have joined the secret societies, but who continue, in spite of their excommunication, to receive the sacrements, Freemasonry tries to make good Catholics join their society, holding out to them enticing temporal gains, and pretending that their society is the most charitable in the world. Accursed hypocrites !

> They clothe their naked villany
> With odd old ends stolen forth of Holy Writ,
> Appearing saints when most they play the devil.

They exercise great power everywhere. Why? Job tells us the reason when he says: "God maketh hypocrites to reign on account of the sins of the people." (Job xxxiv. 30.) Ah! let us never forget the curse which the son of God has pronounced upon all such hypocrites. Let us live in such a manner that our interior will always correspond to our exterior life, our faith to our works and our heart to our words. "Be not a hypocrite in the sight of men," says the Holy Ghost (Ecclus. i. 37), for, "the hope of the hypocrite shall perish; his joy lasts but for a moment." (Job viii. 13; xx. 5.)

3. *Calumny or Slander.* Calumny is to ascribe to another a crime which he has not committed, or to exaggerate a real fault of our neighbor. Can there be any crime so odious and so full of malice as that of ascribing to an innocent person crimes and guilt? So detestable is this sin that it is a matter of surprise that a Christian should ever be guilty of it. And yet this crime is but too often committed even by Christians.

When an altercation takes place between them, they calumniate each other in the most frightful manner, they reproach each other with the most infamous crimes and the most shameful acts. Listen to two women scolding, and what a scene! They are not even content with branding each other with the most opprobrious epithets and the most scandalous crimes, but must charge each other's ancestors with every species of wickedness and dishonesty.

This sin of calumny is so degrading, that of itself it inspires us with horror and affright; and when a Christian descends to such vileness and infamy, malice, indeed, must have taken deep root in his heart. One should think that no Christian, except one lost to all honor and respect, could be guilty of a vice so degrading and malignant, and yet there are to be found persons who charge others with various crimes of which they have not only not been guilty, but of which they never thought of committing.

Calumny, whenever it is greatly injurious to our neighbor's reputation, is a very grievous sin; a grievous breach of justice, charity and truth. For when the evil we say of our neighbor is false, the telling of it robs the absent of his good name and of the favor of others, and that is certainly doing him a great injustice; for if the robbing one of his property be a grievous breach of justice, the robbing him of his good name and of the kind regard of others is much more so, because the Scripture says: "A good name is better than great riches, and good favor is above silver and gold." (Prov. xxii. 1.)

Of the vice of calumny or slander, the Scripture speaks with the greatest horror. The Prophet David says of calumniators "that they have whetted their tongues like a sword, they have bent their bow, a bitter thing, to shoot in secret the undefiled." (Ps. lxiii. 4.) And again he declares them hateful to God and man. "Thy mouth," he says, "hath abounded with evil, and thy tongue hath framed deceits;

sitting thou didst speak against thy brother and didst lay a scandal against thy mother's son; these things thou hast done, and I was silent, thou thoughtest unjustly that I should be like to thee; but I will reprove thee, and sit before thy face." (Ps. xlix. 19.)

These declarations of Scripture clearly point out to us the detestation and horror in which God holds the vice of calumny. It is a base vice—it is a malignant vice, and one attended with the direst effects. It produces the most fatal consequences, as for example, in Joseph's imprisonment, Susanna's condemnation, and the murder of the eighty-five innocent priests by king Saul, on account of the slanderous accusation of Doeg. It is often thrown back on the calumniators, in their severe punishment, as in the elders that accused Susanna, and in the enemies of Daniel.

We may easily understand the grievousness of the sin of slander from the severe punishments with which God often has visited this crime.

Thomas of Canterbury tells us that he knew a man who was in the habit of tearing to pieces, with his treacherous tongue the good fame of his neighbors, and recklessly shedding the blood of their reputation. Being at the point of death, he fell into a paroxysm of such rage as to mangle his tongue with his teeth, and what was still more strange, whenever he opened his mouth an intolerable stench escaped from it. (Apum., cap. 37)

Baronius (Tom. iii. An. 397, n. 34) relates that a certain man, called Donatus, while at table cast reflections injurious to the happy and illustrious memory of St. Ambrose, and that another man called Mauranus, on like occasion, spoke evil of the glorious actions of St. Augustine. They were both struck with mortal blows by an invisible hand, and covered the table with their own blood. Having been carried on the arms of others from the table to their beds, they miserably expired.

We read in the life of St. Alphonsus, that, after he had established himself with some of his missionary priests in the diocese of Cajazzo, in Italy, at a place called the Villa there were several persons who tried by most vile calumnies, to ruin the zealous missionaries because they could not endure seeing their immoral lives censured. Their efforts to see the devoted missionaries banished from the place were crowned with success. But God was not slow in punishing everyone who had a share in the calumnies.

The tongue of the wretched woman who had falsely accused St. Alphonsus and his companions was eaten up by worms, in so frightful a manner, that she was unable to receive holy Communion; she was moreover so horribly tormented by remorse of conscience, that she was forced, as it were, to avow publicly that all she had said against the missionaries was but an infamous calumny.

Nicholas Masucci, who had joined in the calumnies, died soon after in despair, uttering the most frightful cries.

John Baptiste Riccardi, who was one of the principal slanderers, terminated his life in the most horrible convulsions, and howling like a perfect maniac.

The hand of Peter Jsolda, which had written down the testimony of the false witnesses whom he had procured, withered, and his only son died soon after; not long after he became an idiot and expired in great misery.

Another healthy young man, Peter Paotillo, died suddenly, immediately after the departure of St. Alphonsus from the villa.

Anthony Masello, who had attested all the calumnies for a sack of grain which Carmen Festa, the chief calumniator, had promised him, died impenitent. Not one of those who had a hand in the calumnies escaped the divine vengeance. Carmen Festa, the most guilty of all, seemed, for the moment, to have escaped, as if God, in his mercy, would give him more time to repent. God sent him a warning, but this wicked man did not heed the warning. Scarcely had the missionaries left the place when a tremendous storm arose; the lightning flashed, and a thunderbolt fell at the feet of this man as he sat in his room; it stunned him, and for a short time he remained unconscious and motionless. When he came to himself he would not recognize the warning. Ere long he fell into disgrace with the prince, was ill used and persecuted, and within a year after the departure of Alphonsus, he was found one morning lying dead under his bed and bathed in his blood.—[*Life of St. Alphonso*, Vol. I., p. 154.]

Detraction. Detraction is to make known, without sufficient cause, the *real*, but *secret*, faults of our neighbor. The sin of detraction, then, consists in making faults of our neighbor known that were not known before, and in making them known to others without sufficient cause. There may be reasons which make it lawful and even necessary to speak of another's faults to those whose duty it is to correct them. A girl, for instance, is too familiar with a young man, or a young man goes to a house of ill-fame. Now, if one makes such conduct known to the father of that young woman or young man, in order that he may apply a remedy, he is not guilty of the sin of detraction.

Again, if we know of some one whose influence is likely to prove injurious to others, it is lawful for us to warn them of their danger, or make the circumstances known to a superior. In this case we do not commit the sin of detraction.

Again, there is question of some projected alliance, or some other affair of importance. We know all about it. Now, if we are consulted by persons interested in ascertain-

ing it, it is no detraction if we give a correct, though disad-
vantageous information about a certain party.

We may even sometimes be obliged to report the fault of
another, when it can be done without danger of grievous
evil to ourselves. In all such cases, however, the faults
should be made known only to those who ought to be
acquainted with them, such as parents, masters, guardians
and superiors. To speak ill of another, says St. Thomas,
is a sin only when it is done to blacken his character, but
not when it is done to prevent his sin, or injury to others.

Hence, when we have no solid reason to believe that good
will be effected by speaking of the fault of another, it is
wrong for us to speak of it. Thus, it is wrong to make the
faults of another known to those who are not likely to suffer
by them, or to those who have no authority to correct them.
It is wrong even to speak to a superior of the fault of another
when we do so from an uncharitable, selfish motive.

To speak of the secret fault of another without sufficient
cause, in such a manner as is very injurious to his character, is
a mortal sin, because the person thus defamed retains his good
name as long as his fault is hidden; but if you make it known
to others, you rob him of his reputation, and when his reputation is lost he can no longer show himself before the public. "*He that filches from me my good name, robs me of that
which not enriches him, and makes me poor indeed.*"

To speak without a just cause of a person's fault which is
public, to one who knows nothing of it, is not a mortal sin,
but it is a venial sin against charity; but remember that it
is a mortal sin to reveal a sinful fact which was once notorious, but is now hidden; because the person who had lost his
reputation has now regained it.

Backbiting. It is backbiting when we speak with malicious
pleasure of the known faults of our neighbor.

Backbiters are, indeed, very common amongst Christians; for, to judge from the conduct of the greater number of them, one would suppose that no restraint was laid on the tongue with respect to our neighbor's failings, and that the good name of our fellow-creature might be sported with at pleasure. In some people we witness a natural itching for *backbiting.* We cannot be in their company five minutes without hearing some piece of scandal or other. We cannot converse with them concerning any one, but they have something or other unfavorable to say. They have good memories for evil. No hearsay story is forgotten by them. Their minds are well stored with scandalous anecdotes of every one of their acquaintances. *Backbiting* is their predominant disposition, and scandal is their delight. They attack friend and foe, with this only difference: their friend they defame with a sneer of pity; their foe with all the rancor of a wicked heart. Some take particular delight in watching the conduct of those whom they do not love, or against whom they entertain feelings of hatred; and when they see or seem to see anything that is not strictly correct, blazon it forth with all the freedom, and make it the common topic of conversation amongst their acquaintances. It matters little to them what injury the person may receive or what scandal may be raised.

It is related of St. Augustine, the illustrious doctor of the Church, that he had an extreme horror of all uncharitable conversation. To prevent any discourse of this nature from being held in his presence, he caused the following inscription to be painted in large letters upon the walls of the room where he usually entertained his friends:

"Slanderer, beware, this is no place for thee;
Here naught shall reign but truth and charity."

It happened one day that some of his guests began to speak in his presence of the faults of an absent neighbor. The holy bishop, with a grave and severe look, immediately reproved them, saying: "My friends, you must either cease to speak on such a subject, or it will be necessary for me to have those verses blotted out from the walls of my room."—[*Catech. de Perseverance.*]

Tale-bearing. Some are in the habit of listening and of relating afterwards what has been said—they are called tale-bearers. They hear a person speak ill of another, and instantly go to that other and tell what they have heard, and by that means cause quarrels, dissensions and animosities among their neighbors.

By this base and sordid vice of backbiting friendships are severed, disorders sown, hatreds cherished, and misunderstandings and ill-feeling spread through communities, and charity and meekness banished from them. Owing to *backbiting* and tale-bearing the husband is prejudiced against his wife, the servants are set against their masters, and masters against their servants. Often-times it happens that children are induced to behave disrespectfully to their parents or superiors, and even flocks to be prejudiced against their pastors, and subjects against their rulers by the defamatory remarks which proceed from the tongues of others. Oh! who can reckon up the evils caused by a backbiting disposition? The Scriptures declare *backbiters* and tale-bearers accursed, and that they and all that are with them shall be held in detestation and shall be hated. "The tale-bearer shall defile his own soul," says Ecclesiasticus, "and shall be hated by all, and he that shall abide with him shall be hateful." (Ecclus. xxi., 13.) "The whisperer and the double-tongued is accursed, for he hath troubled many that were at peace." (Ecclus.

Now, we become guilty of the sin of slander, detraction or back-biting in several ways, namely :

1. When we ascribe to our neighbor a fault which we know he has not committed, or a defect which he has not.

2. When we exaggerate his faults. *

3. When we proclaim those of his faults as certain which are uncertain.

4. When we make those faults of his known which were hidden before.

5. When we insinuate the faults of our neighbor, by saying, for instance, "Such a person goes often to confession, but......"
I can say no more. It is sometimes less injurious to tell the fault openly ; for the insinuation will make persons think that the fault is greater than it really is.

6. When we put an unfavorable interpretation on the good action of our neighbor. Some persons, for instance, cannot find fault with their neighbor's conduct because it is quite blameless. What then do they do? They censure his motive or intention. They say, "He acts this way in order to deceive others."

7. When we deny his good qualities and try to diminish his merit. There are persons, who, when they hear their neighbor praised for some good which they cannot deny, they will say : "Ah! Well! he is not the man the world takes him to be. For my part ;—but I will say nothing ; for least said is soonest mended." Or they will shake their head and put on a significant smile, with,—" I could say something if I chose."

8. When we praise our neighbor coldly, but only to give great effect to the detraction ; if, for instance, we say : "He is a person I have great esteem for ; he has several good qualities. But I am sorry he is given to such and such things. I always looked upon him as a good man ; but it is

27

a pity he is not more on his guard against such a practice."
These *buts*, at the end, are like the sting in a serpent's tail;
they carry poison with them. "Their words are smoother
than oil, and the same are darts," says the royal Prophet.
(Ps. 44. 20.)   .

9. When we repeat the unfavorable reports about our
neighbor, by saying, for instance: She was led into the
secret by a friend of hers, who had been told it by an acquaintance, who had it from a near relation, who had been
informed of it by an intimate friend, who heard it from the
best authority. Thus:

> "Cutting honest throats by whispers,
>   And all who told it added something new,
> :   And all who heard it made enlargements too ;
>   · In every ear it spread, on every tongue it grew."

10. When we, by our silence, approve of the evil which
others are retailing, or disavow the good which they relate
of our neighbor.

11. We may also injure the reputation of our neighbor by
signs. We are, for instance, in society and a certain crime
is spoken of as becoming rather general. No person in particular is mentioned as being guilty of that crime. But there
is one present who, by some sign, such as a glance of the eye
points to another, and insinuates as much as: "such a one
there is guilty of that crime." Now he who gives such a
sign is guilty of the sin of detraction. Such a man is called
in Holy Writ "a man full of tongue." "A man of tongue
shall not be established in the earth." (Ps. 139, 12.) By
a man "full of tongue" is meant a man of many tongues,
who injures the reputation of his neighbor not only with his
tongue, but also with the hands, with the feet and with the
eyes.

12. Detraction and defamation are committed not only by the tongue, but they are also committed in a far worse way by the press, in newspapers and other publications.

13. It is not less forbidden to calumniate a religious order or any kind of community than any individual person. To calumniate a community, all other things equal, is far worse than to slander an individual.

It is also forbidden to defame the dead, because their memory should be respected, and also because by defaming them, their relatives may be seriously injured.

Now, not only detraction, but also to listen with pleasure to detraction is forbidden by the eighth commandment. He who consents to the sin of detraction and takes pleasure in hearing his neighbor ill spoken of is guilty of sin.

For St. Paul, when speaking of crimes, among which was enumerated the sin of detraction, says that, "Not only they who do such things are worthy of death, but they also who consent to them that do them." (Rom. i. 32.) "Hedge thy ears with thorns, and hear not a wicked tongue." (Ecclus. xxviii. 28.) Indeed, if there were no listeners, there would be no slanderers and back-biters. The pleasure with which the detractor is listened to, encourages and hardens him in his wicked habit, and therefore the listener becomes a sharer in his guilt.

Hence St. Bernard says that the detractor has the devil on his tongue urging him to speak, and the listener in his ears making him eager to listen. And Planters says that those who carry about accusations as well as those who listen to them should be hanged—the tale-bearers by their tongues, and the listeners by their ears.

Let every one who wishes to lead an innocent life, fly all converse with persons whose habit it is to censure their neighbor's conduct; let him obey the commandment of the Holy ·

Ghost, who says: "Have nothing to do with detractors; remove from thee a forward mouth, and detracting lips put far from thee." (Prov. 24, 21. 4, 24.) Should you happen to hear any detraction of importance, be on your guard to give no token of complaisance, in order not to take part yourself in the detraction, nor have any share in the sin of another.

Trample under foot, all human respect, lay aside all unnecessary regards for the dignity of the speaker, and rebuke the detracting tongue (if due and lawful respect for the detracting person forbids it not), and remind the defamer of the damage he is doing to his neighbor.

Let him take for himself, in such a case, the advice given by St. John Chrysostom: " If any one wishes to detract, say to him, with all freedom, 'if you wish to speak well of your neighbor and to relate anything that redounds to his credit, my ears are open to listen. But if it is your intention to speak evil of him, to reveal his faults and failings, or to blame his doings, I will close my ears against you. My ears are accustomed to receive the balm of good discourse, not the filth and ordure of backbiting.'" (Homil. 3.)

But if the station of the slanderer is such that he is your superior in rank or authority, and does not allow you to address him in that style and to rebuke him so freely, try at least to divert the conversation and to start another subject more in keeping with Christian charity.

But should you find that even this is not practicable, you may at all events cast down your eyes, put on a serious look and show by your exterior what you are not allowed to express in words; that is, show him by the serious behavior which you put on that such talk is unseemly in itself and an annoyance to you. By this means you will administer a silent but effectual reproof, for, as the wise man says, " the north wind driveth away rain, as doth an angry countenance a backbiting tongue." (Prov. 25, 23.)

Cassian relates that a certain man, called Machetes, had received such grace from God that when the conversation was on pious or useful subjects, he was ever alive to what was going on, and was self-possessed though the conversation might last ever so long; but whenever the conversation was uncharitable, he immediately went off into a deep sleep. (Libr. v., cap. 20.)

You may not be able, by miraculous slumber to show him who backbites in your presence, the displeasure you feel at this talk, so repugnant to charity, but you may make him sensible thereof by your silence and by the sadness of your countenance, whenever it will not be possible for you either to divert the conversation or to rebuke the backbiter.

The sin of detraction is but too frequent even among Christians. "You will find but few persons," says St. Jerome, "who do not easily censure the conduct of others." Find me a man, says St. James, who does not sin with the tongue, and I will admit that he is a saint. "If any man offend not in word, the same is a perfect man." (James iii., 2.)

> The faults of our neighbor with freedom we blame,
> But tax not ourselves though we practise the same.

> None, none descends into himself to find
> The secret imperfections of his mind,
> But every one is eagle-eyed to see
> Another's faults and his deformity.

There are many who often go to confession, holy communion, say the Rosary every day, and perform many other works of piety and charity, and try to avoid sin as much as possible except the sin of detraction. Now, though the number of backbiters is great, yet no one likes to be looked upon as a backbiter. Hence every backbiter has an excuse to palliate his fault. Thus, for instance, one will say, "I said nothing but what was strictly true, and the person of whom I spoke had lost all title to his good name."

We are very much deceived if we imagine that we can, without sin, recount the evil doings of our neighbor, because what we say is true. Let us suppose that some one of our neighbors had stolen some article, that another had got drunk, another had been guilty of blasphemy, and another of immoral conduct, and that it comes to our knowledge; can we, because all this is true, tell it here and there without sin? Dissensions, enmities and quarrels result from detraction; and to be the cause of all this mischief and ill is no sin? What is become of that principle of charity, *Do not to others that which you wish should not be done to yourself,* if we can, without sin, speak of the crimes and faults of others? Would you wish that others should speak of your own faults, though in doing so they should not transgress the truth?

You say, has not a person lost all title to his good name when he has transgressed? But allowing that he has lost all title to it, by what authority can you take it from him? If you knew a person had goods in his possession to which he had lost all title, can you or any private person, in justice, take them from him? If you knew a person had murdered his neighbor, and by that means lost all right to his own life, could you, in justice, take his life from him? Certainly not, for the punishing of crimes of any sort does not belong to any private person, nor to any other till the guilty person be properly tried and convicted and his crime legally known; consequently, though your neighbor had done anything ill, until his crime become manifest he is accountable only to God, he is amenable only to the divine tribunal, and, therefore, you have no title to publish it to others, and deprive him of the good opinion they still have of him.

But on what grounds do you say he has lost all title to his good name? Is it because he has done some evil action? Who is there that has not done some such action in his life? Does every one then lose all title to his good name because he has done an evil action? Certainly not; one may be a very good man, and very justly esteemed, though in some things he fails, and, therefore, while his failings are secret, or known to a few, it is a manifest injustice to publish them, and thereby rob him of his good name and the esteem in which others hold him. With regard even to the evil itself committed by him, which is known in secret to you, how do you know but he has repented and made his peace with God? And if such be the case, he has as full a right as ever to his good name, and, therefore, it would be a great act of injustice to deprive him of it by publishing his secret faults. Yes, carry this truth with you: He that was yesterday a sinner may be a saint to-day, and the moment that his crimes are published is often the moment of mercy which completes his conversion. Remember what is recorded of the penitent Magdalen. The proud Pharisee reproached her with her crimes, and yet in that very instant her love and her tears effaced them at the feet of the divine Redeemer.

Another one says, "I mean no harm in speaking of my neighbor's faults." Let me ask you what would you think of him who robs you of your money and says, I mean no harm?"

Now, is not detraction far worse than robbery or theft? What great blindness! If you had committed some twenty or thirty thefts in your life-time, would you not be ashamed

of yourself and deem yourself unworthy to live in the society of honest men? But, after having injured your neighbor's reputation twenty or thirty times, which is a greater
sin, you hardly feel any remorse, or sorrow, as if you had
done no evil! What a delusion! What blindness!

But suppose even that in detracting your neighbor you do
not always commit a mortal sin; but remember that anything that injures our neighbor in the least in his reputation,
should never be looked upon as a slight evil. Our reputation is as dear to us as the apple of the eye. Now, even as
the least touch of so sensitive a part as the eye is ever most
painful, so, too, every wound in our reputation caused by
the tongue of another is always most intolerable, and ought
not, in all justice, to be accounted a slight evil.

Besides, though detraction sometimes may be but a venial
sin, yet it has a certain deformity of its own for which it deserves to be considered a serious evil. To steal a trifling
thing is, of course, not a mortal sin. But were a nobleman
or some other person of honorable position guilty of it, he
would, if it became public, be more ashamed of it than if he
had committed a grievous sin of revenge or the like. The
reason is, because theft is infamous which, even in trifling
matters, retains its special deformity, rendering disgraceful
all those who commit it, and imprinting, in every instance,
a stain on their honor. Can we not say the same of detraction, which is a real theft, and what is worse, robs a person
of that which is most precious, even of that fair name and
good repute which he enjoys in the minds of his neighbors?
Therefore granting, that the detraction, in certain instances,
be slight; granting that it be venial; still, it always is a
great evil, as it robs our neighbor of what is most dear to
him, ever cuts him to the quick, and puts him to torture.
Though ever so trifling, detraction is an infamous theft, an

action ever unbecoming in a Christian, who ought to have at heart the virtue of charity more than anything else.

To understand still better the heinousness of detraction, we have but to consider what Holy Writ and the Fathers of the Church say of it.

The Scriptures denounce in the strongest language the vice of detraction and declare that the detractors' tongues cause the most disastrous results. "Detract not one another, my brethern," says St. James; " he that detracteth his brother or he that judgeth his brother, detracteth the law, and judgeth the law." (James iv., 11.) The teeth of a detractor are poisoned darts, and his tongue is a sword that inflicts death, for the Prophet David tells us so! "Whose teeth are weapons and arrows, and their tongue a sharp sword." (Ps. lvi., 5.) The detractor according to the wise man is a serpent which glides imperceptibly on us, and stealthily bites us: "If a serpent bite in silence, he is nothing better that detracteth secretly. (Eccles. x., 11.) And in his comments on these words, St. Jerome says, that as a serpent instils his poison into the wound which his venemous sting has made, so, too, the detractor who hacks in secret the reputation of his neighbor, infuses into the wound all the poison of his wicked heart." "My son,"........ says the wise man, "have nothing to do with detractors, for their destruction shall rise suddenly; and who knoweth the ruin of both?" (Prov. xxiv., 21.) With reason then, therefore, has St. James called the tongue, "a fire, a world of iniquity, a restless evil, full of deadly poison." (James iii., 6, 8.)

In truth, a detracting tongue is a "restless evil;" "a world of iniquity;" for it outrages every virtue. It outrages religion, for, if any one, as the same apostle says, believes that he has religion, and yet does not put a curb on his tongue, his religion is vain. It outrages humility, for pride it is that hurries us on to crush down and destroy the character of others. It destroys justice, for what right have we to deprive our neighbor of his good name, which is dearer to him than everything else; for, as we have just said, is not a fair character the most valuable of all temporal blessings? *Is not a good name preferable to much riches?* as we learn from the book of Proverbs. It may lead the poorest and most destitute man to rank and comfort; but a fair name, once sullied, cannot be recovered with all the treasures of earth. What an injury, then, must it be? What an act of injustice is it, then, to deprive a person, by detraction, of what is in itself valuable?

"Who would believe it," says St. Bernard, "that so small a thing as a word of detraction could cause such dreadful havoc." The person detracted becomes like a dead member in the community, says St. Francis of Sales. He sinks into an object of infamy and public contempt, and when the sun rises it is only to enlighten his shame, and let him see his shattered character.

Detraction, I repeat, is therefore a very grievous sin, when it seriously injures the honor and reputation of our neighbor. Hence it is not without reason that the book of Proverbs declares *the detractor the abomination of men;* that St. Paul excludes them equally as adulterers from the kingdom of heaven. Yes; their poisonous tongues shall never sing the praises of God in heaven, but shall for an eternity be drenched with the hatred and bitterness which they have shed on the wretched and afflicted heart of their brethren.

Besides these declarations of Holy Scripture, it may be observed, that to speak ill of our neighbor is quite contrary to the example of Jesus Christ, who was so tender with the reputation of others, that he would not make him known who was to betray him, though it gave him so much pain, but allowed even Judas to receive the holy communion unworthily, rather than reveal his crime to the other apostles; and though he knew that a few hours after he would be made known to the whole people, yet for our instruction he would not be the one to make it known.

St. Bernard calls the *detractor's tongue a two-edged, nay, a three-edged sword, with which he commits three murders at one stroke.* The detractor, in the first place murders his own soul when he destroys his neighbor's fair fame. Secondly, he murders the character of the person he detracts, for he destroys that civil life by which he lived fair in the esteem of others. Thirdly, he murders the souls of those who listen with pleasure to the detraction, and encourage and spread it around; for whoever encourages and gives ear to the detraction, is equally criminal with the detractor. Detraction is also a base and cowardly vice; for, when we detract our neighbor, we stab his reputation behind his back, and at a time when he has no opportunity of defending himself. Of this holy Job particularly complained, when he said: "Even fools despise me, and when I was gone away from them, they spoke against me." (Job xix., 18.)

There is still another consideration that ought to make us detest and avoid the sin of detraction, it is this:

Those who have given false evidence against a neighbor, or who have spoken ill of him, or injured his character in any way must repair the injury done him, as far as they are able, and give him satisfaction by restoring his good name as soon as possible, otherwise the sin will not be forgiven.

He who has injured the character of another must not only repent, but must also repair the injury done him as far as he is able. If, for example, our neighbor should be unjustly imprisoned through our false evidence, and thus be deprived of the means of supporting his wife and children, we would be obliged to support and provide with everyth.ng necessary, the prisoner's wife and children, and to repair all the losses sustained on account of the imprisonment. If we have spoken ill of our neighbor, we must make him satisfaction by restoring his good name, for it is a certain truth that to obtain the remission of any sin we must first make reparation for it.

If we have injured our neighbor in his property, the property must be, if possihle, restored, otherwise the sin will not be forgiven. There is the same obligation when we have spoken ill of him or injured his character in any way. We are as much bound in one case as in the other. The only difference is, that in the latter case, there is greater difficulty than in the first. It is easy to take away a good name and injure one's character, but it is most difficult to restore the good name and repair the injury done to the character. An injurious word is soon spoken, but cannot be soon repaired. Can a severe wound be closed without leaving a scar? But the injury done to our neighbor's character must be repaired, otherwise the sin will not be forgiven.

When a persons good name has been taken away by falsehood the author of it is obliged to retract his calumny in the presence of all those before whom it was uttered, even at the risk of injuring his own reputation, because it is not just that the innocent should suffer, in order to screen the guilty. True, this is exceedingly difficult, but the difficulty does not remove the obligation. Menochius relates that a certain nobleman defamed a married lady. He was afterwards advised by a Dominican father to retract the calumny. The nobleman replied "I cannot do that, for I cannot destroy my own reputation by declaring myself a slanderer." The father told him that until the calumny was retracted he could never receive absolution.

If one's character has been injured by detraction, or by

making known some hidden vice to which he was subject, there is also an obligation of making satisfaction by restoring his good name. But in this there is still greater difficulty. For if the person really committed the sin, it cannot be said that he was innocent of it, for that would be a lie, and it is never lawful, as we said before, to tell a lie. What then is to be done? We must adopt the best means in our power. Sometimes it is better to speak well of the person, whose good name you have taken away, without mentioning the particular sin you have told of him, especially when you have reason to persume that this would be more pleasing to him, than to revive the remembrance of his fault. The great difficulty there is in restoring a good name and making satisfaction for injuring one's character, points out in a particular manner, how dangerous it is to speak ill of our neighbor, or injure his character in any respect.

We are also obliged to make satisfaction to our neighbor when we have treated him with contumely, or in other words, when we have insulted him. Contumely, or an insult offered to another is, indeed, unjust to him, as it takes away his honor, which is no less dear to him than his reputation. But injustice of any sort must be repaired if at all possible ; anything unjustly taken from our neighbor must be restored. But how restore honor to the person from whom it has been ravished? In making him satisfaction proportionate to the outrage offered him.

The nature of the satisfaction to be made, must be regulated by the nature of the offence, the rank of the person offended, and also by the rank or position of the person who has offered the insult or offence. And first, with regard to the insult offered, it is evident, for example, that he who has given a blow to another has more satisfaction to render than if he had offered him only a slight offence.

Secondly, with regard to the rank of the person offended : if the person offended be an inferior, it will be sufficient to testify our regret by some marks of tenderness and kindness ; if there be question of an equal, we are to make an apology to him and ask pardon. But if the person offended be a superior, or one of exalted rank, it will not be enough to ask pardon merely—to make a simple apology—it will sometimes be even necessary to ask pardon on our bended knees, and to ask it in public.

In the third place, with regard to the character of the person who has given the offence : bewailing the offence and asking pardon on bended knees requires very little sacrifice from some and is done without trouble or pain ; but there are others who would be prepared for any sacrifice sooner than ask pardon for an offensive word ; and as for asking it on bended knees, nothing could prevail on them to do so. It is, then, quite evident, that the nature of the satisfaction which would be required from the first, should not be exacted from the second, and that a slight apology from the second would be more than equivalent to a thousand pardons, asked even on their knees by the persons of the first description.

Rash judgment. To judge evil of our neighbor without a reasonable cause is a rash judgment, forbidden by the eighth commandment. Two things, therefore, are implied in the sin of rash judgment : 1, That the matter of the judgment is *something injurious* to our neighbor, or in other words, that the opinion which we form about him, lessens his reputation in our mind. 2, That the judgment is formed without a *reasonable cause*, and it is precisely in this that its rashness consists.

It is not a sin to have a bad opinion of another when we know that our opinion is correct. Thus, for instance, it is no sin to doubt a man's word if we know that he has often told lies. It is no sin to think that a man whom we caught in the act of stealing is dishonest.

The sin of rash judgment is committed in several ways.

The most ordinary ways in which we become guilty of this vice are the following: 1, When we form an ill opinion and conceive a dislike of any one at first sight, from his looks and words; and resting upon no other foundation, judge him guilty of this or that vice. 2, When we misrepresent a good or indifferent action of our neighbor, which may arise from a good motive, and to which we should attribute it if we were influenced by justice and charity. 3, When, upon seeing any one committing a sin, we at once without any other reason, judge him addicted to that sin. 4, When we misrepresent the good dispositions of one, judging his humility to be mean-spiritedness; his meekness to be cowardice; his patience in bearing crosses to be constitutional indifference.

The sin of *rash judgment* is greater or less, according as the matter on which we frame our judgments, and the grounds we have for framing them, are of greater or less moment. If without sufficient evidence and without due reflection we judge another to be, for example, a robber, an adulterer, or a drunkard, we are guilty of mortal sin, though we should confine the judgment we have formed within our own breast, for if we make known the rash judgment to others we become guilty of another sin, that of detraction or slander.

Rash judgment is contrary to *charity* which " thinketh no evil," and commands us to do unto others as we wish them to do unto us.

Rash judgment is also opposed to *justice*, because it destroys within us his reputation by destroying the good opinion we had of him, to which he has a right until he forfeits it by some evident crime.

Rash judgments are expressly forbidden by Christ, and under a very severe penalty: "Judge not," he says, "that you may not be judged; for with what judgment you judge you shall be judged." (Matt. viii., 1.) And St. Paul, in his epistle to the Romans, warns us in strong language against *rash judgments:* "Wherefore," he says, " thou art inexcusable, O Man, whoever thou art, that judgest, for wherein thou judgest another, thou condemnest thyself, for thou dost the same thing which thou judgest." (Rom. ii., 1.) Usurp not, then, the place of God, for to God belongs judgment. The heart of man is a sanctuary, into which God alone has a right to enter. He alone can know its movements, penetrate its most secret folds, and clearly behold what passes there; as for us, we can only behold the exterior.

To judge aright of others in our own hearts, and to guard against *judging* others *rashly* we should follow as near as we can the mode of proceeding used in courts of justice. In the tribunals of justice no one is condemned until proofs of his guilt be clearly established, and the accused person be heard in his own defence. We should observe their manner of proceeding before we pass judgment upon others; we should hear what they can say for themselves, how they relate the matter, and what plea they can offer in their justification.

Daily experience shows us that if we wish to find out the truth, we must hear both sides of the case. There are usually in current reports so many exaggerations and errors, so much malice and partiality, that we should be very slow to believe them.

We cannot conclude, then, from mere report, neither can we judge justly from mere appearances or mere circumstantial evidence.

Had we seen Joseph while a slave in Egypt rushing out of

the chamber of his mistress, had we heard her cries and her terrible accusations, how would we have judged him? Would we not have reasons enough to consider him guilty? And yet he was entirely innocent, even a martyr of innocence.

Again, had we been in court during the trial of Susanna, and heard the two grave and venerable elders swear solemnly against her, would we not naturally have judged her guilty? And yet she was quite innocent, and her venerable accusers were really the guilty ones.

Again, were we to see a beautiful lady adorning herself with all the skill and finery that art and nature could afford, and thus gorgeously attired go and visit a general of an army and spend the evening alone with him in his tent, what opinion would we form of her? Would we not believe her to be a person lost to all shame and honor? And the fair and virtuous Judith did all this. She visited the lascivious Holofernes, and yet she remained innocent, and saved her people from slavery and death.

We should, therefore, be very slow in judging ill of others. "If," says St. Beanard, "you cannot excuse the act, excuse the intention Attribute the fault to ignorance, weakness, surprise ; or, if you cannot do that, at least attribute it to a violent temptation, and say to yourself: 'If I had been tempted so violently, perhaps I would have done worse. Perhaps he has been tempted many times before this and always resisted nobly. Would I have done as well?'"

Those who condemn others harshly very often fall themselves into the very same sin that they themselves condemned. God permits it to punish their pride and their want of charity. "Judge not, that you may not be judged."

It is related in the Lives of the Fathers of the Desert that the Abbot Isaac, being one day present at an assembly of the religious, formed a bad opinion of one of the monks

28

whom he met there, and, from some trifle or other which he noticed, judged him to be worthy of correction. Upon his return to his cell he found an angel waiting at the door, who opposed his entrance. Filled with awe, the Abbot humbly begged to know the object of his mission. " I am come from our Blessed Lord," replied the angel, " to inquire from you what you wish to be done with that monk whom you have already condemned in your own mind?" The holy Abbot at once cast himself upon the ground, acknowledged his fault, and implored pardon of God. " Go," said the angel, " God pardons you, but in future be more careful about judging your brethren, and condemning those whom God himself, perhaps, has not condemned."—[*Lives of the Fathers of the Desert.*]

In the days of Totila, king of the Goths, there lived at Narni, in Italy, a holy bishop named Cassius. It happened that Totila, seeing him one day, formed a bad opinion of him, on account of his red and fiery complexion. " This man," said he to himself, " is certainly a drunkard." But Almighty God undertook upon the spot the defence of his servant. At the same moment he permitted a devil to enter into the person of Totila's sword-bearer, who became grievously tormented by the evil spirit. The bystanders, in the greatest alarm, carried the poor possessed man to the feet of the holy bishop, who at once delivered him by simply making over him the sign of the cross. Thereupon Totila retracted his unfavorable judgment, and ever after esteemed and reverenced Cassius as a saint.—[*St. Gregory the Great.*]

Some years ago a pious and learned Jesuit Father, named Tanner, was travelling from Prague, in Bohemia, to Inspruck, in Tyrol. Before reaching his destination, however, he fell sick and died in a village on the road.

Thereupon the magistrate of the place immediately repaired

to the house where the good priest had died, and took an inventory of his effects.

Among other things, the magistrate found a small mysterious box, that thoroughly roused nis suspicions. Impelled by curiosity he raised the lid and peeped in. O horror! Instantly the box falls from his hands, and the good man, pale with terror, cries out: "Begone, Satan! I renounce thee, Satan!" Others came and looked into the box, and each one protested that Satan himself must be there. In fact, they all beheld a huge monster moving about, black and hideous, of enormous length and armed with frightful horns.

A young student, who had just finished his course of philosophy and had graduated with distinguished honors, happened to be in town. He soon examined the box; he, too, beheld the frightful monster. "My friends," said he, addressing the gaping crowd, "it is a principle of philosophy that the container must be greater than the thing contained. Now here we see precisely the reverse; we behold a huge monster contained in the insignificant space of this little box. This is contrary to all the laws of philosophy; it is contrary to all the laws of nature. Hence, I conclude that the monster contained in this box cannot be a material being; hence it must be a spirit. Now, as a good spirit would not take so hideous a shape, and would, moreover, not suffer itself to be imprisoned thus in a box, it follows that this monster must be an evil spirit; therefore, it must be Satan himself."

Here the voice of the new-fledged philosopher was drowned in a burst of applause. Encouraged by this evident proof of his wonderful reasoning powers, the youthful philosopher continued: "Now, my friends, what are we to think of a man who carries Satan himself about with him in his travels? What are we to think of a man who has been clearly in league with the arch-enemy of the human race? It is evident that the deceased must have been a wicked man, a true sorcerer.

Thereupon it was unanimously agreed that the good priest should be deprived of Christian burial, and that the box containing the infernal monster should be solemnly burned.

The news of the strange adventure spread like wild-fire through the entire neighborhood; and many a thrilling tale was told of priests and Jesuits; and wiseacres shook their heads and solemnly declared that they *always* knew that these priests and Jesuits were in league with the devil.

As the worthy villagers were about to consign the mysterious box to the flames, a learned professor happened to pass through the place. He was immediately regaled with the startling news of the terrible Jesuit and his infernal prisoner. At the urgent request of the villagers the professor went to view the box. On beholding it, he burst into a loud laugh. "Why," said he, "you foolish people; this is a microscope." "A what?" they exclaimed, in amazement. They had never heard of a microscope before, and many began to suspect that the professor, too, was perhaps a sorcerer or a Jesuit in disguise. Hereupon the professor opened the microscope, shook it a little, and out crawled a small horned beetle.

At this the villagers burst into a loud laugh. The professor explained to them the mystery of the microscope, and they returned to their homes wiser and happier.

But the affair did not all end here. Busy tongues were not wanting to spread the report about of the mysterious box, about wicked Jesuits, etc., but they were very careful not to breathe a word about the beetle or the microscope. That would have spoiled the story and destroyed the sensation.

This story teaches us never to judge rashly and condemn any one for anything before having made a thorough investigation; it teaches us not to view the faults of others through a microscope, so that they appear much greater than they really are. This microscope is our wicked heart, so full of jealousy and envy. Take away this lens and you will see something deserving of praise, or at least of compassion, in your neighbor.

This story also teaches us not to believe evil reports too readily. Those who speak of their neighbor's faults have seen them in a microscope. If they repeat what others have said, they see them through a double lens. Each new reporter adds a new lens of his own; it teaches us never to speak of the monster in the box without telling the sequel; never to speak of any one's faults without adding whatever can exculpate him. "Do unto others as you would wish that they should do unto you."

Suspicions. To suspect evil of another without any reason is a venial sin; it is hardly ever a mortal sin unless when one wilfully and without any reason suspects his neighbor as guilty of a very grievous sin. I say without *any reason*, for when there is some good reason for the suspicion, such a suspicion is no sin. Good Christians, however, always think well of their neighbor, whilst the wicked think badly of him. "The fool . . . whereas he himself is a fool, esteemeth all men fools." (Ecclus. x., 3.)

How many persons are there not who have repented of believing too readily either their own rash suspicions or the hasty accusations of others? A duke of Bavaria, Louis the Severe, who lived in the thirteenth century, had a hard experience in this way. He was in one of the provinces bordering on the Rhine, when he received by chance from his wife, Mary of Brabant, a letter that was not intended for him. The duchess had written two letters on the same day, both dated from the castle of Donauwœrth; one was meant

for her husband and the other for one of his officers, named
Henry Rucho. Unhappily she made a mistake in directing
them, and the duke received the letter intended for the officer.
As it contained some kind of cordial expressions, he instantly
supposed that his wife had betrayed him. A gloomy jeal-
ously then took possession of his soul; he hastened to Donauwœrth, entered the castle in rage, knocked the sentinel
down, killed a person he met on his way, flung the duchess'
first waiting-woman from the top of a tower, threw the
duchess into prison, and, next day, regardless of either piety
or justice, or the earnest protestations of his wife, he had her
beheaded. This was in the year 1255 or 1256. The unhappy
man failed not to discover that his wife was innocent, but
the discovery came, alas! too late. He was so grieved
thereby that his hair became suddenly white in the space of
a single night. Such was the chain of crimes and misfor-
tunes that resulted from a rash suspicion and a hasty judgment.—[*Schmid et Belet, Cat. Hist.*, II., 341.]

From this sad story we learn the wholesome lesson that
when doubts and suspicions or derogatory judgments arise
in our mind about our neighbor, we should not dwell on
them, but rather disapprove and reject them as soon as we
perceive that they are rash and unjust.

The suspicions and doubts of superiors, of parents and of
masters, concerning their subjects, are, generally speaking,
not unjust or blameworthy, because they are obliged to
watch over their inferiors and even mistrust them to a certain degree, in order thus to prevent them from doing wrong.
In such cases they act from motives of prudence.

Of a similar nature are the doubts which we form in order
to prevent some harm, or to take precautions against the
possible occurrence of evil that might happen. A person,
for instance, who receives a stranger into his house, may

prudently provide for the safety of his possessions, just as he would if the stranger were a person whose honesty he suspected.

Contumely. By contumely is meant an insult offered to a person in his presence, by injurious expressions to vex and annoy him, such as reproaching him with any defect spiritual or corporal, true or false; upbraiding him with any crime, true or false; branding him as ungrateful for benefits received, or as guilty of dishonorable conduct; upbraiding his humiliations or his poverty, etc.; and all this with a view to wound his feelings.

As the unhappy Queen Marie Antoinette was on her way to the scaffold, a shameless woman sprang into the cart that bore her and spat in her face. She continued to insult the queen till her head fell beneath the guillotine. She even insulted the lifeless body, and there, on the blood-stained scaffold, in presence of the vile rabble, she danced the shameless dance known as the Carmagnole. The real name of this degraded woman was Marie Angelia Loyson; but she was known all over Paris by the nick name of La Carmagnole. In all Paris there was none more shameless and degraded than this woman. And yet—how wonderful is the mercy of God—this monster so vile and degraded was converted. She not only gave up her sinful life, but was the means of bringing back to God hundreds, that, like herself, had strayed away from the path of virtue. She spend the last twenty years of her life in this glorious work. She lived in a poor garret in the Rue de Valois and dressed as a common beggar. She entered the third order of St. Francis. She prayed, wept, and performed the most rigorous penances to atone for the sins of her youth. Whatever money she earned or received as alms she spent in caring for those unfortunates whom she had led back to a life of penance. She even succeeded at last in establishing an asylum for these penitent Magdalens. After death she was placed, according to her own wishes, in a simple pine coffin and buried in a pauper's grave. But her good deeds were not unnoticed. A wreath of costly flowers was placed by loving hands upon her simple coffin; and members of the first families in France — among them the prince Marshal of Ponte Rosina and the Duchess of Chateau-tremlent—considered it an honor to accompany her remains to the grave.

O wonderful mercy of God! "On what day soever the sinner turns from his evil ways," saith the Lord, "I shall no longer remember his sins. As I live, I swear by my divine life, I do not wish the death of the sinner, but that he be converted and live."

Detraction destroys the character of our neighbor, contumely takes away his honor. And St. Paul says, that all who treat a neighbor with contempt are hateful to God; "contumelious, hateful to God." (Rom. i., 30.) If we examine into the cause of contumely, we will find that the tongue is the restless member from which the evil proceeds. This contumely is generally caused by quarrels; and these quarrels are the contentions of the tongue; generally it originates from a fault on one side or the other—words ensue; one party becomes warm and the other party equally warm; the dispute increases; one party criminates and the other party recriminates. When one is accused and cannot exculpate himself, he retorts upon the other party by an accusation of some old failing. Words and speeches follow words and speeches, and then old sores are opened, old grievances renewed, the most serious evils introduced, and in a short time gain such deep root as seldom to be eradicated. These are, indeed, serious evils, and to no other cause are they to be attributed than to the malevolence of the tongue.

When contumely contains defamatory matter it is a double sin, because it injures the honor as well as the good name of our neighbor.

It is also a species of contumely to disclose, without sufficient cause, a secret which is entrusted to us, or which we promised to keep. We are, however, not bound to keep a secret: 1, When it has become notorious and public, for then it is no longer a secret. 2, When the revelation of the secret is considered necessary for the public good, or for some other very important reason. We are, of course, speaking of natural secrecy and not of the sacramental secrecy of confession, which, under no circumstances and for no consideration whatever, can be broken and which is guarded by the seal of God himself.

The law of secrecy not only forbids us to betray what has been entrusted to us; but it also forbids to pry into the secrets of others. If a tale-bearer is a contemptible creature, a prier into secrets is even more so, though not perhaps equally dangerous. He is ever on the watch to gratify a morbid curiosity by listening at doors, peeping into drawers and boxes, and opening and reading letters and secret papers. To do these things is not only mean, but it is actually sinful, it is a species of contumely which may even amount to the guilt of a mortal sin; for instance, if you were to open and read a letter that is likely to contain something that the owner would be very much grieved to have known to others. Always resist, at the beginning, these itchings of curiosity and go away from the temptation. Look upon it as a mean and contemptible practice, unworthy of a noble and generous soul, to attempt to pry into the secrets of others.

A letter of another, however, may be opened by legitimate authority, or for a sufficient reason, or when there is a very good reason to suppose that the writer of the letter, or the person to whom it is sent, has no objection to our reading it. In this, as in all else that regards the law of justice and of charity, we must be guided by the grand principle of doing to others as we should reasonably wish they should do unto us.

What is commanded by the eighth commandment?

By this commandment we are obliged to be truthful in all things, and also to speak of others with justice and charity. To tell the truth at all times, should be a fixed rule with you. Nothing should induce you to violate the truth.

Never say, as a great many do, how can I be expected to witness the truth, when by so doing I shall endanger the life, or if not the life, the character and reputation of those that are nearest and dearest to me. What crime can it be to tell a lie, when the character of my very dear friend is at stake? Speak not so, for God will not, under any circumstances allow you to depart from the truth. You must witness it in all things.

One day a companion of St. Thomas of Aquin wished to have a good laugh at Thomas. So all of a sudden he exclaimed: "Behold an ox flying through the air!" St. Thomas looked up, as if it were true what his companion said. Thereupon he was laughed at by his companion, who remarked at the same time, "How can you be so foolish as to believe that an ox can fly?" St. Thomas calmly answered: "I would rather believe that an ox can fly than that a Christian can tell a lie."

The author of Bibliotheca of Pastors (p. 179,) relates that the Emperor Maximinian sent his officers to incarcerate St. Anthimus, Bishop of Nicomedia. The soldiers, who were in search of him, went by chance into the very house of the saint, and asked for something to eat. He treated them kindly; they asked where they could find Anthimus the bishop. The saint answered: "Behold him; I am Anthimus." The soldiers through gratitude said: "We will not bring you to the emperor; we will say that we have not been able to find you." The Saint replied: "No, my children, I do not wish you to be guilty of a lie; I am willing to die rather than advise you to tell a lie" He then went with them to the emperor.

If you have committed a fault, and should be accused of it by your parents or superiors, deny it not, but at once candidly confess it, no matter what the punishment may be, that you should receive for your fault.

The illustrious George Washington, who afterwards became President of the United States, had received as a present, when he was six years old, a little hatchet, with which he kept chopping everything that came in his way. He one day amused himself stripping the bark off a magnificent English cherry-tree, which appeared to be completely spoiled. His father perceiving this mischief, angrily inquired who had done it, adding that he would rather have lost a hundred dollars than that tree, which he had prized very highly. No one could find out the culprit. At length little George, who was not present at the moment, being one day in the garden with his hatchet, his father perceived him and immediately guessed that he was the author of the mischief. He asked him if he knew who it was that had spoiled his cherry-tree. The child hesitated a moment and then answered: "I cannot tell a lie, papa; it was I that cut it with my little hatchet." Hearing this confession so frank and honest, Washington's father could not be angry with the child. "Come to my arms, my son," said he, "the honesty with which you confess your fault repays me a hundredfold for the loss of my cherry-tree. I value your candor and sincerity more than I would a thousand cherry-trees, though they were loaded with the finest fruit." In after years it was observed that the great man never could and never did violate truth in any case whatever; so true it is that people retain all their lives the good habits contracted in their youth.—(Noel, *Cat. de Rodez*, v. 467.)

Let no earthly gain or profit induce you to tell a lie, for it will not bring any blessing upon you.

Do you who are engaged in business or trade wish to make great profit? Always tell the truth. Cesarius (lib. iii., chap. xxxvii.) relates that two merchants, who had always to accuse themselves in confession of having told lies in their dealings with others, were always in poverty. The confessor said to them; "Tell no more lies and I promise you great success in your business." They obeyed, and his words came true. By always telling the truth they soon established the reputation of being honest men. Thus they gained more in one year by telling the truth than they had gained in ten years by telling lies.

Let nothing induce you to swerve from the truth; witness it in all things. Though property, parents, friends, and even your life should be sacrificed by your witnessing the truth, yet let the property go, and the parents and friends be ruined, and let your life be sacrificed sooner than tell a lie, and not witness the truth.

Some years ago I read a story that went the round of the papers and which I could not read without shedding tears. I am sure it will affect every one the same way. An American paper mentions the case as being brought before the authorities in the town of Madison. A good little boy of nine years of age, an orphan from his earliest infancy, who was adopted by a farmer named Marquete, from the hospital in Milwaukee. Some time after his installation in his new family, the little boy having had occasion to remark some very bad conduct on the part of the farmer's wife, thought it his duty to inform the husband. But the woman denied the charge so vehemently that the farmer was convinced that his wife had been calumniated. The wife then insisted that the boy should be whipped till he retracted what he had said; and the husband taking a scourge, suspended the child from a beam in the room and whipped him for nearly two hours with such barbarity that the blood streamed on the ground. He stopped then and asked the child if he still persisted in what he had said. "Father," said he, "I have told the truth and I cannot retract to tell a lie." Trampling under foot every better feeling, the cruel woman again insisted that her husband should continue what she called his duty. The blows commenced again with renewed fury, and continued till the poor little fellow fell almost lifeless into the arms of his executioner, to whom he said throwing his little arms around his neck: "Father, father, I am dying! I have told the truth!" And he expired. The court at Madison took cognizance of the affair. The miserable woman was convicted of the crime of which she was accused, her husband was condemned as guilty of murder on the person of his adopted child; finally, the young orphan was proclaimed the martyr of truth. (*Recompenses Hebdom.*, No. xlix., p. 24.)

Though the whole world should be destroyed and brought to ruin by your *witnessing the truth*, the truth *should be witnessed* by you, for God will never allow a violation of it for any purpose or through any motive. Let your speech, then, be frank, open and sincere, free from equivocation, artifice, or dissimulation. Never tell a deliberate lie by way of excuse or otherwise, remembering always that God is the God of truth.

During the great French revolution at the end of the last century, the Catholic churches were everywhere pillaged throughout the country and closed for public worship. The priests were also proscribed, and forced to conceal themselves in private houses, or even to seek shelter in the thickets of the forests or in the caves and fastnesses of the mountains. It happened about this time that a young girl named Magdalen Larralde, of the village of Sare, on the borders of Spain, fearing to have recourse to her own parish priest in his place of concealment, was wont to cross the mountains whenever she desired to approach the sacraments, in order to seek spiritual assistance from the Capuchin Fathers at the convent of Vera, on the Spanish side of the Pyrennees.   One day, however, in returning from the convent, she fell in with an outpost of the French army, which was then stationed along the frontier, in consequence of the war which raged between the two countries. The soldiers immediately seized her as a spy and dragged her before the general, who questioned her as to the object of her presence in Spain.   Magdalen answered simply and without a moment's hesitation that she had been to confession. The officer, touched by her youth and innocent bearing, and anxious, if possible, to save her, quickly replied: "Unfortunate woman, do not say that, for it will be your sentence of death. Say, rather, that the advance of the French troops frightened you, and drove you to seek shelter on Spanish ground." "But then I should say what would not be true," answered the girl, and I would rather die a thousand times than offend God by telling a lie." In vain did the general urge and solicit her to yield ; her firmness never gave way, and she was conducted before the tribunal of St. Jean de Luz. Before her judges Magdalen again with unflinching courage refused to save her life by a lie. She was therefore condemned to the guillotine, and as she walked to the place of execution her step never faltered, and she ceased not to invoke the assistance of God and to sing the Salve Regina in honor of the Queen of Heaven.—[*The Month.*]

THE NINTH AND TENTH COMMAND-
MENTS.

" Thou shalt not covet thy neighbor's wife."
" Thou shalt not covet thy neighbor's goods."

Human judges forbid and punish only external crimes, because the secrets of hearts are hidden from human tribunals. " Man seeth those things that appear, but the Lord beholdeth the heart." (1 Kings xvi., 7.)

The sixth and seventh commandments forbid all actions contrary to chastity and justice. The ninth and tenth commandments forbid even all wilful thoughts and desires contrary to these virtues. From this we clearly see that God is not satisfied with mere outward chastity and justice ; he also commands us to have a chaste and just will and heart. Whatever it is unlawful for us to do, it is also unlawful for us to desire or wilfully think of with pleasure. All the commandments, therefore, may be broken by sins of thought and desire ; but God quite especially forbids sins of thoughts contrary to chastity and justice, because those sins are more dangerous for various reasons :

First. Sins of thought are more easily committed than sins of action. The occasions of sinful actions are often wanting ; but sins of thought are often committed without the occasion. When a soul has turned her back on God, the heart is continually intent on evil, which causes delight, and

[439]

thus multiplies sins without number. "All the thought of their heart was bent upon evil at all times." (Gen. vi., 5.)

Secondly. At the hour of death sinful actions, generally speaking, cannot be committed; but we may then still become guilty of sins of thought, and he who has been in the habit of consenting to bad thoughts during life, will be in danger of indulging them at the hour of death, for then the temptations of the devil are very violent. Knowing that he has but little time to gain the soul of the dying person, he makes greater efforts to make it fall into sin. The devil is come down unto you, having great wrath, knowing that he has but a short time. Surius relates that when St. Eleazar was in danger of death he was so frightfully tempted with bad thoughts that, after his recovery, he said: "Oh! how great is not the power of the devils at the hour of death!" The saint overcame the temptations, because he was accustomed to reject bad thoughts. But wretched the man who has contracted the habit of consenting to them. Father Segneri relates that a certain sinner frequently consented to evil thoughts during life. At death he made a sincere confession of all his sins, and was truly sorry for them; but, after death, he appeared to a person and said that he was damned. He stated that his confession was good and that God had pardoned all his sins; that before death the devil represented to him that, should he recover from his illness, it would be an act of ingratitude to forsake a certain woman who had a great affection for him. He banished the first temptation. A second came, which he also rejected; but having continued to think of it for a little while, he was tempted a third time, yielded to the temptation, and thus he was lost.

Thirdly. God forbids especially sins of thought contrary to purity and justice, because they are the source of all other sins.

. The reason why people are tempted to do wrong is not from any real love of vice as such, but rather from an imaginary hope of pleasure or gain which they promise themselves to obtain from doing what their conscience or the law of God forbids. Could they then be prevailed upon not to seek any sinful pleasures and unlawful gains, the sources of temptation would be dried up.

Now, the object of the ninth commandment is to check every desire of unlawful pleasure, and of the tenth to check every desire of unlawful gain. In a word, the ninth and tenth commandments teach us the proper government of the heart.

Nothing is of greater importance than this government of the heart, because the neglect of it is the cause of all the other sins we commit. For " from the heart (when not properly governed) come forth evil thoughts, murders, adulteries, fornications, thefts, false testimonies, blasphemies," indeed all kinds of wickedness. (Matt. xv., 19.) " For out of the abundance of the heart the mouth speaketh. A good man, out of a good treasure, bringeth forth good things ; and an evil man, out of an evil treasure, bringeth forth evil things." (Matt. xii., 34,35.) Therefore, according as the desires and dispositions of the heart are, so will our outward conduct be—good or evil. How important, then, it must be that we should properly govern and regulate our thoughts and desires according to the law of God.

Immodest thoughts and desires. In explaining sins of thought, we must distinguish three parts of an evil thought. The first part is the *suggestion*, or the simple idea of the evil presented to the mind. This is no sin, but when rejected, is an occasion of merit. "You are crowned," says St. Antonine, "as many times as you resist sin." There are many persons, who have the fear of God, are scrupulous, and afraid that every bad thought which presents itself to the

29

mind is a sin. This is an error. It is not the bad thought, but the consent to it, that is sinful. All the malice of mortal sin consists in a bad will, in giving to sin a perfect consent, with full advertence to the malice of sin. Hence St. Augustine teaches that, where there is no consent, there can be no sin. Though the temptation, the rebellion of the senses, or the evil motion of the inferior part of human nature should be very violent, there is no sin as long as there is no consent.

Even the saints have been tormented by temptations. The devil labors harder to make the saints fall than to make the wicked sin, because he looks upon the saints as a more valuable and more glorious prey. The prophet Habacuc says that the saints are the dainty food of the enemy. "Through them his portion is made fat, and his meat dainty." (Hab. i., 16.) And therefore the prophet adds that the evil one stretches out his net for all to deprive them of the grace, and he spares no one. "For this cause, therefore, he spreadeth out his net, and will not spare, continually to slay the nations." Even the great Apostle St. Paul, after he had been made a vessel of election, groaned under temptations against chastity. "There was given me a sting of my flesh, an angel of Satan to buffet me." (2 Cor. xii., 7.) He several times implored the Lord to deliver him from the temptation. "For which thrice I besought the Lord that it might depart from me." The Lord refused to free him from the temptation, but said to him : "My grace is sufficient for thee." And why did God refuse to remove the temptation? That by resisting it, the apostle might gain greater merit.

St. Francis de Sales says that, when a thief knocks at the door he shows that he is not inside the house. In like manner, when the devil tempts us, we have a strong proof that the soul is in a state of grace.

The great St. Catharine of Sienna, that favorite spouse of
our Blessed Lord, who bore in her body the stigmata or marks
of his sacred wounds, was at one time of her life subject to
the most violent temptations of Satan. That wicked spirit,
envious of the angelic purity of her soul, was wont to fill her
mind with filty imaginations, and to assail her heart with the
most impure temptations. Unceasingly did she call on God
for help, but she seemed to receive no answer. Her mind
was obscured with frightful darkness, and she seemed on the
very brink of the precipice. Often indeed, she was unable
to distinguish between temptation and consent, but an invisible hand always preserved her from falling. Upon one
occasion after her temptations had ceased, our Blessed Lord
came to visit her, filling her with heavenly consolations.
"Ah, my divine Spouse," she cried out, "where wast thou
when I lay in such an abandoned and frightful condition?"
"I was with thee," he replied. "What," said she, "in the
midst of the filthy abominations with which my soul was
filled?" "Yes," answered our Lord, "for these temptations
were most displeasing and painful to thee. By fighting
against them thou hast gained immense merit, and the victory was owing to my presence." Thus did St. Catharine
learn that God is never nearer to us than when we appear
the most desolate and abandoned, and that he is never wanting to those who call upon him with humility and confidence.
[*Butler's Lives of the Saints.*]

"God," says St. Alphonsus, "permits his servants to be
tempted in order to try their fidelity and purify them from
their imperfection. Hence I here add, for the consolation of
timid and scrupulous souls, that when a person who fears
God and hates sin, is in doubt as to whether he gave consent
to a bad thought, he is not bound to confess it as long as he
is not certain of having consented to it. Had he really fallen

into mortal sin, he would have no doubt about it; for mortal sin is so detestable, that it is impossible for a person who fears God to admit it into the soul without his knowledge."

The celebrated Gerson, Chancellor of the University of Paris, in the fourteenth century, relates that a poor solitary was tormented in this way long and violently, but without daring to acquaint his director of his trouble. "I am lost!" said he to himself; "it is frightful to have such bad thoughts; if I tell my spiritual Father he will be scandalized, and will have a very bad opinion of me." Nevertheless, after having borne these interior torments for full twenty years, he re-solved to speak of them to an old father of the desert, in whom he had great confidence; he dared not even tell him by word of mouth and wrote what he had to say on a piece of papyrus. The holy old man having read it, began to smile and said to him: "My son, place your hand on my head (the solitary having done so) I take your sin upon my-self, so trouble yourself no more about it." "How, Father," asked the solitary, much surprised at these words, "it seems to me that I have already one foot in hell, and you tell me not to trouble myself about it?" "But, son," said the old man, "do you take pleasure in these thoughts?" "On the contrary, Father, they have always given me great sorrow and much pain." "That being the case," replied the man of God, "it is a proof that you did not consent to them, and that it was the devil who excited them in you in order to make you despair. Therefore, son, take my advice, and if any such thoughts again present themselves to you, say to the devil, who is the author of them: ' ' Woe to you, spirit of pride and impurity; on your head be your abominations and your blasphemies! I will have nothing to do with you; I hold to what the Church believes, and I would die a thou-sand times rather than offend God.' " These words of the

Holy old man so consoled and strengthened the solitary that he was never again attacked by the thoughts that had so long tormented him.—[*Rodriguez, Christ. Perf.*, iv., 88.]

The second part of an evil thought is the *delectation* which takes place when the person stops to look, as it were, at the bad thought, which, by its pleasing appearance, causes delight. This delectation is not a mortal sin when the will does not consent to it; but it is a venial sin, and if not resisted the soul is in danger of consenting to it; but when this danger is not proximate the sin is only venial.

However, it is necessary to remark that when the thought which excites the delight is against chastity, we are, according to the unanimous teaching of theologians, bound, under pain of mortal sin, to make a positive act of resistance to the delectation caused by the immodest thought, because if not positively resisted, the delight easily obtains the consent of the will. "Unless a person resists delectations," says St. Anselm, "the delight passes into consent and kills the soul." (Simil. cxl.) Hence, though a person should not consent to the sin, if he delights in the obscene object and does not endeavor to resist the delectation, he is guilty of a mortal sin by exposing himself to the proximate danger of consent. "How long shall hurtful thoughts abide in thee?" (Jerem. iv., 14.) Why, says the prophet, do you allow hurtful thoughts to stay in the mind? Why do you not make an effort to banish them from the heart? God wishes us to watch over our hearts with great care, because it is on the heart, that is, the will that our life depends. "With all watchfulness keep thy heart, because life issueth out from it." (Prov. iv., 23.)

From what has just been said it is clear that certain persons, who are not scrupulous, but are ignorant and have a lax conscience, are in great error when they imagine that evil thoughts, though wilfully indulged in, are not mortal sins if the corresponding actions are not consummated. Into this error the Scribes and Pharisees fell.

In the law of Moses punishment was imposed only on actual external crimes, and hence the Scribes and Pharisees drew a false conclusion, that internal sins were not prohibited; but in the New Law our Redeemer has explained that even wicked desires are forbidden.

"You have heard that it was said to them of old: Thou shalt not commit adultery; but I say to you, that whosoever shall look on a woman to lust after her, hath already committed adultery with her in his heart." (Matt. v., 27–28.) This stands to reason, for if we do not reject evil desires, it would be very difficult to avoid actual external sins. We must then remember that we are not allowed to desire what we are not allowed to do. Hence it is that the bad thought to which a person consents has the same malice as its corresponding action. As sinful works separate us from God, so also do sinful thoughts. "Perverse thoughts separate us from God." (Wisd. i., 3.) And as all bad actions are known to God, so also he sees all wilful evil thoughts and will condemn and punish them.

St. Alphonsus relates that a woman, who had the reputation of a saint, was assailed by a bad thought regarding one of her servants, she neglected to banish it immediately, and in her heart consented to sin. She afterwards fell into a more grievous sin, because she concealed, in confession, the complacency she had taken in the bad thought, and died miserably. But she was believed to be a saint; the bishop had her buried in his own chapel. In the morning she appeared to him, enveloped in flames, and confessed, without profit, that she was damned on account of the bad thought to which she had consented.

The third part of an evil thought is the *consent* of the will. Evil thoughts are not our own as long as our will has no part in them. But if we deliberately and fully consent with our will to any evil which is proposed to us by our thoughts and which we clearly know to be a mortal sin, then such thoughts become our own and make us guilty of mortal sin.

Suppose we are often thrown into the company of a person whom we very much dislike. He has perhaps been very harsh and unkind to us; he has done us a great injury, or his manners are very disagreeable. In our intercourse with such a person we may naturally experience uncharitable feelings; we find it difficult to think of him and behave towards him in the same way that we do towards others. And though we try to overcome our aversion, we may often be in doubt as to how far we have been wanting in charity. Now, we cannot repeat too often that sin does not consist in having uncharitable thoughts or feelings, but in giving way to them, or in wilfully keeping them in our mind, instead of trying to get rid of them or reject them. The thought and feeling often come in spite of ourselves, and we cannot always get rid of them as soon as we would wish.

When we are low-spirited we cannot at once feel happy and cheerful by the mere desire to be so. So, in like manner, when we feel uncharitable toward another, we cannot at once feel kindly towards him, however much we wish to do so. When, therefore, we have evil thoughts, we mean, by consent to them, such a state of the will as would be correctly expressed by saying: "If I had the power of banishing these thoughts at once, I would not use it; or, if I could at once rid myself of this temptation I would be unwilling to deprive myself of the pleasure which I experience in its continuance."

A person may sin grievously by thoughts in two ways:
by *desire* and by *complacency*. A person sins by desire,
when he wishes to do the bad act which he desires, or
would wish to do it, if he had the opportunity. Such a desire may be a mortal or a venial sin, according as the
corresponding action is either a mortal or a venial sin,
for sins of thought and desire are of the same kind as
the corresponding actions. However, in practice, the external action always increases the malice of the will,
either because it ordinarily increases the complacency in
which the will indulges, or causes it to continue for a longer
time. Hence if the action follows the desire, it is necessary to mention it in confession.

A person sins by complacency when he does not desire to
commit the sinful act, but delights in it as if he had committed it or were then committing it. The main difference therefore between sins of complacency and sins of desire is, that
the sins of complacency represent the sinful object as past
or present in the imagination and feed the mind on the guilty
thought, while the sins of desire represent the sinful object
as future and seek after its enjoyment.

The sin of complacency is called *morose delectation*, and
may be committed in a moment. It is called morose, not because the complacency in the thought of the unchaste action
lasts for a considerable time, but because the will dwells wilfully with delight on the thought. We say *wilfully*, to remove scruples from persons of timorous conscience, who suffer against their will, certain carnal sensations and delights,
although they do all in their power to banish them. Though
the inferior part of human nature should feel a certain delight, there is no sin, at least no mortal sin as long as the
will does not fully consent.

"Motion of concupiscence," says St. Alphonsus, "which

precede advertence are neither mortal nor venial sins, but
only natural defects proceeding from our corrupt nature and
for which God will not blame us. The sensations which precede consent are at most only venial sins when we are careless
about banishing them from our minds after we perceive them ;
for, in' that case, the danger of consenting to the evil desired, by not positively resisting and banishing that sensation
of concupiscence is only remote and not proximate. Theologians, however, usually except sensations of carnal delectation, for in them it is not enough to remain passive, but we
should make a positive resistance, for otherwise if they are
any way violent, there is great danger of consenting to
them.

As for other sins of concupiscence, however, the full wilful
consent alone to the desire of a grievous evil is a mortal sin.

If one advertently consents to a wicked desire, or takes
morose delectation in thinking on it, he is then guilty of a
grievous, or at all events, of a light fault, for our Lord himself says : "Follow not in thy strength the desires of thy
heart." (Eccl. v., 2.) ; "Go not after thy lusts." (Eccl.
xviii., 30.) "Let not sin therefore reign in your mortal body,
so as to obey the lusts thereof." (Rom. vi., 12.) I say "a
light fault," because the delectation of a bad object is one
thing ; the thought of a bad object another ; this delectation
of thought is not mortally sinful in itself, but only venially
so ; and even if there be a just cause, it is no sin at all.
This, however, must be understood to be the case only when
we detest the evil object ; and, besides, that the consideration
of it should be of some utility to us, and that the consideration of it should not lead us to take pleasure in the evil
object, because if there was a proximate danger of this, the
delectation would, in that case, be grievously sinful. When
then, on the other hand, concupiscence assails us against our

will, then there is no sin, for God only obliges us to do what is in our power. Man is composed of flesh and of spirit, which are always naturally at war with each other; and hence it is not in our power not to have many times sensations that are opposed to reason. Would not that master be a tyrant who would command his servant not to feel thirst or cold? I repeat with St. Augustine: "that, what is not voluntary is by no means sinful."—[*History of Heresies, Refutation* xi. 5.]

We can never be secure against evil thoughts and desires. Bad thoughts, evil desires and the corrupt inclinations of the heart are what we shall have to fight against all the days of our life. For the human heart is corrupted by the fall of Adam; it is naturally bent upon evil. This is what makes "the life of man upon earth a warfare" (*Job.* vii., 1); and puts us continually in danger of sin, unless we use proper means for curbing and correcting our natural inclinations.

The prophet Isaias says: "Take away the evil of your devices." (*Isai.* i., 16.) What does he mean by taking away the evil of our devices? He means that we should take away the occasions of evil thoughts, such as reading bad books, looking at immodest objects, keeping bad company, immodest dancing, profane comedies, intemperance, etc. Again, when thoughts against chastity present themselves to the mind, we must try to banish them the very instant we perceive them without giving ear to them or examining what they represent to us. "As soon as lust shall suggest evil" says St. Jerome, "let us exclaim: "The Lord is my helper."

Should the temptation continue to trouble us it will be very useful to make it known to our confessor. St. Philip Neri used to say "that a temptation disclosed is half conquered." But, as this cannot always be done immediately, the masters of the spiritual life advise us to treat temptations against chastity with contempt, turning our mind on our employment, or any other subject which will most easily take up our attention. If these temptations are continual and very troublesome, it would be imprudent always to make positive acts contrary to them, for to do this would be too fatiguing for the mind. In this case, says St. Alphonsus, it is sufficient resistance to pay attention to the will that it may not take any part in them.

In temptations against chastity some saints had recourse to very severe mortifications. St. Benedict rolled his naked body among thorns. St. Peter of Alcantara threw himself into a frozen pool. "But I believe," says St. Alphonsus, "that the best means to overcome these temptations is to have recourse to God that he may strengthen our will to detest them and conquer them, saying: "Lord, give me strength to resist this temptation; do not permit me to be separated from Thee; deprive me of life rather than allow me to lose Thee."

EVIL THOUGHTS AND DESIRES FORBIDDEN BY THE TENTH COMMANDMENT.

It is not a sin to desire what belongs to another, if we seek its possession by lawful means and for a good end. It would not be wrong, for instance, to desire to purchase a house, or a piece of land to which we have taken a fancy. The desires which God, by the tenth commandment, forbids us to entertain are those which cannot be lawfully gratified. Thus, we are forbidden to covet that which we can possess only by unjust means. We are forbidden to desire the death of a relative in order that we may inherit his property, or of a successful rival, in order that we may succeed to his place. We are forbidden to set our hearts on riches so as in their pursuit, to neglect other duties; for instance, almsgiving, the frequentation of the sacraments, or the performance of any other religious obligation. We are forbidden to seek riches for any bad object; for instance, that we may be enabled by them to gratify our passions and indulge in sinful pleasures. Merchants are forbidden to desire the dearth of food and other necessities, that they may become rich; officers and soldiers are forbidden to desire war, that they may pillage the vanquished; medical men are forbidden to desire the prevalence of disease; magistrates and lawyers are forbidden to wish for feuds and lawsuits. The best means to overcome such desires is to attach ourselves more and more to God and use the perishable goods of this world only as a means to do good, in order thus to become worthy of the everlasting goods of heaven." "Blessed are the poor in spirit, for theirs is the kingdom of heaven." (Matt. v., 3.) At a time when the scarlet fever made great havoc amongst the poor in Paris, and the priests of St. Marcel were not able to administer the last sacraments to all the dying, the Capuchin Fathers came to their assistance. One of these, a most venerable man, began his visits of charity with a low stable, where a victim of the contagion lay suffering. What did he see on going in? A dying old man, stretched on some filthy rags. He was alone; a bundle of hay served him as a bed; no seat, no furniture; he had sold all, during the first days of his illness to obtain a little broth. On the black, bare walls hung an axe and two saws; that was all he had, that and his arms when he could move them; but then he had not strength to lift them. "Take courage, my friend," said the Capuchin; "God is dealing mercifully with you; he is going to take you out of this world, where you have had nothing but troubles." "Nothing but troubles!" repeated the dying man in a feeble voice; "you are mistaken, Father, I lived contented enough, and never complained of my lot. I never knew either hatred or envy; my sleep was calm; I worked all day, but I slept soundly all night. The tools you see there procured me my daily bread which I eat with a thankful heart, and never envied those whose tables were better served. I saw the rich more subject to disease than others. I was poor but until now I got good health. If I recover my health, which I do not expect, I will go back to the wood-yard, and continue to bless the hand of God, who has hitherto taken care of me." The confessor, much surprised, knew not how to talk to such a penitent. He could not reconcile the sight of his wretched pallet with language so content. He composed himself, however, and said to him: "My son, although this life has not been wearisome to you, you must nevertheless, make up your mind to quit it; for you must submit to the will of God." "Undoubtedly," replied the dying man calmly and firmly; "every one must pass away when his turn comes; I knew how to live, and I know how to die; I thank God for having given me life, and for making me pass by death to him. But, I believe the moment has come; yes, I feel it—farewell, Father!" He had barely time to say these few words, when he tranquilly yielded up his soul into the hands of his Creator.—[Guillois, *Nouv. Explic. du Cat.*, 266.]

THE COMMANDMENTS OF THE CHURCH.

In the volume "The Church and her Enemies" we have shown that Jesus Christ established the Church to continue his work upon earth. He gave her the same commission that he himself had received from his father (St. John xx., 21.) He entrusted her with the keys of the kingdom of heaven, and promised to ratify in heaven whatever she should bind or loose upon earth. (St. Matt. xvi., 19.) He commanded the faithful to regard those who refused to obey her as heathens and publicans: "If thy brother shall offend against thee, go and rebuke him between thee and him alone. And if he will not hear thee, take with thee one or two more, that in the mouth of two or three witnesses every word will stand. And if he will not hear them, tell the Church. And if he will not hear the Church, let him be to thee as the heathen and the publican." (St. Matt. xviii., 15–17.) He assured the pastors of the Church that the disobedience and disrespect shown to them was the same crime as though it were shown to himself: "He that heareth you heareth me; and he that despiseth you despiseth me." (St. Luke x., 16.) It is clear, therefore, that the Church has received power and authority to make laws and precepts which are binding on the consciences of her children, and to transgress her commands is as much a sin as to transgress any of the ten commandments, which have been already explained. This authority of the Church is derived immediately from God, and consequently is independent of any other authority. Hence St. Paul, addressing the clergy of

Ephesus, says: "Take heed to yourselves, and to the whole flock, wherein the Holy Ghost hath placed you bishops, to rule the Church of God." (Acts. xx., 28.) Hence, in the exercise of their power, the apostles made laws binding on the faithful, without consulting the civil rulers, and they claimed for their ordinance a divine authority. "It hath seemed good to the Holy Ghost and to us to lay no further burden upon you than these necessary things, that you abstain from things sacrificed to idols, and from blood, and from things strangled." (Acts. xv., 28-29.) Hence we read that St. Paul "went through Syria and Cilicia confirming the Churches, commanding them to keep the precepts of the apostles and the ancients." (xv. 41.)

The Church possesses also legislative power by virtue of the natural right. As she is a perfect and independent society, she has the right of self-government and that of prescribing what is necessary for its preservation or conducive to its end. By virtue of this power, the Church can establish laws, watch over their observance and punish the transgressors, by excommunication and the refusal of the sacraments and Christian burial.

As a parent has a right to command his child to do one thing or avoid another, to impose an obligation where none existed before, so that the very same action that would otherwise have been harmless becomes sinful by its opposition to a lawful command, so in like manner the Church can impose on her members precepts which are binding on their consciences.

The object of the Ecclesiastical law is: 1, To maintain order and peace throughout the body of the Church by a stable and prudent administration. 2, To prevent abuses. 3, To render the observance of the divine law and the practice of all that Jesus has taught and prescribed more easy to the faithful. Thus we are commanded by God to serve and worship him; and the Church fixes the days, and instructs us in the manner in which we are to fulfil this duty. The Sacred Scripture frequently inculcates the necessity of fasting and abstinence, as well as acts of mortification generally; and the Church appoints the days, and lays down rules for fasting and abstinence. The very institution of the Sacraments of Penance and the Blessed Eucharist implies an obligation to receive them; and the Church commands her children to fulfil this duty at least once a year.

There is, therefore, the closest connection between the commandments of God and the precepts of the Church. There is, however, an important difference between them. The commandments of God never vary, they are always binding, and binding in all places, and upon every man without exception; whereas the commandments of the Church bind only those who are members of the Church; they may, moreover vary in different ages and different countries. The reason of this difference is, because the commandments of God are simply the expression of those principles of right and wrong which are as unchangeable as God himself; whereas the precepts of the Church, being in their nature human laws, are not binding when it is impossible or very difficult to keep them, and therefore, admit of dispensation. To do something that is forbidden by a commandment of God is to do something that is bad and wrong in itself. To commit murder, to rob a person of his money, or to take away another's character unjustly, is to do something that is bad in itself. He who eats meat without necessity on a Friday, or performs unnecessary work, or neglects to hear Mass on a Sunday commits a sin not because he does something that is bad in itself, but because he disobeys a lawful command. In these cases, the sin that is committed consists in the act of disobedience. Hence, where there is no disobedience there is no sin. Thus the authority of the Church which imposes the obligation, may relax or entirely take it away. If, for instance, the Church dispenses certain persons, or if circumstances arise in which she does not intend that her precepts should bind, there would no longer be any sin in doing what under ordinary circumstances is forbidden. The authority of the Church over the body of the faithful may be compared to the authority of a parent over his children. A father may lay down a rule for his children to go to school every day, and if they refuse to do so, they are guilty of disobedience; but he might relax this rule, or he might not wish to apply it to wet days or times of sickness; so in like manner the Church imposes her commands; but she still retains the power of modifying them, as often as circumstances render it expedient. She may dispense with her own laws, but she cannot change the law of God. Thus she may exempt invalids from the obligation of fasting or abstinence, or from hearing Mass on Sundays; but she cannot, in any case or under any circumstances, allow a person to tell a lie or to deny an article of faith. This will explain what is meant by the phrase which we often hear, that the doctrine of the Church is always one and the same, while her discipline may vary. By the doctrine of the Church we understand the revelation or teaching which she has received from God, and of which she is the divinely-appointed guardian and interpreter; by her discipline we mean those rules and laws which she has received power to frame for the government of the faithful dispersed throughout the world. The truth of God, it is evident, is one and the same at all times, in all places, and under all circumstances; but the regulations which are best adapted to the wants of different times or countries may vary.

30

THE FIRST COMMANDMENT.

The laws of the Church are numerous. Some of them regard hierarchical superiors; others regard the clergy and religious Orders; others again have reference to the sacraments, worship, and the benefits of worship, and lastly, others regard all the faithful. The principal ones of these last are called *the Precepts of the Church;* they are six in number.

The first commandment of the Church is:

" To keep certain appointed days holy, with the obligation of resting from servile work, and to hear Mass on all Sundays and Holy-days of Obligation."

A feast-day, or festival is, generally speaking, a day of joy, a day of solemn assembly, or public rejoicing, established either in honor of some distinguished person, or in commemoration of some great event.

There are civil festivals and religious festivals. It is only of religious festivals that we are here about to treat. Men are accustomed to erect monuments to commemorate extraordinary events, achievements, victories, and the like. The works of God, however, infinitely surpass those of men in greatness, power and wisdom. But men are apt to forget the works of God, and the divine favors which they have received, especially those which are long past. What a contrast between "Hosanna to the son of David: Blessed is he that cometh in the name of the Lord. Hosanna in the highest," and "Away with this man. Crucify him !" What a contrast between spreading their garments in the way before him and stripping him of his garments, casting lots for them, and putting on him the scarlet cloak of mockery !

What a contrast between cutting branches of palm trees and strewing them where he passed, and platting a crown of thorns and putting it upon his head and a reed in his right hand, bending the knee before him in mockery, and saying: "Hail, king of the Jews!" What a contrast between "King of Israel" and "We have no king but Cæsar!"

As God knows this fickleness and instability of the human mind and heart, what, then more natural than to read in Holy Scripture that he instituted, in the Old Law, seven principal feasts for the Jews, to be as it were, so many monuments of what he had done for them.

The first feast was perpetual; for a lamb was immolated every morning and evening to represent the duration of eternal happiness. The second was the festival of the Sabbath, which was celebrated every week, in memory of God's rest on the seventh day after the work of creation. The third was that of the Neomenia, or new moon, in opposition to that celebrated by the pagans at full moon. It was solemnized every month to remind the Jews of the benefits and protection of divine Providence.

The other festivals were celebrated but once a year. They were the solemnities of the Paschal Lamb, in memory of the escape of the Jews from their captivity in Egypt; and of the Pentecost during forty days, in commemoration of the law given to Moses. Three other festivals took place the seventh month, the whole of which was employed in constant solemnity, corresponding to that of the Sabbath. The first day of that month was the festival of Trumpets, in memory of Abraham's sacrifice, who immolated, instead of his son Isaac, a ram with long horns, and hence is represented at this festival by trumpets. The sound of these instruments apprised the Jews to prepare themselves for the tenth day of the same month for the festival of Expiations, established

in memory of the pardon that God granted them by the intercession of Moses for having adored the golden calf.

Then followed the festival of the Tents or Tabernacles, to
commemorate the miraculous protection of the Hebrews in
their journey through the desert, where they dwelt in tents.
They had to offer, at this festival, the finest fruit of the trees,
and branches of the finest verdure and of the most delicious
odor. All this was found in abundance in the Promised
Land, and was to signify that God had brought them from a
barren land to a country of delightful fertility. The last
festival was that of the Collection. During this day they
had to contribute towards all that was necessary for the divine worship.

Now, as God, in the Old Law, commanded his chosen
people to keep certain festivals, so he also commands Christians to keep certain days holy.

In the Old Law it was through Moses that God prescribed
certain festivals. In the New Law it is through his Church
that he commands certain days to be kept holy.

In the Old Law, no doubt, great events were honored by
festivals; but, great as they were, they were only a shadow
of far greater events, and the religious solemnities recalling
those events to the mind of the people, mystically or figura-
tively signified those greater events in the New Law; for
instance, the daily immolation of a lamb represented the perpetual sacrifice of the Lamb of God on our altars. The festival of the Sabbath represented the spiritual rest brought
into the world by the Saviour of mankind. The festival of
the new moon prefigured the light and grace of the Catholic
Church by the doctrine and miracles of the Son of God. The
festival of Pentecost pre-announced the descent of the Holy
Ghost on the Apostles, and that of Trumpets their preaching the Gospel. The festival of the Expiation prefigured the

purity of the Christian people and the remission of their sins. The festival of the Tabernacles represented our pilgrimage and exile in the world of misery and desolation; and that of the Collection or Assembly the reunion of all the saints in heaven.

These three last festivals came in immediate succession to denote that the Christian soul ought to advance incessantly from virtue to virtue, till it comes into possession of eternal, happiness.

Alas! what are all the wondrous works which God performed in favor of the Jews in comparison with the stupendous prodigies which the Son of God performed on earth for thirty-three years and a half? What then, more natural than that the Catholic Church should have instituted festivals to commemorate the unspeakable blessings which God has bestowed, and still continues to bestow upon us through his well-beloved Son, Jesus Christ, our Redeemer, through the Blessed Virgin Mary, his immaculate Mother, and through his angels and saints? We have, therefore, festivals in honor of the Most Holy Trinity, in honor of our Lord, Jesus Christ, and in honor of the Holy Ghost.

We, also, have festivals in honor of the Blessed Virgin Mary, the Mother of God. She is the tabernacle in which God concealed the created wisdom, nay, the uncreated and incarnate wisdom itself. It was in her that the Son of God was conceived and made man and dwelt for nine months; so that, if we call him our Redeemer from all eternity, we may also, with great propriety call his Blessed Mother our Redemptrix, that is, an instrument or *perpetual help* in the work of our Redemption, and in the whole order of grace wrought and instituted by Jesus Christ.

It is impossible carefully to study the history of Jesus and Mary, as it is recorded by the evangelists, without perceiving a uniform law of Providence uniting them in the great events of their lives for the work of our own salvation and sanctification. Ignorance and forgetfulness of the treasures which we have in Jesus Christ and his ever Blessed Mother cause the ruin of millions of men.

Hence it is that the Church has consecrated so many days in the year to the honor of Jesus Christ and of the Blessed Virgin Mary, and so solemnly celebrates the feasts of our divine Redeemer and his ever blessed Mother. We also have festivals in honor of the angels to commemorate the blessings which God through them has bestowed upon us and to thank him and them for these blessings. Finally, we have festivals in honor of the saints.

From the beginning the festivals of martyrs were celebrated. According to our ancestors' way of thinking, the death of a martyr was a victory for him, an example for his brethren, and triumph of religion. The blood of this victim was cement to the edifice of the Church. The day of his death was solemnized; an assembly met at his tomb, and the holy sacrifice of the Mass was celebrated there. The courage of the faithful was thereby roused. This custom appears in the acts of the martyrdom of St. Ignatius and St. Polycarp—the second century—and undoubtedly it was followed in Rome immediately after the martyrdom of SS. Peter and Paul.

The testimony of the apostles and their disciples, sealed by their blood, was too precious not to be brought continually before the eyes of the faithful.

The same notice that led to the establishment of the festivals of the martyrs gave rise to the festivals of confessors, that is to say, of saints who, without having suffered the death of martyrdom, had edified the Church by their heroic virtues. Their life was a glorious testimony of the holiness of the Catholic Church and a proof that her morals can be practised by every one.

Now, the festivals which we are commanded to observe as Holy-days of Obligation in most of the dioceses of the United States are:

1. New-Year's day, or the Feast of the Circumcision.

2. The Epiphany, or the manifestation of our Lord to the Gentiles in the persons of the Magi.

8. The Ascension of our Lord into heaven.

4. Corpus Christi, or the festival in honor of the Real Presence of Christ in the Blessed Sacrament.

5. Christmas-day, or the feast of the Birth of our Lord.

6. The Annunciation of the Blessed Virgin Mary.

7. The Assumption of our Blessed Lady.

8. The Feast of the Immaculate Conception of the Blessed Mother of God.

9. The Festival of all Saints.

As the obligation of hearing Mass and abstaining from servile work as well as other questions concerning the santification of Sundays and Holy-days of Obligation have already been explained in treating of the third commandment, we here omit the manner in which Sundays and festivals of obligation are to be kept holy.

THE SECOND COMMANDMENT.

" To keep the days of fasting and abstinence appointed by the Church."

Abstinence and fasting are often confounded in the minds of many people. The obligation of abstinence, however, differs from that of fasting. Abstinence implies a restriction as to the quality of food; fasting implies a restriction both as to

quality and quantity. On abstinence-days we are allowed
to take our usual number of meals, but are forbidden the use
of certain kinds of food. On fasting-days we are not only
restricted as to the quality of food which we are permitted
to use, but we are also forbidden to take more than one full
meal.

According to the present discipline of the Church, the law
of abstinence, as applied to days out of Lent, simply forbids
all kinds of flesh-meat. During a part of Lent the prohibition is more extensive.

On abstinence-days, therefore, we are strictly forbidden to
eat flesh-meat, or anything which is made up with flesh-meat;
but, by a recent Rescript of Pius IX., the use of lard and
dripping is permitted on all days throughout the year except
Good Friday. The essence of the precept of abstinence
consists in the prohibition of certain kinds of food; the essence of fasting consists in taking but one meal, and that
not before midday. The abstinence is broken as often as a
person partakes of prohibited meats on an abstinence-day.
He may therefore sin against the abstinence several times on
the same day. The precept of fasting, on the contrary, cannot be broken more than once on the same day.

Nothing is more clear than that fasting and abstinence are
both inculcated in Holy Scripture. The earliest command
of which we read was one of abstinence. Adam was allowed
to partake of the fruit, of all the trees of Paradise except
one, from which he was commanded under pain of death to
abstain (Gen. ii., 16, 17). Again immediately after the
flood Noe was commanded by God to abstain from flesh with
blood (Gen. ix., 4). In the Levitical law the Jews were
commanded to abstain from the flesh of divers kinds of animals (Levit. xi.) When the angel foretold the birth of
Samson, he commanded his mother to drink no wine nor

strong drink, nor to eat of anything unclean (Judges xiii., 4). We see, therefore, that the precept of abstinence held a conspicuous place among the ordinances which God delivered to his people under the old law.   In the new law, too, it is remarkable that of the few precepts which are recorded in the New Testament not belonging to the moral law, the most prominent is one of abstinence :   " It hath seemed good to the Holy Ghost and to us to lay no further burden upon you than these necessary things, that you abstain from things sacrificed to idols, and from blood, and from things strangled," &c. (Acts xv., 29).

So strictly were the laws of abstinence observed, that during the Babylonian captivity, Daniel and his three companions lived on pulse and water, rather than defile themselves with the forbidden meats which came from the king's table ; and God so blessed their obedience to his command, that, " their faces appeared fairer and fatter than all the children that eat of the king's meat " (Dan. i.)   Still more remarkable was the constancy of Eleazar and the seven Machabees, who chose rather to lay down their lives than to eat of the forbidden meats (2 Mach. vi. vii.)   The particular forms in which the law of abstinence is enforced, in these and other instances recorded in Sacred Scripture, are now no longer obligatory ; still it is obvious that the same principle is implied in these cases as in the precept imposed by the Church.

We sometimes hear certain persons say in a tone of levity : "What use is it to impose such privations upon one's self? What goes into the mouth defiles not the soul. "   This they say in order to justify the violation of the holy law of abstinence.   At the time of Louis XV., an unscrupulous prince, it was customary at the court of Versailles to serve both fish and flesh on days of abstinence when there was a grand hunt. But no sooner had the pious king Louis XVI. come to the throne than he abolished this scandalous abuse. Thereupon an old officer complained and said: What goes into the mouth does not defile the soul. He thought himself dispensed by this famous axiom from following the rule which the Church imposes on all children. "No sir," replied the king vehemently, "it is not precisely eating the meat that defiles the soul and renders it guilty, but it is the revolt against a lawful authority, and the violation of one of its formal precepts; it then remains to ascertain whether Christ gave to his Church the power of giving commandments to her children, and whether he ordered the latter to obey them. The catechism assures us that he did; and since you read the Gospel you ought to know that Our Lord somewhere says: 'Whosoever heareth not the Church, let him be unto thee as the heathen and the publican.' Now, sir, I am of the opinion that neither you, nor any one here present, would wish to be considered in that light." These words, coming from the mouth of a prince, and a prince who practised so well what he said, produced all the effect that might be expected. There was no talk of eating meat even after the chase on days of abstinence.—[Filassier, *Dict. d'Educ.*, 1, 5.] .

It would, indeed, be superstitious and sinful to believe that any kind of meat is in itself unclean, or defiles the soul more than another, or that it is more lawful to take it on one day than on another; but this is a very different thing from believing that a person is guilty before God by violating the commands of a lawful superior.

It is therefore clear that the precepts of abstinence, or the prohibition of certain kinds of food, has been enforced, both under the old and the new law. The days on which abstinence is commanded may vary at different times and in different countries. Formerly Wednesday was observed as a day of abstinence, because on that day the sorrows and sufferings of our Lord's Passion *commenced*. Saturday also was at one time generally kept, and is so to this day in some countries, as an abstinence-day in honor of our Lord's burial, and as a preparation for the due observance of Sunday. Friday, however, in memory of the crucifixion and death of Christ, has always been considered the most appropriate day for the practice of penance and mortification. For a long time it was observed as a rigorous fast, and is still kept throughout the Church as a day of abstinence. According to the present discipline of the Church, we are required to abstain on all Fridays throughout the year, "except the Friday on which Christmas day may fall, and on Sundays in Lent, unless leave be given to eat meat on them." Those who, by reason of their age, or for any other cause, are not bound to fast, are yet required, unless they are otherwise dispensed, to abstain on all fasting-days during the year on which flesh-meat is not allowed.

It may be well to remark here that to diminish our ordinary quantity of food, or to abstain from a certain kind of food is in itself not a real virtue, for one is not virtuous by merely abstaining from eating or drinking. Every physician often prescribes abstinence in quantity and quality of food for the good of the health of his patients. But if we keep abstinence in conformity to the principles of religion and reason, in the spirit of penance, or if, in accordance with the precepts of the Gospel, "we add virtue to faith, knowledge to virtue, and abstinence to knowledge" (2 Pet. i., 5.), then abstinence is a real virtue and renders our works meritorious in the sight of God and his holy Church. We should therefore, never be prevailed upon to violate the law of abstinence for a trifling reason, such as human respect, which is one of the worst enemies of virtue and duty.   People do not dare to act differently from others, and hence it is that when they have neither firmness, nor resolution, they allow themselves to be drawn into this weakness.   Happily every one is not so.   A celebrated physician, who was at the same time, a great naturalist, was invited to dine at M. Buffon's.   There were at dinner some philosophers, still more famous for the incredulity they made show of, than for their knowledge of mathematics or belle lettres.   It was on Friday, and the host, who had perhaps forgotten that it was a day of abstinence had only meat soup served in the first course.   The Christian doctor took none, and was determined to wait for the desert, rather than violate the rules of abstinence.   Most of the guests perceived this, and many of them knew the cause.   Amongst these was Diderot, unhappily so well known for his hatred to religion.   He first put this question to the doctor: "Doctor, why do you not eat?" and he immediately added with a mocking smile : "Is it because to-day is Friday, and you see nothing here you can eat?   Now, do you really think that flesh meat is not as good on some days as on others."   "Yes, sir," answered the physician ; "yes, I am satisfied that flesh meat is injurious every day on which the Church has seen fit to prohibit its use ; I am a physician and a Christian, and am, therefore, more capable of judging than others, who are, perhaps, neither one nor the other."   This modest and courageous answer produced its effect.   Buffon called his butler, and told him in a low voice to remove the dishes and serve no meats in the second course.   It was accordingly done, and Diderot was not the last to applaud it, for we cannot help admiring a generous, upright man, even when his conduct is a reproach to ours.—[Guillois, *Nouv. Explic. du Cat.*, 293.]

We can still less help admiring the generous conduct of a

child under trying circumstances. In the town of Avignon there was a child who was about to make his first communion. The parents of this child were not very religious; like many others now-a-days, they did not observe the laws of the Church, and, what is unhappily too common, every one in the house followed their bad example. The child's confessor explaining to him the danger there was for him in following an example so pernicious, and the real sin he committed thereby, forbade him to imitate his parents and ordered him to observe the abstinence prescribed by the Church. When the following Friday came the pious child, docile to the advice of his confessor, refused to eat meat. The Father was angry with him, and said: "See that you obey me, and do as I do myself." "Father," said the sweet child mildly, "give me whatever orders you please; in all that is not contrary to the laws of God, I will always obey you; but if I obey you in this, I should have to violate that law, and I cannot do it." The father became furious. He began to swear at his son and threaten him, but the child still answered in the same mildness: "Father, you order me to do what the Church forbids, I cannot obey you." Then the father's fury was at its height; he ordered his son to go to his room, not to leave it, and to eat or drink nothing but dry bread and water. The child instantly obeyed. Soon after, the father was obliged to go out on business. The mother, who had no more piety than the father, but loved her son very tenderly, took the opportunity to go in haste to the child's room with some delicacies for him to eat. "My dear," said she, "your father is gone out. So I have brought you something to eat." "Thank you, mamma," the child replied, "but my father forbids me to take anything but bread and water; his prohibition is not contrary to the law of God, and I will obey him; mamma, I cannot accept what you have been so kind as to bring me." These words of the child made a lively impression on the mother; her heart was torn; she went away in tears, and hastened to tell her husband what had passed. The father could not withstand the sight of this so wise and Christian conduct on the part of his son; his harshness was overcome. He sent for the child, and, with tears in his eyes, clasped him in his arms, saying: "My son, not only will we not force you to eat meat on Fridays, but from this day forth, we will give you no more the bad example we have heretofore given you; we will abstain from meat ourselves on days when the use of it is forbidden." The father kept his word, and ever after the whole family observed the laws of the Church.—[*Etrennes a la Jeunesse Chret., Années* 1852-63.]

FASTING—ITS OBLIGATION, AND THE SEASONS FOR IT.

Fasting is more frequently inculcated in Holy Scripture than abstinence, and it has been more diligently practised by the servants of God. Thus fasting is commanded as a part of the penance we should perform for our sins: "Be converted to me," said the Lord, "with all your heart in *fasting*, and in weeping, and in mourning" (Joel ii., 12). Our Blessed Lord himself foretold that his disciples would fast after his departure from them: "The days will come when the bridegroom shall be taken away from them, and then they shall fast" (St. Matt. ix., 15). He also lays down rules which we should observe when we fast: "When thou fastest, anoint thy head and wash thy face, that thou appear not to men to fast, but to thy Father, who is in secret; and thy Father, who seeth in secret, will repay thee" (St. Matt. vi., 17, 18). We are told of the greatest servants of God that they fasted. Thus Moses and Elias fasted forty days, as, indeed, our Lord himself did. The royal prophet fre-

quently makes mention of his fasting (Ps. xxxiv; 13, lxviii.
11 ; cviii. 24), Esdras (2 Esdras i. 4), Daniel (ix. 3), Esther
(xiv. 2), and the prophetess Anna (St. Luke ii. 37), were
remarkable for their fasting. The faithful of Antioch were
ministering to the Lord and fasting when the Holy Ghost
said to them: "Separate me Saul and Barnabas for the
work whereunto I have taken them. Then they fasting and
praying, and imposing their hands upon them, sent them
away" (Acts xiii., 2, 3). And when the apostles ordained
priests, they fasted and prayed (Acts xiv., 22). Fasting
moves God to show mercy. Thus the Ninivites proclaimed
a fast and were pardoned (Jonas iii., 7–10). It makes
prayer more efficacious (Tobias xii., 8 ; Judith iv., 12 ; Dan.
ix. x. ; St. Mark ix. 28). It also obtains temporal benefits. "We fasted and besought our God," says Esdras (viii.
23), "and it fell out prosperously unto us." (See also 2
Chron. xx. ; 2 Esdras i. 4 ; Esther iv. 16.)

The holy fathers also frequently inculcate the duty of fasting, and enforce its observance by the teaching and practice
of Holy Scripture, and by the consideration of its necessity
for our fallen nature. They tell us that fasting is a part of
the penance which is required of us if we have sinned ; and
if happily we have preserved our innocence, it is necessary
as a discipline to strengthen us against the danger of falling.
"Fast," says St. Basil, "because thou hast sinned, and fast
also to prevent the danger of sinning."

St. Augustine sums up the spiritual benefits of fasting in
the following words: "It purifies the soul, enlightens the
spirit to subdue the flesh, inspires the heart with contrition and humility, dissipates the clouds of concupiscence,
quenches the fire of passions and makes the brilliant light
of chastity shine all over the body."

Times of fasting. Though the Sacred Scripture clearly

inculcates the obligation, and sets forth the advantages of fasting, it nowhere lays down any precise rule as to the time and manner of fasting. One of the reason for this silence is no doubt owing to the fact that the same regulations are not equally well adapted to all times and circumstances.

Yet, on the other hand, if the duty of fasting were left to each one's discretion, it is much to be feared many would neglect it altogether. The Church has therefore received power to determine the times and rules of fasting, and to modify them as the necessities of each age or country may require.

We fast to atone for our past faults, to avoid them in future, and lift our souls to heaven by penitential works. These means of sanctification are employed at certain periods of the year, as prescribed by the Church.

Lent. The fasting-days which we are commanded to observe are: "The forty days of Lent, the Fridays of Advent, in most of the dioceses of this country, the Ember days, and Eves, or Vigils, of certain festivals."

The fast of Lent is frequently spoken of by the most ancient Fathers as of apostolic institution. It is the most solemn season of penance throughout the year. In imitation of our Blessed Lord's fast of forty days, and in order to prepare her children for the solemn commemoration of his sufferings and death on the cross, the Church commands them to fast during Lent. This penitential season begins on Ash-Wednesday and continues, during the six following weeks, till Easter Sunday, and thus embraces a period of forty days, exclusive of the Sundays.

Advent. What the Vigils are to ordinary festivals, or what Lent is to Easter, Advent is to Christmas. It is a time of penance and devotion to prepare the faithful to celebrate in a fitting manner the Advent, or coming of our Lord, by his birth into the world. Its institution seems as ancient as Christmas itself; though its duration, as well as the manner of its observance, have varied at different times and in different places. Like Lent, it for some time comprised a period of six weeks or forty days, part of which was kept as a strict fast. It now begins with the Sunday nearest the festival of St. Andrew, November 30th; so that the earliest day on which it can begin is the 27th of November, and the latest the 3rd of December. It thus embraces four Sundays and three full weeks together with part of a fourth. As the Catechism states, we are bound in most of the dioceses of the United States to fast on the Fridays during Advent.

Ember-days. Each quarter of the year consecrated to God by the observance of a three days' fast. The weeks appointed for this purpose are, the first week of Lent for the spring season; the week of Pentecost for the summer; the week following the Feast of the Exaltation of the Cross, September 14th, for the autumn; and the third week of Advent for the winter. From very ancient times these weeks have been called Ember-weeks, and the Wednesdays, Fridays, and Saturdays occurring in them—the days on which the fast is kept—are called the Ember-days. The date of the institution of the fast of the Ember-days cannot be clearly ascertained. They are mentioned in a decree ascribed to the Holy Pope St. Urban in the year 224, and are reckoned by St. Leo the Great as of apostolic origin. The object of the institution of the Ember-days was to consecrate each season of the year by acts of penance and mortification, to beg God's blessing on the fruits of the earth, and to thank him for those which had been gathered in; and likewise, as the Ember-weeks are the times specially appointed for the ordination of

31

the ministers of the Church, to pray for a zealous priesthood, and for the abundance of the divine blessing to descend on those who are chosen as the spiritual fathers of the faithful and their guides in the way of salvation.

Vigils. It was formerly the custom of the faithful to spend the day preceding the great festivals of the Church in prayer and fasting. In particular, they passed the night in watching and in exercises of devotion, as a preparation for the solemnity they were to observe on the following day. From this custom of watching, or keeping vigil during the night, the eves of these festivals were called Vigils. In course of time, the meeting of the faithful during the night, for purposes of devotion, gave rise to disorder and inconveniences, and, therefore, it fell into disuse; but we have a remnant of the ancient practice in the fasting-days or vigils which precede the festivals of Whit-Sunday or Pentecost, the Assumption, All Saints' and Christmas-day.

RULES OF FASTING.

It has been already said that the essence of the fast consists in taking only one full meal on the same day, and that not before midday. Formerly it was the custom to take nothing on fasting-days till the evening. In process of time, however, the single meal began to be taken at an earlier hour in the day, and this practice prepared the way for the further relaxation, by which a little was taken in the evening in addition to the full meal. The regulation which is enforced at the present day allows those who are bound to fast to take a full meal any time after midday, and a small supper, or, as it is called, a collation, in the evening. The Church has nowhere defined the quantity which may be taken at the evening collation, but the general custom, which, in the absence of any authoritative declaration, may be considered the best interpreter of her laws, fixes the quantity at not more than about eight ounces. Besides this restriction as to the quantity allowed for collation, it is necessary to bear in mind that we are also bound to the strictest abstinence. Not only is all kind of flesh-meat forbidden at collation, but also eggs, butter, cheese, and milk. The collation will therefore generally consist of bread and fruit or vegetables.; and, in virtue of the rescript of our Holy Father, to which reference has already been made, the use of dripping and lard is permitted on all days except Good Friday. It is also customary in some countries to take a very small quantity in the morning, but this should never exceed two ounces.

At one time it was forbidden to drink wine on fasting-days, but this prohibition no longer exists ; and, as a rule, liquids, such as beer, water, tea, or coffee, do not break the fast. Such liquids, however, as soups, milk, and generally those of a nourishing kind, are not allowed, except at the principal meal. All fasting-days are also abstinence-days, unless leave is expressly given to the contrary. When meat is allowed on fasting-days, whether by a general dispensation granted to all, as is commonly done in Lent, or by a particular dispensation granted to one or more, fish and meat are not allowed at the same meal. This prohibition of the joint use of fish and flesh-meat extends also to the Sundays of Lent, but not to any of the other abstinence-days throughout the year.

The proper order to follow on fasting-days is to take the principal meal about midday or after, and the collation in the evening ; but according to a declaration of the Congregation of the Sacred Penitentiary, those are not to be disturbed who for any reasonable cause invert the order, and take the collation after ten in the morning, and the dinner in the evening.

Each Bishop has power to modify to a certain extent the Lenten dispensations in his own diocese.

OF THOSE WHO ARE EXEMPT FROM THE OBLIGATION TO FAST AND ABSTAIN.

1. The Church does not intend her laws to bind where their observance would cause serious inconvenience, or where it interferes with duties of a higher kind. Thus the law of fasting only comes into force when persons have completed their twenty-first year, because at an earlier age fasting would often be injurious to the constitution. But no such inconvenience, as a rule, attends the observance of abstinence, and therefore children, no less than adults, are bound to abstain. No age has been fixed by the Church after which fasting ceases to be obligatory; but, according to the opinion of many theologians, those who are past sixty may with a safe conscience consider themselves exempt.

2. Those whose means of support are altogether precarious, or who are seldom sure of a full meal—those who live by hard labor, and generally those who require to eat several times in the day to enable them to fulfil the duties of their state of life—are not bound to fast.

3. In times of sickness or of delicate health, where fasting would be injurious, the Church does not wish that this law should bind. Abstinence is not so frequently attended with inconvenience as fasting; and, therefore, those who are dispensed from fasting are still bound by the law of abstinence, unless the contrary is implied. Where, however, the observance of abstinence is attended with serious inconvenience, it may be dispensed with. If, therefore, there be any who, from the state of their health, or from the nature of the duties in which they are engaged, believe themselves unable to comply with the precepts of the Church, they should, if pos-

sible, apply to their parish priest or confessor for a dispensation, and not take the matter into their own hands. They should also bear in mind that a dispensation always supposes a reasonable cause, and therefore they should not seek to obtain it without some proper ground of exemption.

THE THIRD COMMANDMENT.

"*To make a good confession of our sins at least once a year.*"

It has been shown in its proper place that the Sacrament of Penance is the divinely-appointed means for the remission of the sins committed after baptism, and, therefore, that confession, which is a part of this Sacrament, is a matter of strict obligation for those who have fallen into grievous sin after baptism. But though the devine law enjoins the confession of sins, it nowhere determines the time for the fulfilment of this duty. For a long period it was not necessary for the Church to lay down any law on the subject. The necessities of the faithful, and the great benefits to be derived from this divine institution, where sufficient inducements to ensure a frequent approach to the Sacrament of Penance. In process of time, however, when the charity of many had grown cold, and a spirit of carelessness and indifference was widely prevalent, many began to neglect confession for years together. It became necessary, therefore, for the Church to impose a distinct command, and to enforce its observance under threat of separation from her communion. The law, which is still in force, was made at the fourth Council of

Lateran, A. D. 1215, and requires all faithful of either sex, after they have come to the years of discretion, to confess their sins to their pastor at least once a year. The Council does not determine the particular time of the year at which the confession should be made; but as the same decree goes on to enforce the obligation of receiving Holy Communion at Easter, it sufficiently indicates that confession should also be made at Easter, as part of the preparation for communion. But while inculcating the obligation of confession, the Church guards with jealous care the right of the faithful to choose their own confessor. It matters not whether the priest to whom they confess belongs to their parish or not, provided only he be approved by the bishop in whose diocese he exercises his faculties.

The precept requires us to confess our sins *at least* once a year, in order to intimate to us that though this is sufficient to comply with the obligation which the Church imposes upon us, it is not sufficient to satisfy her desires. No general rule can be laid down as to the frequency of confession, because much depends on each one's state of life and facilities of going to confession. Thus much, however, may be said, that it is very important for each one to have a regularly fixed time for approaching this Sacrament, and not to depart from it without some good reason. There are few if any, who might not with advantage make their confession once a month; others, by the advice of their confessor, might do so once a fortnight, or once a week. But whatever may be a person's state of life, or whatever may be his regular time of going to confession, he should always make it a point to go as soon as possible, when he has the misfortune to fall into mortal sin. Knowing, as we do, the uncertainty of our lives, and that we may any moment be summoned before the tribunal of God, it is the height of imprudence to remain a single day in the state in which, were we to die, we should be forever lost.

As confession is the remedy for sin, it always presupposes the existence of sin. So long, therefore, as children are incapable of committing sin, they are incapable of receiving the Sacrament of Penance. But when they begin to come to the use of reason, and are able to distinguish between good and evil, they are able to commit sin, and with the evil comes the necessity for the remedy. The age of seven is generally considered the time when children are capable of committing mortal sin, and when, consequently, they should be instructed and taught to make their confession.

THE FOURTH COMMANDMENT.

"*To receive worthily the Blessed Sacrament during the Easter-time.*"

Our Blessed Lord tells us in the most emphatic manner, "Except you eat the flesh of the Son of man, and drink His blood, you shall not have life in you. (St. John vi., 54.) So great was the desire of the early Christians to partake of this heavenly banquet, that many received the Holy Communion daily. St. Luke tells us of the early converts to Christianity, "that they continued daily with one accord in the temple, and breaking bread from house to house." (Acts ii., 46.) As time went on, however, this first fervor began to cool; and the same reason which obliged the great Council of Lateran to enforce the precept of yearly confession, also led to the command to receive the Holy Communion at least at Easter. Many of the observations which have been made in reference to confession equally apply to the precepts of Easter Communion. For example, the command to receive the Blessed Sacrament belongs to the divine law, and the Church only determines the time of its fulfilment. She requires us to receive Holy Communion at least once a year, but her desire is that we should do so much more frequently. But though the explanation of this precept has much in common with that of the foregoing one, there are some points of difference which should not be passed over. Thus, while we are simply commanded to go to confession once a year, the exact time of the year at which the obligation of communion must be complied with is defined. The general law of the Church requires all the faithful to receive the Blessed Sacrament between Palm Sunday and Low Sunday, both days included. In the United States however, where, on account of the small number of priests, it would be extremely difficult for all to approach the Sacraments during this fortnight, the time for complying with this obligation has been lengthened so as to include the whole of Lent, beginning on the first Sunday in Lent, and ending on Trinity Sunday, that is eight weeks after Easter.

Again, the reverence due to so august a Sacrament requires that children should not be admitted to their first communion till they are capable of being well instructed in its nature, and the dispositions which are required to receive it with fruit. While seven is the age at which children should be thaught to make their confession, they are not generally admitted to Holy Communion till between the age of ten and thirteen. But it should be carefully borne in mind, that when they are able sufficiently to understand the nature of this Sacrament, they are bound to prepare themselves to fulfil the precept of receiving it.

In Catholic countries, where the regular distinction of parishes exists, each one is bound to make his Easter Communion in his own parish church, or at least to ask the permission of the parish priest or Bishop, if he wishes to communicate elsewhere. This practice is important, both as an example to the rest of the faithful, and as a means of enabling the pastor to know those of his flock who are living in the neglect of their Christian duties. Though it is not of precise obligation in countries such as our own, still the general law of the Church sufficiently indicates her desires on the subject.

THE FIFTH COMMANDMENT.

" *Not to marry within certain degrees of kindred, nor to solemnize marriage at the forbidden times.*"

The explanation of this commandment is found in Volume " Grace and the Sacraments," p. 510 to 514 and 518.

THE SIXTH COMMANDMENT.

" *To contribute to the support of our pastors.*"

See the explanation of this commandment in Volume "The Greatest and the First Commandment," p. 408—409 ; and especially in Volume " Grace and the Sacraments," p. 419—428.

www.ingramcontent.com/pod-product-compliance
Lightning Source LLC
Chambersburg PA
CBHW032020110726
47901CB00004B/1140